TOM O'DORNIN was born in Eire, but now lives in England with his wife and son. Following university he worked in a variety of roles for a few years, but then went travelling, taking a keen interest in the history and myths associated with the places he visited, especially Greece, Turkey and Tibet. Since returning from his travels he has been focusing on a writing career. *Empire of the Moon* is his first novel.

EMPIRE
OF THE
MOON

Tom O'Dornin

SilverWood

Originally published in 2015 by SilverWood Books
This edition 2020

SilverWood Books Ltd
14 Small Street, Bristol, BS1 1DE, United Kingdom
www.silverwoodbooks.co.uk

ISBN 978-1-78132-965-8 (paperback)
ISBN 978-1-78132-966-5 (ebook)

British Library Cataloguing in Publication Data
A CIP catalogue record for this book is available from
the British Library

Set in Adobe Garamond Pro by SilverWood Books

EMPIRE OF THE MOON

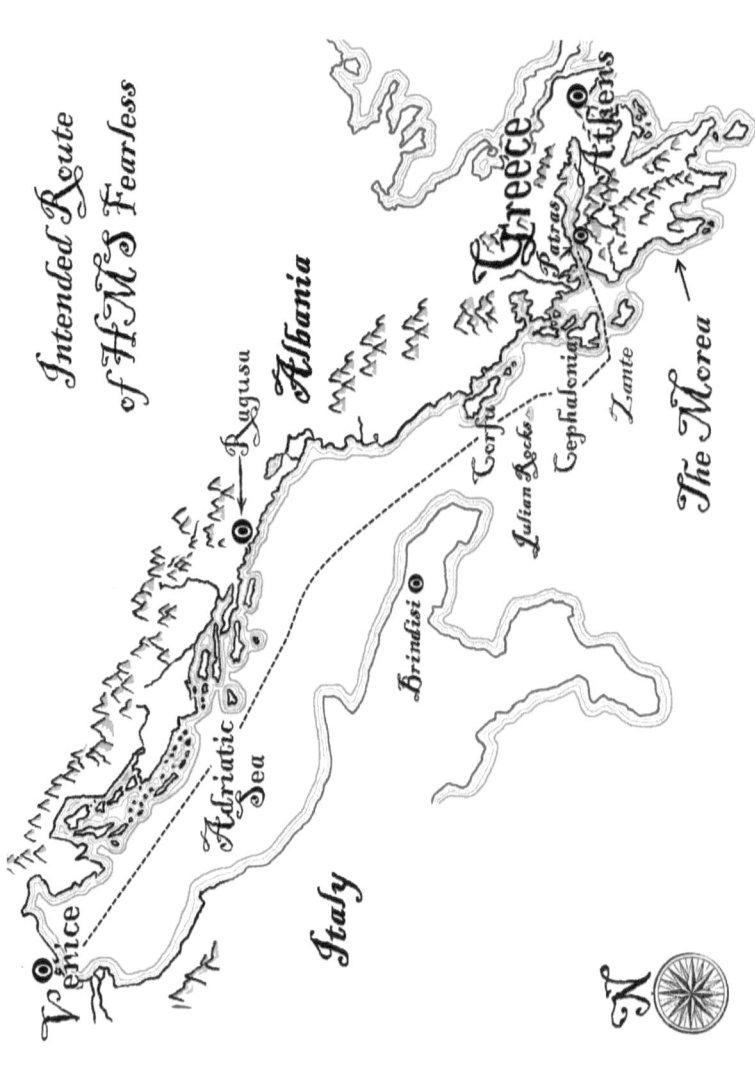

Intended Route of HMS Fearless

Venice

Italy

Adriatic Sea

Brindisi

Ragusa

Albania

Greece

Corfu

Julian Rocks

Cephalonia

Zante

Patras

Athens

The Morea

N

CHAPTER 1

Helena fidgeted in her chair, glanced at the clock again, and sighed with impatience. Their ship had become becalmed that morning, and freezing mist had driven Helena and her younger sister Isabelle into the warmth of Captain Todd's great cabin. Since then they had been huddled round the wood stove, Helena reading in the captain's smoking chair, while Isabelle embroidered. All around them were the comforting sounds of the ship's crew going about their duties – the dull thud of footsteps up and down the oak decks, muffled voices, and the occasional ringing of the watch bells.

Their trip around the Continent, thus far, had been everything Helena had hoped for, and she had already filled several notebooks and sketchbooks with details of the sights they had seen in France and Italy. The highlight of the trip had been Florence, where she had been spellbound by the works of art in the Uffizi Gallery. But on arriving in Venice, their chaperone – one of her father's men – had returned to their lodgings with tales of unrest in the air, and the threat of attack from the Turk. The news sent Isabelle into a panic, but to Helena the story did not ring true – the Venetians themselves seemed perfectly calm and appeared to be going about their business as usual. Nonetheless, within hours the British ambassador himself had been summoned, and he had personally escorted them via longboat onto HMS *Fearless*, which happened to be visiting Venice on some sort of diplomatic mission. Literally minutes after they had boarded, the ship had set sail, and then they were on their way to supposed safety in the Greek port of Patras, from where they would be able to take a passage to Gibraltar.

Helena tried to concentrate on her travel book again but found her thoughts wandering. At first she had been incensed by the abrupt end to their travels, despite the captain putting his own cabin at their disposal.

Her anger, however, had dissipated on the first night, when a young Lieutenant Hurst had joined them for dinner at the captain's table. In spite of herself – who had turned down the numerous suitors her father had paraded before her, and who considered most men to be scoundrels, rakes or spineless dandies – she had been completely smitten by him.

He was tall, of medium build, with an aura of unshakable self-confidence and authority, tempered by a dry sense of humour. And, as Isabelle never tired of pointing out, with his athletic physique, flaxen hair, and piercing blue eyes set in a chiselled face, he had the looks of a young Norse god. He knew of their father, the Earl of Salisbury, and his father was one of the finest silversmiths in London. Best of all, there was no wife or fiancée involved, information she had – subtlety she thought – wrung out of him less than an hour into the dinner. Helena knew that a man like Lt Hurst could quite easily have a woman in every port, and yet by the end of their first evening together – unless he and his fellow officers were expert dissemblers – she was convinced there was no other woman in his life. At Helena's request he had given them a tour of ship on their second day on board, and in the course of the tour it had become obvious to Helena that the feeling was mutual.

'Or maybe I am deluding myself,' she thought, glancing at the clock again, 'due to the desperation of an old maid!'

She shook her head to dismiss the notion; the Fates had brought them together, she was sure of it, and since meeting him a constant feeling of joy had welled up within her, together with a sense of barely contained excitement whenever she thought of him. She looked for every excuse to be on deck when he was on duty, ostensibly sketching the coastline or painting sea views, hoping to catch sight of him. He would acknowledge her if he passed by, but rarely spoke to her as he went about his duties, as was fitting.

The evenings had quickly settled into a pattern that had taken on something of a dreamlike quality. The sisters would make their way up to the high deck above Captain Todd's cabin to watch the sunset, where Lt Hurst would join them after his watch, pointing out the constellations as they appeared in the crystal clear Mediterranean sky. By the light of the whale-oil lanterns, and with the sound of fiddle and accordion music coming from below deck, they would then join the other officers for dinner in the candle-lit cabin. The food provided by the captain's Genoese cook was of exceptional quality, and the meals themselves passed in a blur of fine wine and polite conversation, despite the captain himself being quite reserved and somewhat aloof.

She yawned, had a luxurious stretch, and made herself more comfortable in the chair. The late nights and several weeks of travelling though Europe by carriage and horseback had tired her. Logs in the stove crackled and spat, while the ship's timbers creaked and groaned as it moved on the gentle swell of the sea. Helena's eyelids began to droop and her book slowly slipped out of her grip, before resting on her lap.

*

The watch bells rang out again, rousing Helena. She glanced at the clock and felt a thrill of excitement as she realised what the time was.

'I'm going outside,' she declared, standing up to stretch her long frame. 'This cabin is getting too far too stuffy.'

'Really? Or are you hoping to meet the gallant Lt Hurst on your travels?' teased Isabelle, smiling but not raising her eyes from her work. Once she had got over her shock at Helena exchanging more than two civil words with a man, Isabelle now found the whole business hilarious, and she wasted no opportunity to rib her sister about it.

The sisters' looks were similar in that both had pale skin, blue eyes, and full, ruby-red lips. They differed in that Helena was tall and had auburn hair and strong, well-defined features with pronounced cheekbones. Isabelle, meanwhile, was petite and blonde, with more delicate features and larger eyes, giving her a somewhat childlike appearance. Both were considered to be beauties in their own right.

'I may be,' replied Helena, smiling as she swept her cloak round her travelling habit of riding dress and boots.

'You should not lead him on, you know,' declared Isabelle suddenly, looking directly at Helena now, her voice taking on a more serious tone.

'How do you mean?'

'Well, to be blunt – at day's end you are a lady – and he is a commoner!'

'But his father is a master silversmith…'

'Really? With a busy school of apprentices working under his direction – or surviving hand to mouth on the odd commission?'

'Well then, Alex is a leader of men – a rising star!' retorted Helena.

'Come now, these military chaps always talk themselves up – and their brother officers will back them to the hilt! If he is such a natural leader of men, why is he not in line for higher command? You know as well as I that at his age – if he were that accomplished – he would be on an admiral's flagship, if it were thought he had the potential to be a captain.'

'You have a point,' conceded Helena, her good mood deflated somewhat, resting her hands on the back of the chair she had just vacated. She cast her eyes away and sighed. 'If only his were family were landed – we would know exactly where he stood.'

'If his family were landed, he would most surely be married already!'

'But Isabelle, if it were not for the fact we occupy different stations in life, he would be the perfect man for me – I am sure of it!' She paused. 'And, regardless, I have already invited him to Wilton in June – he has leave then.'

'Well, that is all for the good. It will give us time to have proper enquires made of him, to see if his family is of substance – and if he really has higher prospects in the navy. If all is well, you will then just have to persuade Papa.'

'That, though slightly underhand, does sound like a good course of action,' agreed Helena, perking up as she fastened her cloak. 'I just pray to God that he does not meet some other woman in the meantime!'

'Do not fret so!' said Isabelle with a smile. 'He will be on a warship from now until then!'

'Why don't you come out also, and get some fresh air?'

'No, thank you,' replied Isabelle, her smile turning to a frown. ''Tis too cold outside – and I don't care for the way the men leer so as we pass. No, I will stay here in the warmth until dinner.'

'Please yourself,' said Helena, as she corralled her mane of long auburn hair into a ponytail. 'How's your embroidery progressing?'

'Well, in view of the events that have occurred in the last few days,' Isabelle replied, looking pointedly at Helena, 'I've decided to start a new one.'

She held up the cloth with the outline of the embroidery just appearing in it.

'"All things come to those who wait",' Helena read aloud, and then laughed. 'How apt!'

'Oh, and just before you go, remember one thing, sister,' said Isabelle, a concerned edge to her voice.

'What would *that* be?' asked Helena, pausing at the door.

Isabelle half rose to her feet and jabbed the air dramatically with her free hand. 'Marriage is nothing more than *legalised prostitution*!' she declared, quoting her sister's favourite saying back to her, before collapsing into a fit of giggles.

'Well, 'tis true where there's a dowry involved,' retorted Helena. 'But I intend to marry for love!'

*

Outside, Helena stopped in her tracks as the freezing air literally took her breath away. The drop in temperature that had occurred in the last few hours was remarkable. Over to her right, the sun was a pale disk, barely cutting through the thick vapour that surrounded the Fearless in a sound-deadening embrace. The sea was now perfectly still and the ship floated there in the half-light, seemingly surrounded by towering walls of ethereal mist.

Several yards in front of her, a seaman stood dutifully at the ship's wheel, while several others swabbed the decks down for the final time that day, a slight sheen of ice forming on the deck as water from their mops froze. About a hundred feet ahead of her, shadowy figures moved around the bow of the ship. Hens, pigs, and goats held in cages on the deck made the odd noise as they settled down for the evening, as if protesting against the change in the weather. The two burly marines guarding Captain Todd's cabin, the tips of their noses blue with the cold, turned to look at her as she stood there on the threshold.

'Everything alright, Miss?' asked one, his gaze lingering on her longer than she felt comfortable with.

'Quite,' she replied, pulling her cloak more tightly round herself and looking directly ahead. She didn't care for such familiarity from the lower orders, but ship life appeared to be quite informal.

'Ship's Master says this weather's most unseasonable,' ventured the other, older marine. 'By rights we should have been in Patras this evening, but it'll be more like…'

Without warning something hit the deck, just ahead of the ship's wheel, with a hollow ringing sound accompanied by the tinkle of breaking glass. The long, bright cylindrical object bounced, and then rolled across the deck to the base of the ships rail – a spyglass, Helena realised. No sooner had the instrument come to a rest than a much larger irregular object caught Helena's eye as it fell silently through the air. An instant later, the body of the lookout hit the deck with such sickening force that the planking buckled, making Helena jump with shock. All movement and sound on the ship halted momentarily, and then seamen and officers rushed over to the man's aid – though to Helena it was obvious he was dead from the unnatural angle of his head. He had died without uttering a cry, and even in the poor light she could see a pool of crimson blood forming on the deck around him. The men around him now had him on his back, and to her horror Helena realised there was a shaft of wood, the length and thickness of a broom handle, protruding from his chest.

One of the figures who crouched around the fallen man now stood up and appeared to be looking for something out to sea, first on one side of the ship, and then the other – it was Lt Hurst, flaxen hair visible below his tricorne hat. Helena's heart skipped a beat and she made to move towards him, but he was already running back along the deck towards her, pointing out to sea and shouting urgently at the men around him.

'Enemy on starboard bow! Bos'un, pipe all hands on deck!'

Seamen who had gathered around the fallen man at first looked up in surprise, but as a man near the ship's wheel blew on a loud, shrill whistle, they were galvanised into action, some sprinting off below deck, while others began to climb the rigging.

'There!' Lt Hurst shouted again, still pointing to Helena's right as he reached the wheel, where he furiously rang the ship's bell, oblivious to her presence. 'All hands on deck!' he bellowed.

Helena followed his direction, but at first she could not comprehend what she was seeing. Several hundred yards away something had appeared out of the veils of mist that surrounded the ship, its shape obscuring the now feeble disk of the setting sun. For a moment, it looked like some sort of giant insect lurching towards them, a multitude of legs on either side driving it forward, with the grey sea foaming as each leg struck. She blinked and looked again – and felt a chill of fear in her stomach as she realised she was looking at a war galley head on, its oars moving to a faint drum beat, powering it on to a collision course with their right-hand side. It would surely be on them in less than a minute.

Around her the ship then seemed to explode with activity, men streaming on deck from every corner of it. Officers barked orders, and red-coated marines took up positions along the ship's rail, while still more had slung their muskets over their shoulders and were climbing the netting to the tops.

'Mr Johnson,' Lt Hurst shouted at a seaman near to him. 'Prepare for starboard broadside!'

The man darted to the nearest hatch, shouting down it to relay the order. Captain Todd then appeared from the doorway to Helena's left, fastening his coat buttons with one hand – a yellow coat Helena could not help noticing, instead of his usual navy blue one – while steadying himself on the ship's rail with the other. His unsteady gait, overly careful movements, and glassy eyes staring rigidly ahead reminded her of their father – when he was intoxicated.

'What the devil is going on, Mr Hurst?' he demanded as he reached the ship's wheel, apparently in the grip of a rage. 'Mr Johnson, hold fire – they'll be no guns fired on this ship without my direct order.'

'But Captain,' Lt Hurst protested, pointing to starboard. 'We're being attacked!'

Following Alex's direction, Captain Todd turned to starboard – and seemed to be stunned at what he was seeing, his mouth opening, but still not issuing the critical fire order.

Helena glanced over to her right – the galley was within three hundred yards of them – and back to Captain Todd. Surely he was not so drunk that he could not see the danger they were in?

'Captain!' implored Lt Hurst.

At last Captain Todd seemed to comprehend the gravity of the situation and belatedly began to issue the order. But it was too late.

From the moment Helena had seen the galley, no sound had come from it save for the remorseless drumbeat and faint sound of its oars cutting through the water. Now a strange, shrill chorus of a battle cry could be heard, which carried with such intensity across the small divide between the two ships that it seemed to physically hit her in the solar plexus.

Captain Todd was shouting 'Starboard guns...' and then his voice trailed off, seemingly overcome by the battle cry that resonated unnaturally in the cold air.

To her consternation, Helena felt raw fear sweep through her body, radiating out from her stomach and weakening her. She staggered back to the cabin door for support, and then the sounds and shapes of the ship seemed to fade away, as if a heavy veil were falling in place around her. She felt rooted to the spot, her head like lead, and it was only with a supreme effort of will that she managed to raise it and view the scene on deck.

All about her appeared to be in a similar state. Some had fallen, a number were slumped against anything upright, while others stumbled around like drunks with blank, uncomprehending visages. She then heard muffled shots and noticed, in an almost detached manner, the marines who had made it to the ship's rail falling slowly to the deck, the cries of their death throes echoing through her mind, while their muskets crashed uselessly around them. The galley surged on, its relentless drums growing louder with each stroke of the oars, as it bore down on them like a demon from the pit.

Her heart began thudding against her chest so hard she thought it would burst, while she gasped for breath. In the nightmarish state she was in, an aura seemed to emanate from the galley – of an ancient evil that was poised to engulf them all.

'We are defenceless,' she thought, burying her head in her hands. 'We are all going to die!'

Then, at that point of utter hopelessness, there came a faint voice that sounded as if it were a lifetime away, but which created a small ray of hope in her heart.

'Prepare to… repel boarders!' it urged, echoing around the unnaturally silent ship. The voice sounded familiar, thought Helena. Someone she knew from a long time ago, in a different place. Then she slowly realised, with a pang of longing, that it was Lt Hurst, and tried to reply to his call, but could not break free of the sorcery.

'Prepare to repel boarders!' bellowed Lt Hurst, his voice now so loud he seemed to be next to her, cutting like a sabre though the veil that had descended about her.

Around her there was a brief moment of stunned silence, followed by what appeared to be a collective intake of breath as all realised the desperate situation they were in – and then pandemonium broke out, with each man resuming his task, shouting furiously to urge one another on. The galley was now barely fifty yards away, and the drumbeat staccato as the oars sliced through the water in perfect time.

'Fire at will!' ordered Captain Todd, finally completing the crucial order.

'Thank God,' thought Helena, still shaking from the effects of the demonic battle cry. 'We have a chance!'

Suddenly the Captain became aware of Helena's presence and turned to her.

'Miss Montagu,' he thundered, 'get below deck now! The quarterdeck is no place for a woman.' He gestured pointedly at the marines on either side of her, and then turned his back on her.

'Captain, I protest!' began Helena, but then found herself being pulled back to the cabin, her arm grasped from behind with a vice-like grip. She tried to call to Lt Hurst, but he was already engrossed in the business of battle.

'Come on now, Miss. Captain's orders,' urged the older marine, genuine concern in his voice.

'No, I want to stay on deck,' she cried, trying to pull away, but the next moment she found herself in the cabin, the door pulled shut behind her.

'Barricade the door, Miss!' shouted the marine from outside.

*

'Damn them!' Helena exclaimed, glancing at the door bar, but ignoring the order. The initial fear had now completely dissipated, her fighting

15

spirit was up, and she wanted to be on deck with Lt Hurst, not stuck in the cabin like a child. She decided she would wait until the marines were distracted and then slip back out on deck – but she would need a weapon. Then she remembered – the bedroom! She staggered towards it, her legs still weak.

'Helena, what's happening?' croaked Isabelle, her face drained of all colour, and slumped on the floor by the smoking chair. 'I'm frightened!'

'No time,' she replied. 'Into the bedroom,' she commanded, as she half-dragged Isabelle in the right direction, scattering her embroidery across the floor.

'Brace yourself,' she warned as they entered the bedroom, physically placing Isabelle's hands on the side of the bunk. 'The ship will shake at any moment.'

A muffled explosion, followed by half a dozen more, sounded from outside.

'At last,' she exclaimed. 'The ship's guns.'

And yet – she had expected to hear a barrage. How many large guns were on either side? Two dozen? Something was not quite right. The guns did not sound as loud, nor shook the ship so much as when they had watched a drill some days previously. Had they misfired? As if to confirm her fears, there was a further muffled explosion, and then the guns fell silent.

Without warning a tremendous crash then reverberated around the ship, as the galley impacted on the *Fearless*, throwing them both to the floor and causing Helena to strike her head on a bulwark. At the same instant, all hell seemed to break loose outside as dozens of firearms were discharged, grenades exploded, and men cried out and screamed in pain.

Helena was back on her feet in an instant, pulling Isabelle up from the floor and propping her against the bunk.

'We are under attack,' she explained, as calmly as possible.

'But from whom?' demanded Isabelle, seizing her sister with fright.

'Turks? Barbary corsairs? I don't know. But do not fret – the crew will see them off.'

'Helena – your head is bleeding!'

Helena glanced at herself in the looking glass to see a gash across her forehead, with blood trickling down the side of her face.

'It is but a scratch,' she declared, staunching the wound with a handkerchief. 'Never mind that now,' she continued, pulling free from Isabelle and dropping to her knees to fish round under the lower bunk. 'Ah-ha, got them! Those pistols we found yesterday,' she explained as she pulled out an ornate walnut box. 'I'm going to load them.'

'But I thought you said the crew would protect us!' wailed Isabelle, beginning to sob.

Helena placed her hands on her sister's shoulders.

'Just a precaution, sister,' she said, looking into Isabelle's eyes. 'This is one of the most powerful ships in the Royal Navy. If anything, these corsairs – or whoever they are – have signed their own death warrants! Now get up and stay there on the bed while I get these loaded.'

With renewed urgency she turned her attention back to the wooden box. She sprang the catches and opened the lid, a rich aroma of wood polish and gun oil wafting up from it. It contained two duelling pistols and a ladies pistol, together with plugs of gunpowder and ramrods. She pulled out the ladies pistol and examined it for a moment. It was only accurate over a short range, but it might be of use at some point. She thrust it into one of her riding boots, the gunpowder and small ramrod into the other.

She then levered out one of the duelling pistols from its velvet-lined recess. It was exquisitely crafted, and perfectly balanced – obviously a gift of some sort and probably never used. She pulled a plug of gunpowder from the box and began ramming it into the pistol with well-practised skill, while Isabelle threw herself on the bed sobbing with fear, her face in her hands.

'There, one done,' she said as she laid the firearm carefully on the bed, trying to affect a casual air.

Outside, there finally came the reassuring sound of a barrage from the ship's heavy guns, accompanied by chilling screams. Presumably they were finding their mark, Helena thought, with grim satisfaction.

The sound of the cabin's outer door being flung open, together with a rise in the roaring background noise, then caught her attention. She poked her head out of the bedroom – and to her astonishment saw Captain Todd stride in, countenance grim and set like stone. He was closely followed by a shorter swarthy man, also dressed in a yellow coat, whom Helena recognised as his cook.

Though astonished at the captain's appearance, the ghastly scene outside shocked her to the core. Bodies of red-coated marines lay strewn all over the deck, and her heart chilled as she realised there was no sign of Lt Hurst, or the other officers. Black-garbed figures with closely fitting silver helmets seemed to be everywhere, some engaged in brutal hand-to-hand fighting with the ship's crew, while others were slipping though hatches to get below deck.

'God help us', she thought. 'We are being overrun!'

The marine who had manhandled her into the cabin was now almost directly outside it, struggling with one of the intruders. He had lost his musket and sabre and was now grasping one of his assailant's wrists with both hands, desperately trying to prevent the intruder from deploying a curved scimitar, while the other hand rained blows on him. Though he appeared bigger and heavier than his opponent, and seemed impervious to the punishment he was taking, it was clear he was outclassed. With a swift movement, the assailant broke the impasse by raising his sword hand high and then kicking the marine's feet from under him. The man fell heavily on to his side, but still grasped the other's arm, forcing his opponent to kneel awkwardly on one leg. Then, despite his own desperate predicament, the marine looked with shock at the cabin door as he realised it was open.

'The women!' he bawled, barely audible over the roar of the fighting, and seemed to look directly at Helena, though she would have been unseen in the shadows of the cabin. 'The women!'

His opponent took advantage of his kneeling position to draw a knife strapped to his boot. He casually flipped it, the silver blade glinting in the light of the whale-oil lanterns, caught it so that he held it at a better angle, and then brought it down with murderous force towards the marine's chest…

The door slammed shut, making Helena jump with shock, her blood running cold at the cry of pain from without. She turned to look at the cook for some sort of explanation of the situation, but he just stood there by the door, staring insolently at her.

'For God's sake, bar the door, man!' she now implored, having to shout to hear herself above the commotion outside. 'We have been boarded!'

The cook made no move other than to fold his arms and to continue staring at her.

'Captain?' She turned to him. 'What in God's name is happening?'

'Everything is in order, Miss Montagu,' Captain Todd slurred, confirming her earlier suspicion, as he strode over to the desk. 'Now kindly stay out of my way, I have work to do!'

As he reached the desk, a deafening explosion occurred, seemingly from the bowels of the ship. It was far louder than the noise of the ship's heavy guns. Captain Todd staggered and half-fell onto his desk, while Helena only just managed to steady herself in time. Once again a shocked silence fell across the ship, and in those moments Helena felt the ship begin to list almost imperceptibly. The two men exchanged questioning glances but said nothing. The cook then made for the cabin door to look through its small barred window.

'The corsairs? Have they been repelled?' she asked, still shaken by the force of the explosion and mystified as to why Captain Todd was present.

'Get in the bedroom now, woman,' snarled Captain Todd, his wig askew as he struggled to his feet, 'and stay there till I give you leave to come out!'

He then ignored her again and began methodically unlocking the drawers of his desk and emptying their contents into a large oilskin bag, as well as charts and books that were lying around.

Helena glanced at the cook – he had a similar oilskin bag already slung over his shoulder, bulging at the seams. How could he have been so prepared? Unless...

Captain Todd glanced up to see her still watching him.

'Gustavo!' he ordered, and the cook strode across the room towards her, his intent obvious.

'Don't you dare touch me, you Italian cur!' she shouted, stopping him in his tracks and giving her time to withdraw and slam the bedroom door in his face. 'My father will have you horse-whipped!' she continued, locking the door as he rattled the handle.

She then maintained a stream of threats in a similar vein, to cover the sound of her loading of the second pistol, as her mind raced, trying to make sense of the situation. The previous day Lt Hurst had explained to her that in the case of a ship being overrun, all documents and charts that could be of use to the enemy would be gathered into a lead weighted bag and dropped over the side. Was this what Captain Todd was doing? But why had the cook not already got rid of his? Whatever was happening, the situation was becoming more nightmarish by the minute, and all romantic thoughts of joining Lt Hurst on deck to help repel the corsairs were now thoroughly dispelled. Leaving the cabin would be suicidal, so she determined that the best course of action was to stay put until the marines regained control of the ship and were able to free them. What use the two men would be if the corsairs entered the cabin, she had no idea – neither seemed to have been armed.

A shout then came from above them, ringing out above the roar of battle.

'Head shots!' the voice called. 'Head shots!'

'Lt Hurst!' Helena exclaimed, gasping with relief that he was still alive.

The second pistol loaded, she removed the key from the lock, and crouched down to see what was happening outside.

Captain Todd had finished clearing his desk and now stood beside the cook, facing the door, the oilskin bag slung over his shoulder. Both men had their hands, bereft of any weapons, high above their heads.

They were surrendering?

A shadow passed across the window of the cabin door – a pause – and then suddenly it was flung open, and a horde of the black-garbed corsairs flooded into the cabin, helmets and scimitars glinting in the lantern light.

Helena caught her breath in shock, fully expecting the two men to be slaughtered before her eyes – but the horde swept around them like the incoming tide around a breakwater – and then the leader shoulder-barged into the door of the bedroom. Helena sprang back with an involuntary scream, and then pulled Isabelle from the bed and back as far as they could go. She then faced the door, with the pistol in her right hand raised and ready. Another body slammed into the door, but the thick oak held. There was a hiatus. Commands were issued in hissing, guttural voices; there was the sound of something heavy being dragged across the floor – and then the door almost buckled on its hinges as something struck it with incredible force. They had a battering ram, she realised with dismay.

'Lt Hurst,' she shouted in desperation. 'Alex, for God's sake help us!'

The door would not hold for long, and to make matters worse, a glance at the lantern confirmed what her sense of balance now told her – the *Fearless* was starting to list. If they managed to stay in the bedroom much longer they would most likely drown, but if the corsairs managed to break in…She pushed the thought from her mind, and after a moment's deliberation she reached out to the lantern with her left hand and turned the wick down until it was extinguished, leaving them in darkness save for the slivers of light seeping in from the sides of the door. Her heart had been pounding with fear, but she felt a deadly calm settle on her as she cocked the pistol and prepared to kill the first corsair who made it through the door.

Two more blows on the door followed, each causing a shriek of terror from Isabelle, now cowering in a state of abject fear behind her.

'I will protect you, sister!' Helena shouted, as another blow struck the door.

The next blow brought the door down with a splintering crash, and the lead corsair sprang into the room with the litheness of a cat. For a moment he was silhouetted in the doorway – and the next he was staggering back, screaming in agony, his head half blown off by Helena's pistol shot.

There was a moment's hesitation by the attackers, giving Helena enough time to swap hands and cock the second pistol. She realised she could be close to death but maintained her deadly calm. Time slowed down. Another corsair ran into the room, and was almost at the outstretched pistol before Helena coolly fired it at point-blank range into his face.

The powder flash lit up the cabin for a moment, and as she maintained her gaze along the barrel of the pistol, her heart sank as she saw more of the fiends gathered outside the door, ready to charge, hands shielding their faces from the gunpowder discharge. The flash had barely faded when they began to move, and Helena flipped the pistol in her hand to use the handle as a club. She managed to strike the next assailant with a glancing blow to the head, but then they swarmed on her, overpowering her and forcing her to the floor.

'Alex!' she shrieked in desperation, kicking and gouging with her nails as best she could, as they dragged her out of the bedroom and into the centre of the cabin. She was now on her back, her arms and legs pinned down by a corsair on each limb, shaking her head violently from side to side lest they should touch her face. She was helpless. She tried to call out again but terror choked the cry in her throat.

Her assailants, having immobilised her, now did nothing. She stopped shaking her head, acutely aware of her pounding heart. Over to her left she could hear Isabelle sobbing. She was almost frozen with terror, not daring to look any of them in the eye, but sensed they were waiting for something to happen.

Another shadow appeared at the doorway, and then a hooded corsair clad in robes of scarlet strode purposefully in, a small leather bag slung across his shoulder and seemingly oblivious to the carnage taking place outside. He quickly knelt down by Helena, produced a dark green bottle and white cloth from the bag, and then casually threw his hood back to better attend to his work. Their eyes met – and Helena gasped in shock at what she saw before her.

His visage was not that of a man but of a demon – bright red reptilian-like eyes set in a deathly pale face, a hook nose, and sensuous, sneering lips, from which protruded rotting jagged fangs. Unable to believe her eyes, she whipped her head over to look at the corsair on her right arm – the same, but younger in appearance, thick pale white hair visible from under his helmet. The same was true of the corsair on her left. The newcomer had now soaked the cloth in some pungent liquid from the bottle. Helena arched her back, desperately trying to push herself back along the floor, but sobbed as she realised her efforts were futile. His free arm snaked out, savagely grasping her hair. He yanked her head back and she smelt his foul breath assail her nostrils. The cloth bore down on her mouth, his merciless gaze drilled into her very soul, and all the fear and tension of the day welled up inside her, producing a scream of terror that rang around the ship.

CHAPTER 2

Helena gradually became aware of her surroundings as she slowly woke from a deep, dreamless sleep. For some time she hovered in that empty region between sleep and waking, but aware that the bed she lay in was comfortable, the sheets crisp and the pillows deep and soft. Despite the comfort, her head throbbed and her mouth was parched, but she was too much in the grip of slumber to stir. Then, events in Captain Todd's cabin started to invade her mind – the corsairs illuminated by the muzzle flash from her pistol, crouched beyond the bedroom door like a pack of animals waiting to pounce...

She sat bolt upright, her eyes wide open, and her heart beating like a drum. She glanced to her side and was almost overcome with relief when she saw Isabelle sleeping soundly in another bed a few feet away, and beyond her an open window. She cast back the sheet and made to go over to her sister – but was halted mid-way by an explosion of pain in her head. She collapsed face-down back on the bed and lay there for a few minutes until the pain subsided somewhat and then slowly opened her eyes. Through habit she reached under the bed and, to her surprise, found her travelling bag more or less where it should have been. Rifling through it she found a small velvet bag containing strips of willow bark. She took one out and chewed on it, and then wondered who had changed them into their nightdresses.

She then remembered lying on her back in the outer cabin and a terrible thought crossed her mind. Had she been violated? She grew cold at the thought, but then realised that, other than her headache, there was no pain or tenderness anywhere in her body. She gave a huge sigh of relief and closed her eyes again.

Sometime later she felt well enough to move again, and managed this time to swing her legs over the side of the bed. A washstand was located at the foot of the beds, which held a pitcher and cups. Slowly and stiffly, she made her way over to the stand and stood against it, supporting herself with one arm as she used the other to pour out several cups of water, until she had slaked her thirst. As she did, she saw her reflection in the looking glass and was shocked to see the cut on her head had almost healed – they must have been senseless for days. Looking closer, she could see the wound had been skilfully stitched, with fine sutures that seemed barely thicker than a hair's breadth. She then sat back on the bed, head in her hands, trying to recall what had happened since the horror in the cabin. Some minutes later she gave an exasperated gasp – her memory was completely blank on the issue.

'Well, at least we are safe,' she thought. The marines must have won the day and pushed the corsairs back. Were they now in Patras? She got up and walked unsteadily to the window to look out. They were in some large building, and that in itself reassured her – this was no corsair lair, but it was surely far larger than she had expected the Consul-General's house to be.

Above and below her were other windows, still shuttered, which struck her as slightly odd. The sun was quite high in the sky and it could have been either mid-morning or mid-afternoon. Stretching out and taking a few deep breaths to help clear her head, the air smelt fresh and cool, so she decided it was not yet noon and that she was looking out to the east. Down below her were numerous courtyards and alleyways that, though festooned with a riot of luxuriant bougainvillea, geranium, and oleander, were devoid of human life. Shielding her eyes from the sun with her hand, she looked out beyond the walls of what she now realised was an actual fortress. Almost immediately ahead of her, about a mile away on the coast, and far below, was a large dock with dozens of ships moored in it. Over to the left of the port were a large number of warehouses and what looked like workshops, some with chimneys from which black smoke trickled out. To the right of the port were well-tended fields of grey and brown, delineated by drystone walls that stretched off in the distance towards the deep blue of the Mediterranean Sea. Further away on the horizon were thick heavy clouds, which suggested to her that a storm would soon be rolling in. Patras, she knew, was in the bounds of the Ottoman Empire, but there were no minarets in sight, and what she could see had a more European feel about it. She wondered if, after the attack, they had diverted over to the Italian coast and were now in Brindisi, or some other large Italian port.

Though somewhat reassured by the orderly scene before her, she found it strange that no one was up and about at what must be a relatively late hour. Turning back to the room, she surveyed it with a critical eye. The furnishings, although of good quality, were a curious mishmash of style and origin. The pitcher was clearly Chinese, yet the cups were English. The washstand, chest of drawers and wardrobe were of French design, with expensive veneers and inlays, yet the washbowl and chamber pot appeared to be Russian. Beyond her bed was a plain rough-hewn table, with two chairs that she guessed were also Russian. The wall hangings and rugs in the room all appeared to be of Ottoman origin, bar for one French tapestry. It was not what she had expected of an Italian nobleman – for surely only such a high ranking man could own a fortress like this – but then again, maybe he was just well travelled and liked to impress his guests.

She sat back down on the bed and wondered when her sister would awake. Isabelle lay there, breathing gently, her golden locks scattered on the pillow and glistening in the morning sun – a perfect picture of innocence. As she gazed at her, Helena was filled with sisterly love for this beautiful creature who had been her childhood playmate, lifelong companion, and confidante. Not as intelligent as Helena by half, to be sure, but far more adept at the social graces, with the effortless ability to light up any company that she entered. Helena, on the other hand, had a prickly personality – she just could not bring herself to suffer fools gladly – and that together with her height and acerbic wit kept most men at bay. This meant that in most company she would keep to the periphery, quite happy to play second fiddle to her glamorous sister. Though Helena could not have realised it at the time, the vision of Isabelle that morning, and the desire to restore her back to that state of innocence, would be her mainstay through the months and years of horror to come.

*

Presently Isabelle began to stir, so Helena went over to her side. She also awoke in a state of panic, shouting out in fear, and it took Helena several minutes to calm her down.

'Where are we?' asked Isabelle, after she had drunk several cups of water that Helena had brought over to her.

'Brindisi, I hope,' replied Helena. 'In a nobleman's fortress – though, truth be told, I am not totally sure. Once you are feeling more yourself, you must dress, and then we can go and find someone from the ship's crew who can tell us what happened.'

'What about Lt Hurst?'

'God willing he has survived,' answered Helena, a shudder of dread running through her at the thought of any other eventuality. She dismissed such thoughts from her mind, determined to hope for the best. 'Now, we must get dressed and find out who our host is,' She opened the wardrobe in the corner of the room. 'My riding dress!' she exclaimed as she pulled it out. 'And is has been cleaned as well. Excellent. We…'

'Did anything happen to us?' interrupted Isabelle. 'While we were drugged?' She was now sitting up in bed, looking worried, her arms folded across her breasts. 'I can't remember anything after the cabin.'

'Nor can I,' replied Helena, sitting on the side of her bed. 'But nothing untowards happened – I am sure of it. I do not feel any different. And yourself?'

'No,' said Isabelle, with some hesitation. 'But *would* we?' She looked directly into her sister's eyes. 'If we had been *raped*?'

'Isabelle! No, I am sure nothing has happened to us,' Helena repeated as she crouched down by the side of Isabelle's bed and took her hand. 'The marines must have re-taken the ship. Take a look outside if you want reassurance – this is a nobleman's palace, not a lair of degenerate corsairs. All our luggage has been brought here and our clothes have been cleaned – which I hardly think are the actions of corsairs.'

'It's just…' Isabelle's face crumbled as she spoke. 'If anything had happened to us…then what man would ever look at me again? I would never be married!' She burst into tears, burying her head in her hands.

'There, there,' murmured Helena, as she stroked her sister's head.

'We are both unsullied – I am sure of it.' She waited until Isabelle's sobs had subsided somewhat before speaking again. 'Come now, we must meet our new protector. He must surely be a nobleman, and there must be many fine young men in his household that we will meet.'

'Well, let us hope so!' exclaimed Isabelle, with a wistful smile. 'Maybe I will have better fortune with men here than in England.' She wiped the tears from her eyes with a handkerchief. 'Right then, we must dress immediately,' she declared as she cast back the bed sheet and swung her legs out of the bed, before fixing Helena with a coy smile. 'Come sister, what detains you?'

*

When both were dressed, and Isabelle had checked her appearance in the looking glass for the hundredth time, Helena moved to the door and attempted to open it – but it was locked.

'For our protection, no doubt,' she remarked, and then knocked loudly on the door. 'Hello!' she called out in Italian. 'We wish to leave this room!' There was no reply, so she now pounded on the door. 'Is there anybody there?'

This time there was the sound of some movement outside, and they heard the sound of laboured breathing coming up to the door – and then passing it.

'Hello! We are in *here*!' called Helena, but the heavy silence of the palace once more descended on them.

'This is most odd,' exclaimed Isabelle. 'Why did they not unlock the door?'

'Let us wait a few moments,' replied Helena. 'They may be fetching a key.'

Sometime later, Helena was about to pound on the door again, when they heard movement, and the same laboured breathing. A key was inserted in the lock and the door swung inwards to reveal a toothless old woman with dishevelled long snowy-white hair that almost hid her eyes from view, dressed in a simple grey smock. She looked at them both for a few moments, uncertain of what to do, but then her attention seemed to be drawn by Isabelle, and for some reason she gaped open-mouthed at her.

'We wish to see your master,' requested Helena in Italian, annoyed at the woman's rudeness. The woman now looked questioningly at Helena. She had obviously not understood what had been said.

'*Sequere me*,' she eventually requested, stumbling over the words as if she was unused to them.

'What did she say?' asked Isabelle. 'It was not Italian.'

'No, 'twas Latin,' explained Helena. 'Although why a servant is speaking it, instead of Italian, is beyond me.'

Helena switched to Latin. 'Come now, out, out!' she ordered, as she shooed the woman back into the corridor, and the two sisters followed her out.

The woman scowled briefly at Helena, but then turned and led the way down the gloomy corridor, lit only by strange lamps on either side that emitted a soft blue light. Intrigued, Helena walked up to one and peered inside it. It was similar to a candle holder but with the opening covered in a wire mesh. Inside were a heap of large blue crystals that appeared to be lit up from within. She held her hand close to the mesh and was surprised to feel no heat being emitted from the lamp. She looked below the lamp itself, trying to find the source of the light.

Realising she had stopped, the servant woman turned and gestured urgently.

Helena reluctantly tore herself away from the lamp, her initial sense of wonder at the cold blue light turning to one of foreboding.

'Where on earth are we?' she thought, as she hurried after the servant.

The ever present, deathly silence of the palace began to unnerve her. The servant continued to a wide flight of stairs and led them up it, huffing and wheezing as she went. At the top of the stairs were large double doors that, even in the cool blue light, Helena could see were covered in arcane and somewhat disturbing symbols. Her sense of foreboding increased, and she began to wish she had found her pistol and brought it with her. This was not the palace of a God-fearing man – that was almost certain. She glanced at Isabelle, but she seemed blissfully unaware of the significance of the symbols, her head filled, no doubt, with images of handsome Italian noblemen waiting within.

It was too late to go back – the servant was opening the doors in front of them. Taking a deep breath Helena walked in behind her – and gasped as the smell of pungent incense assailed her nostrils. The smell was quite disgusting, forcing them both to pull handkerchiefs to their faces. The servant urged them forward, to the far end of what appeared to be a large audience chamber, which lay wreathed in gloom. Continuing on, they could now make out a large throne-like chair on a raised dais, and Helena's heart skipped a beat as she saw a shadowy figure sitting perfectly still there, face hidden from view by a cowl. No sound came from the figure, but Helena had the overwhelming sense they were being watched and critically assessed by some cold and higher mind. They reached the steps of the dais and stopped, unsure of what to do – and then both started as the doors shut loudly behind them.

The noise prompted Isabelle into action and she executed a graceful low curtsey towards the shadowy figure.

'My Lord, we are your humble guests,' she said in Italian. This drew no reply from above, and Isabelle glanced furtively at Helena for some inspiration.

'May we know the name of our protector?' asked Helena in Italian, as she also curtsied, though a tad awkwardly.

Following her question, there was a moment of silence, and then the figure above gave a short, harsh bark of a laugh. He rose smoothly from the throne and began slowly walking down the steps towards them, his hands reaching up to his cowl.

'Forgive me, ladies. I have been rude. Let me introduce myself,' said the figure, with a voice that was deep, commanding and resonant, his Italian grammatically perfect, albeit with a slight Eastern European accent. He was on the last step now. Helena's heart began to race with fearful anticipation and the sisters instinctively retreated back as he neared them.

He drew back his cowl to reveal – as she had feared – luxuriant shoulder-length white hair, which framed a wickedly handsome face of pronounced cheekbones and a square jutting jaw, though his eyes were hidden by smoked lens spectacles.

'My name is Zentar, son of Korthdan and heir-in-waiting to the Empire of the Moon.' He smiled at the end of this statement – and both sisters screamed in unison when they saw the fangs protruding from his upper jaw.

*

The sisters fled from the audience chamber in blind panic, pushing the servant to one side and wrenching the large double doors open, before half stumbling down the stairs and back to their room. Once there, they had only just barricaded the door with the heavy chest of drawers when it was pushed slowly but firmly open, its wooden feet screeching as they scraped over the stone floor. The sisters screamed again. Isabelle ran to the furthest corner of the room, while Helena reached under her bed to pull out her travelling bag, tipping its contents out on to the bed itself. She was still rummaging through them when the creature entered the room.

'Is this what you are looking for?' he asked in his resonant Italian, holding up a small pistol.

Helena abruptly stopped searching and stepped back to join Isabelle near the window.

'How dare you go though my belongings,' she exclaimed, having recovered some of her composure. 'That belongs to me!'

'I think not,' Zentar replied, putting the pistol away in a pocket. 'Captain Todd said it belonged to *him*.'

'Captain Todd is here?' exclaimed Helena. 'What about the rest of the crew?'

'And *where* are we?' demanded Isabelle, emboldened by Helena's offensive.

'Ladies, please,' the creature requested, holding up one hand to silence them. 'One question at a time,' he insisted. 'Here, sit,' he commanded, picking up the two chairs near the table and moving them to their side of the room, before retreating back, near to the door.

He then spoke, in a coarse guttural language that Helena had never heard before, to someone outside in the corridor, in the tone of someone giving instructions. That done, he shut the door and perched on the edge of the table behind him, as the sisters reluctantly pulled the chairs over and sat down themselves, both with their legs crossed and arms folded.

'Well, who exactly are you?' demanded Helena, once she had sat down, the initial fear she had felt fading as she observed him more closely. His fang were hideous, but he had a commanding, aristocratic presence about him, and she sensed he was rational and of even temperament. 'And, pray, explain what you mean by "the Empire of the Moon."'

She felt his gaze boring into her for a few moments, clinically assessing her again, and just as she was beginning to feel uncomfortable, he looked away.

'The Empire of the Moon,' he began, 'is the domain of my people – the Rakshasa. It exists on both the physical and astral planes, as well as others that you will not be aware of.'

'Sir – please speak plainly. We do not know of this "astral plane" you speak of…'

'But you do,' insisted Zentar. 'You visit it each night.'

'You have lost me,' exclaimed Helena, eyebrows raised as she shot a look of exasperation at Isabelle.

'It is simple enough. When you sleep, you lose awareness of your physical body, and that allows you to perceive the higher reality of the astral plane – which you know through dreaming. We can act on that plane as easily as on this – whereas you are like infants on it. You are vaguely aware of events going on around you – memories playing out, emotions, colours, and sounds that sometimes you remember – but on the whole you have no ability to act on that plane, nor manipulate it.'

'Please,' requested Helena, becoming impatient now, 'enough of this high philosophising. Where are we right *now*? On the "physical plane", if you will?'

'At this moment, the physical boundaries of our empire are the shores of this island.'

'We are on an island?' exclaimed Helena, exchanging a shocked look with Isabelle.

'Yes. The island of Santorini, in what you will know as the Aegean Sea,' he replied.

The sisters exchanged a puzzled glance.

'But...we were supposed to be going to Patras. If we are in the Aegean, then we are far south of Athens, is that not so? What on earth are we doing here?'

'You have been brought here for your own protection.'

'Protection?' echoed Helena, in disbelief.

'Yes,' he insisted. 'Ladies, you are obviously not aware of it, but your ultimate destination was *not* Patras.' He paused. 'It was Cairo.'

'Why?' protested Helena. 'And what is all this talk of protection? We were on a Royal Naval warship. Why, you are just trying to confound us, sir!'

'Documents given to us by Captain Todd will prove what I have stated...'

'Was he working for you?' demanded Helena.

'Yes. He aided us in your rescue.'

'You mean he *betrayed* us,' Helena spat the words out, hatred rising up within her. 'How long are we to be kept here – for our *protection*?'

'You will be returned to your own people when we judge it safe to do so, and not before.'

Both sisters were stunned into silence at this. Zentar stood up.

'And now, I must leave you. The servants will bring you some food at sunset. We will talk again, in a few days hence.'

He walked over to the door to leave.

'Wait,' asked Helena, unable to keep a tone of pleading from her voice as panic rose up within her. 'You said you had spoken to Captain Todd – but what about the rest of the crew?'

Zentar gave a deep sigh. 'I am afraid to say that...' he hesitated, '... that during the action we took to rescue you...all of the remainder of the crew perished.'

Helena gave a cry of horror and leapt to her feet, taking several steps towards him with her hands clasped, before pulling herself up short of him. 'No!' she cried. 'Say 'tis not true! Please, for the love of God...'

'The loss of life was regrettable,' said Zentar, 'but there was no other way.'

He then turned away from them, opened the door and stepped through, pulling it firmly shut behind him. They heard the sound of a key turning, and were locked in again.

Black despair gripped Helena and she collapsed on to her bed, weeping uncontrollably.

CHAPTER 3

Tired, unshaven, and filthy, Alex rounded the corner of a derelict building and breathed a heartfelt sigh of relief. Ahead of him, its white washed walls gleaming in the afternoon sunlight, was a large fortified compound – with the Union Flag flying overhead. It was located on the west side of a harbour that lay before him, and to the north was the road to Athens. The harbour was huge, easily capable of sheltering a considerable navy and surrounded on all sides by the ruins of ancient walls. Because of this, Alex was shocked at what he saw about him as he sat on his horse near the quayside – the port of Piraeus was practically deserted and eerily quiet. Other than the British compound and a French one on the other side of the harbour, near which stood a small Greek monastery, the only buildings present were a mean Turkish custom house and a few sheds. A handful of ships were anchored in the harbour and some small fishing boats were tied up to two ruined moles. The harbour, with its glistening ruined walls of white stone and marble gave the impression that a mighty civilisation had once been present here but had faded away, leaving only its bones to bleach in the sun.

He remained there for a few moments, then roused himself from his contemplation and quickly headed towards the British consulate. Eagerly now, he dismounted and presented himself at the gates, thrilled just to hear the English voice of the gruff marine on the other side, who challenged him in a broad Norfolk accent. Sometime later, a marine sergeant appeared at the gates.

'And who the devil are you?' he demanded, from behind the wrought iron gates, flanked by two musket-touting guards.

This was not quite the reception Alex had been expecting, but given the fact he probably now looked like a Greek bandit, unshaven and with the tan of a peasant, it was probably understandable. He took off his hat to reveal his blonde hair, came to attention, and saluted smartly.

'First Lieutenant Alex Hurst of HMS *Fearless*,' he replied. 'I was shipwrecked over a week ago…'

'HMS *Fearless*?' countered the sergeant. 'Never heard of it – but you better come in before the Turks start sniffing around.' He gestured towards the customhouse where two Turkish soldiers were looking over in curiosity.

One of the gates was opened, and Alex was about to enter when suddenly there was the sound of horses' hooves behind, and he saw a coach-and-four bearing down on him.

'Make way for Admiral Blake!' called out the coachman; the other gate swung open, and Alex barely had time to enter the compound before the coach thundered into the courtyard.

The coach came to a sudden halt, the door sprang open, and out stepped a fresh-faced chap wearing a lieutenant's uniform.

'Sergeant Clark – what is that peasant doing inside the compound?' he demanded, pointing at Alex, before his feet had even touched the ground.

'Says he's a naval officer, sir,' retorted the sergeant, snapping to attention.

The carriage creaked as an older man in a black cloak descended from it. He was an archetypal Leo – tall and well-formed, with fine features, a high forehead, and long swept-back sandy hair that was greying at the temples.

'Lieutenant Jenkins, take charge here,' he commanded, not even glancing at Alex. 'Get this man cleaned up and bring him to my office at three o'clock.' He then strode off in the direction of the main building.

'Certainly, Admiral,' responded Lt Jenkins and began issuing orders.

Another well-dressed man stepped from the coach, standing on the carriage step as he supervised the unloading of luggage, and taking not the slightest interest in Alex as he was led away to the barracks.

*

Less than an hour later, Alex was in the anteroom to Admiral Blake's office. After a scrub down, the barber had shaved him, and then he had been given fresh navy issue clothes from the stores. He now sat in a comfortable chair, his stomach full, relieved and elated to have reached safety. Presently the double doors to Admiral Blake's office opened.

'The admiral will see you now,' announced Lt Jenkins.

Alex went into the large office and sat at the chair indicated, while Lt Jenkins joined Admiral Blake on the other side of the table. The light from the late afternoon sun streamed in through the Venetian blinds, lighting the whole room up in a hazy glow. Admiral Blake presently finished with the document he was reading, signed it, and pushed it over to one side. He then straightened up and looked Alex in the eye with a steely gaze.

'Well, sir! Who are you and where have you come from?' he demanded.

'Sir, I was on HMS *Fearless*…'

'What!' exclaimed Admiral Blake in shock, his businesslike attitude vanishing in an instant. Lt Jenkins had also literally jumped with shock at the mention of the *Fearless*, and his hands were on the arms of his chair, as if ready to leap over the desk at Alex.

'Jenkins – the *Fearless* manifest,' commanded Admiral Blake. The warmth had evaporated from his eyes and was replaced by a cold stare. Lt Jenkins dived into a bag that was down by the side of the table, pulled out a dog-eared sheaf of papers, and passed them to Admiral Blake, who ran his finger down the list of men, holding the papers closely so that Alex could not read them.

'Who was your captain?' the admiral demanded.

'Captain Todd.'

'That's not what I have here!'

'Captain Iserwood fell ill some three days before we sailed from Gibraltar – Captain Todd was drafted in as a last-minute replacement,' explained Alex.

'I handpicked Iserwood myself,' murmured Admiral Blake, 'and now I remember you being discussed for the *Fearless* also. What is your first name?'

'Alex, sir,' he replied, gaining confidence as he felt events moving his way.

'Good God, man!' exclaimed Admiral Blake. 'Then what are you doing here? What's happened to the *Fearless*?'

Alex hesitated before speaking. 'The *Fearless* was destroyed, sir – in a corsair attack.'

'My God!' exclaimed Admiral Blake, his voice almost a whisper. 'We have lost the *Fearless*?'

'Unfortunately, sir – yes.'

Admiral Blake leaned back momentarily in his chair with his hands resting on its arms, looking at Alex as if he had seen a ghost. He then hurriedly conferred with Lt Jenkins, and the next moment Lt Jenkins was halfway out the door.

'And bring some paper and quills back with you – we need to record this,' called Admiral Blake after him. He turned his attention back to Alex. 'No!' he commanded, raising his hand and stopping Alex before he could speak. 'I don't want you to say anything until we are all assembled.' He suddenly looked tired and seemed to have aged ten years in the space of a few moments. 'That cabinet over there,' he said gesturing across the room. 'Be a good chap and get the brandy out will you? And four glasses? We're going to need it.'

*

Admiral Blake flopped back in his chair, glass in hand, distractedly tapping the desk with his fingers as they waited for Lt Jenkins to return. Alex sat silently, mystified by the other's reaction. Presently the double doors opened and Lt Jenkins slipped in, closely followed by the man Alex had seen supervising the unloading of the coach. The man glanced at Alex as he made his way to the spare chair near the door, bringing in with him the smell of stale tobacco, but otherwise ignoring him.

The newcomer was tall, of medium build, with a thick shock of black hair that was a trifle curly and reached almost to his neck. Dark eyebrows were permanently arched in a faint expression of surprise, and his eyes brown and heavy lidded with long eyelashes more like those of a woman. Below his Roman nose were full-bodied lips and a firm, jutting jaw. Though his features were finely chiselled, they also spoke of a lifetime of good dining – his otherwise fine cheekbones being slightly padded.

He wore a light blue brocade suit consisting of a coat, waistcoat, and knee breeches, finished off by knee-length stockings. The white ruffles of his shirt were visible at his wrists and the buckles on his highly-polished black shoes gleamed. Manner, posture, and clothes all spoke of someone of great wealth, power and confidence.

Admiral Blake had stood as he entered. 'Lord Charlemont, please have a seat,' he said indicating a spare chair on Alex's side of the table.

Lord Charlemont sat without a word, crossing his knees and supported his hands to one side on a silver topped cane. Several rings on his manicured, tobacco stained fingers glistened in the sunlight, and he looked as if he should be sitting in an expensive coffee house in London, not in this far-flung outpost of England. Alex found that he had also automatically risen to his feet at Lord Charlemont's entrance and now stood there awkwardly, waiting for some acknowledgement from the man.

'Lt Hurst – Lord Charlemont,' said Admiral Blake. 'Special Consul to the Levant Company.'

'My Lord,' replied Alex, coming smartly to attention.

'And, Lord Charlemont, this is Lt Hurst.'

Lord Charlemont barely turned his head in Alex's direction, and gave a very slight nod, before turning his attention back to Admiral Blake and ignoring Alex again. Alex sat down, somewhat irritated at the man's attitude.

'I hope this will not take long, admiral,' began Lord Charlemont. His voice was deep and melodious. 'I have an appointment in Athens later this evening.'

'Well, Lord Charlemont,' Admiral Blake said with a wry smile, as he glanced over to Alex, 'you may decide to cancel that!'

Lord Charlemont tilted his head a fraction towards Admiral Blake, raising his eyebrows quizzically.

'Lt Hurst here is the only known survivor of a corsair raid barely a week ago…'

Lord Charlemont's expression changed ever so slightly to one of disinterest, mixed with polite patronisation.

'…on the *Fearless*.'

For a brief moment Lord Charlemont froze as Admiral Blake's words seemed to hang in the air. Then an instant later he was on his feet, cane raised in one hand as he bore down on Alex.

'What happened?' he roared, all affectation discarded. 'Where are the women?'

'Lord Charlemont!' exclaimed Admiral Blake. 'Please calm yourself. That is what we are here to find out!'

Lord Charlemont ignored him and continued to bear down on Alex, who was already off his seat ready to fend off a blow from the cane.

'Sit down, sir!' bellowed Admiral Blake.

Lord Charlemont halted, shocked at the way he had been spoken to.

'*Please*,' persisted Admiral Blake, in a more reasonable tone, his demeanour changing in the space of a heartbeat.

Lord Charlemont reluctantly returned to his chair, throwing his cane onto the table, and drawing a cry of anguish from Admiral Blake.

'Careful now, I have just had that polished!'

Lord Charlemont ignored him as he kicked his chair round so that it faced Alex, and then sat down, glaring at him.

The doors opened a crack.

'My Lord?' asked a harsh Germanic voice, the owner of which was hidden from view.

'All is well,' replied Lord Charlemont, still glaring at Alex. 'I will call if I require you.'

Almost instantly the doors shut again.

'Well, gentlemen,' said Admiral Blake, in a conciliatory tone, 'the sooner we start talking, the sooner we can find out what happened to the *Fearless*. Lt Jenkins here will take notes.'

Lord Charlemont said nothing, but moved his chair closer to the table so he could rest his arm on it, and from a pocket he drew out a slim silver case. From this he took out a cheroot, lighting it carefully from a tinderbox Lt Jenkins slid over to him.

'Good,' commented Admiral Blake, taking this as agreement. 'Well Lt Hurst,' he said, stretching his arm out towards him. 'From the beginning – but keep it succinct. Please make a note, Jenkins, that Lt Hurst arrived in Piraeus on the 17 April, 1735.'

*

'We were attacked four days out from Venice, and had just passed the Julian Rocks, south of Corfu,' began Alex. 'We were dead in the water, a thick mist had settled around us, and by late afternoon the temperature had dropped to freezing. I had just come on deck for the last dogwatch when the lookout fell to the deck. Initially, I thought he had fallen asleep on duty, but then I realised he had been shot with a machine launched crossbow bolt. The next moment we were under attack from a galley…'

'A galley?' echoed Admiral Blake as, by his side, Lt Jenkins scribbled away valiantly. 'What armaments did it have?'

'Deck mounted crossbows, obviously, but no heavy guns that I remember.'

'You mean an unarmed galley took on a fifty gun ship? That would be tantamount to suicide!'

Alex found his face burning with embarrassment at Admiral Blake's observation but pressed on. 'It came out of the mist from starboard. I gave the order to open fire, but then Captain Todd appeared on desk and countermanded it.'

'Why?'

'I have no idea, sir. I was the senior officer on deck when I sighted the galley and had every right to issue the command. By the time I had persuaded him to open fire again, a battle cry arose from the galley that literally froze everyone in their tracks.'

'A *battle cry*?'

'Yes, sir. Just before they rammed us.' Alex paused. In the warm light of day, in a civilised consulate office, it seemed implausible even to him that the events of that evening had actually happened – but he knew there was a rational explanation for it. 'The sound and intensity of it was incredible, and it effectively disabled everyone on the ship for a few moments.'

Lord Charlemont suddenly seemed to lose his bad temper and appeared intrigued.

'I've been in quite a few engagements, and I think what we experienced was a combination of surprise at the strange nature of the battle cry – and the raw shock a surprise attack can induce.'

Admiral Blake nodded in agreement, but Lord Charlemont did not seem so convinced.

'I recovered first, and then shouted out several times at the crew to repel boarders. This snapped them out of the shock, and from then on all acted normally.' Clearing his throat, he pressed on. 'Captain Todd then issued the fire command but our guns didn't work due to the cold and damp – or at least we just had misfires…'

'Had the gun stoppers been in place?' interrupted Admiral Blake.

'Not before I came on watch, sir. Captain Todd had ordered them to be removed some four hours previously, in case of a surprise attack. My view was that the guns' charges could be adversely affected with the damp – as was the case – so I had ordered them to be replaced.'

'Good grief,' muttered Admiral Blake, taking a swig from his brandy glass. 'Go on.'

'So the galley managed to ram us with minimal damage and a raiding party got on board before it pulled away.'

'What did they look like?' interrupted Lord Charlemont, leaning forward in his chair. 'And what were they armed with?'

'Well, they were dressed in a black garb similar to North African Arabs, but with silver helmets that were partially masked around the eyes. They had pistols and carried large rectangular shields on their left arms – the insignia of which was the head of some creature wrought in silver, with fanged jaws. More weapons hung from their belts – pistols, a *kilij*, knives, and grenades. They also wore some sort of chainmail vest which appeared to provide protection against our muskets.'

'And what in God's name were your marines doing at this point?' demanded Admiral Blake, an undercurrent of anger in his voice.

'Snipers on the galley shot most of those who had made it to the starboard railings or up into the shrouds during the period of time we were all affected by the battle cry.'

Admiral Blake grunted in disgust at this.

'Shortly after they boarded, I withdrew the command party back to the poop deck.' A questioning frown crossed Lord Charlemont's face. 'The high deck at the rear of the ship,' he added.

'And Captain Todd?' demanded Admiral Blake.

Alex took a deep breath. 'After issuing the fire order, he passed command back to me and went below to his stateroom.'

'He did what?' Admiral Blake gasped in horror. 'He *deserted* his post?'

'Yes, sir. That, and his subsequent actions, led me to that conclusion.'

Admiral Blake's gaze dropped to the table, a look of rage on his face. Lord Charlemont glanced over to Admiral Blake and then nodded at Alex to continue.

'At first we seemed to be containing them, but then some of them got down to the heavy gun deck. Using grenades, and God only knows what else, they overcame the starboard gun crews, allowing the galley to draw alongside. Another raiding party boarded and forced its way to the poop deck steps, where we managed to pin them down for a while. At this point, some of these raiders went below – the captain's stateroom was directly beneath us – and shortly afterwards I heard a door being broken down. Then there were shots…' He paused, his voice breaking slightly. 'Women screaming. Cries for help…' He swallowed hard to control his emotions. 'And then silence.'

Lord Charlemont closed his eyes, his shoulders drooping slightly and sighing as a look of pain crossed his face. Finally he opened his eyes again, but now they were downcast. Admiral Blake also appeared to be in shock and just stared ahead of himself. Alex was puzzled – if Lord Charlemont had been expecting to meet Helena or Isabelle, how was it that the sisters had failed to mention this to him?

'Go on,' Admiral Blake requested, his voice weak.

'The raiders re-appeared from below, carrying two female figures with them.'

'The women – then they were still alive?' demanded Lord Charlemont, snapping out of his despondency.

'I hope to God they were, but honestly I don't know,' replied Alex, not wanting to raise his own hopes, let alone theirs. 'They were like rag dolls. Helena was bleeding from a head wound and there was blood on her riding dress.'

'They could have been drugged,' postulated Admiral Blake, his voice rising with enthusiasm. 'I take it they were transferred to the galley?'

'Yes.'

'Then they're alive!' declared Lord Charlemont with absolute confidence, striking the table with his fist. He leapt to his feet, blue smoke from his cheroot swirling around him as he did so. 'Admiral Blake, we must send out warships immediately and track down these curs down!'

'Lord Charlemont, please!' requested Admiral Blake. 'We need to know what else happened.'

Lord Charlemont huffed with annoyance, but Admiral Blake insisted. Once again he reluctantly took his seat.

Alex was about to continue when he visibly flinched as a memory from that night suddenly came back to him – something he had seen but not realised the significance of until now.

Admiral Blake saw the look of shock cross his face. 'Lt Hurst?'

'There were also two men who transferred to the galley, sir. Two men in black hooded cloaks – carrying bags – just in front of the Montagus. I had thought they were corsairs at the time, but now…'

'Go on,' prompted Admiral Blake.

'I saw a flash of yellow from where the cloak of one of them had ridden up… My God, sir – it was Captain Todd!'

'You are absolutely sure?'

'Yes. Captain Todd had appeared on deck wearing a yellow frock coat.'

'Then, who was the other man?' asked Admiral Blake in exasperation.

'At a guess, I would say his cook, Gustavo.'

Admiral Blake shoulders slumped and he buried his head in his hands. 'It just gets worse,' he croaked. 'Desertion *and* treason!'

'There is also something about one of the raiders you should know,' continued Alex. Admiral Blake looked up at him warily.

'One actually made it up to the poop deck. I struck him down, and once he was on the deck, I pulled his helmet back.' He paused. 'He had long blonde, almost white hair, and his face was deathly white. The eyes were all wrong, too,' said Alex, shaking his head as he tried to describe what he had seen. 'They were a similar shape to a snake's eyes, and yet bright red and his eye teeth were hideous – unnaturally long and sharp.'

'Well, what of it all?'

'I had delivered a death blow to his temple, so that could have accounted for the eyes looking wrong – burst blood vessels and so forth…'

'And the Barbary corsairs frequently sharpen their teeth to points to terrorise their victims,' interrupted Admiral Blake.

'My thoughts also, so I can only think he was an albino; but so were the others that attacked the poop deck – their hair was visible below their helmets.'

Lord Charlemont was once again intrigued and appeared to want to pursue this matter, whereas Admiral Blake was dismissive.

'Unusual for corsairs, I grant you – but hardly of any relevance,' he declared. 'All sorts of scum join their ranks in pursuit of fortune, even Christians from Europe – please continue.'

'Well, we managed to hold them off the poop deck for few more minutes, but then they overwhelmed us. I would have been shot dead at that point by one of them, had not the aft magazine gone up and blown me over the stern.'

'And then?'

'Well, that was it as far as our resistance went. By the time I had recovered my senses, the raiders had complete control.'

'How long did all this take?' inquired Lord Charlemont.

Alex shook his head. In battle it was difficult to gauge the passage of time. Engagements that seemed to take hours would subsequently be found to have been over in a fraction of that. He quickly relived the sequence of events in his mind before speaking again. 'I estimate around ten to fifteen minutes.'

Admiral Blake shook his head in disbelief. 'A fifty gun ship overpowered in fifteen minutes,' he murmured. 'Unheard of.'

'There's even worse to come, sir,' Alex said, trying to keep his voice steady – this would be the most difficult part to recount. 'I hid in part of the floating wreckage from the explosion and was able to observe the raiders. More of them, dressed in scarlet, boarded the *Fearless*. One by one, they put the crew, living and dead, through some sort of selection procedure.'

'What sort of procedure?' demanded Lord Charlemont.

Alex shook his head. 'It's difficult to say. They were brought before the leader of the scarlet-clad raiders who held his hand over their heads...'

Lord Charlemont's eyes narrowed. 'Could you see anything hanging from his hand?' he persisted.

'No. But whatever he was doing, some of the crew were rejected and run through, before being tossed into the hold.'

'And the others?'

Alex took another deep breath. 'They were beheaded – held upside down – and their blood drained into a barrel.'

The scratching of Lt Jenkin's nib stopped abruptly. There was absolute silence in the room. All looked at him in horror, Lord Charlemont sitting back in his chair, arms folded, eyes once again narrowed. He was the first to break the silence.

'What did they then do with the blood?' he asked, voice low, and in a tone that implied he already knew the answer.

'The black-clad raiders gathered around – and drank the blood from bowls given to them by the scarlet ones.'

'Good God,' Admiral Blake said, his face pale, voice barely a whisper. He looked at Lord Charlemont. 'Who are these *barbarians*? Who would *do* such a thing?'

'I swear it is true, sir – on my mother's grave.'

Admiral Blake shook his head in disbelief. Finally he spoke again. 'Continue.'

The scratching of the nib renewed.

'The galley cast off and the *Fearless* sank fairly quickly. I swam around after it had gone down, but I could find no other survivors. I made it to shore, was found by a hunter, and managed to persuade him and his brother to bring me here.'

'Why did you come here, instead of Patras?' cut in Lord Charlemont.

'The hunter told me the area to the north of Patras is teeming with brigands. He knew the road to Athens so it made sense to make for the consulate here.'

'Deuced good of them to help you – you gave them some incentive, I take it?' asked Admiral Blake.

'I've a few gold sovereigns sewn into my belt, in case of shipwreck.'

'Stout fellow,' muttered Admiral Blake, looking away, his thoughts elsewhere.

*

For a few moments no one spoke, and the room was silent save for the sound of Lt Jenkins's quill scratching across the paper, his notes catching up with the spoken account.

Glancing back at Lord Charlemont, Alex realised he was staring intently at him, a suspicious look on his face.

'You referred to Lady Helena as "Helena",' said Lord Charlemont, his tone accusing.

'That is correct.'

'A remarkably familiar way to refer to a lady, is it not?'

'Lady Helena and I became acquainted in those four days on the *Fearless* – we found we had a great deal in common and became close. We arranged to meet up again in England later in the year and...' he paused. 'And I was going to ask her to marry me.'

Silence once more descended on the room and the other three men looked at him with a mixture of shock and, for reasons he could not even begin to guess at, embarrassment.

'Ha, I knew it! A bounder!' sneered Lord Charlemont, breaking the silence and slapping his hand down on the table.

Admiral Blake gave an embarrassed cough. 'Easy now, Lord Charlemont. These things happen.'

There was a brief pause, and then without apology for his outburst, Lord Charlemont began questioning Alex about the corsairs again – insisting on going through every detail of their appearance, from their robes to the way they held their *kilijs*. Admiral Blake eventually joined in the questioning but he, on the other hand, was more concerned with how the crew had reacted to the attack, and whether proper procedures had been followed.

It was almost another hour before all their questions had been exhausted. Admiral Blake and Lord Charlemont then conferred briefly in hushed voices before the admiral turned to Lt Jenkins.

'Mr Jenkins, order us some coffee, will you?'

'Yes, sir,' replied Lt Jenkins, rubbing his eyes from the strain of scripting.

'And Mr Hurst – please leave us,' requested Admiral Blake. 'We have much to discuss. Also, speak to no one of these matters – though I fear news of your ordeal will have already spread beyond the walls of this compound. Jenkins will show you to the wardroom and the guest quarters. Meet back here at six o'clock.'

'Certainly, Admiral,' said Alex, and got up to leave the room.

Opening the double doors, Alex walked through the anteroom and saw the man whom he presumed had briefly spoken to Lord Charlemont. He was of medium height and strong build, with closely cropped auburn hair and a hard, tanned weasel-like face, set off by intensely bright blue eyes. His clothes were of a good cut, but practical and those of a servant. Alex assumed he was Lord Charlemont's manservant and gave him a nod as he passed; the man, however, did not return his acknowledgement and just glared at him.

*

On returning to Admiral Blake's office later that evening, Alex found that a fire had been set in the hearth to offset a slight chill in the evening air, and candelabra had been produced, giving the room a homely feel. Places had been set and various dishes were gathered in the middle of the table, and the room was dominated by the enticing aroma of roast lamb. Alex suddenly felt hungry again. Admiral Blake and Lord Charlemont, seated with their backs to the portrait of the king, stood up as Alex entered the room. He waited for Admiral Blake to sit down again before taking his own place.

'Gentlemen, let me say grace – then we can eat,' declared Admiral Blake. 'We'll speak of other matters later,' he said, gesturing pointedly to the serving staff.

The food was excellent. Admiral Blake had no great love of regulation salted beef and preferred to eat fresh local produce. As well as lamb, the dishes contained rice, tomatoes, aubergines, peppers, and olives, as well as thick lamb gravy stock. Following the main dishes, a thick milk-like substance named *yogurt* was served up. Admiral Blake insisted that Alex try some, mixed in with an aromatic honey that he described as 'The finest honey in the world – from the slopes of Mt Hymettus!'

It transpired that Admiral Blake was a born raconteur, and Alex soon found himself often near helpless with laughter at the man's anecdotes. A lot of the tales involved well-known figures in the government being caught with their trousers down, both literally and metaphorically, described in a most disrespectful way. During the meal even Lord Charlemont thawed somewhat and recounted some raunchy stories about the aristocracy that surprised Alex in their frankness and the rank of those involved. Most seemed to centre around some club that Lord Charlemont was a member of, but the name of which he did not let slip. Eventually, having drunk several toasts to King George II, the plates and dishes were cleared away, the cigars and port passed round, and the serving staff dismissed. They pulled their chairs up to the hearth and gathered around the dying embers of the fire.

*

'Now,' announced Admiral Blake in his businesslike manner. 'Let us return to the matter in hand. As you may be aware, Lt Hurst, most European trade with the East Indies, Middle and Far East in spices, silks, carpets, and so forth, is now carried by shipping travelling round the Cape of Good Hope. The main reason for this is the dominance of the eastern Mediterranean trade routes by the Ottoman Empire who levy *outrageous* charges on all goods travelling through their lands.'

'The major overland caravan route from the east,' cut in Lord Charlemont, 'terminates at Aleppo in Syria. Before the Portuguese discovered the sea route round Africa, the Ottomans had total control of this land based trade, as well as the maritime route that terminated in Alexandria – any ship entering the Red Sea had to pay tax duty at Mocha. By the time goods had passed through their land, with all the attendant custom duties, protection money, and bribes, the price of spices in Alexandria used to be up to *two thousand percent* higher than their original cost in India,' he said, his voice rising with anger.

'So you can imagine the advantage it would give us over the sea route if we could ship goods between the Red Sea and the Mediterranean but avoid these costs altogether,' continued Admiral Blake. 'Now, recently there has been a split in the Ottoman Empire, and Egypt has effectively become independent of the sultan. A few years ago, the emir of Egypt dismissed the Ottoman governor – Kaburli Pasha – and refused to accept a replacement. He has now declared himself ruler of all Egypt. His name is proclaimed in Friday sermons and has also been inscribed on coins. It is thought that the current sultan, Mahmud, will move against him eventually, but at the moment – according to our colleagues in Constantinople – he is preoccupied by some Russian incursions into the Crimea. In the breathing space this has given him, the emir has been looking for ways of forging a military alliance to protect himself against the inevitable wrath of the sultan. So, some time ago he secretly offered a monopoly on a fixed rate route through Egypt, from Port Said to the Red Sea.'

'A set price per ton of goods, regardless of their worth,' explained Lord Charlemont. 'Up until now, all goods travelling over their land had to be examined, and a tax imposed based on the perceived value of the goods.'

'Quite,' agreed Admiral Blake. 'This route was offered to all the main western European seafaring powers – England, the Netherlands, Portugal, and Spain. However, the latter is not interested – the Treaty of Tordesillas restricts it to the New World. Portugal does not have the necessary army and fleet, and France was not offered it due to the close ties between it and the Sublime Porte…'

'Ever since the Franco-Ottoman alliance,' interrupted Lord Charlemont.

'Given our long-standing presence and contacts in the Levant, the king passed the negotiations to us, and it ended up as a two horse race between us and the one other seafaring power in Europe that was capable of fulfilling the treaty conditions,' continued Admiral Blake. 'But, after almost a year of negotiation – of which Lord Charlemont has been a major part – we persuaded the emir to award the route to us.' He paused again, as if awaiting a reaction to momentous news.

'Well. That does sounds like good news, sir,' remarked Alex, struggling to see what any of this had to do with him.

'It's not just *good* news,' exclaimed an exasperated Lord Charlemont. 'It's the best thing we have done since we won Gibraltar twenty years ago! This will enable us to cut *weeks* off the time required to bring goods from the East Indies by the sea route. All other European nations will have to come through us if they want to shift goods via the shorter land route and we will be able to charge *them* custom duty. The figures involved are astronomical, man!' he said getting more excited as he went on. 'This will consolidate England's position as a major player in Europe – it will be the making of us as a nation!'

'Except for one small detail,' interrupted Admiral Blake. 'The emir extracted from us agreements on military aid to prevent the Ottoman Sultan invading, as well as promises of numerous 'gifts', all of which we managed to fulfil, or at least negotiate a suitable replacement for. However, one of his more unusual and inflexible requests was...'

He hesitated, casting his eyes down momentarily before looking at Alex directly.

'...for an English woman, of noble birth, to join his harem in Cairo.'

CHAPTER 4

It must have been the effect of the port, but it took Alex a few moments to register the implications of what had been said. When he did, the warmth that had enveloped him over the course of the evening dissipated in an instant.

'What?' he roared, jumping to his feet and knocking over his chair. 'Lady Helena is to be given in marriage…' his voice choked, 'to a heathen?'

'No,' replied Lord Charlemont. 'It is her sister, Lady Isabelle.'

'But…this is barbaric! The women know nothing of this! Admiral Blake…'

'Lady Isabelle has not yet attained her majority,' insisted Lord Charlemont. 'As her sole parent and guardian, the earl accepted the emir's proposal of marriage on her behalf.'

'Then the man is an imbecile,' retorted Alex, his fists clenched in anger. 'This cannot be allowed to happen!'

'Lt Hurst, calm yourself!' thundered Admiral Blake. 'Sit down, sir, and hear us out! The situation is quite different from what you may imagine.'

Alex hesitated, taken aback at the sheer weight and authority of Admiral Blake's voice, then retrieved his chair and reluctantly sat down, his mind still reeling at the revelation.

'Be aware that this arrangement has been requested before by rulers in India and Persia for trade deals there, but each time the monarch has refused to approve it,' explained Lord Charlemont, somewhat bluntly.

'This time, the king was minded to approve it,' continued Admiral Blake, 'in view of its importance to the *nation*,' he concluded, with a slight look of distaste. 'Lady Isabelle was chosen from a number of portraits put forward by various members of the aristocracy…'

'All fools to a man – and all of whom have huge debts, run up at the race course or card table,' cut in Lord Charlemont. 'The father of the selected woman was to have his debts paid off by the king, and be provided with a generous pension for life.'

'I would have put it perhaps slightly differently but yes, that is the essence of it,' conceded Admiral Blake. 'The Montagus, due to their father's gambling are, in reality, as poor as church mice. Without this deal, the earl's Wiltshire estate, as well as his houses in London and Dublin would have been seized by late March. The family would have been turned out on to the street and the women would have become destitute.'

'Destitute? That's ridiculous,' exclaimed Alex. 'What about their friends and relatives?'

'The Montagus have no close relatives in England,' answered Admiral Blake.

'And all their friends have been driven away over the years by the foul temper of old man Montagu,' added Lord Charlemont.

'Well, I could take them in then,' insisted Alex.

'Oh, you think you could, do you?' retorted Lord Charlemont. 'Just marry Lady Helena, then settle down and pretend that nothing had happened? Why do you think Lady Isabelle – a renowned beauty – is still a spinster? Lady Helena is, of course, another matter altogether.' He shot a contemptuous look at Admiral Blake as he said this. 'Back in the day when old man Montagu still had money, she turned down every suitor presented to her and even *he* did not dare force one on her. Nowadays, however, all of society knows of the earl's debt, and no dowry-seeking suitor in his right mind has gone near the place for years. If you married her, then all of Earl Salisbury's *countless* other creditors would be dragging you through court for the rest of your life. You would end up as penniless as they are!'

Alex said nothing, stunned for the second time in so many minutes.

'This arrangement, distasteful as you undoubtedly find it, is the only way out of bankruptcy and disgrace for the Montagu family,' continued Admiral Blake. 'With it they can retain their family estates, their good name and, above all, their honour. Lady Isabelle, instead of living in squalor, will live out her days in the luxury and comfort she is used to – albeit on a foreign shore – and you would be free to marry Lady Helena.'

Alex said nothing for a few moments, as he thought through the implications of what had been said. When he finally spoke, he chose his words carefully, struggling to contain the anger he felt welling up inside him.

'Pardon sir, but you are not telling me the whole story. All of this – the attack on the *Fearless* – was no chance occurrence. What corsair would dare attack a heavily armed warship flying the Royal Ensign, unless he knew there was something of great value on board?' Alex demanded. 'They knew what they had come for – they'd even brought a battering ram, for God's sake! How much more prepared can you be?'

'Agreed,' said Admiral Blake.

'We were betrayed by Captain Todd – but for whom was he acting? Who was behind this?'

'We believe Captain Todd was working for the Seventeen Lords of the Dutch East India Company,' replied Lord Charlemont. 'For well over a century they have refrained from interfering with the affairs of the British East India Company and the Levant Company – but now it would appear that the temptation of this prize proved too much. If they controlled the overland route themselves, they would have the lion's share of goods sourced and shipped from the Middle and Far East to Europe. To achieve this, we believe they stage-managed the attack on the *Fearless* to obtain the one treaty demand they could not duplicate – Lady Isabelle.'

'The corsairs were probably recruited from the Red Sea, most likely Arab slavers working the East African coast,' continued Admiral Blake. 'Their ferocity is legendary. Apparently they make the North African corsairs look like children. Kitted out at a port in Palestine, no doubt, with the galley and suitable slaves,' he mused. 'Then made their way along the Greek coast until they came across you near the Julian Rocks – though how they knew your exact location in that fog is beyond me.'

'When the treaty had been signed, Lady Isabelle would have entered the emir's harem, and once inside she can never leave. Given that no man can enter the harem on pain of death, and that all the Negro guards are castrated deaf-mutes, no word of the attack would ever come from her. The Dutch would then have no more use for Lady Helena, and given their demonstrable disregard for human life...'

Lord Charlemont let his words hang in the air.

This third shock rendered Alex speechless again. That this whole nightmare had been cold-bloodedly orchestrated by merchants back in Amsterdam was almost beyond belief.

'This whole business...is insane,' he finally mumbled.

'But it all becomes academic unless we find the women – and we need your seafaring and fighting skills if we are ever to do that.' The admiral's preternaturally bright blue eyes bored into Alex. 'You know practically the whole story now, man, so what d'you say? Are you with us or not?'

Alex looked blankly at Admiral Blake for a few moments, and then dropped his gaze. To his military mind the course of action was obvious – striking out on his own would be futile, and if he were ever to see Helena again, then he had to take part in the enterprise. Moreover, better he did it than entrust the task to some parchment scratcher like Lt Jenkins. He had no idea how he would explain to Helena how her sister had been sacrificed in such an underhand way – but that had not been of his making, so he pushed those thoughts aside. He took a deep breath.

'Very well, sir,' he said, raising his eyes to look directly at Admiral Blake. 'I'm with you.'

'Excellent,' exclaimed Admiral Blake, glancing at Lord Charlemont, and then letting out a sigh of relief as Lord Charlemont harrumphed in a non-committal manner. 'Best man for the job, without a doubt, eh, Lord Charlemont?' He paused to re-fill his port. 'As for the rest of it, Lord Charlemont and I had arranged to meet the *Fearless* at Patras, around the beginning of April. From there we were to travel with you to Alexandria and thence to Cairo. Anyway, we waited at the house of the Consul-General of the Morea until last night, but other matters came up and I decided to return here – most fortuitously, as it has turned out.'

'So when was Lady Isabelle due to be,' Alex grimaced. '*Presented* to the emir?'

'Around the end of April…'

'Good God,' exclaimed Alex, jumping to his feet again. 'Then we have barely two weeks!'

'Steady on,' urged Admiral Blake with a wry smile. 'As luck would have it, I received word only this morning that the emir has been called away on urgent business to the Nubian border, in the south of his kingdom. Reading between the lines, it would seem there is some sort of rebellion going on there. Anyway, the upshot of it all is that he has instructed the presentation be put back until the 20 May, by our calendar. You have just over one month in which to aid Lord Charlemont in his search for the women. Once they have been found your job will have been done. I will organise the necessary military force to free them and with luck may yet get Lady Isabelle to the emir in time.'

'We *will* find them, I assure you,' Lord Charlemont stated, looking directly at Admiral Blake and ignoring Alex.

'Carry out this task successfully,' declared Admiral Blake, 'and you'll be looking at a substantial increase in pay – together with an invitation to join me on my flagship.'

'That is…most generous of you sir.' Alex was momentarily taken aback by what the admiral had said. Then again, finding the Montagus would probably line the pockets of both men considerably, so it was the least of what the admiral should have offered him.

'Now, I want you both to leave here at dawn, just after the curfew has been raised, with Lt Jenkins. He'll drop you off outside Athens, and then continue in to obtain the necessary *firmans* from the *vaivode* – the local governor, that is. Make a show of entering the city, and get some lodgings there at a *khan* that I know of. You will act as Lord Charlemont's personal secretary, and his manservant, Fredrich, will relay any messages to me if necessary, but otherwise you will be acting on your own. Clear?'

'Perfectly. Right, I must go, gentlemen,' declared Lord Charlemont, draining his glass and moving to stand. 'I have matters to attend to.'

Admiral Blake then stood up and walked over to Alex, proffering his hand. 'Glad to have you on board, Lt Hurst. I'm sure my confidence in you will be vindicated.'

And with that, he and Lt Jenkins left the room. Alex made his way to his own room, and as he opened the door he suddenly felt very tired. The emotionally charged low and high points of the day had exhausted him, and a tide of fatigue washed over him. After a week on the road, sleeping in ditches and hedgerows, the simple single bed, with crisp sheets and pillows, seemed like unimaginable luxury. Not bothering to undress, he stretched out on the straw filled mattress, and was asleep in an instant.

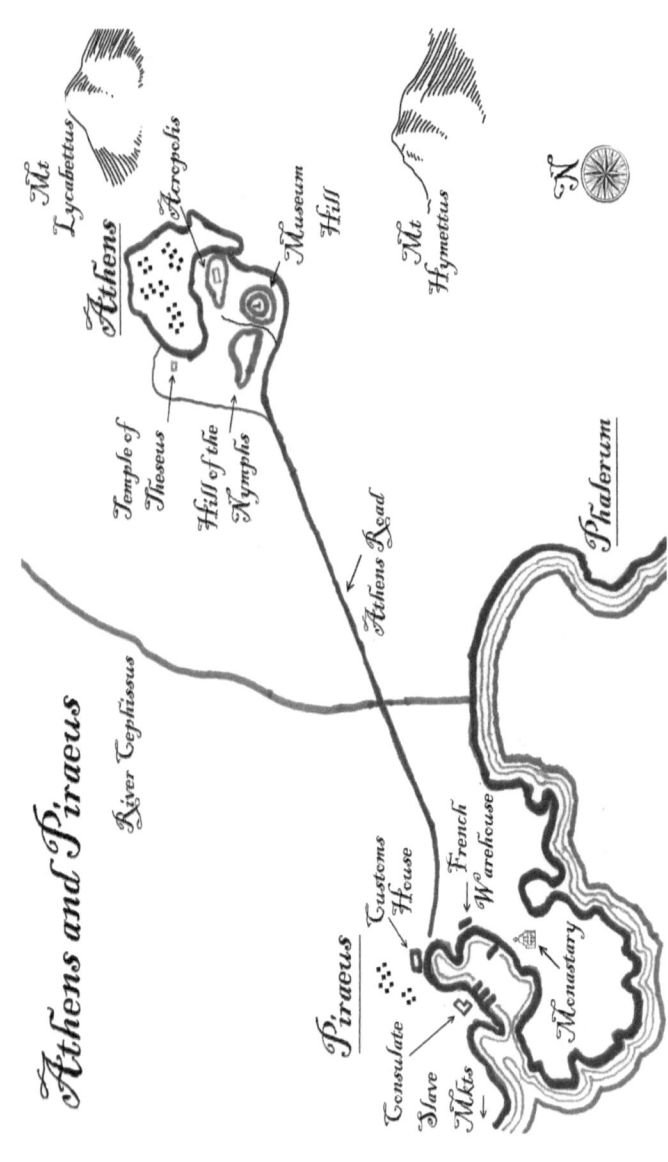

Athens and Piraeus

Mt Lycabettus

Athens

Acropolis

Museum Hill

Mt Hymettus

Temple of Theseus

Hill of the Nymphs

Athens Road

River Cephissus

N

Phalerum

Customs House

French Warehouse

Piraeus

Consulate

Slave Mkts

Monastery

CHAPTER 5

Someone was shaking his shoulder – it was Fredrich holding a lantern above him.

'You sleep like the dead!' he exclaimed with ill temper. 'We are to leave in an hour. Get ready.' He paused to light a candle on the chest of drawers from his lantern, and then stomped out of the room.

Alex reluctantly rolled out of the bed. It was still dark outside, and shivering slightly with the cold, he washed his hands and face in the washbowl. He then gathered the few things he had drawn out from the stores, stuffed them into a kit bag, and made his way to the meeting room. A fire was lit in the hearth, and Admiral Blake and Lord Charlemont were already there, eating a breakfast of mainly leftovers from the night before.

'Ah, Lt Hurst,' said Admiral Blake, 'please join us.' He took a sip from his coffee cup and then ordered a fresh pot for Alex.

Lord Charlemont acknowledged his presence with a curt nod, and continued eating.

Alex then ate in silence, attentively listening as Admiral Blake went through some procedures – stating how letters were to be sent to him, what to do if aid were required, and a few coded messages that could be used if they were detained for whatever reason by the Turkish forces.

Presently Lord Charlemont stood to leave, and with a slight feeling of shock Alex realised it was time to go, even though he had no idea how they were to even start looking for the two kidnapped sisters. He drained his coffee cup and stood up, as Admiral Blake led them to the doors.

'Well gentlemen, this is it,' he said as he halted at the doors. 'I still have a mountain of paper to work my way through, so I will say goodbye now.' He shook their hands warmly. 'Good luck to you both. I hope to see you, with news of the women, in due course.'

They left without further ado in Admiral Blake's coach-and-four. Alex sat back in his seat and watched as the deserted roads of early morning Piraeus rolled past him. Lord Charlemont sat next to him and almost immediately dozed off, while Lt Jenkins sat opposite with Fredrich who steadfastly ignored Alex, his arms crossed as he stared out of the window.

*

They quickly left Piraeus, which was not much more than a small village, and got on the road to Athens. Presently, in the faint light of dawn, he could see on either side of the road the remains of the Long Walls, which had once protected the road from the port to the city. As they approached Athens, with the bare Mt. Lycabettus in the background, the nature of the plain changed from corn fields and became thickly planted with olive trees and vineyards.

Soon the road approached two small hills, the one to the right having some sort of monument on it, and at first Alex thought they would pass through them. Instead of continuing towards the city, however, their coach veered off on to a rutted track that led to the left of the two hills. Once they had rounded the hills, he could make out something of Athens ahead, the walled city itself dwarfed by the Acropolis that rose above it. They bumped along for some time before finally coming to a halt outside the city walls behind a plainly adorned but almost perfectly preserved Greek temple set on a small hill, which had goats wandering in and out of its columns.

'The temple of Theseus,' remarked Alex, recognising it from the accounts of earlier travellers to Greece.

'I say,' carped Lord Charlemont who had woken as the carriage came to a halt, 'you're very knowledgeable – for a sailor. I thought you chaps all went to sea at fourteen and just learned how to tie knots!'

Alex caught a weary look from Lt Jenkins.

'Actually, I read Mathematics and Natural Philosophy at Oxford – but the ancients have always held a fascination for me.'

'Well I never – an *educated* sailor,' declared Lord Charlemont as he strolled away, leaving Fredrich to haul his luggage over to the temple.

The luggage was quickly unloaded, and the coach sped off through a nearby gate into Athens itself.

'Admiral Blake has arranged for a cart to come here after the Mussulmen's morning prayers,' announced Lord Charlemont, shivering slightly with the cold as he seated himself on one of his cases. 'Until then, Fredrich, be so good as to procure for us some coffee.'

With that he took out and lit a cheroot and began smoking it, looking into the middle distance and ignoring Alex, as Fredrich walked off towards the nearby city gates.

Alex did not mind the Lord Charlemont's silence, as he was taken by the elegance of the temple and so walked round it, startling some of the grazing goats. A lot of its metopes were quite weathered, and so were difficult to make out, but he recalled that they depicted the exploits of Theseus and Hercules. As the temple was set on a small hill, at one point he found himself looking over the city walls at Athens itself; his impression was of flat roofs, minarets, cypress trees, isolated marble columns, and the domed roofs of mosques crowned with stork nests. Blue vertical columns of chimney smoke rose lazily in the still morning air, creating something of a haze over the city, and he could hear the sound of dogs barking in the distance. Finally, having completed his circuit, he returned to where Lord Charlemont sat.

'Impressive, is it not?' asked Lord Charlemont on his return, his initially patronising attitude thawing somewhat. 'The problem is the Ottomans don't care for the past; I spend half my time here seeking out antiquities and shipping them back to England to protect them from further damage or misuse. Go anywhere in this city and you'll find maimed statues and pedestals with inscriptions that are just half-buried in the earth. Also, both the Turks and Greeks have taken to using the smaller marble pillars to mark their graves.'

He gestured over in the direction of the Acropolis, which was to the south, now just outside of the current city walls.

'You can't see it too well from here, but the whole hillside below the entrance to the Acropolis now looks just like one big graveyard. No doubt there used to be houses there, lapping up to the edge of the Acropolis itself when it was inside the city walls, but most of that area is deserted now. It's more "Necropolis" than "Acropolis" – ha!' he said, laughing with a snort at his own pun.

'And what of the Parthenon itself?' asked Alex, realising with some relief that they seemed to have a common interest. 'It seems half-ruined.'

'Well, the Goths have always been portrayed as barbarians, but when Alaric captured Athens from the Romans he left most of the main buildings intact. Even the Turks – under Mahomet the Second – did not destroy the ancient temples when they captured it almost three hundred years ago. No! It was left to our fellow Christians, Venetians under the command of General Morosini, to commit what must be the most heinous crime upon our ancient heritage. During an attack on the city a mere fifty years ago, they fired cannon at the Parthenon itself,' he said, pointing back to the hill with the monument that Alex had noticed on the way in. 'From Museum Hill, over yonder. It set off a powder store and brought down most of the central part of the building.' He took another long drag from his cheroot.

'What is it used for now?' asked Alex, looking back towards the Parthenon, having to shield his eyes from the rising sun. 'There appears to be another building within it.'

'Well, the Turks had converted the entire building to a mosque – one of the most magnificent in the world, apparently. But after the Venetians almost destroyed it, they built another small mosque within the central part of the ruins.'

'Really?'

'You shouldn't be so surprised. Before the Turks invaded, it was used as a Christian church dedicated to the Virgin Mary; before that, it was a Greek temple dedicated to the goddess Minerva. Every religion builds on the sites of those that have come before it.' He inhaled deeply from his cheroot again. 'Why, even St Paul's cathedral is built on the site of a Roman temple dedicated to the goddess Diana.'

Neither of them said anything for a moment. Alex was slightly unsure of what his role was in the task they had been set, while Lord Charlemont seemed lost in thought.

'Well, that's enough talk of the past; we now need to concentrate on the task in hand,' Lord Charlemont said presently, dropping the cheroot stub to the ground and stubbing it out with the heel of his boot. 'In any situation, be it in war, commerce, or domestic,' he continued, his tone suggesting he was mounting a well-worn hobby horse, 'to find out what is *really* going on, one must find those who are in power. Not those who are elected, or act as mouthpieces for others, but those who wield power on a daily basis and who know what is happening in their sphere of influence – down to the last detail.'

He then paused as he dragged on a new cheroot to light it.

'You have someone in mind?' cut in Alex.

'Of course – Ibrahim Bin Kaslm. He is the foremost merchant on the Balkan Peninsula, with over a hundred ships in his trading fleet. He will have heard something on the wind, I've no doubt.'

'Well, that sounds promising,' admitted Alex. 'How do we get to meet him?'

'Oh, I've already arranged that,' replied Lord Charlemont. 'We're due to meet him just after noon tomorrow. Ah, here's Fredrich with the coffee. Excellent.'

Fredrich had returned with a copper pot and three crockery cups on a tin tray, together with some small almond flavoured pastries that Lord Charlemont informed him were named baklavas. The coffee had been made in the traditional Turkish manner – strong, bitter, and thick as syrup. The three of them drank it sitting on Lord Charlemont's luggage, as he critically surveyed Alex's clothes.

'Hurst, you are to act as my secretary – however, before we go anywhere near Bin Kaslm's house we must first find you some decent clothes. You look as though you've just jumped ship. We'll find a shop in Athens and kit you out, and then find a barber who can give you a proper haircut and a shave.'

There was a sound of hooves approaching on the road followed by the rumble of wheels.

'Excellent!' exclaimed Lord Charlemont. 'The cart is here,' he continued as he consulted his pocket watch, 'and it is only half past seven.'

CHAPTER 6

Later that day, back at the consulate, Admiral Blake looked up as Lt Jenkins entered his office.

'Ah, Jenkins, good! I need you to encode a signal to the Company HQ.' He picked up a piece of paper from the table and handed it over. 'Use three pigeons,' he continued. 'This may be the most important signal we ever send.'

'Three, sir?' repeated Lt Jenkins looking askance at the length of the message – it covered most of one side of the paper.

'Yes, you'd better get started now – may take a while, what?'

With that Admiral Blake walked over to the cabinet containing his strongbox, unlocked it and took out the Admiralty Cipher Tables, a book over 400 pages thick. Before handing it over to Lt Jenkins, he carried out a mental calculation based on the current date, the algorithm of which he was forbidden to commit to paper. Having done this, he opened the tables at the calculated page, flattened out the book and handed it over.

Each double page spread contained a table of around one thousand commonly used words, each with a corresponding six-digit code. All the codes within each table appeared in other tables in the book, but assigned to different words, allowing a signal to be encoded so that only a recipient using the correct table could have any chance of decoding it.

Lt Jenkins rooted around the room until he found a pad of rice paper, and then began the painful process of encoding the signal on to the wafer-thin paper. Two hours or so later, the signal had been encoded and written out three times. Admiral Blake ensured the correct date was written, un-coded, onto each piece of paper, and then they carefully folded the papers up and pushed them into small tin canisters.

The signaller was called for, and he arrived with a basket of three carrier pigeons. He and Lt Jenkins carefully attached each of the canisters to a pigeon with Admiral Blake keeping a watchful eye throughout the whole process. The three of them then went to the roof of the consulate and released the pigeons at ten-minute intervals.

Admiral Blake watched the last pigeon as it fluttered into the bright blue vault of heaven above them, orientated itself, and then headed off to the northwest.

'God's speed,' he found himself muttering under his breath.

With luck, one or more of the pigeons would arrive at the British embassy in Vienna in about two days time. The ambassador there was under orders to immediately send on any messages he received from Athens using London-bound pigeons, so that the signal should be received at the Levant Company headquarters in about four days hence.

*

Quite separately to the signal that Admiral Blake had sent, the following advertisement appeared in the last week of April and first week of May, 1735:

English lord requires men for well-remunerated work abroad,
duration unknown. Those interested should meet
in Athens during May.

The advertisement was carried by several European daily newspapers, including:

The Daily Courant, London
La Gazette, Paris
Courante uyt Italien, Duytsland, & C, Amsterdam
Vossische Zeitung, Berlin
Wiener Zeitung, Vienna

CHAPTER 7

The Englishmen spent the early part of that morning settling into rooms in the large *khan* in Athens to which Lord Charlemont had directed the cart driver to, while Fredrich went off to procure an *araba* – a Turkish coach. The *khan* was quite luxurious and consisted of a gated house with its own courtyard and stables on the ground floor. There were windowed rooms above, each with a bed, its own fireplace, and shared toilets at the end of the building. A black-clad Turkish widow showed them around, gave them keys to the rooms and then retreated downstairs to the kitchen next to the stables. Shortly after ten o'clock, a messenger appeared with the *firmans*.

'Excellent,' exclaimed Lord Charlemont. 'That means we can go to the bazaar now.'

He slung a bag over his shoulder, and they immediately left the *khan* and set off by foot through the streets of Athens, giving Alex a chance to observe the inhabitants of Athens up-close. The Turkish men – mainly bearded – wore long robes and turbans, while the Greeks dressed in short jackets, a sash around their waist with loose breeches, all topped by a red skullcap. The Turkish women were dressed, to Alex's eyes, like nuns. Their heads were covered with white linen, so that only their eyes and nose were visible and wore bulky, shapeless dresses that reached almost down to their ankles, with loose leather boots of red or yellow. The Greek women, on the other hand, wore what looked like long petticoats that fell in folds to the ground, with a thin veil of muslin thrown over the head and shoulders. A third distinct people could also be seen – Albanians. From what Lord Charlemont said, they did most of the manual labour. Both men and women were dressed in a simple smock that came down to their knees; the men's heads were adorned with white skullcaps, the women's with large hoods.

'Would you believe that a mere ten thousand people now live in this once proud city, this former centre of civilisation and emporium of the world?' Lord Charlemont declared, waving his hand dramatically around as they walked. 'I rode round the modern city walls once – and did it in less than half an hour! The old city walls would have taken almost two and a half hours, if you included the walls down to the port. Yes, the pageant of history has moved on from it – for now, at any rate.'

'It's difficult to believe that such a great city could fall into such decline,' remarked Alex as they continued through the narrow streets.

'As long as the Turk stays here, it will remain so,' observed Lord Charlemont. 'They do little or nothing to encourage trade through here, which was the life-blood of the city…'

'Speaking of trade,' cut in Alex, 'what *exactly* does the Levant Company trade in?'

'Oh, for goodness sake!' spluttered Lord Charlemont as he stopped dead. 'Do I have to tell you everything?'

'Now look here,' retorted Alex, turning to face him, 'we are visiting this merchant tomorrow, and I am supposed to be your secretary. How will it seem if this fellow asks me some simple question about the Company and I cannot answer?'

Lord Charlemont huffed and puffed in his supercilious way, but eventually carried on walking, his hands behind his back as if he were lecturing to a university student.

'Well, thanks to the trading factory Good Queen Bess and the Levant Company established in Constantinople, we in England are no longer forced to buy Levantine goods from the French and Venetians – the Ottomans' original trading partners – via their entrepôts of Marseilles and Venice, and so avoid their attendant levies.'

'In terms of structure, we have a governor in England, together with a deputy governor and eighteen council assistants. Then there are consuls and vice-consuls all around the Levant, depending on the size of the trading factory. Our main trading factories are at Constantinople, obviously, as well as Aleppo. Aleppo is nearly equidistant from the Mediterranean and the river Euphrates, giving it a strategic position for trade – and as I mentioned last night, the old Silk Road ends there. In fact, Aleppo accounts for over half of the total imports from the Levant into England.'

'As for the rest, we also have consuls at the Levantine ports of Smyrna and Acre, one on the island of Zante, the Consul-General in Patras, of course, and here. Our main Levantine imports are spices, salt, silk, coffee, cotton, medicinal drugs, indigo, and currants. Our main exports to them are most of the base metals, including Cornish tin…'

'For manufacturing bronze cannon?' interrupted Alex.

'Exactly. Also muskets, pistols, sword-blades, saltpetre for making gunpowder, and broadcloth – which the Ottomans use for the *janissary* uniforms.'

He paused and looked at Alex with a glint in his eye. 'As you can imagine, this has not made us that popular with the rest of Christian Europe – they see it as active collusion with Christendom's greatest foe! The Venetians and French, in contrast, are forbidden by the Bishop of Rome to export any weaponry to the Ottomans, and so mainly trade luxury items, such as jewellery, fine plate, ceramics and so forth.'

By now they had reached the bazaar.

'Anyway, that is the Company in a nutshell. But if Bin Kaslm asks you anything more, just deflect him to me.'

*

The rest of the morning and afternoon was spent in the bazaar, frequented by both Turks and Greeks, and scented by the dry, pungent perfume of unfamiliar spices. They first found a barber, who gave them both a shave with a cut-throat razor and then removed the hair from their nose and ears by holding a lit taper close to them, to burn away the unwanted hairs. He then cut Alex's hair according to Lord Charlemont's precise directions. When he was finished, even Alex agreed the cut was for the better, it being more stylish than his usual regulation navy cut.

Following this, Lord Charlemont had Alex measured up for the clothes necessary for his role, the wizened Jewish tailor taking no notes as he deftly measured Alex. They selected the cloth to be used and, from pictures of European styles, the cut of the breeches and jacket. It was late afternoon when they had finished ordering all the clothes necessary, which the tailor assured them they would be ready and delivered the next morning. As they left his shop, he pulled the shutters across and set to work immediately, calling out to his assistants in Greek. Lord

Charlemont then decided Alex's shoes looked too military in their appearance and so took him along to a cobbler.

After that, Alex roamed around by himself, searching for items he would need. All that he had read of bazaars emphasised the multitude and quality of goods they sold, and yet he was not impressed by what he saw. In fairness, there were slippers, boots, coarse muslin, pipes, tobacco, coffee, and drugs for sale, but no paper, quills, ink or well-made shoes or hats. He could have easily found all these items, and many more, back in London, in the shops of Cheapside or Fleet Street. Another item he could not find was a pocket watch. He mentioned this later to Lord Charlemont.

'In all my travels in the Ottoman Empire I have never seen a public clock, let alone a pocket watch,' declared Lord Charlemont. 'The only clockwork timepiece I have seen here was in a *vaivode's* house. If you think about it, such devices could undermine the authority of the *mullahs* – the holy men. Who would need a call to prayer if each household had a clock?'

'Well, how do the *mullahs* know the time?'

'Through the use of sundials and water clocks.'

*

They returned to their lodgings before it got dark to find that two Ragusan salt traders had also taken some rooms, and had stabled their packhorses down below. They all sat around the same table as the widow served them lamb stew, but conversation was stilted, even though the Ragusans could obviously speak fluent Latin. They seemed to view Lord Charlemont and his companions with suspicion, as if they feared they would be robbed of their precious salt, and left the table quickly.

Later on in the evening, in Alex's room, Lord Charlemont went through the etiquette that would be expected of them the next day, and briefed Alex on the answers to questions the merchant might ask him, as well as insisting that Alex use the surname of Jackson so that he could not be connected with the *Fearless*.

'And for goodness sake, Hurst,' Lord Charlemont concluded, 'try not to clip your words so much, you're not on a warship any more. And don't hold yourself so stiffly at table – relax, man! Slouch a bit – look more normal!'

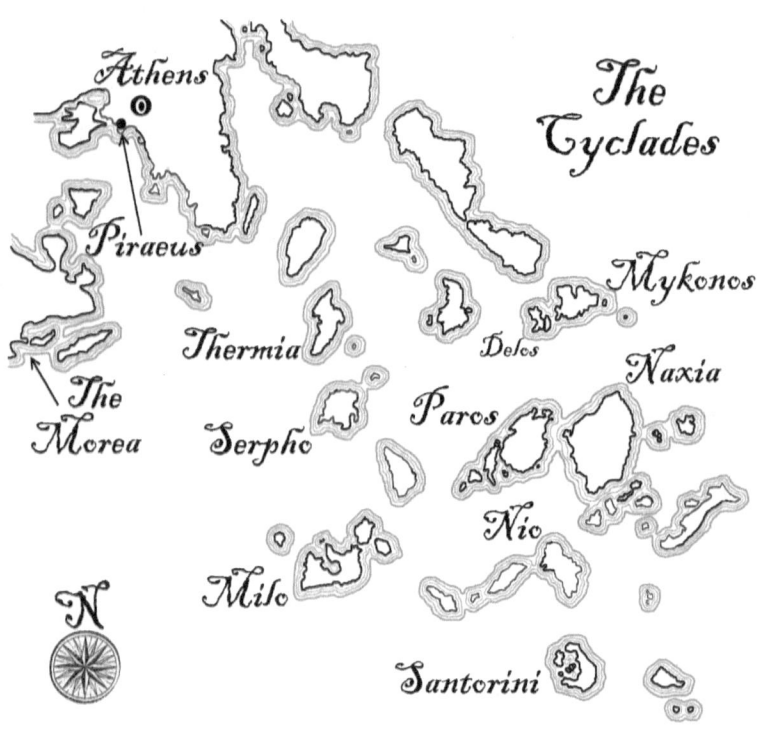

CHAPTER 8

Noon the next day found the Englishmen at the large gates of a house on the fringes of Athens. Lord Charlemont introduced himself to the two guards just inside the gates in fluent Turkish, and they shouted out to others, their gaze not leaving the Englishmen for a second. The branches and leaves of vegetation inside spilled out through the tall railings and onto the walkway outside, making it difficult to see the house from the roadway.

'Remember,' whispered Lord Charlemont as a servant came to the gates to let them in, 'you are my private secretary – I will do the talking. Only speak if I ask you a direct question and take careful notes – Bin Kaslm may ask to see them.'

They walked in, following the servant. Glancing round, Alex noticed an armed man standing some feet away from the gates, just on the inside of the railings. He was facing outwards, looking through the vegetation, but probably invisible from outside. A glance to the other side revealed another, and he guessed more were stationed all around the house. The house itself was ochre, built in the European style with a pitched roof and large windows, behind which Venetian blinds guarded against the sun.

Two more armed guards were stationed at the double doors to the house. At Lord Charlemont's prompting, Alex took his shoes off there, swapping them for silk slippers, and once inside he found himself in a cool and airy hallway lit naturally from above, complete with a crystal chandelier and marble staircase. To the left and right, bouquets of fresh flowers stood delicately arranged in porcelain vases, on elegant tables gilded with gold. The floor was tiled with marble, in a geometric, repetitive pattern. The whole room was decorated in an understated way, but it was obvious that only the most expensive materials had been used in its construction. Alex was impressed – this seemed to him to be the residence of a lord, not that of a merchant. They were left there for several minutes.

'We may have to wait some time, as they will still be at midday prayers,' remarked Lord Charlemont.

Inside the house all was quiet. They stood in silence for a few moments until Alex felt compelled to speak.

'There is something I do not understand here,' he exclaimed, his voice barely above a whisper.

'Go on,' said Lord Charlemont, also keeping his voice low.

'Back in England, I'm sure I read that all subjects of the sultan are his slaves. But how can this be so? This man must be a rich as a lord!'

'Well, I see it has also fallen to me to educate you in the mores of Ottoman society,' retorted Lord Charlemont, a touch of sarcasm in his voice. 'Society here is divided into the ruling and subject classes. The ruling class are the true Ottomans – they have to be a Mussulman, profess absolute loyally to the sultan and his state, and devote their life to his service. They also have to know and practise the complex system of customs and behaviour known as the 'Ottoman way', as well as being able to speak Ottoman Turkish – a blend of Arabic, Persian and Turkish. These people are known as *Osmanh* and their relationship to the house of Osman is by tradition that of a slave – but, in actual fact, it means that their life and property are maintained at the discretion of the sultan. This ruling class consists of the military, administrators, and holy men, above all of which are the sultan, his Grand Vizier, and the Imperial Court. In the course of carrying out their duties they may accrue some wealth, but it could all be taken from them, on a whim of the sultan. Also, if an *Osmanh* abuses his position in any way, or fails in his duties he is garrotted with a bowstring – probably a punishment from the days the Ottomans were just a horde of mounted archers – and his head delivered to the Sublime Porte in a velvet bag.'

'A bit harsh, surely?'

'Yes, but effective – I'll wager the Ottoman Empire is run far better than parliament could ever run England!'

'So Bin Kaslm is an *Osmanh*?'

'No! Though he is a devout Mussulman, he is a member of the more populous subject class, the *Reyahs*, which consists of people who actually generate the wealth that supports the empire – merchants, artisans, fishermen, farmers, and so on. All the wealth he generates, bar tax, is kept within his family and as long as he does not break the law, he cannot be stripped of it, nor can his life be arbitrarily taken. Consequently there are a lot of *Reyahs* who are far wealthier than most *Osmanh*.'

*

The double doors above them were suddenly opened, and a servant beckoned them to come up. They walked up and stepped into a long airy room, bounded on both sides by windows and the ubiquitous Venetian blinds, with silks hanging between the windows. A huge Persian carpet covered almost the entire marbled floor, and two large divans, their backs to the windows, faced each other across the width of the room, with a low table between them. A small brazier in the middle of the room gave off an aromatic perfume.

At the far end of the room there was a small platform covered with cushions, backed by a white curtain that ran from floor to ceiling. Seated cross-legged on the cushions was an elegantly dressed man who rose up as they entered and came over to greet them. Bin Kaslm was bearded and his white cotton robes were elaborately embroidered, and fell gracefully from his tall frame. He had something of a hawk-like face, but otherwise would have been thought quite handsome. To top it all, as Lord Charlemont later explained, he wore the green fez of one who had completed the *Haj*. He did not appear to be older than his mid-thirties and yet was controlling a vast shipping empire.

'Greetings, esteemed visitors from *Frankistan*,' Bin Kaslm declared in excellent Latin, as he shook Lord Charlemont's hand. 'It has been a long time – how are you my friend?'

'Ibrahim, I am well. It is indeed an honour to see you again. Please let me introduce my private secretary, Mr Jackson.'

'An honour to meet you also, Mr Jackson,' said Ibrahim graciously turning to also shake Alex's hand.

The charm of the man was genuine, and Alex felt flattered by the manner in which he was greeted.

Bin Kaslm gestured for them to sit on the right-hand divan,and then sat back cross-legged on his cushions, clapped his hands and ordered them some coffee from a barefooted slave who appeared from behind the curtain. 'Please,' he implored them gently, 'sit down.'

Lord Charlemont gracefully sat down, also in the Turkish manner. Alex sat down more awkwardly, unused to sitting cross-legged, and ended up perching on the edge of the divan, one leg stretched out with the other bent under it, resting on the carpet.

While Alex was trying to get comfortable, Lord Charlemont had handed some gifts for Bin Kaslm to one of his assistants – some fine English cloth and a box containing a pair of English silver-handled pocket pistols. In return, another man brought over two large muslin handkerchiefs, edged with gold lace.

'Now my friend,' Bin Kaslm began, 'what news do you have from England?'

Lord Charlemont quickly went through the main news of late: The Whig first minister, Walpole, was sensibly continuing to resist military involvement in European squabbles, thereby allowing the country to prosper; a public lottery was to be held to build a second bridge across the Thames; there was a push in parliament for the laws on witchcraft to be repealed, and finally there were rumours that the Young Pretender was beginning to gather support in France for another Jacobite rebellion.

An attractive young servant girl then appeared with a silver bowl filled with a sort of thickly perfumed marmalade, from which a golden spoon protruded. As instructed the night before by Lord Charlemont, Alex took a spoonful and placed it into his mouth, and then passed the bowl back to her. A second, even more attractive servant girl then appeared with the coffee in silver cups. Alex had to force himself to concentrate on his note taking to avoid staring at her – she had a curvaceous figure that her light silk dress barely covered or concealed.

'And what of trade?' asked Bin Kaslm, at the same time leaning forward by a fraction.

The servant girl was now directly in front of Alex and she carefully placed the coffee cup in front of him. He raised his eyes briefly from his notepad and found himself looking directly into her deep brown eyes, all too aware that her well-formed breasts were just below his line of sight and partly in plain view thanks to her low-cut dress. He thanked her but found himself blushing slightly. Humour danced across the girl's eyes, and under her gossamer veil she smiled, and then straightened up to move away.

'One trend that I have observed, and which I feel will be of interest to you, is that the taste for coffee is declining.'

Bin Kaslm eyes narrowed slightly and he grew more attentive.

'When I was a boy there were three thousand coffee houses in London alone, but now there are more closing than being opened.'

'What is replacing it?' asked Bin Kaslm.

'Chinese tea,' replied Lord Charlemont. 'People seem to prefer the taste and it is thought to stimulate the mind without straining the nerves...'

'How much is being imported?'

'Well in 1720, the East India Company imported two hundred thousand pounds in weight. Last year it was more like one and a quarter million pounds.'

'And coffee?' continued Bin Kaslm.

'Five hundred thousand pounds in 1730, and just over four hundred thousand pounds last year.'

Bin Kaslm looked impressed. 'What price does the tea sell for on the dockside?'

'Around five shillings, four pence a pound.'

'It certainly sounds like an interesting opportunity,' Bin Kaslm said, unconsciously stroking his beard with his right hand, while carrying out some mental calculations, 'but which classes are drinking it? If it is only the aristocracy then the market will be almost saturated already.'

'All classes,' replied Lord Charlemont emphatically. 'From layabouts to lords,' he added with a smile.

'But why is it becoming so much more popular than coffee?' Bin Kaslm asked, a touch of exasperation in his voice.

'Tea leaves can be used several times without a marked taste difference,' answered Lord Charlemont. 'Although this is done only by the lower orders, I hasten to add!'

'This is indeed interesting,' conceded Bin Kaslm and leaned back, bringing his hands together in a prayer like way, index fingers gently rubbing his beard again. His internal conjugation lasted for a few more moments, and then he sat up straight and called again to his servants. 'Now,' he said with a smile and an expansive gesture of his hands, as a servant appeared from behind the curtain with more silver cups, 'how can I help *you*?'

'To get straight to the point my friend Ibrahim,' Lord Charlemont said, sitting up very straight and looking at him directly in the eye, 'I am having problems with piracy.' He then turned away to Alex. 'The map please,' he requested.

Alex dutifully pulled a map out of his shoulder bag and handed it to Lord Charlemont, who spread it out on another low table in front of Bin Kaslm, orientating it for him. Meanwhile the servants had given them all a silver cup each that contained liquid chilled *sherbet*. Alex cautiously tasted it, discerning the flavours of orange and liquorice, and found it quite agreeable.

The four colour map, from the Dutch cartography house of Jansson, portrayed the Greek mainland, the Morea, and several islands including Crete to the south, as well as Macedonia, Albania, and Serbia to the north, and the Italian peninsula opposite them. Lord Charlemont tapped his finger on the Julian Rocks, just south of Corfu.

'Here, about a week ago, a Levant Company ship was attacked by corsairs.'

'What did they look like?'

Lord Charlemont also took a sip from his *sherbet* and then described the corsairs, their black robes, rectangular shields, chain mail, and the way they conducted their attack, without of course mentioning that they had been almost one hundred percent successful. In his version of events, the attack was repulsed by the bravery of the crew.

'My friend,' Bin Kaslm said, after Lord Charlemont had concluded, 'this is indeed terrible news for us both. I have actually heard only recently of these corsairs that you speak of. They also attacked a British warship barely a week ago and all were lost, save one.'

Lord Charlemont feigned surprise at this – the news had travelled fast, as Admiral Blake had predicted.

'I can only think they are new to this region,' Bin Kaslm continued, 'in which case I will soon find out where they are based. Alternatively, it could be that they came from some distance away, with the knowledge that your ship contained something of great value. If this were the case, I would guess the corsairs came from Nio. We call it "Little Malta", due to the number of corsairs who use it as their base,' he continued, pointing to an island well to the north of Crete. 'No matter how many times the Turkish navy goes in to clear them out, they always go back, and the loss in shipping never seems to end. But I swear to you, by the beard of the Prophet, that wherever they come from, I will help you hunt down these corsairs that threaten the free passage of the sea!'

Lord Charlemont looked doubtful. 'Mr Jackson – how long would it take for a galley to reach Corfu from Nio?'

Alex leaned over the map, noting the scale. 'If they could keep up a rate of four knots, then around ten to twelve days,' he replied. 'But that would be way beyond the limit of a galley's range. Normally a galley can only carry enough provisions for a journey two days out from its base and back again. Nio seems too far south – unless they were able to re-provision en route.'

Lord Charlemont was obviously disappointed and was about to roll the map up when Bin Kaslm pointed to an island between Crete and Nio.

'Before you go, Lord Charlemont,' he declared, 'you should know that your map is out of date by some years.' They all gathered around again. 'This archipelago, marked here as "Santorini", can no longer be reached.'

'How can that be?' asked Alex, puzzled, unaware of Lord Charlemont's warning glare. 'This map was made...' he consulted the side of it, 'less than one hundred years ago.'

'Those islands were well-known for suffering earthquakes, and had mines of brimstone beneath them that would frequently break out on to the surface,' explained Bin Kaslm 'In the year 1060...' he then paused to carry out an internal calculation, 'or 1650, by the Christian calendar, the islands were shaken by a mighty eruption in one of these mines. A noise, like that of countless cannon shots, was heard all over the region. Huge clouds of ash were expelled by these explosions, filling the air and reaching as far as Constantinople. A giant wave appeared, causing grievous damage on nearby islands, and ships of the Turkish fleet were swept away from their moorings on the island of Dia, to the north of Crete.'

Lord Charlemont nodded, as if agreeing.

'The flames of the eruption could be seen from Heraklion in Crete, and so much of the floating stone…' he paused, obviously searching for a word.

'Pumice' volunteered Lord Charlemont, and Bin Kaslm nodded in acknowledgement.

'…appeared on the sea – some of those stones were as big as this house – that the Turkish general there assumed the whole of Santorini had sunk and so sent a galley to investigate.'

'And what did they find?' asked Alex, thoroughly intrigued.

'We don't know. The galley was discovered weeks later, drifting aimlessly off Crete amongst the pumice. None of the crew was on board, and all the slaves were dead, still chained to their benches. It is thought they had died of poisonous vapours.'

'So all three islands just disappeared?'

'No – the top of the highest mountain of the three islands can still be seen, with a strange blue light shining on it. But the rest of the islands, if they still exist, are obscured by what look like raging storm clouds. It is thought that the explosion caused mines of brimstone to open up all around the islands, boiling the water above them and throwing up steam, spray, and poisonous fumes for several hundred leagues into the air.'

'I do remember vague tales about an archipelago that had been destroyed by a volcano in this part of the world,' remarked Alex, turning to Lord Charlemont, 'but I just assumed it was just a legend.'

'No, it is true,' insisted Bin Kaslm calmly, 'I have seen the raging walls of water myself. All shipping that attempted to penetrate them has never been seen again – hundreds have tried to, but none has succeeded.' He looked at Lord Charlemont, and then Alex. 'In fact, most shipping that even goes within ten miles of it is lost. And so we avoid it,' he concluded, holding both hands up in an empty handed gesture.

'Obviously, most of the trade routes go round it now,' said Lord Charlemont in a dismissive manner. 'I too have seen the convulsions of water, though a spyglass.'

'I take it, Mr Jackson, that you have not spent much time in the Levant,' observed Bin Kaslm suddenly, almost imperceptibly changing the tone of the conversation.

Alex sensed trouble if they continued down this line of questioning. 'That is correct. I only recently become Lord Charlemont's secretary,' he admitted.

'I see,' remarked Bin Kaslm and sat back on his cushions, coolly surveying them both as he took the first sip from his sherbet.

Alex quickly thought of how he could divert attention from himself. In his desperation, an idea occurred to him. 'My Lord,' he said, with due reverence in his voice to Lord Charlemont, 'there is one fact we haven't mentioned yet, regarding the attack, which might be significant.'

Lord Charlemont's eyes flashed another warning to him, but he played along. 'And what is that, Mr Jackson?'

'It's true that most of the attackers wore black robes, but there were a few who wore scarlet robes. They did not take part in the attack but were observed to be on the corsair's ship.'

'Scarlet robes?' exclaimed Bin Kaslm suddenly, leaning forward again. He was going to speak, but then stopped himself as if he were weighing up whether or not he should divulge something. His introspection lasted a few moments more, and then he spoke. 'Now, that is interesting. For more years than I wish to remember, probably from the time of my grandfather, scarlet-clad traders have been regularly seen in the slave markets of Piraeus. It is said that they come from the north, due to the pale skin of their hands and so they are called the Northerners…'

'What about their faces?'

'They are always hooded and wear spectacles of smoked glass, so their faces have never been properly seen. But,' he raised a hand as if to halt further questions, 'this is probably a coincidence, because if they had anything to do with these pirates you speak of, I would have known and dealt with them by now.' He seemed to weigh up a few more possibilities in his mind, and then dismissed them. 'That is the only piece of information, for what it is worth, that I can give you gentlemen. I hope your journey here has not been in vain.'

'Not at all,' replied Lord Charlemont, a determined glint in his eye. 'I would be grateful if you could give me a letter of introduction to the slave traders, in order to guarantee their co-operation in this matter, as it is of mutual interest to us both.'

'Certainly,' Bin Kaslm replied, clapping his hands and then speaking rapid Turkish to the servant who appeared.

'I shall have the slave markets watched around the clock for the next few weeks,' continued Lord Charlemont, turning to look at Alex. 'To see if I can find these people you speak of.'

'There is no need for that, Lord Charlemont,' Bin Kaslm said, as he scribbled out a letter on a notepad passed to him by a servant.

'My friend...' began Lord Charlemont, turning back to him, puzzled at this remark.

'They come every month, on the night of the new moon, though that is not common knowledge, so I would appreciate it if you were to be discreet regarding the matter.'

He folded the paper and then used wax to seal it with his signet ring, before handing it, and a separate piece of paper, to Lord Charlemont with a smile.

'Here is your letter of introduction and the details of the trader they usually deal with. I have instructed him to allow you to observe the Northerners, so you may determine if they are similar to the ones seen on your ship. May Allah aid you in your work, and be so good as to keep me informed.'

On the way out of the room, to Alex's surprise, a bowing servant sprinkled them with rose scented water from a long-necked silver bottle.

CHAPTER 9

They were barely out of Bin Kaslm's gates when Lord Charlemont turned to Alex.

'What did I tell you?'

'What can I say?' exclaimed Alex. 'Your approach worked.'

A smug smile settled on Lord Charlemont's face as they climbed into the *araba*.

'Fredrich, take us to the slave markets!' he commanded dramatically on the step, before ducking into the *araba* and pulling the canvas cover closed behind him.

Alex smiled and shook his head at this – the man's manner was so melodramatic, it bordered on the comical.

'So, a strong lead already and it's only day two of our enterprise,' Lord Charlemont continued, rubbing his hands together, as he looked through a gap in the canvas at the retreating house. 'I have a good feeling about this.' He turned to Alex. 'Now, when is the next new moon?'

'In a few days,' replied Alex.

'Can't you be more exact?'

'No, not without an almanac. But it's around two days from now, I'm sure of it.'

'Well, that's good. It will give us time to reconnoitre the slave markets and get set up before these characters arrive.' He turned to Alex and noticed he had undone his collar.

'Now, for goodness sake, button up your collar before we reach this man's house. It's important you stay in character while we are in the city.'

'I'll do it when we get there,' replied Alex tetchily, feeling again as if he were back at school. 'It's far too tight. I can hardly breathe with it. Anyway,' he said, changing the subject. 'Bin Kaslm was completely different to what I was expecting.'

'That does not surprise me,' observed Lord Charlemont, 'considering the bizarre ideas most Europeans have regarding the Ottomans.'

'What do you mean by that?'

'The Ottomans consider European languages and culture as being unworthy of their attention – which was all very well when their empire was one huge military machine that could expand by conquest and looting of its neighbours. But now it's almost fifty years since the Grand Vizier, Kara Mustafa, threatened to stable his horses in St Peters – Christendom is holding them back to the west, the Russians to the north and the Persians to the east, and so there is nowhere left for them to conquer. Their recent setbacks have forced them to employ others to act as dragomen for them, as even at the highest level of government they only speak Ottoman Turkish. So Bin Kaslm is unusual in that he is Turkish, but decided to trade with the infidel, and learn Latin in the process. Most merchants in the Ottoman Empire are Greeks, Armenians or Jews. Indeed, the Grand *Dragoman* to the Sublime Porte is a Greek, and it's Greeks who act as dragomen at most levels of government.'

'That is remarkable,' agreed Alex in a neutral tone, 'but just one thing – did you see that servant girl back there? Why was she dressed in such a provocative manner? I thought all these Mussulmen's women were locked up in harems.'

Lord Charlemont adopted his pompous tone once more. 'That *slave* girl, dear boy, was nothing more than a probe by Bin Kaslm.'

'I don't understand.'

'He was probing your weaknesses – and it was patently obvious he discovered what yours is.'

'Well, it's hardly a weakness to find a pretty girl attractive!'

'True enough,' agreed Lord Charlemont, 'but it's something that he noted, and if your paths ever crossed again he would try and use it against you. Last time I was there, he offered me hashish.'

'Hashish?'

'A weed that is smoked in a pipe but is the complete opposite of tobacco – more soporific than stimulating. It was very good too – you should try it sometime,' he said, smiling wryly at the younger man's reaction.

*

As they approached Piraeus they came across large crowds of Turkish sailors walking from the port in the direction of Athens. Their spirits were high and they had the carefree mood of those on shore leave. The Englishmen presently entered Piraeus and headed for the western side of the port, to the slave markets. En route they skirted the main harbour. Two days previously the harbour itself had almost been deserted save for a few British ships tied up at the Company quays on the western side, but now it was teeming with Turkish war galleys.

'What is happening?' asked Alex.

'Admiral Yildiz's fleet,' answered Lord Charlemont. 'The Ottoman Empire traditionally goes to war between April and October,' he continued, 'but there are no major campaigns planned this year, and it's too late to start one now, so their fleets are effectively lying idle. Instead, they are about to start a joint operation with a British fleet coming in from Gibraltar in a few days hence, to flush out known corsair nests in the Aegean – the piracy in these parts has been disgraceful for decades now.' He cast he eye over the Turkish fleet. 'No doubt we will end up doing most of the work – now that Yildiz has docked the fleet, he may find it hard to drag his men out of the fleshpots of Athens!'

The fleet looked a formidable force, but then Alex reminded himself that the *Fearless* could have taken on any ten of its galleys, all things being equal.

'Did you see anything of Venice when you were there?' asked Lord Charlemont suddenly.

'Yes,' replied Alex, slightly puzzled at the question, 'all the main sights. We had arrived earlier than anticipated, so I had a couple of days of shore leave. Why do you ask?'

'Did you notice the large marble lions in front of the arsenal, one sitting on its hind legs, about ten feet high?'

'Why, yes, I do recall them. In fact our guide pointed them out and said they were a gift from the people of Greece...'

83

'Such naivety!' hooted Lord Charlemont. 'General Morosini stole them from here – one of them used to stand just over there, in fact, by the entrance to the outer harbour. Until then, Piraeus had become known as "Porto Lione". Yet another act of desecration by the Venetians! Also, following his brief occupation of Athens, he rounded up all the local inhabitants he could find, and sold them into slavery.'

'What? He sold fellow Christians into slavery?' exclaimed Alex, shocked to the core.

'No – Greek Orthodox Christians – whom most Venetians considered to be heretics,' replied Lord Charlemont, amused at Alex's reaction. 'You have a lot to learn about how the world works out here. Remember, the Venetians were instrumental in the Forth Crusade that took Constantinople, when thousands of Orthodox Christians were put to the sword.'

*

They left the harbour behind and arrived at the address Bin Kaslm had given them, one of the few houses adjacent to the slave markets. As it turned out, the trader was not at home and was not expected back for a few days, which put a dent in Lord Charlemont's good mood. Leaving Bin Kaslm's letter with the man's servants, they headed back to Athens in the *araba* and considered their next move.

'We may have to leave at a moment's notice to follow these characters to their stronghold,' began Lord Charlemont. 'So it would be best if we use the next day or so to get all our equipment together.'

He saw a look of concern on Alex's face.

'What are you thinking?' he demanded.

'Well, Bin Kaslm says they are thought to come from the north, but I don't believe that – I think they are based somewhere at sea. I think once they have bought their slaves, they will transfer them onto a ship.'

'My thoughts exactly. The Ottoman Empire's principal strength lies on land, not at sea. If these characters were land based, they would have been discovered and flushed out many years ago. We will therefore prepare for a sea trip.'

'Assuming they use a galley again, it would be useful for us to get a couple of grappling hooks on short ropes.'

Lord Charlemont raised his eyebrows slightly in a questioning look.

'After the attack on the *Fearless* I noticed a possible stowaway space on one side of the galley's bow, in with the anchor rigging,' Alex explained.

'That sounds reasonable. Let us waste no more time.' Lord Charlemont stood up and, leaning out of the covered area, gave whispered instructions to Fredrich in German.

'Why the whispering?' Alex asked as Lord Charlemont settled back in the *araba*, puzzled by the lack of melodrama.

'We're going to see my armourer here in Athens,' replied Lord Charlemont. 'And I don't particularly want Bin Kaslm to know who that is.'

'Oh, I see,' commented Alex.

'I don't think you do,' said Lord Charlemont. 'One of his men has been following us since we left his house.'

*

'Now!' cried Lord Charlemont, and leapt from the moving *araba*. Alex followed him half a second later, stumbling slightly on the uneven surface of the road. The *araba* had just turned a blind corner, and off to the left was a small alleyway. Regaining his footing, Alex ran after Lord Charlemont down the alleyway, and was grabbed roughly and pulled back into a doorway. There were no sounds for a few seconds, other than that of a crying child in the distance, some women talking nearby, and a few dogs yelping. Then, from the direction of the road came the sound of hooves on the cobbles, growing louder and then fading away.

'Good,' said Lord Charlemont, releasing his grip on Alex. 'We've shaken him off. Follow me.'

Then off they went, half running through the back streets of Athens, down alleyways, and along narrow streets lined with stallholders. The houses they ran past were mean and straggling, with large empty areas or courtyards in front where children played. In airless lanes, high whitewashed walls reflected the heat of the sun, causing Alex to break out in a sweat. Once or twice they came upon an open space strewed with the black ruins of some recent fire, or past mounds containing the rubbish of years, on which large wolf-like dogs lay stretched under the sun as if they were dead. Storks, on low roofs on either side of them, looked gravely down as they passed, and the still air was scented with citron, and pomegranate rinds scorched by the sun.

Occasionally they broke into a larger square that Lord Charlemont was careful to skirt round, behind stalls if possible. Eventually they came to a halt in front of a nondescript door down a quiet dusty alley. Alex had a good sense of direction, but with all the turns they had made even he had become disorientated.

Lord Charlemont then walked up to the door and rapped on it in some sort of pattern. Nothing happened for a good minute or so, and he was about to knock again when there was some movement from within, and presently a barred spy hole opened, and someone briefly looked out before shutting it again. There was a sound of heavy bolts being drawn back and finally the door opened. No word had been spoken, but Lord Charlemont walked confidently in, gingerly followed by Alex, and the door was slammed shut behind them.

*

A couple of hours later, they made their way back on to the street. The door shut with the sound of bolts being pushed back into place, and they were back out in the blinding afternoon sun, the back streets as quiet as ever.

'Why didn't we take the weapons with us?' asked Alex. 'How can you be sure he will deliver them to the *khan?*'

'Non-Mussulmen are not allowed to bear arms – or own slaves, for that matter – so it's best not to be caught with them,' replied Lord Charlemont. 'And I have only paid half of the cost so far.'

'Well, with the amount of weaponry we've bought, I'd guess he's probably shut up shop for the rest of the day,' remarked Alex as they walked away.

'More like for the next month!' retorted Lord Charlemont. 'By God, he drives a hard bargain – I should get him to work for me!'

Fredrich was waiting for them about half a mile away in a square, sitting outside a kahvehane in the shade, drinking coffee. He jumped up as they approached.

'Where is he?' asked Lord Charlemont, quietly.

'Over there my Lord,' replied Fredrich, gesturing surreptitiously to a fruit stall on the other side of the square. A turbaned man was sitting near it eating an apple, his back against a wall, idling and apparently uninterested in what was happening around him.

'Take back us to the bazaar,' Lord Charlemont ordered. 'Don't bother trying to shake him off.'

*

At the bazaar, they stopped at a stall Alex had spotted that sold European books. Here he picked up an almanac, which confirmed that the new moon was close – just three nights away. They also called in at saddler, where Lord Charlemont ordered some oilskin bags to be made up for them for the assumed sea journey.

The two Ragusan merchants had left, leaving them the only ones at dinner. Lord Charlemont wolfed his food down then excused himself, saying he had matters to attend to, taking Fredrich with him.

The sun had gone down, so Alex packed the weapons into his bags, had a few glasses of wine, and skimmed through a book that Lord Charlemont had lent to him – *A Voyage into the Levant*, written by a French botanist, Monsieur Tournefort, almost twenty years previously and translated into English. Most of the islands in the Aegean were described in some detail, together with a potted history, maps, and sometimes illustrations of the inhabitants and the local flora and fauna. As a result of Bin Kaslm's remarks, he read the chapter on Nio in detail, but there not much on Santorini, other than its history up to the middle of the seventeenth century. Then there was a note to say it was now: '...*veiled from sight of man by swirling mists of steam following a most calamitous explosion of the Volcano there.*'

After reading this his eyes grew heavy, so he blew out his candle and went to bed, reckoning he would not be getting much sleep in the next few days.

CHAPTER 10

For a day or so after their first meeting with Zentar, Helena had been inconsolable, causing Isabelle to worry if she were taking leave of her mind. Then, on the second evening, she woke suddenly from a fitful sleep.

'He could still be alive,' she declared, sitting up in bed and staring directly ahead of herself, dark shadows under her eyes from incessant crying.

Isabelle stood up from where she had been embroidering, sat down on the bed beside her, and put her arm round her. 'Why do you say that?' she asked, as gently as she could.

'I heard him – above us – just before they broke into the bedroom, still fighting and urging his men on,' Helena replied. 'He has been in countless engagements with Barbary corsairs – of all people, he would surely know what to do…' she turned to look at her sister, '…to survive.'

'I pray that is so, sister,' said Isabelle, 'but Zentar did say that all had perished.'

'Perished?' exclaimed Helena with a snort of derision. 'Butchered, more like!'

She said nothing for a few moments, staring at the bed sheet before stirring herself.

'Anyway, I must believe that he is alive or…or I will go mad with grief. We *were* meant to be together,' she stifled a sob, 'and I refuse to believe that he has been torn from me.'

'But how could he have escaped? We were in the middle of the sea!'

'He is a strong swimmer – probably one of the few on board that ship who actually could, I would wager! And we were not that far from shore – before the mist came down I saw land away to the east.' She paused. 'He *could* have made it, and if he did he will have made his way back to England, I am sure of it.'

'Well, again, let us pray 'tis so, sister, and we can find him once we are returned to the shores of Albion ourselves…'

'This talk about "returning us to our own",' interrupted Helena. 'It just does not make sense. Why attack a Royal Naval ship if the purpose of the exercise is then to send us back to England? What advantage is there for the Rakshasa in all this – unless there is a ransom involved?'

'Well, I sincerely hope it is the case, whatever the reasons behind it,' exclaimed Isabelle. 'But let us not dwell on all this at present – for there is much we do not know – and pray that matters will become clearer as time goes on.'

'Wise counsel indeed,' agreed Helena, throwing back the sheet. 'We could spend days trying to fathom this riddle and get nowhere. Now, when will the food be arriving?'

Isabelle glanced out of the window. 'Very soon – they have brought it around sunset each day so far.'

*

Helena was dressed by the time their food arrived, and feeling the need to vent her frustration at their incarceration on Zentar if possible or, failing that, one of his underlings. This time, instead of the old servant, a younger female entered the room, and what shocked them most about her were not her red reptilian-like eyes but her attire. She was dressed in a knee-length scarlet tunic, reminiscent of dress that Helena had seen on ancient Greek vases. Her arms were also bare to the shoulder, exposing lithe limbs of sinewy muscle. She wore little jewellery, other than a couple of silver bracelets and ties in her hair. Both sisters stared at her, scandalised; they had never having seen a female bare so much flesh in public. She walked in with a natural self-confidence and a proud, almost arrogant bearing – obviously a fair cut above the old woman. The food she brought consisted of a cold platter of sliced mutton, barley bread, olive oil, some fruit, and a crystal glass carafe of wine. The female initially ignored them, but once she had placed the tray down, she turned to glance over at them, her eyes narrowing slightly as she did so.

'Ah,' thought Helena, 'for some reason she perceives us as a threat.' Her instincts told her the female was somehow connected to Zentar.

For a second, the young female's glance alighted on Helena, and it was obvious that she was impressed by her auburn hair, but then her gaze quickly moved on to Isabelle and, like the servant woman before, seemed fascinated by her. Helena glanced over at Isabelle. What fascinated them so? With her pale skin and blonde hair she was not that much different from the Rakshasa; maybe that was it – they saw her as almost one of their own. In any event, she decided to needle the female and see how she reacted.

'That will be all,' commanded Helena in Latin, in her most haughty tone, waving her hand towards the door.

The female turned look at her, red eyes flashing with annoyance. She seemed to be on the verge of saying something, but then thought better of it and made to leave the room.

'One moment,' ordered Helena.

The female stopped in her tracks and whipped her head round, glaring at Helena.

'Tell your *master* that we wish to take the air outside tomorrow.'

This produced a grunt of exasperation from the female, and she stormed out of the room, slamming the door behind her.

Helena clapped her hands and burst out laughing. 'Ha,' she exclaimed. 'They may look like the offspring of Beelzebub, but their emotions are just as malleable as ours!'

'Sister, have a care!' chided Isabelle. 'Do not provoke them so. Remember where we are!'

'Oh, do not fret, Isabelle. If we are to be ransomed, then in the meantime they must look after us. Besides, goading is good – much truth is spoken in haste, and even more so in anger.'

'But what did you say to her?' Isabelle asked as Helena made for the table.

'I will tell you in due course. Anyway, enough of that now – we must eat!' She poured them both a glass of the wine, which was a vibrant, light yellow colour. Taking a sip of it, she gasped in surprise. The wine – which she later learned was made from the Nykteri grape cultured on the island – had an almost bone dry consistency, but with a pleasing citrus-like flavour.

Isabelle began serving the food, picking up the platter of mutton and sharing it between the two plates. 'What about the dress that creature was wearing?' she exclaimed. 'Outrageous, was it not?'

'I'll say! You could almost see her knees – the shameless hussy!'

*

Later that evening, as they sat by the open window, there was a discreet knock at the door, and the sisters barely had time to stand before Zentar himself strode in, smoked glass spectacles in place, wearing what appeared to be less formal but still purple attire, and carrying a chair. He stood by the door, obviously intending to say something, but before he could say a word, Helena cut in across him, head tilted back slightly, looking at him down her nose.

'Thank you for coming so promptly, Zentar.' With satisfaction she noticed a slight pursing of his lips – her remark had riled him. 'As I said to your *servant*, Isabelle and I would like to take the air outside tomorrow...'

'She was no servant,' Zentar interrupted, a touch irritated. 'She is a wife of mine.'

'You mean, she *is* your wife,' Helena corrected him.

'No – she is but *one* of my wives,' Zentar clarified. 'We Rakshasa can have many wives, if we choose.' He paused, his gaze momentarily alighting on her empty ring finger. 'And we sometimes take females like yourselves to be our wives also,' he added.

A ghost of a smile crossed his lips as Helena felt herself inexplicably blushing at this revelation and had to look away, her cheeks burning.

'Of course,' she muttered. 'We know that the Mussulmen, for instance, are allowed to take several wives, but we Christians prefer monogamy...'

'In principle at least – if not in practice,' remarked Zentar, with a wry smile now as he watched her closely.

'Well, what about our request?' asked Helena, changing tack.

'Ah, yes. Your request to take the air.' He moved the chair into the room and then rubbed his hands together as he sat back in it, looking concerned. 'It may take some time before we can arrange it.'

'Why?' demanded Helena, sensing an opening. 'Are you not masters of this island? Or are there others here that you fear?'

Zentar suddenly shot back to his feet at this, his face contorted with rage. 'The Rakshasa fear no one!' he shouted, slamming the open door in anger and causing the sisters to start. He then caught himself and calmed down almost as quickly as he had erupted. 'It will take several days to arrange because my father – Korthdan – must approve of it, but he is not available.'

'I see,' Helena remarked in a neutral manner. She had a few barbed comments lined up that she might have made, but thought better of provoking him again – for the time being at least.

'Look,' said Zentar, his tone now consolatory. 'My father's word is law. Unless he wills it, there is nothing I can do to change your overall situation.'

'Why did you say we are here for our protection?' cut in Isabelle.

'If we had not…' Zentar struggled for a moment to find the right word. '…extracted you from that warship, Lady Isabelle would be shortly due to enter the seraglio of the emir of Egypt, as part of a trade agreement between the Levant Company and the emir.'

'That is hogwash…'

'Be attentive, I pray. I know this may be difficult for you to comprehend, but this will confirm what I have said.' As he spoke, he drew out an oilskin cylinder from an inside pocket and tossed it over so that it landed gently on Isabelle's bed. 'Assuming you can read Latin, of course.'

Helena gave a contemptuous snort and then stood to gingerly retrieve the cylinder from the bed and sat back down. She opened the cylinder and unrolled the parchment within.

Isabelle leaned over to read it also, but it was indeed written in Latin. 'What does it say?' she asked.

Helena glanced up at Zentar, who was watching her intently. '"Greetings to the most regal Jamal ad-Din Aktai, Emir of all Egypt, from the Governor and Company of Merchants of England trading to the Levant Seas",' she began, then spent a few moments reading more of the flowing copperplate script. 'Then there is a lot of flannelling,' she commented. She scanned further down the page and then gave a gasp of horror, her eyes widening with shock. '"We bring to you this day, Lady Isabelle Montagu…"'

'What?' gasped Isabelle, straining to find her name on the parchment.

'"…as the final gift your majesty requested in order for you to confer your most gracious approval to the commercial trading route across your kingdom…"' She stopped and looked at Zentar again through narrowed eyes. 'This is surely a forgery!' she declared and threw it onto the floor.

'Please, Lady Helena. All I ask is that you examine the signatures at the bottom of the document,' Zentar insisted, not at all flustered by her reaction.

Reluctantly Helena picked up the parchment, straightened it out and scanned it again.

'Oh my Lord!' she exclaimed a few moments later. After a few more moments she handed it wordlessly to Isabelle, casting down her eyes.

'What am I looking for?' Isabelle asked.

'The very last signature. On the bottom right-hand side.'

'Lord Charlemont!' exclaimed Isabelle in English. She placed the document down, shot a glance at Zentar, and then leaned towards Helena. 'But how can we be sure 'tis truly he?' she hissed.

'It has the seal from his signet ring beside it,' replied Helena, in barely a whisper. 'I recognise it from old.'

She felt sick to the stomach and her mind reeled as she tried to comprehend the dire situation they had suddenly found themselves in.

'Well,' asked Zentar. 'Do you believe me now?'

''Tis…it cannot be true,' she retorted, struggling to keep control of herself. 'Even Charlemont would not stoop so low.' She looked at Isabelle, confusion in her eyes. 'Would he?'

'It is genuine, I assure you. And you recognise the seal, do you not?' Both sisters were now silent.

Presently Zentar spoke. 'I can see this is a great shock to you. There is nothing I can do about that, but I can, however, make life more comfortable for you until you are returned to your own.' He gestured at them.

To Zentar's obvious amusement, Isabelle immediately piped up with a request for more clothes and shoes – she had been wearing the same attire for almost a week now and was tiring of it. Helena requested clothes also, as well as notepads, drawing pads, charcoals and paints, coffee, and bottled wine. The wine already served to them had been excellent, but Helena intended to use the bottles for messages – and cast them into the sea at the first opportunity.

*

The conversation then moved on to other topics. It transpired that Zentar was well educated; in addition to Italian, he could also read and write Latin, French, Turkish, and Persian, and had an almost encyclopaedic knowledge of both ancient and recent European history. His intellect, Helena came to realise, was more than equal to her own, and she was suitably impressed when she discovered he could not only recite poetry from Rousseau, her favourite French poet, but also interpret it with remarkable insight.

In due course he told them about the history of the Rakshasa, insisting they were a peace loving people. Helena took this claim with a large pinch of salt, having seen the warrior Rakshasa up-close, but conceded that he appeared to represent another, more cultured side to their race. He explained that, due to their appearance alone, they had been feared and reviled by man and forced to live in a remote land in the far north of Europe '…in the days when the Roman emperors still ruled most of the known world.'

For well over a millennium they had resided there, having little contact with man – and not seeking any – content to live in peace and isolation. That peace had been shattered when their hidden land was discovered by emissaries of the Pope around a century ago, who waged war on them, forcing them to flee their homeland. They had eventually settled on Santorini, raising a 'Wall of Storms' to protect themselves, '… using natural laws not yet known to your philosophers – not even to the great Sir Isaac Newton himself.'

The islanders had welcomed them, he explained, as they liberated them from the yoke of the Turk, and the Rakshasa had enjoyed an almost ideal relationship with them. During the day the islanders could live and roam as they pleased, fishing and growing their crops and vines, the wine from which they supplied to the Rakshasa.

'But they can never leave, as they could give away the secret of your very existence,' Helena pointed out.

'That is true,' agreed Zentar. 'But Helena,' he said, an earnest look on his face. 'They are but simple sons and daughters of the earth – peasants. To them the idea of leaving these islands – their home – would be inconceivable. They are quite happy here, let me assure you of that. And in return for this Arcadian life they enjoy, we only ask that the island become the sole domain of ourselves between dusk and dawn.'

At this point in their conversation another female appeared at the door, this time bearing a tray of glasses containing a dense bright yellow drink, which the sisters politely took when proffered, but sat looking at uneasily.

'Please,' requested Zentar as he saw their reluctance. 'It is but a lemon drink with a touch of spirits in it. It is a favourite of my people.'

'Oh well,' thought Helena as she took a sip of the drink. 'If anything diabolical were due to occur, it would have already happened by now.'

She found that it tasted of lemon as Zentar had said, but not overpoweringly so, and also had a delicate sweetness to it that counterbalanced the bitterness of the fruit. There was, maybe, more than just 'a touch' of spirits in the concoction, but all in all it was delicious and she took a bigger sip. To her surprise, rather than diminishing, the flavours seemed to intensify, and she found herself eyeing up Isabelle's glass, in the hope her sister would reject hers.

When Helena challenged him about why the Rakshasa were only active at night, he shrugged it off.

'Think of us as nocturnal cousins of Man. There is, in reality, very little between us.'

The next piece of information shocked them both, and had Helena's cheeks burning again.

'Indeed, our two races are so similar that offspring have been born of unions between Rakshasa and humans – though it has happened quite infrequently. Almost all of the children born have been well formed and of sound mind. They develop either into pure Rakshasa, pure human, or usually a half-caste mix of both.'

As the evening drew on, Helena began to find herself becoming more well disposed towards Zentar, but she did not discount that this could be an effect of the lemon drink they had been given. Bar the outburst of anger – which she had, after all, deliberately provoked – he had an engaging, easy going manner, and even something of a sense of humour. Also, in his presence she found herself remarkably at ease, as if he were radiating some aura of calm. Their initial shock at his appearance had now faded, and due to his courteousness and engaging manner they were hardly troubled when, some hours into the evening, he permanently removed his spectacles.

Finally, he had revealed, the Rakshasa hoped to move out of the shadows, to a proper land of their own, and be recognised as a nation in their own right. Korthdan would then concede power to him, and he would become ruler, with the intent of negotiating peace treaties with the leaders of all the great powers. Then they would be able to trade openly and freely with other nations, instead of having to plunder their shipping – an activity, he pointed out, that until relatively recently, the British themselves had been famous for. The sisters were so taken up with his tale that even Helena forgot to ask what commodity the Rakshasa would actually use for trade.

It was late when he left. The sisters had no clock and so did not know the precise time, but it felt like midnight. Following their conversation, they both agreed he was actually a stunningly handsome and well-built devil and, in the soft light of a candle-lit ballroom in London, would have set the heart of any English woman aflutter.

CHAPTER 11

The next day a messenger brought word to Lord Charlemont that the slave trader, Mustapha, had arrived back in Piraeus, and had arranged for them to view the Northerners, who were expected the following night. They used the day to make last-minute preparations for what they assumed would be a long sea journey, packing dried meat, fruit, nuts, and bread into oilskin bags. They also obtained a few pig bladders of beer and fresh spring water. The bags they had bought enabled them to carry all their equipment on their backs, freeing up their hands, and each had a short-barrelled musket tied to the outside. With the grappling hooks that the arms dealer had supplied, they tied loops roughly every two feet along the ropes to aid in climbing. Alex finally shouldered up all his equipment, and it was extremely heavy.

'Lord Charlemont,' he declared, 'with all this on we will drown if we have to swim!'

Lord Charlemont looked at him as if he were a weakling, and then shouldered his own bag; Alex looked on in amusement as the other staggered around the room for a few seconds or so, guessing that Fredrich usually did any heavy lifting required for 'm'Lord.'

'You're right,' Lord Charlemont conceded shortly. 'We had better get some more pig bladders and, if needs be, inflate them and use them as floats.'

*

Come sunset the next evening, they were ensconced in a room above Mustapha's courtyard. All three had come over on horses that Fredrich had procured for them and had left in a nearby street in the care of one of Mustafa's lackeys. The slave trader was a cruel, obnoxious individual, but after reading Bin Kaslm's letter he had become compliant to the point of grovelling and had made all the arrangements required for them.

Dusk turned to twilight; twilight to darkness, and there was still no sign of the Northerners. Lord Charlemont still sat by the window noting every movement below; Alex and Fredrich sat at the table further into the room, playing cards by candlelight. Alex had tried to engage Fredrich in conversation but he had proved almost as enigmatic as on the first day they had met. He had only managed to ascertain that Fredrich was a former commander of the Swiss Guard – the elite band of mercenaries traditionally used by the Roman Catholic Popes as their personal bodyguards. How he came to be in Lord Charlemont's service he would not say, and Lord Charlemont himself would not be drawn into the conversation.

The first set of candles had almost burnt out and Lord Charlemont and Alex were stretched out on the floor, sleeping on their cloaks, when an urgent whisper from Fredrich woke them. Lord Charlemont glanced at his pocket watch. 'Midnight,' he said simply before replacing it and blowing out the candles. They all crowded around the window.

Down below in the courtyard there was a buzz of activity, with no visible reason why, save for Mustafa in the centre who was clapping his hands, urging unseen people on and shouting to those within. Moments later, two lines of slaves, chained at the neck, were led out of the building. There were about three score of them in total, an equal mix of young adult males and females, of both black and white. All were clothed in simple knee length sackcloth. One of the girls was crying, but most just stared stoically ahead of themselves.

'Good God!' exclaimed Alex. 'Some of those are Europeans!'

'Of course they are,' hissed Lord Charlemont, 'captured in corsair raids on southern Europe. Where do you think they end up? Now keep your voice down.'

A flurry of extra activity below heralded the arrival of a large caged cart pulled by four black horses – and driven by two scarlet-clad figures.

'It's them,' whispered Alex, his hackles rising at the sight of them.

Lord Charlemont nodded. 'I was expecting more,' he whispered.

The Northerners brought the cart to a halt more or less in the middle of the courtyard and climbed down without a word. They were tall and moved with purpose, though rather stiffly, like old men. Mustafa beckoned to his men, now hardly saying a word as he went through what was obviously a well-rehearsed procedure. One by one, the slaves in each line were brought before the two hooded figures. As they neared the hooded figures they all tried to shy away from them in fear but were forced to their knees. Alex glanced anxiously towards the cart, fearing that he would see a barrel there and that the whole nightmarish episode would be repeated – but it was empty, save for chains.

The Northerners then raised their right arms above each slave's head, in an action similar to the one Alex had seen on the *Fearless*. This time, with the flickering light of torches hung around the courtyard, he could just make out that each had what looked like a plumb line in his hand. The two slaves were pulled to their feet, shoved towards the cart, and the next two pushed forward. Several more pairs passed them, until one seemed to fail whatever test was being carried out and was roughly marked with a charcoal cross on her forehead by her judge. Mustafa, standing between the two lines, cursed and stepped forward, kicking the defenceless girl as she struggled to get to her feet.

'Ah. They are using a pendulum,' whispered Lord Charlemont. 'An occult method of determination.'

He had barely uttered the words when the taller of the two scarlet figures suddenly turned directly towards the window, his face hidden in the shadows of his cowl. They shrank back in shock. Surely the Northerner could not have seen or heard them?

'Stay down,' commanded Lord Charlemont to them both and they waited, not daring to move.

Several minutes seemed to pass, and then the clink of chains from below indicated that the process had started again.

'Fredrich,' whispered Lord Charlemont, 'a mirror!'

Fredrich passed a small mirror over to him and he held it up at an angle, which enabled him and Alex to once more observe the proceedings down below.

'If we gaze only on their reflection, they will be unaware of us,' whispered Lord Charlemont with confidence. Alex was sceptical, but sure enough the Northerners now appeared not to notice them, even when they talked in low voices. He briefly wondered how the other man was aware of this, not knowing that this knowledge of occult matters would shortly bring him to the brink of killing Lord Charlemont.

At one point the Turkish night patrol passed the yard. Mustafa looked over to them and just nodded at the commander, who nodded back and continued on without stopping.

In due course the selection procedure ended and the unlucky ones, as Alex thought of them, were loaded onto the cart by Mustafa's men and chained in place. Only three had failed the selection process. One of the Northerners was conferring with the slave trader and several small bags were passed over, Mustafa receiving them with grovelling thanks while the Northerner turned wordlessly away in the direction of the cart. Both were now on the driver's pew, the reins in their hands. With the crack of a whip the cart was then turning round. A few seconds later it left the dirt floor of the courtyard and with a clatter of hooves made its way onto the cobbles of the street outside.

They waited a few seconds, and then Lord Charlemont sprang up. 'Follow me,' he commanded, sweeping up his bags and racing for the stairs.

Mustafa was waiting for them at the bottom of the staircase. 'It was all right?' he asked anxiously.

'Yes,' replied Lord Charlemont as he raced past him, 'I will pass my thanks to Bin Kaslm,' he called as he disappeared round the gatepost, leaving Mustafa looking relieved.

Their horses were tied up outside a kahvehane that had long closed, the lackey squatting outside it, smoking a long pipe. Fredrich tossed some coins at him and the man stood up, speaking in rapid fire Turkish, obviously demanding more. They ignored him as they secured the bags on the horses until he tried to prevent Fredrich from mounting his. Fredrich roughly barged him away with his shoulder, and then punched him with terrific force, laying him out cold in the dirt. All three then tore down the road in pursuit of the cart, before it disappeared into the night.

*

They soon caught up with the cart, but kept a good distance away. 'Don't look at the Northerners,' instructed Lord Charlemont as they trotted along, 'they can obviously sense it. If you must look in their direction, just focus on the cart.'

The cart quickly rumbled east out of Piraeus, the three horsemen shadowing it, and continued east along the coast road. Alex soon realised they were heading for the beaches of Phalerum, the ancient trireme port of Athens, used for centuries before Piraeus was developed. As there was practically no moonlight, they had to rely on the rumble of the cart wheels to guide them on. After an hour or so, the noise from the cart suddenly became muffled and almost disappeared. Riding on, they made out a hedge-lined lane to their right, barely wide enough for the cart. Feeling about on the ground for the carts tracks confirmed their assumption that it had turned off the road at this point. In the distance they could hear the crash of waves on a beach.

'What do you think?' asked Lord Charlemont.

'If I were them, I'd have this lane watched,' replied Alex. 'I say we take to the fields on foot.'

'My thoughts exactly!'

They led the horses away, slung their bags on their backs and made their way with some difficulty through a corn field, walking with the lane way over to their left. Presently they came to the beach that was backed by high dunes. Carefully they made their way round the dunes and soon came across their quarry – and a galley. It was docked stern first, about a hundred yards away, in a small natural harbour formed by an outcrop of rocks that jutted out from the otherwise smooth coastline. Alex could see it was not fitted out for war – it had no guns, boarding ramps or raised sniper platforms. Its furled sail flapped gently in the almost non-existent breeze. By the faint starlight, Alex could make out a few black-clad figures armed with muskets, silhouetted against its hull, standing guard around it. The cart had only just drawn up and the scarlet-clad ones were going through the motions of unloading their human cargo. They pulled back and rested against the dune, all three of them slightly out of breath.

Lord Charlemont was almost beside himself with joy. 'By God Hurst – it's definitely them! We're on to them. Right,' he said, trying to calm himself down, 'first things first. Fredrich, get the pig bladders out and inflate them. I need to write a note for Admiral Blake.' He untied the oilskin protecting his notepad, lit a small stub of a candle and quickly scribbled a note in flowing copperplate.

Meanwhile Alex stripped off most of his clothes and stuffed them into an oilskin bag, pulling the draw cords tight to seal it. Having finished his note, Lord Charlemont handed it to Fredrich, and then disrobed while Alex helped Fredrich inflate the remaining bladders and tie them to their bags. The grappling hooks were unpacked, and finally they were ready.

'Right, Fredrich, go back to the head of the lane and draw the Northerners up there. Make it as noisy and as long as possible. We'll take advantage of it and swim out to the bow of the galley. Understood?'

Fredrich nodded. 'Good luck, my Lord!' he said, and then was gone.

They waited for a while, occasionally peering round the dune to see what was happening. The slaves were being led over the rocks and the first of them was boarding the vessel. More time passed, and looking round the dunes again, the last of the slaves had just boarded. Suddenly shots rang out from the direction of the road. Peering round the dune again they could see the black-clad figures on the rocks moving uncertainly towards the beach and then with purpose as they were urged on by others.

'Let's go,' whispered Lord Charlemont hoarsely, and they were off, racing across the short stretch of beach, the pig bladders bouncing against them in a way that would have been comical had the situation not been so deadly. Next, they were in the sea. The bags were awkward to swim with, and eventually Alex had to roll over on to his back, holding on to the floating bags and kicking out only with his legs.

It seemed to take an age to reach the bow but they finally made it. The shots from the shore were becoming less frequent and more distant. The anchor chain was positioned on their side of the bow, forcing them to swim round to the other side, which had the rigging and nets that Alex had remembered. The deck overhung the hull at this point and it made an ideal stowaway refuge. Using the grappling hooks Alex pulled himself up first, and then his and Lord Charlemont's bags, closely followed by the man himself. The stowed netting formed a large sort of hammock affair, which enabled them to stow their bags at one end and half sit huddled together at the other. The gunshots were receding into the distance but they used the time afforded to pull their dry clothes back on, and then settled down as best they could as they heard footsteps on the deck.

A lot of shouting, cursing, and whinnying of horses then went on, as they heard the cart and horses being manoeuvred on to the vessel. The anchor chain was then hauled up before an uneasy silence settled over the ship. Alex hardly allowed himself to breathe until the silence was broken by the deep bass sound of timing drums. The ship then lurched forward as its oars bit into the water, and they were off into the darkness of the Aegean Sea, leaving a trail of ghostly phosphorescence in their wake.

CHAPTER 12

After the night of Helena and Isabelle's first proper conversation with Zentar, he began occasionally bringing them gifts of flowers and fresh fruit, and chatted freely to them both for hours at a time. At first they had stayed in the room, but then he had invited them both out to take the night air on the roof of the palace, and view the island by moonlight. Next it was tours for them both around the palace itself and down to the port. Wherever they went, other Rakshasa would defer and bow as they passed, which made the sisters feel like royalty. As the nights went on, however, it became obvious that he was, to Helena's amusement and Isabelle's chagrin, taking more of an interest in Helena. She played along with him, determined to use him in order to aid a possible bid for escape.

Then, on one fateful night he requested that just he and Helena take the air by themselves; a request to which Isabelle could only grudgingly acquiesce. Helena, however, had felt uncomfortable being alone with him; the conversation was stilted, and she was glad when he cut the evening short with some excuse and returned her to the room.

Zentar did not give up, however, and from then on she found herself playing a dangerous game of regularly having to charm and make conversation with her inhuman admirer by night, while trying to extract from him any information that would aid herself and Isabelle. In truth, she could have distanced herself from Zentar and directed his interest towards Isabelle – something she had done with a number of young bucks back in England – but there was something she wanted from Zentar: something she hoped would heal a part of their lives that had been torn asunder that Isabelle did not have the necessary guile to obtain.

The game then quickly moved to another level, one more fraught with risk for Helena: Zentar started taking her out of the palace altogether in his chariot to see various parts of the island by night. This changed matters to Helena's considerable disadvantage. It was one thing for her to correspond and occasionally have chaperoned meetings with men she considered of her own intellect – mainly Alexander Pope and Sir Richard Steele – but she had never found any of them physically attractive and had even laughed at Pope when he had unexpectedly declared his love for her some years previously. Now, however, she found herself spending increasing amounts of time alone – utterly alone in seemingly deserted parts of the island – with a handsome warrior prince, a creature of power and high intellect, and with an interest in her that was clearly much more than platonic. As more time went on she realised that, while during the hours of daylight she desperately wanted to escape from the island and be reunited with Alex, when night fell the powerful aura of Zentar blotted all else out, and she found herself being drawn to him as a moth is to a candle. Events, she realised helplessly, were spiralling out of her control.

CHAPTER 13

It was difficult to hear above the noise of the bow cutting through the water, and the oars creaking and groaning as they relentlessly churned the sea. It was cold, the wind chilling them as they huddled there, unable to move. Judging by the few stars he could make out from their position, Alex could tell they were moving south-east.

As dawn broke they were alarmed to see that directly above them was a trapdoor, presumably to allow access to the area they were hiding in. Because of this, as a precaution they unwrapped their pistols and knives, as well as a couple of hand grenades each, and made them ready – though in reality if they were discovered it would mean almost certain death.

Much to Alex's unease, Lord Charlemont, balancing a bit unsteadily on the netting, actually raised the trapdoor slightly to see what was happening on the deck. As it happened, there was no one about and nothing to report. The sun came up and the air temperature began to rise. An hour or so later the wind picked up, the oars were halted and they heard sounds of the sail being raised, presumably to conserve the energy of the oarsmen, who had been propelling the galley along at an incredible ten to eleven knots. Alex had discerned this by dropping a small branch caught in the netting and counting the seconds it took to clear the stern of the galley. This was fast for any kind of craft, and would have given even a Royal Navy frigate a run for its money. Once they were under sail the apparent wind under the bow eased considerably.

Being on the eastern side of the bow they now started warming up from the sun as it rose further above the horizon. The only disadvantage that the wind brought was that the smell of the galley slaves was now blown forward. At first it was a nauseating odour of sweat and excrement, but after a while they became accustomed to it. The galley rose and fell gently with the swell, and the low angle of the sunlight made the surface of the water look like quicksilver. Seagulls cried out in the distance and water slapped lazily around the bow.

*

Alex woke with a start – the gentle rocking of the boat and warmth of the sun had lulled him to sleep. He turned to Lord Charlemont, who noted his waking with a wry smile.

'What time is it?' he asked.

Lord Charlemont consulted his pocket watch. 'Eleven o'clock,' he said. 'You've been asleep for hours. Any idea where we are?'

Alex pulled the map they had brought out of its waxed cylinder and studied it for a few minutes, comparing it to what he could see.

'I'd say we're about fifty nautical miles south-east of Piraeus. That island over there could well be Serpho, though it's difficult to tell. All these islands look quite similar.'

'Well, if you are right, another ten hours and we could be in Nio,' observed Lord Charlemont, looking over his shoulder at the map. 'It looks like Bin Kaslm was right about where the Northerners are based.'

Midday found them hungry, so they decided to eat, having grown more confident of the security of their hideaway. Despite this, they still remained vigilant, one keeping guard while the other ate. Shortly after midday, his belly full, even the eyelids of the apparently indefatigable Lord Charlemont were drooping, so he settled down to sleep while Alex remained on watch.

During the whole day they sighted only one other vessel, which looked like a French *xebec*. The ships passed without either acknowledging the other. He wondered if the Northerners were flying the Turkish colours. If so, given its appearance, the captain of the French vessel would have assumed the galley was a Turkish naval vessel.

*

The afternoon drew on. Suddenly a female scream came from above, making Alex jump with shock. Lord Charlemont was awake in an instant. Shouts also carried around the ship, coming from the stern of the galley. Despite their predicament, both were almost irrationally eager to find out what was happening – anything to break the monotony of their journey. Being the nearest, Alex cautiously and slowly pushed up the trapdoor, arching his neck back so he was almost peering down his nose through the crack made – but initially he could see no sign of life. Looking around, he realised that instead of the oarsmen being exposed to the elements, as was usual in galleys, their level was covered over by a smooth wooden deck raised slightly in the middle, like a pitched roof, along the length of the ship.

Another scream. One of the slave girls had somehow broken free and suddenly appeared, running furiously on to and around the deck, evading a few hooded Northerners who came out after her, but who seemed sluggish and lethargic in comparison. She was a black African – tall, slim and long-limbed, with her hair shorn short. She ran desperately from one side of the galley to the other, each time halting in uncertainty at the sight of the sea below before turning and making for the other side. One of the Northerners drew his *kilij*, the sound of this action clearly audible to Alex. The girl turned at this, saw the drawn *kilij* and screamed again, this time making for the mast. The swordsman ran towards the terrified girl, twirling the blade above his head as he went, hissing curses.

Another shout came from the stern and one of the scarlet-clad Northerners appeared. The swordsman, now at the base of the mast with the girl several feet above him, turned and halted at this shout and reluctantly sheathed his *kilij*. The girl was standing on a small ledge on the mast, her arms wrapped round it, crying and shouting out in a language that Alex could not make out. A cold hand seemed to grip his heart and he had to stop himself from breaking cover and going to her aid. The scarlet-clad one made his way slowly to the base of the mast, uncoiling a whip as he went. The girl saw this and started to shuffle around to put the mast between them, but he quickly circled round. The black-clad Northerners moved forward and positioned themselves around the mast.

The whip lashed out. The girl screamed and pressed herself tightly against the mast to prevent the whip wrapping itself round her leg. The scarlet-clad one hissed a curse and quickly re-coiled the whip. The whip flicked through the air a second time and found the girl's upper arm, wrapping itself round in an instant. The whip bearer lost no time and brutally pulled the girl down. Two black-clad Northerners caught her before she could hit the deck, but she fought like a wildcat, kicking out, punching and clawing into their hooded faces. The scarlet-clad one moved into the melee, shouting angrily. The girl lunged at him and tore back his hood. Unlike the raiders on the *Fearless*, this one wore no helmet, just smoked glass spectacles, and his now bare head revealed a thick shock of long platinum blond hair that reached down to his shoulders.

'Let me see,' demanded Lord Charlemont and they awkwardly exchanged places. The screaming and shouting went on for a few seconds more and then faded away.

'They took her below decks,' explained Lord Charlemont, gently closing the trapdoor and settling down again.

'You saw his hair?' asked Alex.

'Yes – remarkable. So we do seem to be dealing with a race of albinos after all,' he commented.

'Poor girl,' said Alex, shaking his head.

'Oh, don't waste your time worrying about a slave girl!' shot back Lord Charlemont. 'Slaves oil the wheels of empire. Accept it – it's the way of the world. Some are meant to rule, others to serve.'

'And you were meant to rule, I suppose,' retorted Alex, glaring at him.

'Look,' said Lord Charlemont, adopting a more conciliatory tone, 'she was born in Africa. Her own kind would have kidnapped her from her village, or more likely ransacked and enslaved the entire village, taken her to the coast and sold her to Arab slave traders, who then sold her on to the Turks. It occurs all the time, to tens of thousands every year. As it happens she's ended up in the hands of these Northerners,' he held up his hand to prevent Alex speaking, 'who, I agree, appear evil, but as slave owners I would guess they are no worse than any others.'

'It's just not right,' Alex persisted.

'As long as there is life, there will be the dominators and the dominated,' intoned Lord Charlemont. 'Count yourself lucky you were born an Englishman! We were born to dominate.' He turned away, obviously considering the matter closed.

'Your arrogance,' Alex seethed, 'is scarcely believable!'

'Quiet now,' Lord Charlemont demanded, not in the least perturbed by what Alex had said. 'Things have calmed down. They may hear us.'

More hours passed. Around two in the afternoon, their course changed and they started heading due south. By the time the sun set, Alex estimated that Nio was about thirty nautical miles due east of them – but they were still heading south.

'Well, I don't know where we're going – but I don't think it's going to be Nio,' he said to Lord Charlemont, showing him the map. 'At this rate of knots, we could be in Crete by sunset tomorrow.'

Lord Charlemont raised his eyebrows, but said nothing.

The sun set and more hours passed. A light mist came down shortly after sunset, so Alex could no longer judge their direction. They dipped again into their rations, swapped places every few hours and alternatively slept and kept watch through the night.

*

The mist cleared before daybreak and Alex was able to judge that they were now heading in an easterly direction. As the light grew stronger, Alex looked ahead and saw what he thought were low lying clouds. As they got nearer he could make out what seemed to be great sheets of swirling rain sweeping in all directions. He woke Lord Charlemont.

'What is it?' asked Lord Charlemont.

'I think we are heading directly for the storm barrier that Bin Kaslm described.'

'It cannot be!' Lord Charlemont exclaimed, springing up and twisting around so he could see ahead.

The phenomenon now rose up before them like a wall of raging water, stretching for miles to their left and right, and yet the sea was calm and the skies to either side and behind them were clear. Shouts came from above, the bass drums started up and the oars took over, causing the galley to accelerate noticeably. A fine mist now filled the air as they drew closer to the wall of water, and howling winds seemed to erupt from nowhere. In the deluge ahead, the sea was white foamed and turbulent.

'Unless we change course,' shouted Alex, 'we'll be broken to pieces!'

At that moment the skies seemed to darken and the light around them failed.

'It's too late!' bellowed Lord Charlemont. 'We are going directly into it!'

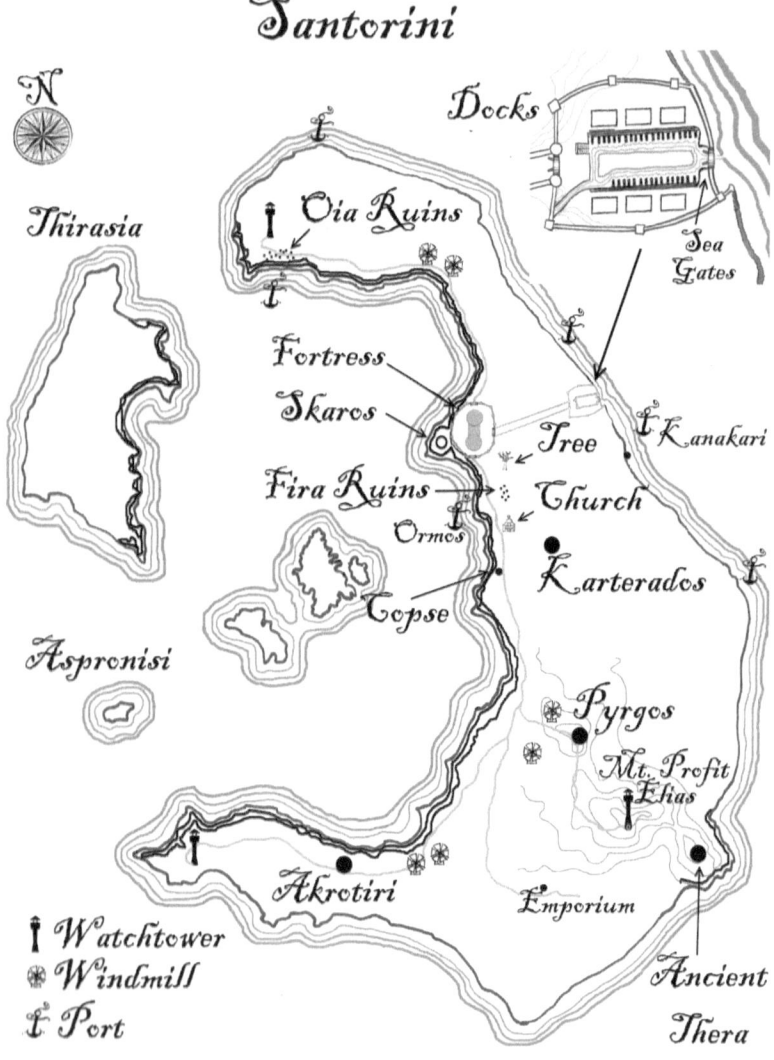

Santorini

N

Docks

Thirasia

Oia Ruins

Sea Gates

Fortress

Skaros

Tree

Kanakari

Fira Ruins

Church

Ormos

Karterados

Copse

Aspronisi

Pyrgos

Mt. Profit Elias

Emporium

Akrotiri

Ancient Thera

🏛 Watchtower
✳ Windmill
⚓ Port

CHAPTER 14

There was nothing they could do but hang on as wave after wave hit the bow with bone crunching impacts. The rigging they were in was awash each time the bow pitched down, the sea sometimes erupting up and forcing the trapdoor open, before it came back down with a crash. They clung to the rigging for dear life, neither able to speak nor hear anything other than the wind and crashing of the waves, their vision blurred with grey water, both caught up in a moment that seemed to last an age.

Abruptly they were out of it. Alex rubbed the water out of his eyes and saw the sea around them was calm once more. Looking back, he just caught sight of the rear of the galley as it emerged from the wall of water. The skies above them lightened in colour and then they were back in warm air and clear skies, with just a stiff breeze whipping up the sea slightly. Behind them, to the left and right, the wall of turbulent clouds stretched for miles, seeming to curve in the distance to encircle them. Lord Charlemont was also looking back. They looked at each other momentarily, and then Lord Charlemont spoke.

'This is insane,' he said simply. 'Sorcery is behind all this!'

'Or mines of brimstone on the seabed – as Bin Kaslm said – boiling the sea water,' retorted Alex. 'I take it you *have* heard of Occam's razor?'

'If that is so, how is it we were not choked by noxious vapours?' Lord Charlemont shot back.

'The rational explanation would be that they have all burnt off by now!'

Lord Charlemont shot him a look of contempt, and was about to respond when Alex saw surprise on his features as he looked forward, past Alex. Alex turned – and his jaw dropped.

Ahead of them, over the foam flecked water, two great masses of rock reared up hundreds of feet out of the sea like two great fangs, separated by an immense gulf. Alex tried to get some sense of proportion, but was unable to. Lord Charlemont looked over at him questioningly.

'It's the Santorini archipelago,' Alex finally replied. 'It must be. We're looking at the northern ends of the two larger islands – but I had no idea they would be this…' his voice trailed off '…spectacular.'

For some minutes they both stared at the sight ahead, still unable to get any sense of scale of them. No other ships were around and there seemed to be no sign of any human habitation on them. Noises from above indicated the sail was going up again, and the oars became idle once more.

*

An hour or so later they were heading straight for the gap between the two cliffs. Now closer, they could see the cliff to the left was made up of stone of a reddish hue punctuated by chutes of grey scree. There appeared to be some buildings along the top of the cliff, but from this distance they looked derelict and there was no sign of life. The only thing that looked in good repair was a graceful yet sinister-looking tower topped by some sort of large lantern that stood almost at the very edge of the cliff. The only living things appeared to be seagulls, wafting round in the currents of air near the cliff face which appeared to be about three hundred feet high. They were surely unscalable, and Alex wondered where the galley was heading for, speculating to Lord Charlemont that they would soon sight and then enter a cave. As he was speaking he noticed flashes of light, as if from a heliograph, coming from the top of the tower. It was some sort of signal, and presumably someone on deck was replying to it.

Shortly after the signals had been exchanged, the galley tacked sharply to port and started heading south-east, around the larger of the two islands, avoiding the gap altogether. The island now swung out of view, hidden from them by the hull. From his recollection of the diagram in Lord Charlemont's book, Alex realised they were now travelling parallel to the east side of the larger island. There could be no doubt this was the Northerners' stronghold, protected by the massive walls of water they had passed through. They began to ready themselves, hurriedly inflating their pig bladders, but as it turned out the galley maintained this new course for well over an hour.

They then heard the sail coming down again and the oars engaging. The galley turned to starboard and the bow wheeled round as the ship now headed directly towards the shore, affording them a view of the east side of the island. Instead of a normal sea shore, the waves lapped against a white crenellated wall that was approximately fifty feet high, and blindingly bright in the early morning sunshine. It started a way over to their right, and continued to their left for almost quarter of a mile. The terrain immediately behind the shore was fairly flat, but then rose up quite quickly in about a mile to what Alex estimated was a height of around one thousand feet. It was as if the island were wedge shaped in cross section and they were now sailing towards the lower end.

At the highest point of the wedge, and furthest away from them, towering above everything was a fortress of gigantic proportions, with sheer walls dropping away from it for hundreds of feet on several of its many faces. At each change in the angle of the wall was a large tower. At the centre of this was what looked like a palace with a low pitched roof of red tiles, decorated with golden cylindrical structures, beneath which large brown shuttered windows peered out, facing east. At the northern and southern ends of this edifice were two identical circular domed roofed buildings, the domes slightly higher than the red tiled roof, each topped with what looked like a lantern. Beneath the walls of the fortress, lapping up to its edges like a sea of vegetation, were hundreds of dwellings, each festooned with so much plant life it seemed that the whole hillside was a huge hanging garden.

'Remarkable' was the only adjective Lord Charlemont could find to describe it.

As Alex's gaze dropped from the fortress, he realised they were heading for two squat sea gates in the wall, maybe one hundred feet wide. He was wondering how the galley was going to fit under such a height when new sounds from above gained their attention. Peering through the trapdoor, he saw the crew were bringing the mast down and laying it horizontally on the deck.

As they drew nearer, he scoured the walls and fortress behind for signs of life, but all he could make out were two guards standing on the battlements above the gates. They huddled down on the netting, and as far under the overhanging deck as possible, to keep out of sight. With about three hundred yards to go, the gates started to open and Alex could hear the creaking of machinery and chains in the background. On they went, passing under the battlements of the wall, which proved to be almost thirty feet thick, and into a fortified harbour area.

The drum beat had slowed down somewhat, and they found themselves cruising past galley after galley tied up parallel to each other in a dock on their port side, the bows facing them as they passed. Automatically Alex started counting, and had reached forty-five by the time their galley slowed. It stopped dead in the water, and then reversed through ninety degrees to place itself stern first to the quayside, between two other galleys towards the end of the line.

As their vessel backed in, Alex realised that an almost identical line of galleys was facing them across a gap of maybe two hundred feet of water. They had effectively come in between two lines of galleys down a long rectangular dock. It had the sea gates at one end, large wooden warehouses lining the quaysides on either side, and at the far end a wide ramp leading out of the water. To the left of the ramp, a spur came off from the dock and terminated against large doors set into the wall that protected the rear of the docks. Behind the ramp were large gates flanked by towers, which presumably led to the fortress and could seal the docks off if necessary.

High up on the ramp were three galleys in various stages of construction, while two older ones had been hauled up out of the water on a huge harness, presumably to have their hulls scraped clean or be repaired. All Alex could do was shake his head in wonder – this was a full scale naval base. From the other end of the dock came the sound of the huge sea gates closing.

Shouts came from above, and it was obvious the cart and horses, as well as its cargo of slaves, was being unloaded. The Englishmen stayed put, the curve of the bow hiding them from anyone on the quayside.

Horses' hooves clattered on the paving stones of the quay, and the rumble of cart wheels and clink-clank of chains echoed around the docks as the slaves were led away. Soon after, they became aware of a large number of people moving around inside the hull. It was the oarsmen, all this time unheard and unseen. There came the rhythmical tramp of feet as an untold number of men marched out of the galley and on to the quayside. Other than a few shouts, very few orders seem to be issued. Between the hull of their galley and the adjacent one, Alex could just see one or two men at a time as they marched silently along the quayside towards the ramp end. They appeared to be Slavic in origin, and on the whole they were well fed and strongly built, wearing simple sweat stained tunics and breeches. All, however, seemed to lack any facial expression and emotion, and moved like automatons, their shorn heads downcast. Alex nudged Lord Charlemont and gestured for him to look. They awkwardly exchanged places on the netting, and he studied them in silence for a few seconds before pulling back.

'Russians and Poles,' he observed, 'captured by Tartars and sold to the Turks, I'll wager. They are thought to make the best galley slaves. Did you notice the scars on their temples?'

'No,' Alex replied.

'I think they've have their temples cut. It's surgery that's supposed to remove the subject's ability to think for themselves, leaving them like docile cattle.' He paused. 'But I've never heard of it working properly.'

'How do you know about this?'

'My grandfather tried it on his plantations in Barbados, but most of the subjects died before they left the operating table,' he replied, matter-of-factly.

'Subjects?' exclaimed Alex in anger. 'You mean your father killed slaves in order to try and make them more docile?'

'No – he experimented on the Irish that were sold to him following Cromwell's conquest of Ireland.'

'That's inhuman.'

'Oh, do be quiet!' snapped Lord Charlemont. 'The Irish are barely human anyway. Look, we can pursue this moral debate at any time – let's concentrate on getting out of these docks for now.' He checked his watch again. 'It's almost gone ten o'clock,' he observed. 'Surely they must start work here soon.'

The galley slaves had been marched somewhere out of their sight, but now the sound of doors opening suggested they were being quartered nearby in one of the warehouses. This was followed by the sound of wooden benches being scraped across stone floors, and then by the scraping of metal utensils on plates.

'Feeding time at the menagerie,' remarked Lord Charlemont. 'We'll have to wait till that lot are finished before we can make a move.'

*

More time passed. The noise of the galley slaves being fed had subsided and they had heard doors being shut and barred before several pairs of boots tramped off into the distance. The only sound now was that of water lapping around the hulls of the moored galleys and seagulls calling to each other. Without warning, a deep resonant horn sounded from the direction of the palace. Alex glanced back to the guards and they seemed to be stretching out and generally relaxing, as if anticipating a change. Sure enough, some minutes later there was the sound of boots on the quayside and two fresh guards made their way over to the sea gate.

They watched the new guards pass the galley, and as they got closer Alex noticed there was something unusual about their heads. They were wearing the close-fitting silver helmets that he remembered from the attack on the *Fearless*, with white hair again visible, but now they also had some sort of mask over their eyes that flashed as it caught the sun. As they drew closer still, he could see the masks consisted of an elongated oval piece of smoked glass, held in place by a strap that went around the back of their heads, giving the wearers a somewhat cyclopean look.

They waited until the changing of the guard had been completed, and then Alex lowered himself into the water and took the bags that Lord Charlemont passed down, arranging the pig bladders around them. Soon they were swimming towards the quay, and then carefully making their way up steps to the quayside. Lord Charlemont stayed down a few steps as Alex peered over the top and looked around for any signs of life. There were none. He returned down to where Lord

Charlemont was positioned and, as quietly as possible, both of them dressed and then slung their bags back on.

On their side of the dock, behind the warehouses, was the dock wall. Beyond it, from what they had seen offshore, lay open fields. They both hurriedly walked up the steps and made the quayside before trotting over to the end of the nearest warehouse, crouching as they went. Once in the cover of the warehouse, safely out of sight, they straightened up and made for the corner nearest the wall. They paused as Alex peered round the corner. All was clear. He turned to signal to Lord Charlemont.

With terrifying speed, a hand reached through a sizeable gap in the planks of the warehouse wall, seized Alex around the throat and pulled him in towards the side of the warehouse. Lord Charlemont half stepped back in shock, and then in the space of a heartbeat drew his pistol with his left hand, his right ready on the handle of his sabre. Alex grasped the arm of his attacker with both hands, barely encircling the massive forearm of the man, and found himself looking into a bearded Slavic face, neat scars clearly visible on both temples. The face, its proportions that of a gorilla, looked back at him like an idiot child who had found a new toy.

'Get…him…off…me,' Alex gasped, desperately struggling for air.

Lord Charlemont paused for a few moments more, and then, to Alex's consternation, he re-holstered his musket and stepped forward towards them both, being careful to stay out of range of the man's other hand, which was gripping the planks of the warehouse wall.

'Release him,' he commanded in Latin. There was no reaction from Alex's assailant, other than to glance briefly over towards Lord Charlemont. He then turned his attention back to Alex, who was on the brink of passing out. Lord Charlemont spoke again, seemingly far away, in a language that Alex did not recognise. Everything seemed to go black.

CHAPTER 15

Alex came to. His assailant had loosened his grip and was looking surprised. Lord Charlemont spoke again, and almost immediately the man released Alex. Alex fell to the ground, choking for breath. Above, his attacker stared down at him through the gap with the look of a dejected infant.

Lord Charlemont helped him to his feet. 'It's a good thing he went for you,' he commented.

'What? Why?' asked Alex, still dazed.

'Would you have known the Russian for "Release him"?'

'It's not funny,' Alex said hoarsely. 'That bastard almost throttled me.'

'Still feel sorry for slaves?'

It had felt like the brute had crushed his windpipe, but all seemed to be in place, and Alex guessed all he would suffer from would be bruises. 'I'm fine now. Let's carry on,' he croaked.

As they passed the man, giving him a wide berth, Alex got a glimpse of the living quarters within through the gaps in the wall. Triple bunks of stark construction stretched off into the gloom inside, each with a large figure prone on it, either sleeping or staring upwards blankly.

'Poor bastards,' he muttered.

They skirted round the dormitories and soon were behind the half built boats, close to the spur. They stopped near some sheds to find a rope.

'This should be long enough,' said Lord Charlemont, struggling under the weight of a heavy hemp rope.

Alex quickly ran it through his hands. 'It's only sixty feet long. We'll need another,' he said. 'We can't leave it tied on – we must be able to pull it down with us.'

They found another similar sized rope and headed back to the wall, staggering under the weight. Soon they were working their way along the base of the wall towards a large stone staircase that would have allowed half a dozen men to march up abreast. Moments later they were up on top of the wall, a small fortified tower affording them some cover from the guards.

Before them lay cultivated fields that stretched down to the sea on their left. Alex quickly tied the ropes together using a sheet bend and they flung both ends over the wall, hanging it loosely around a battlement.

Lord Charlemont was over first, Alex following on closely behind. They pulled the rope down, re-coiled it, then staggered with it through a deep dry ditch filled with undergrowth. Reaching the other side, they trotted off down a dusty lane lined with drystone walls made up of rough-hewn black, red, white and grey rocks the size of cannonballs. They had arrived in Santorini proper.

*

They continued until they were a good quarter of a mile from the dock before hiding the ropes in some bushes well away from the lane. Both were breathing hard with the exertion; the grey soil underfoot was dry and loose. Shortly afterwards they stopped to eat, settling in what looked like a sheep enclosure by one of the fields, and quickly got through more of their rations.

It was a bright day and the sun was now at its highest and strongest. From where he sat, Alex could see fields stretching off to the south of them, becoming gently terraced as they rose up to the higher spine of the island. There were light brown fields of young barley and arid grey fields containing what looked like inverted woven black baskets, each separated by a few feet. The baskets appeared to be made up of the branches of a plant that was just coming into leaf. Other uncultivated fields were a riot of poppies, daisies and violets. A light breeze rustled the leaves of some Mediterranean pines nearby, while down towards the sea were clumps of shady tamarisk trees. A couple of hooded crows cawed as they soared in the clear air above them, while swallows darted round higher still. Further south, in the distance Alex could see a large mountain, shimmering in the heat haze. It was bizarre to think that such a peaceful setting could be the home to the bestial corsairs he had encountered. It all seemed too pleasant; too neat and orderly. The only discordant note was a muted roar in the background, which had Alex puzzled at first, until he realised it was generated by the towering clouds of rain surrounding the island in the distance.

'Well,' said Lord Charlemont, still chewing some dried meat, 'I think the best thing would be to find the land entrance to this fortress, lie up and observe movements for a few days – get a feel for the guard patterns, etcetera – then get in and search for the women.'

Alex raised his eyebrows. He could not help feeling that Lord Charlemont was overly optimistic. He suspected that the reality of the situation would soon dawn on Lord Charlemont and they would end up just mapping out the defences of the fortress before attempting to get back to the mainland with the information.

'Very well,' Alex declared in a businesslike manner, 'I suppose we'd better get started then.'

He stood up and brushed the dust from his clothes as Lord Charlemont packed the remainder of his rations away, and then turned round to climb over the drystone wall.

'Good God!' Alex exclaimed as he found himself looking into the eyes of a man standing on the other side of the wall. The man's eyes widened in shock, and he stepped back, babbling in what Alex recognised as Latin.

'What's wrong?' demanded Lord Charlemont, struggling to get up.

Alex quickly glanced about. Thank God the man was alone and unarmed – but what a fool he had been not to check before breaking cover. He leaned over the waist-high wall and grabbed the man by his jacket, and then pulled him bodily over. He met surprisingly little resistance from the fellow, even though he had the strong build of a farmer.

'Master?' the man implored in Latin as Alex threw him on to the ground of the enclosure.

'Hold him!' commanded Lord Charlemont, and an instant later he had a knife to the terrified man's throat.

Though wide-eyed, the man would not look either of them in the eye. 'No! Please, Master, what is it you want?' he cried.

'Be still,' commanded Lord Charlemont in Latin. He looked at Alex, puzzled. 'Why's he calling you "Master"?' he asked in English.

'I've no idea,' replied Alex, turning his attention back to the man and putting the question to him.

'You are from the fortress,' the man said, his face betraying surprise at the apparent simplicity of the question. 'You must be obeyed. I am your servant,' he continued. 'Please,' he asked again, 'what is it you want of me?'

'He thinks you're one of the Northerners,' postulated Lord Charlemont. 'It must be your hair.'

'Possibly,' Alex agreed. He gestured to the prone man with a downward glance of his eyes. 'He seems a bit simple, but he should be able to tell us what's going on here – where everyone is.'

'Go ahead,' agreed Lord Charlemont, withdrawing the knife from the man's throat to calm him.

'Where is everyone?' asked Alex, addressing the man.

'Where is who?' he asked, obviously puzzled by the question.

'Those who live in the fortress.'

Again, to the man this seemed to be a simplistic question. 'They sleep,' he replied, shrugging his shoulders slightly.

'Why?' Alex persisted.

'Because that is what you do, Master,' replied the man.

The Englishmen looked at each other uncomprehendingly, and then Alex turned back to the man. 'I don't understand,' he said.

'Master, are you unwell?' asked the man, a desperate smile fixed on his lips. 'You have lost your spectacles. Maybe the sun has vexed you. Let me help you back to the fortress.'

'No. Be quiet,' Alex snapped.

'Well, that would explain where all the Northerners are,' said Lord Charlemont. 'Presumably they use the locals to do the farming for them.' He turned to the man. 'Where do you live?' he demanded.

'In my village, Karterados, not far from here,' the man replied, squirming.

'What is your name?'

'Tryphon.'

'Right, Tryphon, is there a head man in your village?'

'Yes,' he replied, now no longer surprised by the simplicity of the questions.

'And is there one who is leader of all the villages on this island?'

'Yes, of course – the Chancellor of Santorini.'

*

The chancellor's village, Pyrgos, was some distance away to the south, and it took them almost two hours to walk there, along donkey tracks made up of the energy sapping soil. They told Tryphon to avoid any villages and skirt round them, but as it turned out they barely saw any. At one point he indicated a gully, saying his village was further up it, but all they could see was the bell tower of a church and no signs of habitation. Alex wondered where everyone was. Here and there were windmills, standing alone in fields, their sails barely moving.

Eventually Tryphon pointed to a collection of houses surrounding a tower on a foothill of the mountain they had seen earlier. 'The *kasteli* of Pyrgos,' he said.

They made Tryphon lead them to a deserted house outside the village, and then he and Lord Charlemont waited there while Alex set off for the kasteli. He was wearing his cloak to conceal his travelling clothes and weapons belt, but with the hood down to display his blond hair. He also wore spectacles of smoked glass that Lord Charlemont had produced from one of his bags. Walking along a drystone walled lane, with fields of the basket-like plants on either side, he noticed that at each corner of the fields were constructions that he first took to be the torsos of scarecrows. However, passing close to one he saw it consisted of willow branches loosely woven into a rough cylindrical shape, with strange geometrical patterns superimposed on it with other branches dyed in bright primary colours. Suspended within was the decomposing body of a rodent, the remnants of its tail wrapped around its body.

He continued on the lane, small lizards scampering out of his way as he strode along past a windmill. Shortly after that he entered the outskirts of the village surrounding the *kasteli*. All the houses he encountered en route were painted in a dull ochre colour – no doubt to camouflage them from prying eyes out at sea – but bushes of geranium created splashes of red along the way. Most of the dwellings were single storey with a vaulted roof and small courtyard, but as the lane became steeper, they adjoined each other in a seamless procession, making it difficult to tell where one house ended and the next began.

Presently he passed through an archway into the *kasteli* itself. If the archway had ever had a gate, it had been removed long ago. As he entered the *kasteli* he noted that the streets, though narrow, were well-paved, with detritus and donkey dung replacing the dust from the lanes. The houses now were larger and better built; some of them were three storeys high with glazed windows, and again ran into each other as the ground rose towards the top of the hill. Most had garlands of fresh wild flowers hung on the front door, as well as globes of garlic and crosses hung from the lintels. The overall impression was that of prosperity – quite different to the rough houses and villages Alex had encountered in rural Greece en route to Piraeus.

Women sat in doorways, weaving or mending clothes, and glanced up at him curiously as he passed before quickly dropping their gaze and continuing with their work. Others swept up their children and ushered them inside at his approach. That reassured him – his appearance was having the desired effect.

It took him a minute or so to reach what he assumed was the centre of the *kasteli* towards the top of the hill; he had passed quite a few narrow streets on either side, and guessed that the inhabitants of the kasteli alone probably numbered a few hundred. Finally he came across a small square, on the other side of which was a Greek Orthodox church with its three bells open to the air, hanging silently above the open door. He stopped there and looked around. There were a few old men playing backgammon at two tables in front of the church, oblivious to his presence, and a couple of dogs asleep in the afternoon sunshine. It all looked perfectly ordinary. He took a deep breath then walked up to the nearest table. The men practically jumped up at his approach, snatching their hats off as they stood up, kneading them nervously in their hands, eyes downcast.

'I am looking for the chancellor,' Alex said in Latin. 'Find him for me.'

The two men exchanged puzzled glances. He repeated himself more slowly, and this time they understood him, with one volunteering to go. The other man stood there for a minute or so, silent but exceedingly nervous, his mood unsettling Alex somewhat.

'Get me a drink,' he demanded to get rid of the man. 'Coffee.'

The man scurried off with much bowing of his head, and Alex sat down in his place, forcing himself to relax and making a show of coolly surveying his surroundings. Presently the drink arrived – in a Venetian cup complete with saucer and silver spoon. Alex dismissed the man with a wave of his hand, sitting back more in his chair. Shortly afterwards, the first man returned with the chancellor.

He was neatly dressed in a simple grey sleeveless shirt, a crucifix on a chain around his neck, loose blue calico trousers and waistband, together with a blue cap on his head and black leather pumps on his feet. He was a strapping man in the prime of health, and there was a quality about him that stood out – an air of confidence and surety of purpose that spoke of natural leadership. He had the light skin of one who did not work in the fields, and thick black hair that was neatly cut and groomed. His large eyes were a deep brown, beneath which was a fine Grecian nose, thick black moustache and a strong jaw. He seemed untroubled by the presence of one of the Northerners in his village.

To Alex's surprise, the chancellor said something to him in the guttural hissing voice he had heard the raiders use on the *Fearless*. He then stood there, waiting for a response.

This threw Alex for a moment, but then he recovered his composure. 'Speak in Latin,' he commanded.

'How can I help you, Master?' the chancellor asked. He looked concerned, but did not raise his eyes above the level of Alex's chest.

Alex dismissed the other man. 'I found Tryphon from Karterados nearby. He is hurt. I need you to come and help me with him.'

'But of course,' the man replied. 'I will get others to help,' he said, turning as if to go.

'No!' commanded Alex. The man stopped instantly. 'The two of us will suffice. Come.'

'Yes, Master,' the man replied, complying instantly with the command.

*

Presently they came to the house where Lord Charlemont was waiting. Alex opened the door, gesturing for the chancellor to go in first, which he did without hesitation, though he now looked slightly worried.

Lord Charlemont had a knife to his throat as soon as he entered. Alex quickly followed him in, drawing out his pistol.

'Don't say a word,' he commanded.

The man's eyes widened in shock as he saw Tryphon tied up and gagged in the corner, but he said nothing as instructed.

'Face me,' commanded Alex again, and Lord Charlemont quickly tied the chancellor's hands and forced him to sit down next to Tryphon.

The chancellor was looking very worried now. 'What is it, Master? What have we done wrong?'

'Be quiet,' Alex ordered, and then led Tryphon out of the hut and into a ditch some yards away.

Back in the hut Alex took off his smoked glasses, squatted down and forced the chancellor to look him in the eye.

'Firstly, I am *not* one of your masters,' he said. 'Secondly, we need to know if you can help us find some women.'

'You have come from outside?' asked the chancellor in astonishment, looking over to Lord Charlemont.

'Yes,' replied Alex.

'This is incredible!' spluttered the chancellor, a huge smile on his face. 'You are the first men from the outside for almost a century...'

'That's all very well,' interrupted Lord Charlemont, 'but we are here to find two women,' he continued, cutting to the chase. 'Do you know anything about them?' He moved in closer to the chancellor.

'Why, yes,' he replied.

'Well, where are they?'

'In the fortress – with the Rakshasa,' the chancellor said.

'Who?' asked Alex.

'Those that rule here – who live in the fortress,' the chancellor replied. 'But the women are under heavy guard. Why do you want them?'

'That is our business,' snapped Lord Charlemont.

'Look,' said the chancellor, turning to Alex. 'If you want me to help you, it would be useful if I knew where you have come from and why you need the women.'

Alex glanced questioningly at Lord Charlemont, unsure of what to say.

'We are from England,' Lord Charlemont replied with a shrug of his shoulders.

'England!' exclaimed the man in wonder. 'You are a long way from home. All the more reason why you will need my help.'

'The women are of noble birth and we are here to rescue them,' Lord Charlemont continued. 'That is all you need to know – now tell us all that you know.'

'Well, the women arrived here about a week ago on a war galley,' the chancellor began. 'There had been heavy casualties, which was unusual. They were carried off in stretchers.'

'Were they injured?' cut in Lord Charlemont, his tone anxious.

'No, probably just drugged. We saw them a couple of days later and they seemed well.'

'Where?' asked Alex.

'In a field,' the chancellor replied, his face taking on a look of distaste for some reason, 'near the fortress gates. We think the Rakshasa allow them to go there in order for them to take the air.'

Lord Charlemont leapt on this. 'How many guards go with them?' he demanded.

'Nine,' replied the chancellor. 'But they are so near the fortress gates you would stand no chance,' he concluded defiantly.

Lord Charlemont clasped his hands behind his back. 'There will be some way to extract them,' he muttered in English.

'Why do you spy on the Rakshasa?' Alex demanded, changing tack and looking directly at the chancellor.

At this the chancellor's jaw dropped and his face went deathly pale, as if some terrible realisation had occurred to him. Lord Charlemont sensed the change in the atmosphere and turned to look at him.

'I don't spy on you, Master, I swear!' the chancellor stammered, all his confidence evaporating in an instant, his gaze now fixed to the floor.

Alex squatted down again and grasped him by the shoulders, forcing the chancellor to look in his eyes again. 'Calm yourself, man!' he ordered. 'We are not the Rakshasa. We are only interested in the women.'

Despite this, the chancellor would not look up, and his breathing was heavy and distressed.

Alex turned to Lord Charlemont. 'I think we've unnerved him – why not show him your *firman*? That might calm him down somewhat.'

Lord Charlemont huffed with exasperation, raising his eyebrows theatrically to the heavens before drawing out a small oilskin package from his coat. He unwrapped it quickly to reveal a waxed cardboard cylinder, from which he pulled out his *firman*.

'Here,' said Lord Charlemont as he thrust the document before the chancellor, 'read this.'

Written on it, in Turkish, Greek and then English, was the following:

To whom this may concern

The bearer of this firman is an English gentleman, Lord Charlemont. He is working with Admiral Blake of the British Royal Navy, based in Athens, and his purpose in Greece is to encourage trade between England and the Ottoman Empire. I demand that he be extended every courtesy and be considered to be under my personal protection.

The Vaivode of Athens
8th Sha'ban 1147 AH

The chancellor cautiously looked up and read the document, curiosity replacing the fear in his eyes as he made his way through it, noting the impressive Ottoman crests at the head of the document and the red wax impression of the Vaivode's signet ring. He read it again, as if to make sure, relief now sweeping over his face.

'Convinced?' asked Lord Charlemont as he rolled up the document.

'You are an English Lord?' the chancellor asked, looking up at him.

Lord Charlemont nodded gracefully, in his effortlessly aristocratic manner.

'Thank God!' the chancellor exclaimed, closing his eyes briefly. 'I thought I had forfeited my life over a simple trick.' He shook his head.

'Listen,' continued Lord Charlemont, keeping up the pressure, 'is there any way we could get those women out?'

'Possibly,' said the chancellor presently, 'but at this moment in time I could not say how. *We* would need to think about it.' He looked up, and said almost as an afterthought, 'If we go back to my village, we could talk there in more comfort.' He glanced at their bags. 'And get some food.'

Alex turned to the chancellor. 'Why should we trust you?' he asked. 'One word from you and these Rakshasa would be all over us.'

'Because you need my help, and I yours,' the chancellor replied. 'For years we have been under the yoke of those devils, waiting, praying for someone from the outside to come to our aid. You could be the answer to our prayers!'

'Every occupying force employs spies,' Lord Charlemont objected. 'What's to say that once we're in your village, word won't get back to the Rakshasa and they come out hunting for us?'

'We dealt with all of the spies years ago, and now feed the Rakshasa all the information we want them to know through our trusted men. It seems to keep them happy.'

'Well, Lord Charlemont, shall we go with him?' asked Alex.

Lord Charlemont glanced at the chancellor and then nodded at Alex. 'Very well. But not until dark. I don't want the whole village aware of our presence.'

The chancellor sat back, obviously disappointed by this. 'No,' he said, his voice taking on a hint of pleading, 'please let us get back to the village by dusk. We must not be any later.'

'Why?' demanded Lord Charlemont.

'Because after dark the whole of the island becomes the domain of the Rakshasa. Any islander found outdoors is executed on the spot,' he replied.

'Look,' said Lord Charlemont rather impatiently, 'what is it about these Rakshasa? Why do they sleep during the day?'

'But surely you already know of them?' exclaimed the chancellor.

The Englishmen shook their heads.

'The Rakshasa,' he continued, 'are what we know as *vrykolakas*.'

Alex was puzzled, but Lord Charlemont's eyes widened slightly as he seemed to recognise the term. He turned to Alex.

'I think he mean vampires,' he said simply.

CHAPTER 16

'Vampires?' echoed Alex. 'What in God's name is a vampire?' he asked Lord Charlemont in English.

'It's a term well-known in northern Europe,' began Lord Charlemont cautiously, as if he were reluctant to divulge what he was about to say. '*Vampir* is a word of Slavonic origin. It refers to one of the undead,' he continued. 'They rise from their graves at night to hunt for the living in order to drink their blood.'

'That's absurd!' exclaimed Alex. 'The raiders who attacked the *Fearless* were as alive as you or me – I killed several of them myself.'

'Look, we can continue this discussion later,' declared Lord Charlemont, Alex detecting in his voice a sudden sense of urgency. 'Now let's get ready to move into the village,' he ordered, indicating to Alex that he should cut the chancellor's bonds.

'Excellent,' said the chancellor as he stood up. 'Let us get Tryphon and go,' he said, leading the way out of the house.

'Surely you do not believe in all this "undead" business?' demanded Alex as they made their way out of the house.

Lord Charlemont glanced at him, and then looked ahead without answering.

*

Cicadas started to drone in the undergrowth as they walked through the cool air of the gathering dusk, past the strange fields of baskets. A goat tied to a post bleated at them as they passed, and from the distance came the sound of dogs barking.

Their entrance into the *kasteli* caused less of a stir than before; the streets were now completely deserted. As they walked into the square, Alex noticed the church door was shut and the backgammon tables were abandoned, their tablecloths gently moving with the breeze, weighed down by rough dark stones. Even the dogs were gone. Examining the houses more closely, he noticed that, though all had doors on to the street, none had windows at ground level. Most had the outline of ground floor windows, but these had been bricked up.

The chancellor walked on purposefully towards his house, which turned out to be one of the larger three storeyed houses near the centre of the village. 'I will send my wife and children away,' he explained as they approached his house.

'Let me hear what you say,' ordered Lord Charlemont. 'And keep your hands in your pockets. I'll be watching you.'

The chancellor called his wife and children to the front door, and as soon as they saw Alex they cast their eyes down.

'Karissa,' said the chancellor, speaking in Latin, 'two of the masters want to use our house for a few days and discuss some things with me.'

Karissa, wide-eyed with fear, momentarily looked over to Alex.

'It is nothing to worry about – take the children to your mother's and I will send for you in a few days.'

They embraced awkwardly, and then, ducking back into the house to pick up a few things, she left with the children before running down the road. They watched her until she had made it to a house about a hundred yards away, where she banged furiously on the door. It opened, casting a shaft of light on to the darkening street. Words were exchanged, and then she was inside and the door shut.

They all entered the house and Lord Charlemont shut the door. They found themselves in a low roofed storeroom with a short flight of stairs leading to double doors above. A door immediately ahead led to a windowless bedroom.

'Good,' commented Lord Charlemont, un-shouldering his musket and casting off his cloak as the chancellor barred the front door. 'Put Tryphon in the bedroom on this floor.'

*

They then moved upstairs to a large long dining room, at the centre of which was a table, with cupboards and a sideboard against the walls. At the other end of the room was a cooking range, and a short flight of stairs led up to the second storey of the house. Lord Charlemont discarded his bags and positioned himself at the table so that he could cover the double doors. The chancellor moved to the range and stirred something in a pot. Alex shook his bags off and settled on a chair, his musket and a pistol also ready. The chancellor then set up a brazier of charcoal at the end of the table before serving them a dish of what looked like mashed potato, but was more yellow in colour and sprinkled with pieces of onion.

'Fava,' he explained. 'It is a bean that grows here.'

'Now, back to the Rakshasa,' insisted Lord Charlemont.

'They invaded our island about eighty-five years ago…' began the chancellor.

'From where?'

'We have no idea, but from their pale skin we guessed they had come from the north, where tales of *vrykolakas* are more common.'

'Do *you* think they are the undead?' persisted Lord Charlemont.

The chancellor pursed his lips and furrowed his brow, as if uncertain what to say. 'We have discussed this amongst ourselves many times. Our bishop certainly thought so. He believed they were originally a tribe of brigands so foul that all were excommunicated from the church. As they died, one by one they were possessed by Satan, who banded them together again in their undead state.'

'Remember,' Lord Charlemont said, seeing the puzzled look on Alex's face, 'we're talking about the Orthodox Church here. One of its doctrines is that the body of an excommunicated man, when he dies and is buried, will remain incorrupt. The body is thereby liable to be possessed by a demon which can then force it to rise at night and go in search of blood.'

'What happens to the victims?' Alex asked.

'They become sick through loss of blood, and if the nightly visitations continue, they eventually die,' Lord Charlemont replied.

'That is correct,' agreed the chancellor, impressed at Lord Charlemont's knowledge. 'The Rakshasa certainly have some characteristics of *vrykolakas*,' he continued, 'in that they sleep during the day, and *occasionally* drink blood, but other than their eyes and teeth they could almost be human. They eat similar food, though it is richly spiced, they sleep during the day in beds like we do, not in a grave, and they mate and raise their young. They live longer than us, but do grow old and finally die. We know this because there were some around at the time of the invasion who have not been seen for decades.' He shrugged. 'So we think they are a *kind* of *vrykolakas* – though of course a *papas* would disagree.'

'Quite. Now, going back to the invasion,' prompted Lord Charlemont.

'It happened in 1650 – which we now refer to as the "Year of Evil" – in the time of my great grandfather, Nikolas Kontaratos. The main town on the island was Skaros, a *kasteli* built on the promontory below where the Rakshasa have their fortress today. Their fortress occupies what was the site of the village of Merovigli.

'Skaros had survived countless attacks from pirates and raiders over the years due to its sheer sides and the fact it could only be entered along one narrow ridge from Merovigli. The dock the Rakshasa have now was just a small natural harbour named Vourvoulos with a quay that we tied our fishing boats to. Another nine villages were scattered over the island, and in total there were probably seven and a half thousand people on the island. We paid almost eight thousand crowns a year to the Porte in *haradj* and land tax, and as long as we paid it the Turks left us alone. For over one hundred years, since the Turks had displaced the Venetians, we had effectively governed ourselves and had a good deal of freedom. We traded with the other islands and the Greek mainland, our Vinsanto wine was used by the Russian Orthodox church for their Eucharistic wine, and many of our people regularly sailed to the Black Sea to do trade there, bringing back wood, as well as to Constantinople.

'For a year before the invasion, earthquakes had shaken the island far more than usual, so much so that many had talked about abandoning Santorini. From March of 1650, these earthquakes grew worse. Many were killed around Skaros as blocks of stone were dislodged and rolled down to the sea. Clouds of thick vapour and flames were seen to emerge from the sea north-west of Santorini. There was sometimes an evil smell to the air and the sea would turn green.

'Finally, on 27 September, when all were in churches praying for mercy from these evil portents, there came a noise like the sound of a thousand cannon. A massive eruption took place in the sea, again north-west of Santorini, throwing huge quantities of pumice into the air, as well as clouds of ash and poisonous gas. For a whole day and night the air was thick with noxious fumes, so bad that thousands of animals died in the fields. Birds fell from the air, over a score of people were killed, and all the crops in the fields that had not been harvested were destroyed. Everyone had terrible pains in their eyes, which swelled up and closed so that all were blind for almost two days. When people could see again, they found that a new island had appeared in the sea where the eruption had taken place.'

'Hold on,' said Lord Charlemont, looking at Alex, 'we passed the north-west coast on our way in here. We saw no island offshore.'

'That is because it sank back into the sea almost four months after it appeared. It is still there as a reef, a score of fathoms down.'

'Hmm,' grunted Lord Charlemont.

'All now implored the bishops to do something...' continued the chancellor.

'You had *two* bishops here?' butted in Lord Charlemont again.

'Yes. One Latin, or Catholic, bishop and one Greek Orthodox bishop. They both lived in Skaros.'

Lord Charlemont still looked sceptical.

'The Latin priests first came here when the Venetians invaded centuries ago, and it is because of their rule that we speak both Greek and Latin. Jesuit missionaries also came more recently – just before the Year of Evil, in fact. The Venetians numbered less than one thousand at most – but they owned most of the land and we Greeks were just serfs. Life under them was like slavery – taxes were crippling and we were allowed no self-government. They also encouraged Latin missionaries to hound us and controlled all commerce. Though you may not believe this, things actually improved when the Turks took over about two hundred years ago.'

'It is said the Turks "justly rule and lightly tax",' remarked Lord Charlemont.

The chancellor grunted at this remark, as if to disagree, but did not pursue it.

'So the bishops took the sacraments, the silver of which had been turned black by the fumes, out from their churches and walked barefoot with them around Santorini, while all were made to fast. The earthquakes receded and everyone began to think the worst was over. None guessed that an even greater evil was poised to strike the island.

'The Rakshasa arrived that night in their black war galleys, landing unopposed at Ormos, the port below the village of Fira. We think an advance party of them had come ashore earlier and murdered all the coastal watchmen before any could raise the alarm. Another group had somehow got inside the *kasteli* of Skaros itself and murdered the watchmen there also. The first we knew of their presence was a huge explosion as the gates of Skaros were blown down. Once the gates were down they swept through them like a black horde. Men raced from their homes with swords and pikes, only to be cut down in the streets by musket fire. Panic and confusion reigned all that night as the warrior Rakshasa worked their way around the town, dragging all from their houses, butchering any who offered resistance, and torching those houses where the inhabitants had barricaded themselves in. The fires spread, and soon the whole town was ablaze. The Rakshasa themselves looked like devils,' he said as he gestured to his face, 'with their red snake eyes and fangs. It was as if hell itself had erupted on to the streets of Skaros.'

He paused.

'My great grandfather was killed defending my grandfather and his sister. It was something my grandfather never got over. When morning came, the town was blackened and burnt. Bodies lay strewn all over the streets. Men, women, children, even livestock – such was the apparent senselessness of it all. But there was a purpose behind it. After such a display of brutality, the Rakshasa knew that no one would dare oppose them. All the fishing boats had been scuttled, and my grandfather said that over fifty war galleys lay tied to the shore near Ormos.'

He leaned back in his chair, folding his beefy arms over his chest.

'At dawn, they gathered those who had survived in fields outside of Fira, speaking to them in broken Latin, and declared that they were the new masters of Santorini and were to be known as the Rakshasa. It was the first time any of us had heard that name, and it meant nothing to us. They then forced the survivors to send word of what had happened to the other villages, promising that all who came to Fira and surrendered would be spared. By mid-afternoon, practically all had obeyed the summons – except the two bishops, who had been in Akrotiri on the night of the attack, and the Turkish *kadi* who was nowhere to be seen. It was then that their leader, who we came to know as Korthdan, told us we were now forbidden to go anywhere north of Fira. He then produced a sand timer and announced that anyone found in Merovigli or Fira by the time it ran its course would be slaughtered. Panic broke out again and people stampeded through the narrow streets, frightened out of their minds, some being killed underfoot. Some were foolish enough to go back to their houses to try and salvage some of their belongings, but the warrior Rakshasa caught up with them and dragged them away. They were hung from the large carob tree just north of Fira.'

The lantern above them flickered slightly as a draught caught it.

'This is something I would expect of the Turks,' exclaimed Alex to Lord Charlemont, vaguely remembering accounts of the siege of Constantinople.

'Wrong,' declared Lord Charlemont, 'the Ottomans are now an honourable people. Even with overwhelming force, they would have given the defenders the chance of an assured surrender. True, those who surrendered would have been sold into slavery, but there would have been no senseless bloodletting. These Rakshasa are nothing more than…barbarians.'

There was a silence as each pictured the nightmarish scene that the chancellor had described. The chancellor looked from one to the other, carefully gauging their reaction.

'Please go on,' requested Lord Charlemont.

'All those who still had homes fled back to them, surviving relatives and friends from the forbidden part of the island joining them. In the next few days the *kadi* was hunted down and hanged from the same tree as the other islanders.' The chancellor grunted. 'He was unlucky – he only came every two years to settle disputes and dispense justice, and had arrived barely a week before the Rakshasa.'

'And the bishops?' asked Lord Charlemont.

'They initially stayed in Akrotiri where the people hid them and looked after them. They then moved to the larger town of Emporium, behind Mt Prophet Elias here. The Rakshasa never came looking for them, and they managed to lead the religious affairs of both communities until their deaths.'

The wind outside moaned as it swept under the door. The chancellor stood up and threw some more charcoal on to the brazier.

'It was two days or so after the fall of Skaros that my grandfather began to notice the weather was changing. After three days of violent and unnatural storms the sun finally came out again. With a spyglass, from the highest point of Santorini it is still possible to see many islands, even Crete on some rare days. From sea-level, however, nothing can be seen, and in time we realised that the Rakshasa had bent nature to their will and caused what we now know as the "Wall of Storms" to be thrown around the island, cutting us off from the rest of the world.'

Alex shook his head in irritation at this, and was about to disparage the chancellor's explanation for the barrier when he heard something that made him pause.

'Wait,' he said, holding up his hand, his head tilted down as he concentrated. He looked up suddenly at Lord Charlemont. 'I hear horses!'

'What's going on?' demanded Lord Charlemont, snatching up his pistol and pointing it at the chancellor. He froze for a moment, staring intently at the chancellor, and then he too heard the horses. He sprang to his feet, black anger in his eyes. 'Traitor!' he shouted, levelling his pistol to the chancellor's head.

The chancellor scraped his chair back across the floor in alarm, trying to move away from Lord Charlemont, his hands above his head. 'No, don't shoot! You don't understand,' he implored, eyes wide with fear.

CHAPTER 17

Alex ran to the double doors, pushing them open to hear better. The sound of the horses' hooves was now audible to them all from the street below.

'There's about half a dozen,' he said, glancing round. The horsemen would be at the door in seconds. 'I say we wait here. If they try to come in we'll have to break cover,' he said to Lord Charlemont, indicating the rear window of the room with his hand.

Lord Charlemont nodded, not taking his eyes off the chancellor.

'There's really no need…' the chancellor protested.

'Shut up! You've betrayed us,' Lord Charlemont spat out, cocking his pistol.

The clatter of hooves on the paved street was almost deafening. Quickly Alex moved away from the doors back to his chair and got hold of the table. He dragged it round then pushed it over, sending the plates crashing to the floor. He crouched behind it, laying his pistol on the floor before unslinging his musket and aiming it at the door.

'When they come through the door I'll shoot this turncoat, then join you,' snarled Lord Charlemont, bracing himself for a shot.

From the bedroom below, Tryphon cried out something in Greek while the wind howled round the house like a wraith, rattling the shutters and banging the doors against their jambs. The sound of the hooves was now like thunder – they were almost outside the door.

And then the hooves were passing down the street, fading away as quickly as they had arisen, carrying with them the sound of harsh male and female voices shouting to each other as if out on a pleasure ride. They waited, frozen in place until the clatter was almost inaudible.

The chancellor breathed a large sigh of relief. 'They've passed,' he declared, an undertone of anger in his voice. 'I told you they would.

During the day we can go where we please and do what we want, but at night Santorini belongs to them. They often ride through here to go to the beach at Kamari.'

'Why?'

'Who knows? We can only guess the next day by what they have left and their footprints in the sand.'

*

They finally returned to their meal, and the chancellor produced for each a small roasted bird, cucumber, goat's cheese and fresh barley bread. Lord Charlemont prodded the bird with his knife.

'Quail?' he asked.

'Yes,' replied the chancellor. 'We catch them in August, and then salt them.'

His appetite having returned, Alex devoured the food, and then took some down to Tryphon. Good local wine was produced and all finally started to relax.

'So,' said Lord Charlemont, continuing their previous conversation, 'do *you* think the Rakshasa were behind the eruption that preceded their invasion?'

The chancellor dropped his gaze, frowned, and absentmindedly tapped his fingers on the table for a few moments. 'We don't really know,' he said eventually, still staring at the table. 'But we think they knew it was going to happen in some way, and timed their invasion accordingly.' He lifted his gaze. 'I don't think that even *they* could control the forces that lurk beneath this island.'

'So what happened after the Wall of Storms had been created?' continued Lord Charlemont.

'Well, the weather calmed down again, as I said, and those who were left – around three thousand – started to try and rebuild their lives as best they could. The Rakshasa for the most part ignored us. They brought in hundreds of slaves with them and they immediately began to build their fortress where the village of Merovigli once stood, working their slaves day and night, building up the fortified palace you can see today.' He paused. 'Did you notice how many towers the fortress has?'

The Englishmen shook their heads.

'Thirteen.'

'A devil's dozen,' Lord Charlemont remarked tartly.

'They also extended the walls of the fortress down to the harbour at Vourvoulos,' continued the chancellor, 'digging out the new dock and using that earth as foundation for the walls around it.'

'The sea gates of the dock *are* impressive,' cut in Lord Charlemont again, turning to Alex. 'I've never seen such a well fortified harbour area.'

'Well, a few of Edward I's castles in North Wales could be resupplied from the sea, but even they had nothing on this scale,' commented Alex.

The chancellor said nothing as he listened to their exchange, but then spoke up. 'Here we have a great advantage when it comes to building stone piers and so on,' he explained. 'Using aspa and mixing it with lime, we get very good cement that hardens well, even underwater.'

'Really?' exclaimed Lord Charlemont. At first Alex thought he was being sarcastic, but then realised the man was genuinely interested. 'The lime you can get from limestone, but what is this "aspa" you mentioned?'

'Aspa? It is compacted ash from the volcanoes we have had here,' the chancellor replied, also surprised at this level of interest.

'Is there much on the island?' persisted Lord Charlemont.

The chancellor gave a short exasperated laugh. 'Much? Come here, Lord Charlemont, and I will show you,' he said as he rose from his chair, knife in hand, and walked over to the nearest wall. He plunged the knife into the plaster, working it round until he had removed a lump of it, which he discarded. He then dug around deeper in the hole, holding his other hand below it to catch what he was scraping out. He turned to where Lord Charlemont stood behind him and held his hand out to show the coarse grey powder he had collected.

'There,' he said. 'Aspa – compacted ash. You may have noticed that this house is partially tunnelled into the earth, as are most in Santorini. We actually tunnel into aspa, which is quite easy to do and supports itself quite well.'

'So the villages are built where there are deposits of aspa?' asked Lord Charlemont.

'In a manner of speaking, yes,' replied the chancellor, an impatient tone to his voice. 'But, Lord Charlemont, the fact is that *most* of Santorini is made up of aspa and limestone.'

At this, Lord Charlemont went very quiet and a ghost of a smile settled on his face as if he had just realised some great truth. The chancellor looked questioningly at Alex as he sat down, but Alex just shrugged, unable to see the significance of what had been said.

'Shall I continue?' asked the chancellor presently.

'Yes, surely,' said Lord Charlemont, but Alex could sense his thoughts were elsewhere.

'All this building activity went on for about a year and a half, at the end of which Merovigli was as it is now. Behind the fortress, further to the north they also built workshops that belch out smoke continuously, the furnaces inside fed by shiploads of charcoal. We think that is where they make their armour and other metal tools.'

'What did you all live on through that time?' asked Alex.

'The survivors only just managed to live on what had been harvested up to the point of the eruptions and plant again for the next season. The Rakshasa, however, shipped in grain, vegetables, fruit and livestock from outside for themselves,' he replied. 'And, of course, slaves. I would guess that you came in with some of the latest from Athens on a Full Moon galley.'

Alex glanced at Lord Charlemont. 'Yes – but that was this morning and the moon is only just new.'

'We call them so because their cargo is…' he searched for an appropriate phrase '…*used* at the full moon by the scarlet-clad ones – their priesthood.'

Alex leaned forward, unsettled at the implications. 'What do you mean?'

'It is not important now,' the chancellor replied, grim faced and dismissing the subject with a wave of his hand.

Lord Charlemont said nothing. He just stared at the table silently, rubbing the stem of his wine glass between his thumb and index finger, his mind still elsewhere.

'Through all this time they ignored us, save for their younger warriors who would frequently terrorise us at night until we learned to block up our windows and bar our doors to them. Then, sometime after the fortress was completed, word came from Merovigli that the Rakshasa Korthdan wanted to see the leader of our people. My grandfather, then barely seventeen, was asked to go and represent the remaining islanders as his father had been chancellor at the time of the attack – every few years the Latin and Greek communities would elect a chancellor to rule them, each with twelve notables, or elders, to aid them in their work. In the Year of Evil, my great grandfather was chancellor for the Greek community. Many of the Latins had lived in Skaros, but after the slaughter very few were left, so the Greek community was in the majority – much more so than before.

'The fiend received him in a large long room at the top of the new palace. He was sitting cross-legged on a raised dais, draped in heavy purple cloth with a priest on either side of him taking notes. It was the first time my grandfather had seen Korthdan up-close. Grandfather knew he was tall from that first proclamation in Fira, but had no idea how old he looked. His eyes were sunken into dark hollows in his face, his skin stretched like parchment over his cheekbones, but his face still had a strong, almost noble, quality about it. His hair was thick and long, almost reaching his shoulders, though time had turned it from white to grey.

'To my grandfather's surprise, Korthdan questioned him about the rebuilding of our agriculture, asking what tools, seeds and animals were required, and promising to supply them on condition we gave four fifths of the wine produced over to them.'

'Wine? Where are your vineyards?' asked Lord Charlemont. 'I have not seen any.'

'We grow our vines in a different way here,' replied the chancellor. 'They are wrapped around…'

'Like a basket?' offered Alex.

'Exactly. It is to protect the grapes from the winds that used to scourge the island – though they are no longer so strong since the Wall of Storms was created. So, my grandfather was given one week to produce the list of requirements and they were duly delivered over the coming months. Korthdan then summoned him and the notables he had chosen to assist him – most of whom were boys like my grandfather – to the fortress. There he stated that my grandfather and his descendants were to represent the islanders in all matters from then on. It was then that my grandfather moved into this house,' the chancellor indicated generally around, 'which had been one of the residences of the *kadi*. Korthdan also insisted that my grandfather and his notables learn their vile language.'

Lord Charlemont took a sip from his wine and gazed into the brazier.

'Since those days things have been relatively peaceful, though there are still some of their activities that are designed to strike fear into us,' he said, eyes narrowing, but without elaborating further. 'The Rakshasa warriors satisfy most of their bloodlust and the demand from Korthdan for gold and other treasures by raiding shipping. What they can't steal from others, they purchase. In these years of peace, the population of the island has grown again, and stands at around four and a half thousand today. Most work on their own land or fish out at sea, the rest work in the fortress during the day doing maintenance, cleaning work, or other duties.'

The chancellor finished speaking and leaned back in his chair. Lord Charlemont leaned forward in his, hands clasped together on the table in front of him.

'So, if you are going to help us, what will you want from us?' he asked.

The chancellor jutted his jaw forward slightly and crossed his arms again, but did not reply immediately. 'I'll need to think about that,' he said eventually. 'Ideally I would like to speak to some of my notables to get their thoughts also.'

'In the meantime,' Lord Charlemont announced, clapping his hands together, 'I suggest we discuss our plan of action for tomorrow. Above all, we need to communicate with the women as soon as possible. Is there any way at all we could do that?'

'Of course,' answered the chancellor. 'They will be at the Hanging Tree. Would you like to talk to them in the morning or the afternoon?'

*

For some time they discussed meeting with the two women, and then Lord Charlemont insisted the chancellor, under protest, join Tryphon in the small bedroom, securing the door with a chain and padlock.

'So what do you think of the Rakshasa now?' asked Lord Charlemont as they made their way back to the first floor.

'This talk of "vampires" is all poppycock!' exclaimed Alex. 'They are a race of albinos, pure and simple. Given they were still burning left-handers in France as witches quite recently, no doubt the Rakshasa have been persecuted down the centuries for the way they look, and have stayed out of sight of the rest of humanity…'

'Really?'

'Of course! It was a pure coincidence that they arrived here when they did, and then they convinced themselves and the islanders that they could manipulate the weather and create the Wall of Storms – which is more likely to have been created by the eruption. It is all superstitious rubbish.'

Lord Charlemont was uncharacteristically silent, avoiding Alex's eyes as he began unpacking his bags.

'I disagree with you, Hurst,' he said presently, straightening up to face Alex. 'I think we have come across a hitherto unknown race here – a superior race, if you will – which *can* manipulate nature to its own ends, using techniques we can only dream about.'

'For an educated man, you surprise me,' snorted Alex in disgust. 'Everything they did on the *Fearless* and the first days of the invasion here was achieved with gunpowder and cold steel – not magic!'

'We shall see,' declared Lord Charlemont in a somewhat pompous manner, dismissing the subject. 'But for now I need to sleep.'

Alex, fatigued by the day's events, could not be bothered arguing further. They laid their cloaks on each side of the brazier, and he settled thankfully down to sleep. At some point in the night he was awoken by the sound of a shutter banging in the wind. He found the source of the noise in a room upstairs, and was about to pull it shut when he felt the ground shift slightly beneath him. He realized he had just experienced a small earthquake, and that the forces that had heralded the arrival of the Rakshasa were not totally dormant.

Reaching out for the shutter, he paused as he noticed strange lights in the distance. There to the north, from two points high up on the Rakshasa fortress shone two flickering blue beacons of unnaturally bright intensity. Below them, pinpoints of yellow light had appeared in the walls of the palace through windows that were now open, and from torches that moved around in the town that surrounded it. He stared at the beacons for a while, fascinated, before finally turning back in for the night. More horses passed back and forth through the village during the night, but none stopped.

CHAPTER 18

That night, just after sunset, the two sisters were sitting at the table finishing off their supper when there was a discreet knock at the door. Helena gave a sharp intake of breath and the sisters exchanged a knowing look.

'Zentar,' Helena remarked, theatrically raising her eyes heavenward in mock disgust – but inside she felt a thrill of excitement run through her. They never knew if he would visit them or not, and that alone put Helena in an agitated state each evening.

'You are spending far too much time with him,' hissed Isabelle, leaning over the table towards her.

'I know, I know,' exclaimed Helena, looking away, 'but there is no harm in it. We are just...companions.'

'Of *course* you are,' retorted Isabelle. 'Honestly, sister, the depth of your delusion is truly wondrous!'

'Please...'

'Remember what you said,' Isabelle reminded her, locking eyes with her sister. 'And remember that *Alex* is the one you love, and he may yet be still alive.'

'Yes, yes. Do not fret,' retorted Helena, casting her eyes down. 'I *will* send him away,' she insisted. 'Once I have the potion,' she added – while realising she did not actually have the will power to reject such a powerful creature as he.

The knock on the door was repeated, this time with more urgency.

'One moment, Zentar,' she called, vaguely aware that her heart was beating with slow heavy throbs and her voice was quaking. She rose from the table unsteadily and opened the door.

He stood there on the threshold, initially looking away, but turning his gaze to her as the door opened. As their eyes met, time seemed to slow down and a feeling of contentment swept over her; all thoughts of Alex faded like dreams at the dawn.

'Come, Helena,' he commanded, his deep voice seeming to resonate through her entire body. 'I have a present for you tonight – something that you have requested of me.'

Helena clapped her hands in delight, and without a word or backwards glance she followed him eagerly out of the room, not even hearing Isabelle's gasp of exasperation behind her.

*

Leaving the palace, they went to the extensive medicinal herb gardens, located to the rear of the fortress. The garden itself was walled, the gates to it guarded by two Rakshasa who bowed to Zentar, but stared with suspicion and annoyance at Helena as she passed them, a reaction she was not used to.

'Why do the guards look at me so?' she asked Zentar as they walked deeper into the gardens, lit by the cold blue lanterns on its inner wall. Here and there, shadowy figures dressed in scarlet worked by oil lantern, watering and pruning the plants, as well as weeding the flowerbeds.

'You must forgive them,' replied Zentar. 'These gardens are most sacred to us. The herbs and plants within provide us with cures for ailments and potions that keep us virile and in health. Even I had a difficult task to persuade its guardians to allow you to enter it.'

They walked through a maze of narrow paths until they came to a flowerbed that Zentar stopped in front of, which to Helena's eye was indistinguishable from the others.

'Here it is,' he declared, and pulled the stalk of a tall nondescript plant with broad leaves towards him.

'It does not look much,' remarked Helena, unsure of what to say.

'No – but it is not the look that is important!' retorted Zentar, a touch of irritation in his voice. 'It is the sap that we can derive from it.' He released the plant. 'Follow me.'

They continued to the rear of the gardens, to what looked like outhouses set into the wall. Zentar entered one and lit the oil lantern within to reveal a room, bare except for a table and shelving on three sides of it that stretched from floor to ceiling. Each shelf held countless labelled bottles of all shapes, sizes and colours, all sealed with corks or complex arrangements of wire holding in glass stoppers, not unlike the shop of an apothecary. Zentar ignored the bottles on the shelves and instead picked one up from the table, where it was sitting on a piece of parchment with the rune-like script of the Rakshasa written on it.

'Ah yes, this is the one,' he said, comparing the label with the notes on the parchment. 'It has been prepared as I commanded. As I explained to you, your father is in the grip of a demon, initially attracted to him because of his love of alcohol, but now it is driving the addiction he has developed. The demon feeds on the astral energy that would normally be dissipated through the body, but is being dammed up, as it were, due to the alcohol preventing his normal nightly experience of the astral plane.'

As was usual in Zentar's presence, Helena was finding it hard to concentrate on what he was saying, but managed to discern the gist of it.

'You mean the alcohol is preventing him from dreaming?'

'Precisely,' Zentar replied with a smile. 'This potion will start to poison the demon, and it will leave within a score of days.' He moved as if to hand the small green glass bottle to her, but then pulled back, a look of slight puzzlement on his face. 'I could give it to you as a gift,' he began, 'but really there is no point, is there?'

Despite the effect Zentar was having on her, through sheer force of will Helena marshalled her thoughts and chose her next words carefully.

'I requested it not because it could cure my father now, but so that it would give me hope that *one* day he could be cured.'

Zentar looked at her quizzically.

'*Maybe*,' she said as she smiled at him in her most beguiling manner, 'one day we will travel to England together, and I will be able to use this to free him from the demon's grip…'

Zentar relaxed, smiled and handed over the bottle.

'Yes,' he agreed, 'maybe we will.'

She held the bottle up to the lantern and gave a small gasp – the liquid inside the dark green glass was just visible, but seemed to be swirling around restlessly of its own accord.

'How does one use it?' she asked, slightly nervous at the liquid's unnatural behaviour.

'Oh, just a small spoon per night till all is consumed,' he replied, reading from the parchment. 'But the treatment must begin at sight of the first crescent of a new moon.' He crumpled the parchment up. 'That is all.'

With a sigh of relief, Helena carefully placed the bottle in a side pocket in her riding dress, one she used to carry her brandy flask when on a hunt, and followed Zentar back into the garden. Once more in the night air, in possession of her prize, she allowed herself to relax and be totally caught up in Zentar's aura.

*

The rest of the night then became like a dream. She was aware of the cool wind blowing back her hair as they rode away from the fortress on his chariot, the hooves of the horses clattering on the cobbled road. Then they were on a secluded beach, walking hand in hand and barefoot along the shoreline, waves gently lapping the black sand as the waxing moon cast a silvery path over the sea towards them. They stopped for a while, both looking up to the moon, totally lost in its serene beauty. Then he gently put his arm round her waist. She turned towards him, and saw his handsome face looking at her in the ghostly light. His lips approached, and she gently pursed her own to receive his kiss...

CHAPTER 19

The next morning, the Englishmen and the chancellor headed north towards the fortress along the higher well-paved road up on the rim of the caldera. In the fields way down to their right, over a high defensive wall for the road, they could see the odd group of people at work. The only gaps in the wall occurred where a lane running up from the fields met the road.

To their left, cliffs dropped away a thousand feet or so down to the sea. Three burnt and blackened islands, which looked as if they had been squat black candles whose wax had spread widely around them before setting, were clearly visible in the centre of the caldera.

Thirasia was almost six miles away on the other side of the caldera, with the much smaller white island of Aspronisi between it and the headland of Akrotiri. At this height it seemed obvious to Alex that the three islands encircling the caldera were the only remnants of an ancient volcanic crater, the dimensions of which were staggering. Once the volcano had spent itself, parts of the crater wall had presumably collapsed, creating the spaces between the islands, and the sea had flooded into the crater itself, forming the caldera. The surface of the water in the caldera now rippled slightly as winds passed across it.

At one point they passed a crude altar, set almost at the edge of the cliff, on which were strewn some offerings of flowers and stalks of barley, weighed down by black and red stones.

'One of the old altars to the north wind god, Boreas,' commented the chancellor. 'Some of the older people still believe in the old gods – though again, the winds now are nothing like they used to be.'

They walked on for a while in silence.

'This is a surprisingly good road,' Lord Charlemont remarked presently. The paving stones were well fitted together and the surface smooth, with drains on either side.

'Yes,' agreed the chancellor, 'the Rakshasa improved on one that was here before they arrived. They widened it so that their chariots can go two abreast on it. It runs all along the spine of the island, on the edge of the cliff, from north to south. Also, if you notice the lanes,' he continued, pointing out a few on the land sloping gently down to the sea, 'none of them run directly from the shore up the hill towards us – it means any body of men can only make short headway up the hill before being forced to traverse along the hillside in search of another lane leading up, if they are to retain what little cover the walls down there afford.'

Ahead, the fortress of the Rakshasa, built on the site of the village of Merovigli, reared up, gleaming in the early morning light. To the left of the fortress, and way below it, was an almost cylindrical huge mass of dusty red rock that rose vertically out of the caldera, connected to the cliffs only by a thin ridge of rock. On it could be seen the ruined *kasteli* of Skaros. It seemed impossible that houses could have been built there in the first place; their remnants seemed to cling to the rock itself, their windows looking out on to drops of hundreds of feet, their barrel-vaulted roofs running into each other in an apparently random fashion. From the middle of the town rose a huge rock on which the remnants of a castle stood. Lower down, they could see the gatehouse of the *kasteli*, and the gap between it and the narrow path that came down from Merovigli which was once spanned by a drawbridge. It was no wonder its inhabitants had been safe there for so long.

They continued on.

'What are these?' asked Lord Charlemont, pointing at one of the cylindrical woven structures that Alex had noticed the evening before.

'Scarecrows,' the chancellor eventually said, obviously embarrassed at the question.

'Scarecrows? Nonsense, man! If they were scarecrows they'd be in the middle of the field, not at the sides.'

'The Rakshasa make them and tell us to use them. They keep disease from the vines.'

'How?'

'I don't know,' the chancellor replied, holding his hands up, 'they just work.' He turned away and walked ahead of them again.

Lord Charlemont looked fascinated at this explanation, but it annoyed Alex.

'Is it not more likely,' he exclaimed, 'that the volcanic ash and noxious gases from the eruption killed all the pestilence which attacks the vines?'

Lord Charlemont harrumphed and said nothing.

After about a quarter of an hour, the fortress gates were clearly visible. At this point they left the main road, going down by the side of a simple Roman Catholic church that stood just off the road.

'There used to be hundreds of Orthodox chapels on Santorini and a few Latin ones,' the chancellor commented as they passed the church, 'but most were destroyed by the Rakshasa.'

Between the church and the fortress were the ruins of a deserted village, which the chancellor told them were the remnants of Fira. They continued down the hill, and then round Fira, along the edges of fields, crouching alongside the drystone walls.

Presently they came to a field about five hundred yards from the fortress gates and set slightly down the hill. In it was a single evergreen tree, around fifty feet high, old and gnarled but in thick leaf. The field itself was uncultivated, measuring a couple of acres and lying fallow, allowing wild flowers to exist there in abundance amongst the grass. To the east of the field the land sloped away below it to the beach, giving good views out to sea. They crouched down behind the southern wall of the field, out of sight of the guards on the fortress walls.

'The Rakshasa bring the women here in the middle part of the morning. They go back in for luncheon, then come out again until the evening,' explained the chancellor. 'Now, the tree is big enough for one of you to climb into it and still remain hidden. You should be able to talk to your women from there without their guards hearing you.'

Lord Charlemont popped his head up above the wall to confirm what the chancellor had said. 'It looks possible,' he conceded, though he looked concerned. 'Where will their guards be?'

'Two at each corner of the field, and one by the gate over there towards the fortress.'

Alex took a quick look over the wall, studying the boughs of the tree, their angles, directions and amount of leaf cover. 'One of us *could* be reasonably well hidden up there,' he stated as he got back down behind the wall.

'We'll toss for it,' replied Lord Charlemont, reaching into a pocket. 'I'll go for heads.'

And heads it was.

'My choice – so off you go,' he commanded, pocketing the coin.

Alex unbuckled his weapons belt, just taking his pistol and hunting knife with him, and then slithered over the wall. Once in the field, he crawled slowly through the grass to the tree. There he got his hunting knife out and used it to dig in and pull himself up. Moving carefully through the lower boughs, he found one where he could comfortably stretch out while remaining hidden. He signalled to the others, and they withdrew to a few fields away, leaving him alone in the warm morning sunshine, the gentle sound of leaves rustling around him.

*

Sometime later the fortress gates opened briefly, though from where he was Alex could not see if anyone had passed through them. Soon after that, his heart leapt as both Helena and Isabelle appeared on the road, surrounded by black-clad Rakshasa. They were dressed in simple petticoats and ankle length skirts, with large brimmed sun hats on their heads, carrying some items under their arms. Eventually he heard female voices from below, and saw the retreating figures of the guards as they made their way to the four corners of the field in pairs. He waited until they had settled, standing in each corner, facing out, and then looked down at the women.

They were almost directly below him. All he could see was the top of their hats, their blonde and auburn hair spilling out from under them. Each had a sketch pad, and had sat down, backs against the tree, and were discussing something in a despondent manner.

He reached into his pocket and took out a piece of paper tightly wrapped around a small stone. Carefully dropping it in front of them both, he then pulled himself in again so as to be hidden from them. The paper read: This is Lt Hurst. I am above you in the tree. Do *not* look up or attract your guards' attention.

'Oh,' Helena said. There was a sound of a skirt rustling and grass being trodden down. 'What's this?' A few seconds passed, then: 'Did you write this, Isabelle? Is this some sort of jape?'

'No,' said Isabelle. 'What does it say?'

'I can hardly believe it,' said Helena, her tone a mix of incredulity and joy. 'Just one moment. No, Isabelle, don't look up!' she chided. A few seconds passed. Then, raising her voice slightly, she cautiously asked, 'Lt Hurst – Alex – are you up there?'

Alex carefully looked over the bough, and to his satisfaction saw that both women were sitting down again, looking directly ahead of themselves, sketch pads on their laps. 'Yes,' he replied. 'Helena, I have…'

To Alex's consternation, Helena clapped her hands with joy as Isabelle gave a little shriek of excitement – and then both burst into tears.

'Yes! Yes!' Helena cried. 'There you are, sis,' she said, turning to Isabelle, 'I told you he would have survived. Oh, thank God! Thank God! I was so worried.'

'Please, I implore you,' said Alex, pulling back to the cover of the bough, 'keep your voices down or all will be lost.'

'Calm yourself, Isabelle,' Helena said sternly. 'No, everything is fine,' she called out in Latin to the guards. 'My sister just saw a spider.'

'Listen,' he hissed, 'how long can we talk for?'

'Less than an hour. We usually go back for luncheon in the fortress,' came the reply. 'Look, is there a ship nearby?'

'Will we be going home soon?' piped in Isabelle.

'No, ladies – calm yourselves! We have no ship.'

Sighs of disappointment wafted up from below.

'And let me tell you now, there is no way on God's earth that we can get you out today,' he said, glancing round at some of the guards.

'Then how are we to leave?' demanded Helena.

'We're working on that. Now…'

'Who is "we"?'

'I am here with Lord Charlemont…' he began.

A cry of horror came up from both of them.

'What?' cried Helena, leaping to her feet, hands clenched in fists of anger, though to her credit she did not look up into the tree. 'That rake?'

She turned her back on the tree and walked several yards away, her back to it.

'After all he has done, he has the impudence to come here to our aid? That charlatan!' she spat out. 'That…mountebank!'

'Damn!' exclaimed Alex, pulling back and pressing himself on to the bough as tightly as possible. He was confused – according to Admiral Blake, the women knew nothing of the trade deal. Glancing up, he saw two of the guards had turned round and were walking towards the tree. He carefully un-holstered his pistol and got ready to cock it.

'No, no, go away!' he heard Helena impatiently order the guards. 'We are just having an argument.' Then, a minute or so later, in a more conciliatory tone: 'It's all right, they've gone now.'

Alex let out a large sigh of relief and realised he had been holding his breath. Looking up, he could see the guards had returned to their positions, and the women to theirs. He said nothing for a few seconds, letting his breathing return to normal. He finally spoke again, his voice slightly choked.

'Do that again, and you can forget about ever going home,' he declared. 'Do you understand?'

'Yes,' came the reluctant reply from below.

'Good. Now, why do you hold Lord Charlemont in such low esteem?' he asked, curious as to how much the women actually knew.

'I'll tell you why,' Helena snapped. 'He turned up at our estate one day and convinced Papa to go into some business with him. All Papa's debts were to be paid off by him, as well as a gift of a considerable sum of money to go towards the refurbishment of the house and grounds. In addition, myself and Isabelle were finally to go on our Grand Tour.'

Alex grimaced – this important fact had been omitted from his briefing in Athens. He had assumed others had approached the debt stricken gentry, not Lord Charlemont himself.

'The Rakshasa, however, told us what was really going on,' Helena continued. She paused for a moment, and, looking down, Alex could see her clenching her fists again. 'At first we could not believe that our own father had conspired to sell Isabelle here to a heathen for the sake of a trade route, as if she were nothing more than' she inhaled sharply 'than a *prize cow*, not his own daughter.'

''Tis a vile disgrace!' exclaimed Isabelle.

'But then we saw a letter that was to be presented to the emir, signed by the rake himself. I tell you, when our dear brother finds out about this, he will hunt Charlemont down and run him through!'

'Listen,' exclaimed Alex, 'you must believe me on this matter – when I met you I had no idea about all this.'

'No? And now you are working with Lord Charlemont? I find this hard to believe,' declared Helena in foul temper, sitting back and folding her arms. 'Another trick, maybe? Where are we to go this time – direct to Constantinople? To join the sultan's harem?'

Alex mulled over what to say next.

'Well?' Helena asked from below.

'Look, regardless of what has happened in the past, the fact remains that, unless you have any great desire to remain here, myself and Lord Charlemont have come to get you off this island.' He paused to let this sink in. 'And to do this I will need your co-operation.'

'Very well,' said Helena, calm now that she had vented her anger. 'What is it you need from us?'

'Anything to get us away from this place,' declared Isabelle. 'We are confined like common criminals here,' she added.

'And your questions?' prompted Helena.

That put Alex on the spot. He thought quickly. 'Firstly, have you been…' he was not sure how to phrase this '*harmed* in any way?'

'If you mean, have we been violated – then no, we have not,' shot back Helena.

'Ah. Good,' he stammered. 'Have they said why they kidnapped you?'

'Zentar told us…'

'Zentar?'

'The son of Korthdan. He is the heir-in-waiting to what they refer to as the "Empire of the Moon" – this island, essentially…'

'Heir-in-waiting? You mean Korthdan is still alive?' Alex was taken aback.

'Why, yes. Granted, I have seen better looking cadavers in my time, but he is most definitely alive. We have met him but once, a few days ago, and he said very little – but seemed to take an unhealthy interest in my sister.'

'The lecherous fiend!' added Isabelle with considerable feeling.

'But he did not act on it,' Helena added quickly. 'And we have not seen him since that day. Anyway, Zentar told us that we had been rescued for our own *protection*, and that in due course we would be returned to our own people. He said we are his guests on the island, and so far he has treated us honourably.'

'Did he mention anything about the Dutch East India Company?'

'The Dutch? Why on earth should he?'

'We believe they may have orchestrated your kidnap in order to claim the trade route for themselves.'

'More scoundrels intent on making money from us?' She gave a sigh of disgust. 'As a matter of fact, no, it has not been mentioned.'

'Well, where in the fortress are you being held?'

'In the palace, near the top.'

'Are you well guarded?'

'I would say so!' Helena exclaimed. 'Nine guards are always with us, save when we are in our room. Look, it must be obvious to you by now that, if any rescue is to be made, it must be well outside the fortress gates, but where we are now is far too near. If anything happened to us, mounted Rakshasa would be out of the gates within seconds, despite their unnatural nocturnal habits. There are stables just inside the main fortress gate, and their riders sleep in the loft, directly above their steeds.'

An uncomfortable silence descended on the trio as they realised they had exhausted the topic of escape for the time being.

'Will you be back tomorrow?'

'Of course,' replied Alex, 'we need to discuss matters further.'

'Oh, good,' declared Helena, obviously relieved for all her initial outrage. She paused for a few moments. 'And may we see the face of our white knight?' she asked playfully.

'I'm not sure that would be a good idea…' Alex began. If nothing else, he imagined he looked quite rough, with the gashes, bruises and powder burns from the battle of the *Fearless* and a few days of stubble.

'Oh, come now,' implored Helena, 'all we see from day to day are these…vile creatures. My heart aches to see a fellow countryman. Especially you. *Please?*'

'Very well,' he found himself saying against his better judgement. 'I'm looking down on you both now. Look up one at a time, but make it brief, for God's sake!'

They both shot up quick glances to him. As Helena's gaze searched upwards for his, he felt his heart leap again, and found himself gazing into her bright blue eyes, now full of warmth and love. He held her gaze for a few heart-stopping moments – but then her look turned to one of doubt as some thought occurred to her, and she cast her eyes down with a slight colour to her cheeks. Isabelle held his gaze for a few seconds also, but with a look of deep gratitude.

'Oh, my dear, thou *hast* been in the wars,' commented Helena presently. 'But how is it that such a good man as yourself is working with a rake like Charlemont?'

'What exactly happened in Captain Todd's cabin?' he asked to change the subject. 'I was above you on the poop deck throughout it all.'

'Well, I saw the galley bearing down on us, then there was that terrible scream that froze our blood – what in God's name was that?'

'I really don't know. Lord Charlemont seems to think they practise sorcery, but…'

'Sorcery? You should talk to Charlemont about that,' remarked Helena. 'He knows a thing or two about it!'

'In what way?'

'You mean you don't know?' retorted Helena. 'His behaviour is the talk of society, man! Why, when he dies, the drawing rooms of London will fall silent for years, such is the scandal associated with him.'

'Look,' protested Alex, 'I vaguely remember some sort of scandal from when I was a boy, but I really don't know what you're talking about. I am a mariner, not a socialite.'

An impatient huff came from down below. ''Tis well-known that as soon as he left Cambridge he fell in with a crowd of idle rakes like himself, drinking, gambling, whoring and duelling over the most petty slights, all over London.'

'Sister!' exclaimed Isabelle, shocked at her sibling's bluntness.

'I'm only telling him what we all say behind closed doors,' Helena snapped back. 'He was so bad that no gentlewoman in London would dare to be seen with him – it would have meant the end to their reputation. After a while he appeared to sort himself out and joined the Coldstream Regiment through a commission purchased by his father. There he learned some discipline, and apparently accounted well for himself. However, when his father died and he came into his inheritance, he resigned his commission and returned to England, immediately joining Lord Dashwood and his *associates*,' she said, emphasising the word with venom. 'Every full moon these degenerates, these members of a "Hell-Fire Club", meet at Dashwood's house in Hanover Square to perform black masses and other such blasphemy.'

'My God!' gasped Alex in shock. 'This is the first I have heard of it.'

'Well, you can now see the sort of man you are consorting with,' remarked Helena, a tone of satisfaction in her voice. 'A scoundrel, a libertine – and a devil worshipper to boot!'

Alex was speechless. Terrible doubts began to creep into his mind. Eventually he recovered himself.

'Look, on the *Fearless*, what happened to you after that war cry?'

Helena recounted the sisters' experience. 'By and by we woke up in the palace,' she concluded.

Alex said nothing for a while. A murder of hooded crows then suddenly flew overhead, cawing loudly. Helena was about to speak further when some movement attracted her eye. 'It's the guards,' she said quickly. 'Time for luncheon.'

'I'll be here tomorrow afternoon,' said Alex, dropping his voice to a whisper. 'We'll have more time to talk then.'

'Thank you, Alex – thank you from the bottom of my heart!' exclaimed Helena. 'It has been most brave of you to come here and talk to us. But take this advice from me. When this is all over, drop your association with Charlemont as soon as you can. The man is a viper who poisons everyone who consorts with him.'

'How did it go?' asked Lord Charlemont when Alex rejoined them. He and the chancellor were sitting in the sunshine with their backs to a drystone wall, each smoking one of the chancellor's clay pipes and getting on famously. His pistol was holstered.

Alex's eyes narrowed slightly – the tone of Lord Charlemont's voice irritated him. Lord Charlemont handed Alex's weapons belt back to him and he buckled it up, kneeling on one leg in the grey soil of the field.

'If you had gone instead of me, I think you would be dead by now,' he declared, glaring at Lord Charlemont. 'I swear, they were so angry they would have given you away – they know about this whole trade deal business.'

Lord Charlemont's heavy lidded eyes blinked slowly, avoiding Alex's gaze. 'I suspected they might – that's why I didn't go out there,' he said, the ghost of a smirk playing across his mouth.

'What do you mean?' Alex demanded. 'We tossed for it.'

Lord Charlemont reached into his pocket and produced the coin used before. 'It's double-headed,' he explained, smirking. 'You're far too trusting.'

'Damn you!' shouted Alex as the doubts flitting through his mind crystallised into a horrifying realisation. He drew his pistol and shoved it violently into Lord Charlemont's chest, forcing his head back against the wall. The chancellor made as if to get up, but Alex snatched Lord Charlemont's own pistol from its holster with his left hand and trained it on him.

'Neither of you move, or – so help me God – I'll kill you both!'

CHAPTER 20

'What's troubling you?' asked Lord Charlemont, arms splayed out on either side of him, but still maintaining his composure. 'What's got into you, man?' he demanded.

The chancellor said something in Latin, but Alex didn't catch it.

'Shut up! I'll tell you what's got into me,' he snarled. 'I've just found out a lot of things about *you*, Lord Charlemont.'

Lord Charlemont tut-tutted and raised his eyes to the heavens as if he had heard this all before.

'One of which is that you, my Lord, are a Satanist!'

'Ah,' said Lord Charlemont, his mood becoming more defensive. 'Now I know what you're talking about, and I can explain everything…'

'Quiet!' Alex ordered. 'It's all starting to make sense now – your knowledge of the occult, and the way we got here so easily and met up with the chancellor. All this talk of the Dutch was just a red herring. It was all prearranged, wasn't it? You and Captain Todd worked it all out – get the women kidnapped then ransom them back to the Levant Company. Brilliant! That way you get a spilt of a huge ransom, and once the trade route's opened, the profits start rolling in.'

'Captain Todd?' exclaimed Lord Charlemont in what seemed to be genuine bewilderment.

'Shut up!' ordered Alex, words tumbling out, his mind making new connections as he spoke. 'No wonder you weren't keen on me coming along on this mission – it could have upset all the careful plans you'd made with your fellow Satanists – the Rakshasa.'

'No. No!' said Lord Charlemont. 'You've got it all wrong…'

'So when were you and the chancellor going to get rid of me? Now perhaps? Just after you've used me to lay the ground work and sweet-talk the women into thinking you're here to rescue them? Would it have been an unfortunate accident?' He glared at the chancellor.

The chancellor was slumped back against the wall, looking totally confused.

Alex turned back to Lord Charlemont. 'Right now, your life is worth less than that of a dog to me, *Lord* Charlemont, when I think of all the men who were slaughtered on the *Fearless*, just so you could make more money!' He paused, breathing hard. 'Why did you do it?' he demanded, pushing the musket harder against Lord Charlemont's chest.

'Listen,' said Lord Charlemont, talking quickly, 'I don't know what they told you out there, but I'm no Satanist...'

'Don't give me that,' spat Alex. 'You're in a Hell-Fire Club, man. The one that meets at Lord Dashwood's house.'

'Ah, yes – that's true, I *was* in that club. But it's nothing to do with the devil,' he protested. 'We met every full moon, and, yes, we wore occult regalia, but at the end of the day it was just an excuse...' he trailed off as if embarrassed, his eyes avoiding Alex's.

'Look at me,' demanded Alex, anger still surging through him.

'It was just an excuse for a debauched feast,' he continued, weighing his words carefully. 'Courtesans were procured and dressed as nuns. Then the members of the club would assemble, dressed for the most part as druids, but masked to conceal their identities. A dinner would be put on, with plenty of wine to loosen everyone up, and then...' he shrugged his shoulders, 'the feast would take place. I alluded to it during our dinner with Admiral Blake. I assumed you knew what I was talking about.'

'What about Captain Todd?' demanded Alex.

'As far as we have ascertained, he's in league with the Dutch. Otherwise, I have never even met the man. Listen, I swear to you I had nothing to do with the attack on the *Fearless*. Anyway, as far as I knew, it was to be commanded by Captain Iserwood. *You* told us that he had been replaced at the last minute due to ill health.'

Alex pulled back slightly.

'That's all I can say about that,' Lord Charlemont concluded, and then changed tack. 'And, if you remember, it was *your* idea to stowaway on the galley, not mine. You made contact with the chancellor, not me.'

'No, but it was your friend Bin Kaslm who led us directly to the right slave market,' Alex persisted. 'And it was your idea to contact the head man of the island when we got here.'

'Bin Kaslm was simply one of many merchants who would have known about the nocturnal visits of the Rakshasa,' Lord Charlemont retorted. 'As regards the chancellor – I've told you how I operate. I always go for those in power. But think about it, man – if I had been behind the raid on the *Fearless*, why would I lead you here, directly to the very place where the women are being held? I could have led you on a wild goose chase round the Aegean for months.'

Alex paused for a moment, his initial certainty unravelling. 'The Rakshasa told the women about the trade deal, but made no mention of the Dutch. All they know is that they will soon be returned to their own people. That sounds to me like a ransom will be involved,' he stated, still looking directly at Lord Charlemont.

Lord Charlemont's eyes widened with surprise, then narrowed again in their usual heavy lidded manner.

'I can't believe that,' he said flatly. 'With all due respect, Lady Isabelle is only of value to the Dutch or the Levant Company. It's quite possible that the Dutch employed the Rakshasa through a proxy and have no idea of who they really are. But any attempt on behalf of the Rakshasa to negotiate with His Majesty's Government would draw too much attention. Undoubtedly the details would leak out, and imagine the outcry in London – not one, but two English roses held hostage by blood-sucking fiends! Why, sir, public opinion would demand a fleet be raised and sent to their rescue. No, a ransom is preposterous – secrecy is both their strength *and* their weakness.'

Alex pondered this for a few moments more. He was almost convinced. 'If you just meet at your club for debauchery, why is it you know so much about the occult?'

'I was interested in the occult as a youth,' Lord Charlemont admitted. 'That's what drew me to Lord Dashwood's club. But all I know is from what I have read – I swear! Look, I was young and lustful with hedonistic friends, and I would defy any man in my position not to do the same…'

'Speak for yourself – some of us have morals, sir!'

'Yes, yes! Look, I have moved on from all that now, and frankly find the whole business distasteful. Some years ago I became a Freemason, and do my utmost to remain true to the oaths I took at my investiture.'

Alex un-cocked the musket and withdrew it from Lord Charlemont's chest. 'Very well,' he said. 'I believe you.' He also lowered the other pistol from the chancellor's direction. 'I apologise.'

'Apology accepted,' said Lord Charlemont with a genuine sigh of relief. 'I'm glad we've cleared that up.' He slowly stood up, brushing his clothes down.

'What was all that about?' asked the chancellor.

'It was all a misunderstanding,' Lord Charlemont assured him in Latin. 'I'll explain on the way back. Now, I suggest we get some food.'

*

On the way back to Pyrgos, Alex recounted in English his conversation with the two women. Lord Charlemont also picked up on the mention of Korthdan.

'He is still alive? Good God, man – that would make him well over one hundred years old! Chancellor?'

'That is correct. I told you they live far longer than we do…'

'Or, he had a son who looks like him, and who inherited his name, for Pete's sake!' exclaimed Alex, almost spitting the words out.

'Calm down, man – we can argue that point later!' retorted Lord Charlemont. 'Now what else did they say?'

Alex took a deep breath. Lord Charlemont's continual acceptance, at face value, of the chancellor's bizarre explanations was beginning to infuriate him.

'So,' said Lord Charlemont when Alex had finished, 'the women's account confirms what we thought about Captain Todd. It would also explain how the Rakshasa knew the women were on board – but *not* how they found you that day.'

'Captain Todd was an excellent navigator,' Alex stated. 'On the day we were attacked he came up on deck just after midday, took a reading on the sun and did some calculations. He then pointed out the Julian Rocks on the chart, and declared that we'd pass them just before the next bell – which we did.'

Lord Charlemont frowned. 'But he still would have had to communicate your position in some way to the Rakshasa.'

'Not necessarily.'

Lord Charlemont stopped abruptly. 'That could be it!' he declared.

'What?' asked Alex.

'They were using thought projection – occult communication by the mind,' Lord Charlemont continued. 'Consider this: Captain Todd worked out your position shortly after midday. He then passed it to the Rakshasa by thought projection, enabling them to becalm you and then track you down. It makes sense!'

'Or they had arranged to rendezvous at the Julian Rocks in the first place!' Alex retorted, exasperated beyond belief. 'The mist was just coincidental, and no doubt delayed their finding us. Why do you insist on looking for such improbable explanations? Has all that reading about the occult warped your ability to reason?'

'Good God, man,' exclaimed Lord Charlemont, gesturing towards the seething walls of water miles out to sea. 'So you really think *that* is a natural phenomenon? I do not – and in comparison thought projection would be a parlour trick for them.'

'You are living in the Dark Ages!' declared Alex through gritted teeth, shaking his head in disgust.

'So, what is the situation?' asked the chancellor, seeing that they had finished their discussion.

Lord Charlemont gave him a brief summary, but left out the details about the trade deal and Isabelle's key role in it.

'So, you *will* require my help.'

'Yes – undoubtedly.'

'Good,' said the chancellor, relieved. 'The first thing that occurs to me regarding your women is for them to persuade the Rakshasa to allow them to attend church every morning. There is a Latin church located about one mile from the fortress gates…'

'The one we turned off at this morning?' Alex butted in.

'Exactly. It is the church of St Catherine. There is a mass there just after dawn each morning.'

'That sounds useful,' said Lord Charlemont, becoming more

enthusiastic about it as he spoke. He stopped and they all turned to look back towards the church. 'It would give us about five minutes' head start on anyone coming from the fortress on horseback. There are no houses around it, but, from memory, it should be possible to deploy men round it and inside it, and in the congregation.'

Alex looked north to the Rakshasa fortress, and then back at Mt Prophet Elias, which was around two thousand feet high, and which prevented the shoreline to the south of it from being observed from the fortress. A thought occurred to him.

He pointed over to the south. 'If we landed a ship behind that mountain at night, we could make our way over here on horseback under cover of dark, spring a trap at the church and still make it back to the ship before the Rakshasa caught up with us.'

Lord Charlemont looked in the direction indicated. 'I think you have a point,' he agreed, and explained the idea to the chancellor in Latin.

'Do not even consider it!' the chancellor declared. 'You may not have seen it before, but there is a fortified watchtower on the top of the mountain. They'd spot you as soon as you came through the Wall of Storms.'

Lord Charlemont took out his spyglass and trained it on the mountain. 'He's right,' he conceded, handing the spyglass to Alex.

Sure enough, partly obscured by the heat haze rising up around it was the top of a watchtower, similar to the one he had seen on their arrival, the base being hidden from their view.

'Well, what about the cliffs here?' persisted Alex, lowering the spyglass. 'There must be some donkey tracks up them.'

'You are right. There *was* one from Fira down to Port Ormos, with a quay at the bottom of it, but the Rakshasa demolished it from the sea upwards for about two hundred feet. Having done that, all they have to watch is the lower eastern side of the island. Even if you managed to land unobserved, what do you think would happen once you put out to sea again in daylight?'

'We'd escape,' said Alex, shrugging his shoulders.

'No, you would not,' declared the chancellor. 'Firstly, shortly after dawn the wind shifts to come onshore – that headwind would slow you down as you made for the Wall of Storms. Secondly, two fully armed war galleys are on constant patrol during the daylight hours. One circles the island one way, the other in the opposite direction, about two miles offshore. It is likely you would encounter one or the other quite soon after leaving shore. Finally, even if you managed to evade them, once you were spotted from any one of the three watchtowers…'

'Where's the third one?' asked Alex.

'At Akrotiri,' replied the chancellor patiently, 'the *kasteli* at the southern end of Santorini.'

He turned, pointing, and Alex could just make it out with his spyglass.

'Any of those watchtowers,' the chancellor continued, 'would signal back to the fortress.'

'By heliograph?'

'Yes. And then a pack of war galleys would be dispatched to intercept you.'

Alex frowned.

'It would be a suicide mission,' the chancellor concluded.

'Why don't they bother patrolling at night when it's their natural time?' asked Alex, unwilling to concede defeat on the matter.

'The night is indeed their natural time. It is easier for their watchmen to see, and in any case, many of them are abroad, so any vessel leaving or approaching Santorini would soon be spotted.'

Alex collapsed the spyglass, raised his eyebrows and sucked in his cheeks slightly. 'It's going to be difficult,' he conceded.

'There may yet be a way,' declared the chancellor. 'But getting the women out to the church, or out on some other ruse, is only the first part of it. We need to talk further about it.'

*

Back at the chancellor's, they remained indoors, out of sight of the passing villagers, while they ate a meal of goat's cheese, cucumber, tomatoes, figs and barley bread. When they had finished, the chancellor sat with them.

'So far I have sheltered you from the Rakshasa,' he began, 'given you food and clothes, and allowed you to talk with your women. Now, if we are to go any further, it is time to talk about a deal.'

'Very well,' agreed Lord Charlemont, 'what is it *you* want?'

'I have some thoughts about that, but I need to talk with the notables of the island before I can tell you exactly.'

Lord Charlemont noticeably stiffened. 'All twelve?'

'Yes.'

'That's too many. The fewer who know about our presence, the better. Get the three you trust the most to come here, and discuss it with them.'

The chancellor reluctantly agreed and made arrangements to send word to them. While they waited for the notables, he told them more about the Rakshasa.

'As I have told you, they sleep during the day and the fortress comes alive at sunset. The artisans then carry out their craft. The warriors practise out on fields to the north, while the priests go into the nearest southern domed tower and chant there till midnight. At midnight the chanting stops, and the priests leave the tower and go into the base of the palace, where they eat in the Great Hall. After they have finished, the warriors go in, and finally the artisans and workers. They all eat again in the Hall shortly before sunrise – none of them appear to cook in their own houses.'

'Then what do they use the northern tower for?' asked Alex.

'That is used for a ceremony connected with the full moon,' the chancellor replied. 'On moonless nights,' he quickly continued, 'they carry torches or oil lanterns around with them, but as soon as the crescent of a new moon appears, as long as the sky is clear, they don't need them.'

'So they cannot really see in total darkness,' said Lord Charlemont.

'Correct. Now, there are very few of their young to be seen – we estimate there have only been around one thousand of them born since they arrived. They are educated in the palace and spend a lot of time learning the martial arts on the fields to the north. On the whole their society appears to be geared for constant war.'

'That would seem obvious,' remarked Lord Charlemont, glancing at Alex.

'In this respect they are like the ancient Spartans,' continued the chancellor, ignoring the remark. 'In fact, they seem to care little for the finer arts, though some of the villagers of Karterados have seen rudimentary musical instruments in the Great Hall, and they have restored an ancient theatre elsewhere on the island – though what exactly they use that for, we do not know.'

*

The three notables arrived towards dusk, as directed by Lord Charlemont as it meant they would be trapped in the chancellor's house until dawn. Lord Charlemont and Alex sat with their backs against a wall on each side of the brazier, smoking clay pipes with their cloaks on, assuming the role of Rakshasa again as the others came in. The notables looked at them nervously as they entered, and sat at the other side of the table in silence until all three had arrived. They were all middle-aged solid dependable types, their deep tans speaking of an outdoor life.

'Thank you for coming at such short notice,' began the chancellor. 'As you can see, I have two guests here tonight, and they are the reason why you are here. Now I must ask you to speak in Latin this night.'

'If there is any way we can serve the Rakshasa…' began one man.

'There's no need for that,' cut in the chancellor. 'My guests are not Rakshasa.' The three looked puzzled, but said nothing. 'Please, Lord Charlemont, Lt Hurst,' directed the chancellor.

They both stood up and pulled down their hoods, eliciting gasps of surprise from the notables.

'This is Lord Charlemont,' said the chancellor as Lord Charlemont gave his trademark nod, 'and Lt Hurst of the British Royal Navy.'

Alex gave a neat salute, and then both sat down.

'They have come to rescue the women who were brought here recently by the Rakshasa.'

There were more gasps at this.

'Lord Charlemont, I give you Spyro, Petros and Talus.'

One of the three stood and turned to the chancellor, his hand on the hilt of a knife. 'We are at great risk harbouring these men here. If the Rakshasa find out…'

'Don't worry, Petros,' the chancellor reassured him, 'the only people who know of these men's presence are in this house right now.'

The chancellor then quickly brought the notables up to date on what had happened. They listened, first wide-eyed with surprise, looking intently at the chancellor and occasionally glancing over to Lord Charlemont or Alex. As the explanation went on, they glanced over again with hostile looks.

'How do we know they are genuine?' demanded Talus, a fairly heavily built man, his hair thinning, but with a thick moustache.

'Lord Charlemont,' requested the chancellor, 'could we see your credentials?'

Lord Charlemont passed over the waxed cylinder. The chancellor unrolled the parchment on the table, and the others crowded round to read the *firman*. Eventually they seemed satisfied, and it was handed back.

'So, they need our help,' the chancellor said with excitement in this voice, 'and this could be our opportunity to break free of the yoke of the Rakshasa!'

The chancellor then requested that they be allowed to speak in Greek for brevity's sake, so the Englishmen settled back with their pipes and watched the discussion take place. At one point, more horses passed. Everyone went silent, looks of fear on their faces, but the horses continued on and the discussion resumed.

'I didn't mention it before,' began Alex in English, 'but Lady Helena shot two of the Rakshasa when they broke down the door to Captain Todd's inner quarters.' He glanced over to see Lord Charlemont's reaction. 'Both in the head.'

Lord Charlemont raised his eyebrows slightly. 'It wouldn't surprise me,' he claimed. 'All of that family's ancestors have served in the military in one form or other. Their brother, Edward, is a captain in the Coldstream Regiment. I knew him when I was serving in the army – he is a fine warrior. I believe he is out in the Americas at the moment.' He glanced over at Alex. 'Lady Helena is, without doubt, her father's daughter – whereas Lady Isabelle is almost a misfit in that family. She does not like the outdoor life, and prefers embroidery and calling on friends to hunting and shooting.'

'How old are they?'

'You mean you never asked? Lady Helena is nineteen, Lady Isabelle seventeen – practically old maids! Listen, I know you've fallen for Lady Helena, but you've been far too long at sea, man!' he declared, waving down Alex's objections with his spare hand. 'There are plenty of good-looking fillies in London Town whose fathers could put up a good dowry. Take my advice: distance yourself from her…' Suddenly his voice faltered.

Alex glanced over at him, and could have sworn that a haunted look flitted across his face for an instant before he managed to recover himself.

'Being too close to her may warp your judgement about what has to be done here, and…' he paused again, looking away, his voice becoming curiously flat '…the less involved you are with either of them, the better.'

'I understand what you are saying…' Alex began, curious as to the reason for Lord Charlemont's behaviour.

'No, I don't think you do!' cut in Lord Charlemont, looking at him intently. He then dropped his gaze and relaxed a bit, taking a puff from his pipe. 'Even if we get them off this island – which is not a foregone conclusion by any means – I'd say to you to forget her. She is the most pig-headed and outspoken hellcat it has ever been my misfortune to meet.' He turned to Alex again. 'And I do mean *ever.*'

'Steady, sir!' retorted Alex. 'You are talking about the woman I love. I will hear no more of this talk!'

'Very well – but do not say you were not warned!'

*

'There is something that bothers me about this whole business,' Alex declared after a while.

'And what is that?' asked Lord Charlemont, turning to him.

Alex hesitated as he knew he was stepping into unfamiliar territory. 'The reason why we are here, why all this has happened, is because of the trade agreement…'

'Quite so.'

'And yet…I don't see that it gives us any real great advantage over travelling round the Cape of Good Hope.'

'Go on,' said Lord Charlemont, turning away, his voice neutral.

'Well, say goods are coming from east. The ships carrying them dock somewhere in the Gulf of Suez, they are unloaded and then transferred, presumably to a camel train.'

'Correct. Camels can carry almost twice as much as horses, and only one in four is needed to carry fodder.'

'Well, just getting the goods from the ships on to camels could take days.'

'True. I was in Aleppo once and saw a camel train come in that took two days and three nights just to settle in.'

'Exactly. All that loading would take time and money, which makes the goods vulnerable to damage and pilfering. Then you have the journey north to the Mediterranean. I'm guessing it is at least one hundred miles.'

'Correct.'

'That would take, say, five to six days, again making the goods vulnerable, with the additional problem of the desert heat, and you get even more problems when you reach the Mediterranean. I don't know that area – I've only seen maps of it – but that's basically where the Nile meets the sea. I can only imagine it is a typical coastal delta, made up of mud flats and salt marshes, which can be difficult to cross at the best of times.'

'Very true,' admitted Lord Charlemont.

'And then you have to load the goods on to ships for the rest of their journey to Europe.' He paused. 'I would say the whole business of getting goods across that stretch of desert would take at least two to three weeks. As well as that, you have the additional considerations of organising ships to be in port at the right times and camel trains always to be available, which will cost money. When you factor all that in, surely it would be faster – and cheaper – to take the goods round the Cape?'

'So,' said Lord Charlemont, turning to him, a touch of exasperation in his voice, 'are you trying to tell me that there's little to no advantage to this trade route?'

Alex paused again. He could sense Lord Charlemont was working himself up to an outburst, but pushed ahead anyway.

'Yes,' he replied – and waited for the expected explosion of anger.

'Well, I'd say you're absolutely right,' declared Lord Charlemont calmly, turning back to observe the conversation going on in front of them.

'What?' exclaimed Alex.

'You're right,' reiterated Lord Charlemont. 'The trade route – as you have described it – could not work.'

'Then why in God's name are we here?' demanded Alex, anger rising up within him.

'Honestly, Hurst, you are provoked so easily,' said Lord Charlemont with a snorting laugh. 'Listen,' he said in a more conciliatory tone, 'you are right in what you say – and I must say that I'm impressed you've spotted that flaw in the route.' He actually managed to say this without sounding patronising. 'However, all of that occurred to us in the Company, and we came up with a solution.'

'Which is?'

'A canal, sir,' replied Lord Charlemont in a solemn voice. 'A canal to link the Gulf of Suez with the Mediterranean. We estimate it will take around ten years to build, but it will be worth the cost. It's the most efficient form of transportation over land, and should pay for itself in less than five years of operation.'

Alex was staggered at the revelation. 'But,' he protested, 'there's not a canal in England longer than ten miles. And you're proposing a *hundred* mile one?'

'Really, Hurst, your ignorance of the Continent surprises me. The Canal Royal de Languedoc in France is almost one hundred and fifty miles long and links Toulouse with the Mediterranean. That took just over twenty-five years to build, and required almost ninety locks. We would need only a few as the Red Sea is only slightly higher than the Mediterranean.'

Alex was awed at the size of the task envisaged. Another thought occurred to him.

'So that's why you were so interested in the aspa.'

'Yes,' replied Lord Charlemont, a smug look on his face. 'In some way I feel the fickle finger of fate in our presence here on this island. From what the chancellor has said, the aspa here will be invaluable to the building of the canal. In fact, it should reduce the time required to build it, if its hydraulic properties are what he says they are. And to think, with a good wind it's probably only three days' sailing from here to Egypt...' His voice trailed off and he seemed temporarily lost in thought. 'I have a good feeling about this whole business. It *will* all work out.'

*

The discussion at the table went on. With the warmth from the brazier, Alex was having difficulty keeping awake. His eyelids were drooping when suddenly the chancellor was standing in front of them. The other three notables were sitting at the table, watching him and Lord Charlemont closely. Talus had his arms folded, a disgruntled look on his face as if he had lost an argument.

'We have reached a decision,' the chancellor announced.

'Good,' said Lord Charlemont, yawning and stretching. The chancellor hesitated. 'Well, man, spit it out!' Lord Charlemont ordered.

'We are willing to give you the necessary aid that will enable you to free your women,' began the chancellor. 'What we propose is the following. We will grant you the necessary help – in the form of safe refuge, transport around this and the other islands and local information – as well as several hundred of my men to supplement an invasion force.'

'You and your men will be putting yourselves at great risk,' Alex interrupted. 'I've fought these fiends – there are no better warriors…'

'We know this,' snapped the chancellor, his voice rising. 'But we cannot just stand by and let outsiders defeat the Rakshasa for us! We have many men secretly trained in the use of swords and fire-arms who are ready and eager to fight.' He moved closer to the Englishmen, his gaze fixed on theirs. 'Our ancestors cry out from their graves for justice,' he declared with tears now appearing in his eyes, 'and we will avenge them!' he shouted, slamming his fist against the palm of his hand.

There was a momentary shocked silence in the room at the strength of this outburst, then to Alex's surprise Lord Charlemont moved forward and embraced the chancellor in a bear hug.

'You are absolutely right,' he said, his voice cracking with emotion. 'It is only just, and we cannot do this without you.' He pulled away from the chancellor, but still held him and looked him in the eye. 'I admire your spirit sir! And in return for all this, what do *you* want?'

The Chancellor looked away briefly as he wiped the tears from his eyes, then took a few moments to compose himself before he spoke again, his voice now resolute.

'You will aid us in driving the Rakshasa from their fortress, preferably killing them all, in order to return our islands to us. Under the terms of a pact that we will draw up, we will then become a British protectorate, with the restoration of the constitution of rights we had under the Turks, and pay your government a small percentage of our income each year.'

Alex gasped – this was a tall order. Lord Charlemont said nothing, preserving an outer facade of calm.

'To make such a commitment would be well beyond the limits of what I can guarantee,' he said, truthfully.

'We realise that,' agreed the chancellor, 'but your Admiral Blake *could* make such a commitment, and organise the necessary force to mount an invasion.'

'So you are saying,' summarised Lord Charlemont, 'that your plan for the rescue of the women requires a full scale invasion?'

'Exactly,' replied the chancellor. 'As we shall demonstrate to you, there is no other way.'

'Well then,' commented Lord Charlemont, 'let's hear it.'

'First, let's get some more coffee on,' requested the chancellor. 'I can hardly keep my eyes open.'

*

With cups of thick Arabian coffee all around, and fresh tobacco in their pipes, the chancellor then went through the plan with them. At first the Englishmen were sceptical, but after another few hours of argument, diagrams and discussion, they were convinced it was the only course of action.

'Remember,' Lord Charlemont intoned at one point, leaning over the table covered with sketch maps of the islands and diagrams of the fortress as they strained their tired eyes in the weak light, 'one incorrect assumption could be the death of us all.'

Stale tobacco smoke hung heavily in the room. Petros and Spyro sat slumped in chairs, asleep, while Talus stood, rubbing his eyes.

'There's only one thing wrong with your strategy,' Lord Charlemont finally said.

'And what's that?' asked the chancellor.

'How do I convince Admiral Blake to deploy all the ships and marines required just to effect the rescue of two women?'

'Well,' began the chancellor, 'there's something in the fortress that should convince you that an invasion is desirable.'

'And what is that?' demanded Lord Charlemont.

'It is the Achilles heel of the Rakshasa,' the chancellor replied, half smiling to himself. 'But it would be better if you saw it for yourselves – I can arrange that.'

'Is it some sort of vulnerability?' asked Alex. 'A forgotten gate into the fortress? An unguarded tunnel?'

'By God, man,' exclaimed Lord Charlemont, 'if this is some sort of trap…'

'No, no, I assure you it is not. I will come with you myself – you will need a guide through that labyrinth!'

CHAPTER 21

The chancellor needed a few days to arrange their entry into the fortress, so in the meantime Alex relayed their ideas to the sisters. He was in position in the tree the next afternoon, and as they walked over towards it, he detected a new eagerness and lightness in their step. Their clothes also looked smarter, and when they removed their hats as they approached, he saw their hair was neatly plaited up and decorated with flowers. Alex's heart skipped a beat as he noticed Helena was wearing a dress with a plunging neckline, revealing some of her ample bosom, while Isabelle wore a simple flowered summer dress. They were obviously looking forward to this meeting – and so was he. The conversation, however, did not start light-heartedly.

'There is something we did not discuss last time,' declared Helena, her mood sombre.

'Go on.'

'We were so glad to see a fellow countryman – especially yourself – that certain aspects of this desperate situation did not occur to us. Lt Hurst – Alex – we appreciate that to get here, and even to talk to us now, you have placed yourself in mortal danger, but all this talk of rescue is misleading, is it not?'

Alex grimaced – he could see what was coming next.

'If you were to free us from these fiends, are we not just jumping from the frying pan into the fire? Zentar has told us that he will return us to our own people – presumably for a ransom – so why should we help you to deliver Isabelle into white slavery? We could quite happily spend the summer here if we knew we were bound for England at some point later in the year. And if Charlemont and his gang of rakes lose money into the bargain, so much the better!'

'It is not as simple as that.'

'No?'

'No. In a nutshell, we believe the Rakshasa kidnapped you and will keep you here until mid-May, when Isabelle is due to be presented to the emir, in order that the Dutch East India Company can win the trade route. All this talk about returning you "to your own" is just a ruse on Zentar's part to put you at ease.'

'In that case, my point still stands,' retorted Helena. 'We could stay here until May and have more precious time together than we would if *liberated* by yourselves.'

'Helena, as far as the Dutch are concerned, you and Isabelle are the only remaining witnesses to what happened on the *Fearless*. They have no doubt allowed you to stay together thus far so that *you* could keep Isabelle company. But – and believe me when I say this – once Isabelle has been handed over to the Dutch, you will be of no use to them. You will be either left here with the Rakshasa, or, as is more likely, murdered outright.'

A shocked silence emanated from below. Nothing was said for almost a full minute.

'It seems we have no choice,' Helena finally said. She briefly glanced up at Alex, her voice hardening. 'But if Charlemont thinks I will meekly allow my sister to be sacrificed in this way, he is *very* much mistaken!'

She then stood up and walked a few yards away, looking out to sea for a good few minutes, hand raised to prevent the wind blowing her hair across her face. Reluctantly she turned back to them, her eyes downcast but her face set with the knowledge of some inner resolution.

'Well,' she asked, 'how do you propose to release us from this "Isle of Demons"?'

Alex summarised the plan hatched the previous night.

'So,' said Helena presently, when both were sitting once more with their backs to the tree, 'you are saying we need to convince the Rakshasa that we want to attend a Roman Catholic mass each morning?' She sounded doubtful.

'Yes,' replied Alex, keeping out of sight above them.

'That may be difficult. It was days before Korthdan allowed us to come here. They do not like us straying too far from the fortress – and may I point out that we are Church of England Protestants who have never set foot in a popish church before.'

'They are unlikely to know the difference. Pray, try and see what the response is,' he exclaimed, slightly exasperated.

'Very well, I will do my utmost.'

'Good. We must also change our place of meeting – the trail I am leaving through the grass is becoming far too noticeable.'

'But what is the alternative?'

'There is a deserted village named Fira, further down the road from the fortress on the way to the church. After your first visit to the church I want you to ask the Rakshasa to allow you to go there so we can talk more easily.'

'Again, I will put the request to Zen…the Rakshasa, but there is no guarantee…'

'Well, use your charms on them! Tell them you wish to sketch the ruins or some other such excuse. Regardless, I cannot come here. If they are agreeable, I will meet you in Fira in four days hence…'

'But where?'

'There is a building with an old wine press inside – there is only the one. Assuming they agree, I will be watching how the guards deploy round the village.'

'Well, what other news do you bring?' she asked presently.

'Not much, I'm afraid,' he replied.

'The guards are beginning to stir,' Helena cut in. 'It would appear we will have to continue this conversation in Fira.' She suddenly turned and looked up into his eyes, blushing as he held her gaze, and then she smiled and surreptitiously blew a kiss at him before turning back.

Isabelle glanced up to him a few moments later. 'Goodbye,' she whispered, before giggling like a schoolgirl, turning to her sister and nudging her.

*

'Well, how did it go with the flame-headed one?' asked Lord Charlemont as Alex and the chancellor entered the house. He was sitting at the table, pistol at his side, almost obscured by a cloud of tobacco smoke.

'Fine,' replied Alex, casting his eyes away from Lord Charlemont's piercing gaze. 'They will put the request to attend mass to the Rakshasa as soon as possible.'

'Good. And chancellor – any news on smuggling us into the fortress?'

'This I must check on,' the chancellor said, walking out the front door.

He returned just before dusk, loaded down with more willow baskets of food that his wife had cooked for them.

'There's a Rakshasa feast coming up in four days time,' he said as he placed the baskets on the table, 'on the first night of the full moon. We usually deliver some of our wine on the day of the feast, so I've made arrangements to get us in with that load.'

CHAPTER 22

'Overcooked! Overcooked!' Isabelle shouted in anger, holding her plate of lamb and rice within inches of the old servant's face.

'Isabelle!' exclaimed Helena. 'Pray do not be so rude to the poor woman. The lamb is quite rare – if it were less cooked, it would be raw.'

'Then how do I ask for it to be raw in Latin?' Isabelle demanded.

Helena told her the phrase, and Isabelle forcibly repeated it to the servant, shoved the plate into the old woman's hand and then turned her back.

'Honestly, Isabelle,' declared Helena after the servant had left the room, 'there is no need to be so rude to the staff.'

'I will talk to her how I wish,' snarled Isabelle, throwing herself down on her bed. 'She is just a lackey.' She looked over to Helena. 'You eat yours now,' she commanded. 'If you wait for the old hag to return, it will be quite cold.'

She then sighed deeply and stared up at the ceiling – a recent habit that was beginning to annoy Helena. She knew it would now be useless to attempt to engage Isabelle in further conversation. These episodes of foul temper were becoming more frequent and intense, but between them Isabelle would return to her old self and apologise profusely for her previous behaviour, blaming it on the heat or their confinement.

In the silence that followed, the discrete knock on the door made Helena start and Isabelle harrumph sarcastically. Their argument had completely taken Helena's mind off the possibility of a visitation from Zentar, and she felt all at sea instead of her usual excited anticipation.

'Your fancy man is here,' remarked Isabelle, a touch of jealousy in her voice. 'What is it about you, sister? Why will no man or Rakshasa ever approach *me*?'

'Isabelle,' hissed Helena, 'I must cooperate with him if we are ever to leave this island.'

'Ah. Yes. *Cooperate*,' agreed Isabelle with heavy sarcasm. 'I swear, sister, your lips were ruby-red when you returned the other night – hours after midnight!'

'Enough!' hissed Helena. Then, raising her voice, she called out in Italian to Zentar. 'One moment, my Lord, and I will be with you.'

'*My Lord* is it now?'

'Did I just say that?' asked Helena, genuinely bewildered.

'You did so,' replied Isabelle, and gave a harsh laugh. 'You are like a love-struck floozy!'

'For goodness sake, be not lying on the bed when he comes in,' beseeched Helena, trying to change the subject.

'Why not?' demanded Isabelle, propping herself up on one arm. 'Are you afraid he will leap on the bed and ravish me? Truth be told, I would not resist – how I long for a man to take me in his arms and…'

'Isabelle! Get off the bed *now*,' hissed Helena, drawing herself up to her full height.

'Oh, very well,' sighed Isabelle, her face a picture of insolence as she rose from the bed. 'You can let our "lord and master" in now,' she huffed as she sat down on a chair.

'*Thank you*,' exclaimed Helena. She quickly checked her appearance in the looking glass and straightened her dress before finally opening the door.

'My Lord…' she began, prompting a sarcastic grunt from Isabelle. 'I mean, Zentar, how lovely to see you. How are you this evening?'

Zentar strode imperiously into the room, sweeping his purple cloak round him. 'I am well,' he said in his deep, seductive voice. 'And how are my Ladies Montagu?'

'Never in better health, *my Lord*,' replied Isabelle in a voice dripping with honey, and with not the slightest sarcasm, as she stood up. She then gave a most graceful curtsey, ensuring her plunging cleavage was directly in his line of sight, making Helena seethe with jealously.

Zentar gave an embarrassed cough and glanced away from her towards Helena. 'And my Lady Helena?'

'Also well, my Lord,' replied Helena, finally feeling the now familiar sense of serenity that washed over her whenever she was in his presence.

'Is he using sorcery on me or am I falling in love with him?' she thought – and then realised, light-headedly, that she did not really care.

'Do you mind if I take your sister out again tonight?' he asked Isabelle without shifting his gaze from Helena.

'No, my Lord. Of course not,' replied Isabelle, her head still bowed. 'If that is your desire.'

'Then come, my love,' commanded Zentar. 'The night awaits!'

*

In the courtyard, Zentar's chariot was waiting for them, the white chargers snorting and stamping with impatience as two servants held their harnesses. The chariot creaked as they stepped onboard, and then with a crack of the whip they were off, passing through the fortress gates at a brisk trot. Helena held on tight as the horses sped up to a canter. The moon had just risen and was casting long shadows across the countryside with its cool silvery light. She looked over at her companion, tall and dark in his flowing robes, his gorgeous eyes reflecting the moonlight like those of a cat.

'Where to tonight, my love?' she asked him.

'The High Watchtower on Mt Elias and thence to Ancient Thera,' he replied, and cracked his whip to speed the horses up. 'From the watchtower we can see all of this island, and others. Hold on!'

With incredible power, the two chargers pulling the chariot surged forward to a gallop, and Helena whooped with delight as they sped along the road towards the mountain, shouting greetings out to other mounted Rakshasa that occasionally passed them, exhilarated as the breeze swept her hair wraith-like behind her. She felt alive, young and invincible, hanging on with one hand to the chariot and to her lover's arm with the other, the cool night air like nectar in her lungs. They glided along through the locked and barred villages of Man on their way to the mountain, the scent of tended jasmine and honeysuckle flitting across her nostrils as they passed by walled gardens and through public squares. Presently the road levelled off, and Zentar had to slow down as another chariot came in the opposite direction.

'Faster,' urged Helena once they had passed the other chariot. 'Now, on to the watchtower!' she commanded, theatrically raising her arm to point at it, and then throwing her head back, shrieking with laughter at her own posturing.

Another crack of the whip and they were off again, getting higher and higher into even cooler air. Eventually they made the foot of the watchtower, bathed in the cold blue light from its huge lantern, and the watchers there welcomed them in, offering them glasses of sweet amber-coloured Vinsanto and thick loaves of barley bread that they dipped in olive oil. Up at the top of the tower, Zentar pointed out the islands visible over the Wall of Storms – large, dark, silent masses, anchored in a glittering sea of silver. Helena peered at them more closely through the watcher's spyglass and made out the faint light of villages of Man scattered here and there. Then they were outside again, back on the chariot and travelling south, away from the summit along a rough track that led to a large rocky promontory that was many hundreds of feet above the sea.

'What is this "Ancient Thera" you are taking me to?' Helena asked as the horses picked their way along a rough track, now barely visible below their hooves.

'I used to come here as a boy,' replied Zentar. 'It is a magical place – but one that cannot be easily described.'

Presently they came to what looked like the outskirts of another ruined town, but as they drew closer, Helena could see the buildings were made of limestone, the larger ones constructed in the Greek classical style and looking ethereal in the moonlight. Then they were standing at the end of a street, easily ten feet wide, that stretched ahead of them, gently sloping upwards into the night and out of sight.

'Ancient Thera,' declared Zentar, dismounting from the chariot and leading her on to the flagstones of the street and into the ghostly town. 'We found it when we first came here in a far worse state than you see before you now, half-buried in pumice stone and lost from the sight of Man. We restored the streets and some of the buildings as best we could as a monument to the noble people who built this over two millennia ago.'

'Who were they?' asked Helena, thoroughly entranced by the sight before her.

'An offshoot of the ancient Greek tribe we admire above all others

– the Spartans. What industry they had, to build an entire city here, so high above the sea! Our priests have divined that they thrived here for almost half a millennium, latterly being part of the Egyptian empire that Alexander bequeathed to his general Ptolemy – the last queen of his great dynasty being Cleopatra.' He smiled at her. 'A beauty like yourself.'

'Flatterer!' she exclaimed, smiling. 'But how can your priests be so sure who the architects of this city were, and where they came from?'

'Using a skill I do not myself possess, they searched for them on the astral plane…' He glanced at her and noticed she was looking puzzled. 'When your physical body dies, that is not the end of your existence,' he explained. 'Your astral body, with all the memories and experiences of your physical life, lives on for countless eons. For most, who did not learn how to act on the astral plane when still alive, this period is spent in a dream. We can, however, temporarily rouse them from this state and question them about events that happened in their lives, before allowing them to slip back into their eternal slumber.'

Helena was silent for a while as she absorbed this remarkable explanation. Finally she spoke again. 'Could I be taught how to act on the astral plane?' she asked. 'It sounds like a wondrous skill to possess.'

'Of course, my love – but all in good time. Let us enjoy this night for now.'

They walked on until they came to a large open space, easily fifty yards in length on one side. 'The agora,' commented Zentar. 'The market, and heart of the city. And over here, a public baths – although this is a later addition, built by the servants of a Roman Emperor.'

'You are right – 'tis an enchanted place,' Helena enthused, looking round her. 'And what a perfect night to experience it!' A thought suddenly occurred to her and she paused, looking up to Zentar. 'But come now – why is there no one else here?' She caught the sly smile that crossed his face at her question. 'Why, Zen,' she exclaimed, grasping his arm playfully and looking up to him. 'Have you, perchance, commanded that no one else visits here this night?'

'Yes, my dear,' he replied, smiling broadly now. 'I wanted you to see it at its best, with no others to distract you from its beauty.' He gazed into her eyes and drew her closer. 'Or to distract me from you…'

He drew her closer still. They embraced and kissed passionately, standing there in the deserted agora as the ghosts of its countless former inhabitants passed silently and unseen around them. Presently, to her surprise he gently drew away from her.

'There is much more to see before this night is out,' he declared, looking directly into her eyes, now half-lidded with desire.

Helena groaned in frustration. 'Must we?' she demanded, pouting. Her physical desire for him was now almost overwhelming, and she ached for it to be consummated. She pulled him back towards her. 'I want you,' she whispered into his ear, barely believing she was being so forward. '*Now!*'

'Soon,' he replied. 'But for now there is the most perfect carving of a dolphin I found when I was a boy that I want you to see.'

Helena gasped in exasperation as he pulled away from her and left her there in the square, seemingly unaware of the level of her carnal desire for him. Evidently it had been some time since he had last seen the carving, as he went from one building to another, examining their walls and pillars, unable to find it. She kicked her heels for a while, and then harrumphed with frustration and decided to have a look around by herself.

She wandered down a side street and came to a small square, in the centre of which was a raised dais, about the height of a table, presumably on which had once stood a statue. She was about to turn back when she noticed something was laid out on it, but she could not make it out properly as it lay in the moon shadow of an ivy covered building. She walked over to it – and gasped in horror as she saw it was a human skeleton, its four limbs shackled by crude chains to each corner of the dais, some tatters of clothing still attached to it. The spine was arched back as if in a death throe, and the skull lay looking to one side, its mouth open in a silent scream. Worst of all, its ribcage had been savagely ripped open. The euphoria of the night suddenly dissipated, and she shivered involuntarily at the scene before her. She turned away just as Zentar walked up, smiling, behind her. His smile and good humour vanished in an instant when he saw the remains, and for the first time in any of their outings he swore harshly under his breath.

'What is it?' demanded Helena, watching him closely. '*Who* is it?'

For a few moments, Zentar seemed lost for words. When he did speak it was with deliberation. 'It was a criminal,' he replied, avoiding her eyes.

'A criminal?' exclaimed Helena, her suspicions aroused by his prevarication. She looked again at the skeleton, moving closer to it. 'Oh, my Lord,' she said, observing the well developed pelvis. 'It was a woman!'

'Helena, there is no need…'

'And why was her rib cage torn apart?'

'Helena, the female was a criminal and she was executed for her crimes…'

'What crimes?'

'I do not know – I was not here,' he replied, becoming increasingly annoyed at her questioning.

A thought occurred to her, and before he could stop her she walked to one of the corners of the square. As she had suspected, human-like bones were scattered there, the odd skull peering sightlessly out from long spiky grass.

'This is a carnal house,' she declared, turning back to him, her fists clenched. 'It is barbaric!'

'Barbaric? Really? Well, answer me this,' he demanded. 'Do you loiter around Tyburn waiting for felons to be hauled out from Newgate prison and hanged?'

Helena hesitated for a moment.

'No. Of course you do not. I have no interest in these executions, but they are necessary – and are carried out by your people also.'

'But the manner…'

'Come, let us leave this place,' he insisted as he grasped her gently by the hand. 'I did not mean you to see this, no more than you would take me to see an execution if I were to visit London Town.'

Helena followed him reluctantly, unsettled by what she had seen. 'I want to go back now,' she declared as they reached the agora again. 'The dolphin, or whatever the carving was, does not interest me in any way.'

'Helena, please let us not leave yet,' he implored her. He took her hands in his, and she did not pull away as she once again felt the soothing power of his aura. 'There is one more part of this city I want to show you,' he continued, 'that I was saving until last.'

Helena made a feeble attempt to pull away, but he held her hands tighter.

'I promise you, once you see this, you will forget all about that… unpleasantness.' He could see her resistance was now faltering, so he turned away, leading her by the hand.

She followed him in silence along an alley that lay in moon shadow, and then they passed through a well-preserved stone doorway into what appeared to be another open space. Zentar paused, turning to see what her reaction would be. The moon now was so bright that it took a few moments for her eyes to adjust to the scene before her – and when they did, she gasped in astonishment.

They were standing at the centre of the top row of seating in an amphitheatre, looking down to the stage, behind which the ground fell away to give a backdrop consisting of the Aegean Sea, glittering in the moonlight, and above it the night sky, as black as ink.

'Incredible, is it not?' declared Zentar over his shoulder as he walked down the central stairway towards the restored stage. When he reached it, the boards creaked under his weight as he turned to face her. She stood transfixed. 'We now use this to re-enact the great victories and acts of our people – but sons of Man built this theatre *two millennia* ago in order to perform the comedies of Aristophanes and the tragedies of Euripides. It can seat well over a thousand souls, and each could hear every word.' He dropped his voice to a whisper. 'No matter how quietly spoken.'

With surprise, she realised she could hear him perfectly clearly, due to the ingenious acoustics of the building.

'Inhabitants would come from all over this island,' he continued, 'and from nearby islands too, to take part in festivities, music and dancing, for men to meet their future wives, and to see these plays performed by day and perchance, as now, by night too, the stage lit with oil lamps…'

'Oh, Zen,' she exclaimed as she joined him on the stage. 'This is beyond words…'

He smiled and let her absorb the scene, imagining the spectacle it must have been, before once more taking her hand and leading her through an opening in the rear of the stage to a small grassy area on the edge of the cliff. He cast his cloak down on the grass, and Helena sat eagerly on it, pulling Zentar towards her side as she lay back on the ground.

They embraced, and presently she was looking down on her own pale naked breasts as Zentar's hand moved up and caressed one.

'I'm not made of butter, you know,' she said, gently chiding the steel sinewed creature that lay beside her.

His hand had moved in further and massaged her breast firmly, causing her to cry out softly as she arched her back in pleasure…

*

'Helena! Helena!' urged Isabelle. 'Wake up – it is almost dawn! We are to go to the church today!'

Helena slowly half-opened her eyes, and then shut them again, the mere effort being too great. She had no headache, but felt deadly tired. 'Where…what time did I get back last night?'

'Way after midnight.' replied Isabelle.

Judging by the pleasant tone of voice, Helena sensed that Isabelle was currently her usual self. Isabelle sat down on the other bed, looking over at her intently.

'What happened last night?'

Helena closed her eyes again and massaged her temple with one hand. 'We went to the High Watchtower on Mt Elias.'

'Lucky you! And you spent most of the night there? What *were* you doing?'

Helena thought back, trying to unpick the whirl of images from the previous night. She remembered the watchtower, the streets of Ancient Thera, the body of the poor woman, the theatre, and then lying on Zentar's cloak. They were osculating…Her hand flew to her mouth to stifle a cry of horror.

'What is it, sister?' asked Isabelle, her expression stern. 'Did you… did he *possess* you?'

'No,' exclaimed Helena, brushing an errant lock of hair from her face. 'No, he did not.' She avoided her sister's penetrating gaze. 'But only just, and so…'

Isabelle gave a loud sigh of relief. 'Well, thank the Lord, for the sake of your virtue, that the man – I mean Rakshasa – is a slow burner.' She paused for a moment. 'Any English Lord would have had your virtue thrice over by now!'

Helena sat there for a few moments, still in shock at the memory, the sheet pulled round her, when an overpowering realisation flitted into her mind.

'Oh, Isabelle,' she cried. 'He is bewitching me!' She looked at her sister, desperation in her eyes. 'I am not myself anymore. He is turning me into one of them – a wanton creature of the night!'

'Sister,' exclaimed Isabelle, her voice firm but gentle, 'are you sure you have not fallen in love with him?'

The question momentarily silenced Helena, but then she turned to look over at the slowly brightening sky framed by the window, hearing the sound of the wind and that of seagulls calling to each other as they wheeled round outside.

'No,' she said. 'No!' she repeated with more conviction. 'Last night – all the nights – are like dreams. But *this* is reality and Alex is the one I truly love…'

And then she burst into tears.

'But I cannot resist Zen!' she cried. 'Once I am in his presence, his aura overpowers me. I am helpless before him!' She looked at her sister, desperation in her eyes. 'What am I to do? Isabelle, my heart is being torn apart!'

Isabelle was by her side now, arm round her, comforting her.

'There, there, sister. Strange, is it not, that I am consoling you? Usually 'tis the other way around.' Helena leaned into her and sobbed uncontrollably for a few minutes, before regaining her composure.

'I dare not go abroad with him again,' she declared suddenly, turning to face Isabelle. 'For if I do, he *will* surely possess me and…' her sobs threatened to erupt again, but she managed to control them '… and I will be tied by a half-caste child to this land and his people *forever*!'

Despair overtook her again, and she buried her head in her hands as she wept.

'Oh, Helena, do not weep so!' urged Isabelle. 'Your virtue is safe – at least for a while.'

Helena managed to stop sobbing and looked at her, puzzled.

'Zentar himself sent word this morning that Korthdan has called him away to carry out some duty or other, and that he will be away for a week or so.'

'Oh, thank the Lord,' exclaimed Helena, lying back on the pillows and wiping her tears away with the sheet. 'I will get some respite at least. God willing, I can use the time to build up my resolve against him.'

'That's the spirit,' said Isabelle. 'Now, pray let us get dressed before our escort starts banging on the door.'

CHAPTER 23

The day after the sisters' first visit to the church, Alex used a spyglass to observe the regular party leave the fortress mid-morning. To his satisfaction, they continued south on the top road, past the Hanging Tree, and on to Fira. Once at Fira, four guards remained with Helena, while the rest searched the village. Having found nothing, they all then deployed round the outskirts of the village, widely spaced – and all facing outwards. Throughout the afternoon they let the sisters wander around the village unhindered, and then accompanied them back. The next day they did not bother searching the village at all and just took up their positions around it, so on the fourth day he decided to keep their appointment as planned.

*

A shadow passed across the doorway of the winery, and a lizard scuttled out of the shadows and into the sun. The wine press stood in the centre of the room, its wood warped and the iron screw of the press thick with brown rust.

'Alex?' Helena hissed as she stood on the threshold of the half-ruined building. 'Are you there?'

'Yes, Helena,' replied Alex, stepping out of the shadows. 'I am here, my love.'

She ran to him and they embraced passionately.

'I can hardly believe it!' she exclaimed presently, drawing herself away so she could look at his face. 'To hold you – 'tis a joy too great to describe. If only we could all leave now and be free of this vile place.'

'Patience, my dear, patience,' he countered. 'Come, let us go outside and sit in the sun.'

'But what about the guards?'

'Do not fret – we will be quite hidden with the other houses around and about.'

They went outside, sat on a grassy bank and ate some food the sisters had brought with them. Isabelle appeared pale, but otherwise seemed fine, and after some small talk she walked away from the winery with her sketch book to allow Alex and Helena to talk privately.

'There is something you should know about Isabelle,' declared Helena when she was sure her sister was out of earshot.

'What is that?'

'Recently she has started having nightmares, terrible nightmares that I cannot wake her from, but about which she remembers nothing the next day.' She glanced over in the direction Isabelle had taken. 'A change is coming over her,' she said in a low voice. 'She has always been sweet natured, but since arriving here has become more argumentative and sometimes quite aggressive. It is quite unlike her.'

'Maybe it is the confinement,' ventured Alex.

'No. I think it is more than that. This place is changing her – they are changing her – I am sure of it.' She shivered, despite the warm sun. 'The sooner we leave this cursed isle, the better.'

They sat in silence for a few moments, then Helena seemed to break out of her sombre mood, and reached over to take his hand.

'Anyway,' she said. 'Let us talk of other things.'

At first Alex was overjoyed to be with Helena again, but as they spoke and the morning wore on, he became aware that she was somewhat reticent when speaking about what had occurred since arriving on Santorini. She seemed preoccupied with some other subject and would frequently avert her eyes from his, or turn away completely, with something approaching a haunted look. Alex began to feel uncomfortable. He had scant experience with the fairer sex – most of the last six years he had been on a warship, and the years before that had been absorbed in study – and Helena's behaviour at first seemed inexplicable. He had expected her to be happy to see him, but she now seemed almost embarrassed to be with him – or embarrassed at something she had done.

He also began to wonder if he had totally misread her intent on the *Fearless*, and that she had really just considered him a charming companion rather than a potential husband. He was, he knew, currently well below her station. They had spoken of this on the *Fearless*, but she had dismissed the subject, declaring she had faith that he would soon make the rank of captain, and with it achieve a far higher social status. Now, though, following all that had happened, was she finding his comparatively lowly rank off-putting and reconsidering her position? With this uncertainty at the back of his mind, their conversation became desultory, and finally petered out. After some minutes of awkward silence, Helena began hesitantly speaking again.

'There is something you should also be aware of…one of the Rakshasa has started making advances towards me.'

'Who?' he asked, his hackles rising.

''Tis Zen…I mean Zentar,' she said, absentmindedly straightening her dress. 'The son of Korthdan.'

'How long has this been going on for?' Alex demanded through gritted teeth.

'A week or so now,' she replied. 'I didn't tell you before because… because I thought 'twas just a brief flirtation – but now I realise he is becoming more serious.'

'In what way?'

'He takes me for walks in the evening, shows me round the fortress and tells me about himself and the Rakshasa.' She paused for a moment, as if uncertain whether to continue. 'He has also told me that the Rakshasa quite often take human women to be one of their wives.'

'Damn him!' exclaimed Alex as he felt jealous rage rise up within him. 'Why in God's name can't he stick to his *own* kind?'

'Alex, Alex!' exclaimed Helena, an uncharacteristic touch of nervousness in her voice. 'Don't worry – he is no threat to you, I promise! I just thought it would be good to talk to him…to see if I can get more information about the Rakshasa, and any other weaknesses you could exploit.'

Alex looked her directly in the eye. 'You swear?'

'Of course,' she reassured him – but then cast her eyes down, looking uncertain. 'Don't worry.'

'Well, for pity's sake do not say anything about myself and Lord Charlemont! One word out of place…'

'Alex, of course I will not! Do you think my head is made of cloth?'

He said nothing for a few moments until the fit of jealousy had passed. 'There is something that has been bothering me.'

'Go on.'

'Have you…' He struggled to find the words, but then just blurted them out. 'Were you and Lord Charlemont ever involved with each other?'

'Whatever made you think that?' Helena exclaimed, sitting up straight with surprise.

'Well…you would have moved in the same circles. And you each talk of the other with such vitriol that I can't help wondering…'

'Well certainly I did know Lord Charlemont socially, through dances and hunt balls, years before all this,' Helena cut in, 'and he did at one point propose to me, but I would have none of it, even though Father was desperately keen on the idea. He claimed he had renounced his old whoring and gambling ways, but, even though I was just fifteen at the time, I knew a leopard could never change its spots and turned him down.'

'So you spurned him?' Alex exclaimed with relief.

'Yes, and I understand he has never forgiven me for it – which might explain his attitude to me. But, before all this I had no real animosity towards him. As far as I was concerned he was just another rakish Lord to be avoided – and there are a lot of them around, I assure you! No, it is the way that he and his cronies have conspired to deliver my sister into the hands of a heathen just so that they could make money – it is that I hate him for.'

'Good – I had been worried…'

'Well, pray, do not be,' she reassured him, 'you have enough to think about.'

*

'Zentar is *courting* her?' exclaimed Lord Charlemont, visibly paling.

Alex was pacing the floor of the chancellor's house in a foul mood, sipping from a glass of wine as he related what Helena had told him.

'What is it about that woman? First you, and now this vampire is throwing himself at her feet!'

Alex stopped his pacing and glared at Lord Charlemont through narrowed eyes. He was about to mention Lord Charlemont's proposal, but then thought better of it.

'My God!' continued Lord Charlemont, looking into the middle distance, horror in his eyes, his voice hoarse. 'To think – we are at the mercy of a vengeful woman! Just one word from her and everything…'

'I know, I know!' retorted Alex, swigging down the rest of his wine. 'But she swears she will say nothing to him…'

'Then we must tell her *nothing* from now on,' declared Lord Charlemont, striking the table with his fist. 'And you must only visit her if absolutely necessary.'

'Go to hell!' exclaimed Alex, turning on him. 'I'll visit her when I please. And if I see that bastard Zentar with her – I swear I will kill him!'

'Now look here, Hurst,' demanded Lord Charlemont, standing and squaring up to him. 'I'm getting worried that your shoulders are not broad enough for this task, that you are starting to let your heart rule your head!'

Alex grunted in annoyance and turned away.

'No, listen to me! If I have *any* doubt that you do not possess the relentless will required to see this task through to the end, then I will relieve you of your duties – here and now.'

Alex looked at him with shock.

'Well?'

'You're right,' Alex declared reluctantly. 'I need to…I *will* control my feelings.' He turned away, rubbing his hand across his face. 'It's just that the thought of her being alone with that fiend…'

'Then console yourself with this thought: if all goes well, Zentar will be dead within a few months – along with the rest of the abominations in that fortress.'

*

The next few days were ones of intense activity for the Englishmen. They would rise at dawn and go riding with the chancellor around the island to familiarise themselves with it. Alex, being trained in cartography and navigation, made sketches of the topography of the island. He studied the composition and angles of beaches near the fortress, and used fishing boats to plumb the depth for several hundred yards from the shore. They also mapped out the lanes leading from the beach to the top road, and for several days observed the prevailing winds at all points around the island.

When possible, Alex would go to Fira in the afternoon, where he would talk to the sisters, and with their help he began to sketch out a map of the maze of streets that existed between the outer walls of the fortress and the gates of the palace. At times Isabelle would politely walk to another part of the field to let them speak privately and more intimately. Alex still felt he was in love with Helena, but worried intensely about the unseen presence of Zentar. Despite what Helena said, and her declarations of love for him, he strongly suspected she had feelings for his inhuman rival.

On the day before they were due to be smuggled into the fortress, Alex was once more in the winery, eagerly awaiting the arrival of the two sisters. Presently Helena entered the building alone, and immediately he could see her face was ashen with worry.

'What is the matter?' he asked her, but she did not answer, and instead buried her head in his shoulder, great shuddering sobs racking her frame.

'It's Isabelle,' she finally said. 'She has been taken!'

CHAPTER 24

'I woke this morning and she wasn't there,' Helena continued. 'They told me she has a distemper and needed treatment.' She stopped and buried her face in her hands. 'I think they must have drugged us yesterday evening and taken her in the night,' she sobbed. 'I'm so worried – what in heaven's name could they be doing with her?'

Alex tried to reassure her as best he could, and despite Lord Charlemont's warning, thought it would help to tell her that they were to enter the fortress the next day. She brightened up considerably at this.

'Swear to me you'll look for her,' she implored him. 'I just pray to God she has not been harmed.'

He promised, but then to his disappointment she decided to finish their meeting early. 'I'm too upset,' she explained. 'And I don't like you seeing me like this.' She straightened up and brushed down her dress as she moved outside. 'When will I see you again?'

'I cannot say when we will be out of the fortress, so most probably the day after tomorrow,' he replied.

Suddenly Helena broke down and started to cry again. 'I'm so worried about little Isabelle!' Huge sobs once more shook her frame, and she had to sit down on the grassy bank, head in hands, until they had passed.

Presently her crying spent itself and she stood up again, wiping the tears from her eyes with a handkerchief. 'I must go now,' she said, and before he could protest, she strode off towards the edge of the deserted village, waving at the guards. 'I want to go back,' she called at them, and was gone.

*

Back at the chancellor's house he related this latest development to Lord Charlemont and the chancellor.

'Well,' said Lord Charlemont reluctantly, 'it would appear that

Lady Isabelle is to be turned over to the Dutch already – but it's far too early. It's weeks to the deadline – so why risk taking her from here? It just does not make sense.' He paused. 'It also begs the question as to what is to happen to Lady Helena.'

'Those were my thoughts,' agreed Alex.

'Chancellor?' Lord Charlemont asked, turning to him.

The chancellor looked pensive. 'Like you, I don't understand it.' He shrugged his shoulders despondently.

'What about this "Full Moon Feast" you mentioned?' asked Alex. 'Is it possible her disappearance is linked with that?'

'I would doubt it,' the chancellor replied, his manner becoming evasive. 'It's very unlikely.'

'We'll continue as planned then,' declared Lord Charlemont. 'Once we've been in the fortress and seen its Achilles heel – whatever that is – then we will have completed our reconnoitre here, and we can think about getting off this island.'

'Fine,' said the chancellor, snapping himself out of his thoughts. 'I'll get the clothes you'll need for tomorrow.'

Lord Charlemont waited until he had left the room, and then dug into one of his bags to pull out a box wrapped in oilskin.

'Leave your pistols here tomorrow,' he said. 'We'll just take knives, garrotting wire and one of these each.'

As he spoke he unwrapped and opened the box, revealing what appeared to be two ordinary pistols, but the handles were metal and quite straight instead of being curved.

'Two special items I obtained from my armourer,' he continued. 'Air pistols – silent killers under ten yards, and an assassin's weapon of choice.'

He grasped the handle in one hand so that the butt was facing Alex. Using his other hand, he pressed a stud at the base of the butt, and a part of it sprang out.

'This is the air pump,' he explained. 'Pump it around fifteen times and you'll have enough air for half a dozen shots.'

He handed one to Alex, who examined it carefully. Looking above the trigger, he noticed the word "Bate" inscribed on the metalwork.

'Bate of London?'

Lord Charlemont nodded.

'But airguns are banned in England – and the Continent, for that matter.'

'Honestly, Hurst, you should have taken holy orders, not admiralty ones! Of course they're banned – but that's never stopped our gun makers manufacturing them on the quiet. And don't be so damned priggish – they may save your life tomorrow without waking up that nest of vampires!'

CHAPTER 25

Just after midday they left the house, their cloaks on to reassume their roles as Rakshasa, and followed the chancellor to where Spyros and Talus were waiting in a donkey drawn cart. There were about sixteen large wine casks on the open cart. The chancellor, Lord Charlemont and Alex got on to the riding seat at the front, while the two notables sat in the back with the casks. With a crack of the whip, they set off.

They had barely started when they came across a large crowd in one of the smaller squares. Lord Charlemont pulled back sharply on the reins, bringing them to a halt again.

'What's going on here?' he demanded, applying the cart's brake.

It seemed like a large proportion of the village had gathered. All looked worried, and there was a low murmur of fearful whispering circulating, which stopped abruptly when they became aware of the cart and its occupants.

'We go on,' declared the chancellor, releasing the brake and cracking the whip again. They set off, aware of a few hundred pairs of eyes watching them furtively as they passed. It was unnerving.

'What was all that about?' asked Lord Charlemont.

'This is one of the ways they control us,' said the chancellor as they swayed from side to side on the cart. 'This wine is for the Full Moon Feast tonight at the fortress, but this is only for the priesthood. The warriors are...' he searched for the right phrase '...in *some* ways more base. They celebrate the full moon in a different way.'

'Go on,' prompted Lord Charlemont.

'All those you saw have to take part in a lottery. The two who lose have to present themselves at the fortress gates at sunset. The same thing happens in all the five villages left on the island. At the gates they are met by the Rakshasa, who braid ribbons of a particular colour into each unfortunate's hair. They then take some of their clothing from them. As soon as the sun has set, they are given a head start of about half an hour, using one of their damned sand timers...'

'You mean they're hunted?' asked Lord Charlemont, a look of fascination on his face.

'Yes, by the warriors hunting in packs, wearing ribbons the colour of the runner they've been assigned to. The clothing is used in order to familiarise them with a particular runner's scent – they don't need to use dogs. The runners' objective is to reach the watchtower on Mt Prophet Elias. If they make it, they are given shelter by the Rakshasa on duty there.'

'And if they don't?' asked Lord Charlemont, verbalising the question that Alex had not had the heart to ask.

The chancellor's shoulders slumped slightly. 'We find what's left of them a few days later – usually with their hearts missing.'

Alex silently shook his head in disgust.

'The warriors then feast up in the ruins of Ancient Thera, eating and drinking themselves senseless until dawn. The next day there is a constant stream of Rakshasa warriors making their way back to the fortress.'

They trundled on through the warm air.

'How is it you, Talus and Spyro were not in the draw today?' Lord Charlemont asked suddenly.

This question obviously needled the chancellor, but he answered it anyway.

'Only those who have come of age but are younger than two score years have to take part,' he explained, his face grim. 'Mothers with suckling infants are excused, otherwise there are no exceptions.'

'So, was your name ever drawn?' Lord Charlemont persisted.

'Yes. Twice. Each time I made it to the watchtower,' the chancellor snapped. 'Is there anything else you would like to know?'

The rest of the journey was spent in silence.

*

They halted at St Catherine's Church and hid their cloaks nearby, helped the two notables climb into empty casks, and quickly sealed them in. They then carried on towards the fortress. As they approached the gates, Lord Charlemont leaned over to the chancellor, taking out a waxed cylinder from his jacket.

'Just before we head in there,' he said, 'please remember I have this list of demands for the pact with your name and seal on it. If you betray us…' He waved the cylinder back and forth.

'There is nothing to worry about,' insisted the chancellor, clearly annoyed.

The gates were opened by a hidden mechanism that they could faintly hear. Two Rakshasa came out carrying muskets, each wearing a close-fitting chain mail suit, tight fitting silver helmets, and their faces obscured by the cyclopean masks. A guttural hissing conversation took place between them and the chancellor, and then they moved closer to the cart. The guard on Alex's side suddenly grabbed him by the sleeve of his coat, pulled it towards him and sniffed the material, Alex having to fight the instinct to draw his pistol. Seemingly satisfied, the Rakshasa released his arm, stepped back and waved them on.

Within a few seconds they were inside the fortress gates. Almost immediately the smell and sounds of horses greeted them – on both sides of the gateway were large stables with rooms above that were shuttered against the afternoon sun. The next moment the cart was heading to the right uphill, and then turned to traverse a road for a hundred feet or so. It went down and then seemed to do a U-turn and head upwards again. This went on for some time as they made their way through the maze of streets that Helena had described. Despite this, Alex managed to mentally track their route from the diagram Helena had drawn for them.

*

At the palace gates, guards came out again and smelt them before letting them pass. There was a spacious courtyard inside, and the cart came to a halt at the far end of it by a large double trapdoor. The chancellor opened the trapdoors. Carefully the three of them unloaded the barrels containing the two notables, lowering them gently from the cart, and then down a short ramp into the cellar. Once the barrels containing the notables were safely out of sight, they slid down the short ramp to join them and found themselves in a wine cellar illuminated by strange blue lamps. Barrels were stacked up on either side of them, and at the far end steps led up to another door. Using crowbars they prised the lids off the barrels and helped Spyros and Talus out.

'We are now below the palace itself,' whispered the chancellor, a torch in his hand. 'That door there,' he said, pointing to the far door, 'leads into the kitchens. From there we will pass through the Great Hall, and then will make our way through the Hall of Trophies. There shouldn't be any Rakshasa about, but we must be careful.'

The Englishmen nodded silently in agreement, and then pumped up their air pistols.

The chancellor led the way through the cellar, up the steps, and then carefully opened the door, checking round before signalling for them to follow. Behind them the two notables had started lowering the other wine barrels into the cellar.

They passed through what looked like fairly ordinary kitchens, but one door to the side, flanked by two bloodied butcher's slabs, attracted Lord Charlemont's attention.

'What is in there?' he asked.

The chancellor followed his gaze. 'Meat,' he said simply.

Alex glanced over and just made out carcasses hanging silently in the gloom within, the shape of which he did not recognise. But then the chancellor was urging them on, and he did not get a closer look.

The kitchen led directly into the Great Hall, the entrance to it being in the middle of two large fireplaces, each big enough to roast an ox. Countless tables, each with its own ivory candelabra, stretched into the gloom. As they skirted round the fireplace, Alex noticed a large banner on the chimney breast above the fire. It had the same silver insignia that he had seen on the shields of the Rakshasa, set on a black background. Now he realised that it was similar to the face of the Man in the Moon – except that it had been warped into a demonic, snarling fanged creature with a flowing mane. Fascinated, he stumbled into a bench and sprawled into a table. The table's three pronged candelabra was knocked over by the force of his collision, and instinctively he reached out and managed to grab it before it hit the table.

'Idiot!' hissed the chancellor.

Lord Charlemont was staring at him – but then Alex realised the object of his attention was not himself, but the candelabra. He looked at it, and to his horror it dawned on him that it was made up of human bones, a skull cleverly positioned mid-way up the base. He almost dropped it, but managed to control himself and carefully place it down.

'Straighten the bench,' commanded the chancellor, then led the way on.

*

Doors at the end of the Great Hall led them into a long, wide hallway, into which sunlight streamed at a forty-five degree angle, illuminating one side of the hall and casting the other into gloom. Along each side of it were what at first glance appeared to be tailors' dummies, each dressed in a different and colourful way. Between the two lines, a thick, lush scarlet carpet stretched out into the gloom at the far side of the hall. On the walls behind them were oil paintings of various sizes, all depicting what appeared to be military figures.

As they drew closer, Alex realised with a shock that each dummy was a mounted human skeleton, wearing the uniform and headdress that its owner presumably had worn when they were killed.

'A trophy room indeed,' muttered Lord Charlemont.

The uniforms themselves were no ordinary ones. None was less than the rank of captain, and they came from all the great seafaring nations – England, Spain, The Netherlands, Portugal and the Ottoman Empire. Most of the skulls were complete; others had parts of jaw bones missing, or holes in the skull where musket shots had entered. Fascinated, they walked slowly past them. There was even an extremely colourful Barbary pirate, canines sharpened to points, complete with the plaited wig he presumably had used during his life. Or was it his actual scalp? A painting behind each depicted a captain from that particular nation, standing proudly in their dress uniform, usually in some nautical situation, their jaws invariably jutting out.

The chancellor was halfway down the hall when he realised they had dropped behind. 'Hurry,' he urged.

They made as if to follow, but Alex suddenly grasped Lord Charlemont by the shoulder, drawing him up sharply.

'What is it, Hurst?' Lord Charlemont demanded.

'This one…' replied Alex, his voice trailing off. The coat was bright yellow – one that you would not expect its owner to be wearing in battle. The skull had a hole in it, exactly in the centre of its forehead. He took the lapel of the jacket between his thumb and index finger, and slowly turned it out. Inside it were embroidered the letters "GT".

'It's his uniform all right.'

'Whose uniform?'

'Captain Godfrey Todd's!'

Alex let go of the lapel, stepping back to get a better overall view. The portrait behind was that of a Royal Naval captain, but was clearly from a much earlier period.

'So is this how the Rakshasa reward their own?' muttered Lord Charlemont in disbelief.

'Come on!' hissed the chancellor from the gloom ahead.

They left Captain Todd there in a bright shaft of sunlight, standing stiffly to attention for his masters, and ran down the hall to join the chancellor.

CHAPTER 26

At the end of the Hall of Trophies, the chancellor led them through another door into a large well lit corridor at right angles to the hall, from which there were a few doors off on either side. It was lined with narrow tables upon which were dried flowers in Chinese vases, and tapestries hung from the walls. This time Lord Charlemont stopped.

'Look here,' he directed Alex.

The tapestry he was looking at was maybe twenty-five feet by ten, and appeared, by the trees and landscape woven into it, to depict some scene in northern Europe. Snow was on the hills in the background, and oaks, ashes and elms could be made out. In the foreground was a fortress, inside which was a palace very similar to the one they were in, with two domed towers and an almost flat roofed mid-section. A battle raged round the fortress and armies were arranged before it. It was a figure in this army that had attracted Lord Charlemont's attention. Alex looked closer – and to his surprise recognised the soldiers as being Spanish, albeit of a previous era.

'You see them?' asked Lord Charlemont.

'Yes, but this would mean the Spanish were aware of the Rakshasa years ago.'

'Quite. Now, look at these,' Lord Charlemont continued, shifting his attention to the rear of the besieging army.

Clearly depicted were members of the Spanish Inquisition, down to their distinctive pointed red hoods and the large crosses they carried before them. They stood near covered carriages by which braziers glowed. The detail was incredible, and Alex guessed the tapestry had been woven from silk.

'And these.'

Further back were what looked like oriental monks, their heads shaven, carrying large scrolls.

'Who are they?' asked Alex.

'Buddhist monks' came the reply, and Lord Charlemont pointed lower down. Into the bottom border of the tapestry were woven rune-like symbols.

The chancellor had doubled back to them and was looking worried.

'We must go,' he said urgently.

'What does this say?' Lord Charlemont asked, ignoring his plea.

'The Day of Shame,' he replied without even looking at it.

'And what does it *mean*?' persisted Lord Charlemont.

'I do not know – look we *must* get out of sight.'

'Very well, but we will talk of this later,' declared Lord Charlemont, and he followed the chancellor down the corridor.

They passed another similar sized tapestry, but Alex only managed to get a glance at it. It depicted a mountainous, arid valley. A mass of what he assumed were Rakshasa were in the base of the valley, with a number of the scarlet ones leading them. On the slopes of the hills all around them were what looked like Ottoman janissaries, armed to the teeth. He had no time for further examination as the chancellor had reached a door to their right and quickly turned into it. He then led them down some stairs into a passageway that sloped gently down, the floor of which was rough stone and gravel in contrast to the paved floors in the rest of the palace. It was pitch dark inside, until the chancellor lit the torch he had brought with him.

'Follow me,' he said, and walked on into the gloom. 'This is one of the original streets out of the old town of Merovigli, leading south,' he explained as they walked along the passageway. 'The Rakshasa built over it, and it is down here we will find their Achilles heel.'

He led the way for a few moments and then halted in front of a door to their left.

'Here it is,' he said. Before either of them could react he sprang forward and, with a flourish, pulled the door open.

The Englishmen both gasped in astonishment as they saw what lay within in the half-light. Before them was a space the size of a broom cupboard – filled from floor to ceiling with every conceivable form of shaped gold possible. If was as if a gold avalanche had swept down from some hillside and finally come to rest in front of them. There were gold goblets, plates, cups, knives, forks and spoons; gold amulets; jewel encrusted gold; gold worked in with other metals in braids; gold necklaces; ornamental gold knives, swords, muskets and armour; gold death masks, funeral decorations, and embalming jars. There was even, Alex noticed, a gold toothpick lying on the floor near to the door. The space contained more gold than Alex had seen in his entire life.

'By Jove!' exclaimed Lord Charlemont, crossing the threshold and looking up into the darkness above the door, then on tip-toes trying to look beyond the gold. 'How far does this room extend back?'

'I'll show you in a moment,' replied the chancellor, watching their reactions, a wry smile on his face.

'How much would you say this lot is worth, Hurst?' asked Lord Charlemont.

'Well, it's been a long time since I worked with my father, and he worked with silver, not gold…' Alex began.

'Roughly, man!' Lord Charlemont snapped.

Alex considered for a few moments. 'At a guess, between one and two hundred thousand pounds,' he finally ventured, looking first at Lord Charlemont and then the chancellor. 'A simple labourer in England earns about fifteen pounds a year.'

'Well, it's hardly a king's ransom,' observed Lord Charlemont, studying the riches before him. 'But it's a lord's ransom – maybe.' He turned to the chancellor. 'Why isn't this guarded?'

'To the Rakshasa, silver is the most highly prized metal. To them, gold is merely a means of purchasing supplies from the rest of the world,' he explained.

'That would make sense,' agreed Lord Charlemont, absentmindedly picking up a gold plate and examining it. 'Esoterically speaking, silver is associated with the moon, which the Rakshasa would appear to worship.'

'So this is their Achilles heel?' asked Alex.

'There is something else you must see first,' replied the chancellor, 'and then all will become clear. Come this way.'

They continued along the passageway for another twenty-five yards or so, then up some stairs into another passageway that stretched off to their left. The chancellor led the way, but after about ten yards stopped abruptly. Alex could just make out the outline of a large circular opening in the wall to his left. To the right were regular sized double doors, elaborately decorated with iron work in the manner he had seen on the fortress gate. He guessed the doors led out somewhere into the fortress.

Without a word, the chancellor stepped over the lower rim of the circular entrance and slipped inside as, by accident or design, his torch began to burn out. Lord Charlemont hesitated, and then drew out his air gun and followed him in. Alex drew his, and stepped after them, just able to make out where he was going before the light faded completely.

Inside, Alex sensed the chancellor was nearby, lighting another torch, and was also aware, from the subtle way that the sound had changed, that they had entered a much larger space than the passageway. They seemed to be on some sort of wooden platform as opposed to solid ground.

'Now, follow me,' commanded the chancellor as he led the way forward, the torch spluttering as it began to catch. They reached a handrail after a few paces and paused on either side of him, waiting for the torch to catch properly.

'The church your women attend each day is the Latin Church of St Catherine,' the chancellor began. 'What I did not tell you is that it was built only fifty years ago, and is a smaller copy of an older one. We are now inside the original, build almost one hundred and fifty years ago by the Dominican nuns. For reasons that we never discovered, the Rakshasa dismantled it, moved it from its original location near Fira, and rebuilt it here, before building the fortress over it.'

They were both watching him cautiously, neither knowing where this was leading.

'What we are standing on now is the choir loft.' The torch finally caught and he held it high above himself. 'And down below us is the church itself,' he continued, gesturing below with his free hand.

They turned in unison to look down – and for the second time that day, both gasped in astonishment. Below them, glittering in the torchlight, was what seemed to be a frozen sea of gold; waves of it ran up the sides of the church, obscuring doors and windows, and one huge wave swept right up to the level of the choir loft, just below their feet. Over to their left, just discernible in the gloom above the sea of gold, was the lintel of the door that the chancellor had opened a few minutes previously, when they thought they had been peering into a small room.

Lord Charlemont dropped his pistol and it fell to the floor with an almighty crash. He then fell to his knees, grasping the handrail in front of himself for support and gasping like a landed fish. Alex was rooted to the spot with awe. The chancellor walked from side to side on the platform, waving the torch round to illuminate different parts of the church, making the gold objects glisten as if they were alive.

'I present you with the results of almost one hundred years of Rakshasa pillaging on the high seas,' he announced. 'African, Egyptian and Indian gold. Gold from the New World, gold from history. Coins from the time of Alexander the Great to the last of the Roman emperors, crowns worn by Cleopatra, golden idols of Baal worshipped in Carthage, and present day gold from the seals of the Celestial Emperor to jewellery intended for Queen Sofia of Spain. It's all here.' His voice dropped to a more sombre note. 'I tell you seriously, gentlemen, this must be the greatest concentration of gold and treasure ever assembled in the history of Mankind!'

He paused, turning to Lord Charlemont.

'Perhaps *this* would be a king's ransom, Lord Charlemont,' he speculated. 'Or, maybe, an *emperor's* ransom.'

Lord Charlemont shook his head in awe at what lay before him. 'An empire,' he muttered.

'What was that?' asked the chancellor jovially, enjoying their reaction.

'One could buy an empire with this,' replied Lord Charlemont, his voice weak, not taking his eyes off the spectacle before him.

Alex lowered his pistol and walked over to the handrail. He too began to feel weak at the knees as the implications of the hoard's value sank in. What was it worth? The church measured about one hundred feet long by forty feet wide, and on average the depth of the gold was probably about six or seven feet. Maybe two million pounds? Three? Even four? Who could say? He tried making a calculation, but was overwhelmed by what he saw and finally gave up. He turned to the chancellor.

'*This* is their Achilles heel?' he asked.

'Yes,' said the chancellor, smiling grimly. 'Which nation would *not* attack this fortress, knowing that this was here?'

'Wait!' exclaimed Lord Charlemont. 'This could be a trick. Chancellor, the torch!' he ordered, pulling himself shakily to his feet.

'Of course,' agreed the chancellor, handing it to him. 'No!' he then shouted, seeing what Lord Charlemont was about to do.

Lord Charlemont had perched himself up on the handrail, and then swung his legs over it before allowing himself to drop on to the gold that sloped up to the choir loft. He staggered in it, crashing round as he tried to find support, before throwing himself back towards the loft and grasping the supports of the handrail. He stood there gasping for breath, searching for solid support beneath his feet. Finding it, he staggered off down the slope, bringing a mini-avalanche with him as he went and taking the sphere of light generated by the torch.

'This can't all be gold,' Alex heard him shouting above the cacophony of sound he had generated. 'It can't be!'

*

It was some time before the chancellor managed to get them out of the church. The Englishmen, still stunned by what they had seen, followed the chancellor back down to the old street, and finally up the stairs to the door leading into the fortress proper. At the door, the chancellor went first, and was halfway out when he suddenly sprang back.

'Rakshasa!' he whispered, and dragged Lord Charlemont by the arm towards a bricked up doorway, Alex following on behind, and they crammed themselves under the stone archway.

The door to the corridor opened and light streamed in. They were, however, in the shadow of the arch, hidden from view. A long shadow was cast on to the passageway floor, and words, spoken in the hissing guttural language, drifted down towards them. There was an expectant silence, and then the door was shut.

'What did he say?' asked Lord Charlemont.

'*She* said: "Is there anybody there?"' replied the chancellor. 'I think we were just unlucky then, they should all be asleep now. Let's try again.'

Gingerly they approached the door. This time the chancellor produced a small mirror on the end of a slender arm of metal that was hinged like a spectacle arm halfway along. Carefully manoeuvring it under the door, he used it to check the lie of the land before he opened the door again. He let them go first, and then carefully closed the door behind him. Alex got to the door of the Hall of Trophies first, and as a precaution ducked down to look through the keyhole. His heart leapt at what he saw – at least two dozen scarlet-clad Rakshasa priests were making their way down the hall towards him, three abreast in a stately even-paced procession, their long white hair swaying gently as they walked.

'Rakshasa coming down the Hall,' he hissed.

The chancellor looked worried. 'I don't understand,' he said. 'They usually don't get up before sunset.'

'We need to get *out*,' Lord Charlemont urged him. 'Think, man! What about the church?'

'No – they are in and out of that all the time they are awake. Down here,' he said, and led them back down the corridor, past the door they had used to get to the old church. After about twenty yards, the corridor turned off to their right. The chancellor stopped at the corner and used his mirror again. 'More coming that way,' he said grimly. 'We'll go back.'

They retraced their steps for about ten yards. 'The ones that I saw will be through that door at any moment,' warned Alex.

They were trapped. As the sound of footsteps grew louder, the Englishmen cocked their air pistols and drew out their hunting knives.

CHAPTER 27

The chancellor suddenly stopped at a table and ducked down. There was a half-height door below it.

'In here,' he ordered, pulling the door open. They scrambled in, the chancellor pulling the door shut gently behind him. They crouched there in darkness and silence, and then heard the measured heavy tread of several dozen feet on the stone floor outside. They waited for a few minutes, and then the chancellor carefully opened the door a crack and used his mirror again. He snapped the door shut suddenly, and seconds later there was the sound of running feet outside.

'The servants are up and about,' he said, obviously mystified.

'What's happening?' demanded Lord Charlemont.

'It would appear that the whole palace is waking up,' the chancellor replied, a tone of resignation in his voice. He lit the torch again, revealing that they were in a low roofed passageway, the end of which was lost in the gloom.

'So, what do we do now?' asked Lord Charlemont with more than a hint of sarcasm.

'Well,' said the chancellor, 'it's too risky to move now. For some reason they are all getting up. I suggest we stay here till tomorrow morning – my men will return then to take back the empty barrels. In the meantime, we can either stay here, or carry on up to the balcony of the northern temple. We'd have more room there, and we won't have to use the torch.'

'That sounds the best option,' agreed Lord Charlemont. 'Lead the way.'

'Hold on a moment,' protested Alex. 'What is this passageway used for?'

'You've seen the blue lanterns on the domes?' the chancellor asked.

Alex nodded. 'This is how they get up to them to replenish the fuel.'

'What is it that they use for fuel?' asked Alex.

'I have no idea!' replied the chancellor impatiently. 'Now, shall we go?'

They followed him along the passageway, almost bent double because of the low ceiling, and then came to a stone spiral staircase.

'I must warn you now,' said the chancellor, 'make the minimum of noise up here. We will be directly above their temple.'

He then carried on, and as they ascended, they became aware of the sound of chanting. 'I do not understand,' he exclaimed, extinguishing the torch as they reached the top of the staircase. 'It is far too early for them to have begun.'

The staircase opened out on to a small curved balcony about three feet wide and twenty feet long, bounded on one side by the wall of the temple and on the other by a wall about two feet high. At the far end was a door that presumably led to the lantern on top of the dome. There was just enough room for them all to stretch out on the balcony. The roof above them was domed, with light streaming in through windows just below its rim, and Alex realised a large circular hall was below them.

*

Time passed. The sickly sweet smell of stale incense hung in the air trapped in the roof of the dome, and it was uncomfortably hot. From below came a ceaseless deep bass chant that now seemed to pulsate around Alex, bringing with it a rising tide of seductive stillness which he could not resist; it was as soporific as a Gregorian chant. His eyelids became heavy and he could no longer keep them open. He sank further on to the balcony floor, his body like that of a ragdoll.

'What time is it?' he managed to ask Lord Charlemont in a whisper.

There was a brief pause as Lord Charlemont struggled to remove his watch from a pocket. 'Half past three,' he replied. 'Though I think it's losing time. Must be the heat…'

Time collapsed to a point, and Alex was in a moment that felt as if it would last forever, until the sound of horns far away summoned him back from the stillness.

'What's that?' he asked drowsily, too tired to open his eyes.

'If I'm not mistaken – hunting horns,' replied Lord Charlemont from some incredible distance away.

The stillness engulfed him again.

*

Alex woke with a start. It was dark, and the chanting below was growing stronger as more voices joined in with it.

'What time is it?' he asked, disorientated by his dreamless sleep, but at the same time feeling refreshed and alert.

'A quarter of eleven. Things are warming up down below – the tempo of the chanting has changed completely. Want a look?' Lord Charlemont passed him the chancellor's mirror-on-a-stick.

He took the device from Lord Charlemont and, propping himself up on one elbow, carefully angled the mirror over the balcony wall to study the temple. The building itself was elegant in structure and now illuminated solely by the full moon that had risen outside. Thirteen large marble pillars around its perimeter would have naturally raised one's gaze upwards to the domed roof that was two hundred feet above the floor. No other supporting structures for the dome were in sight, but its diameter was around one hundred and fifty feet. The dome, Lord Charlemont was later to tell him, compared well with the largest raised by Christendom or Islam. Between the pillars hung long crimson pendants, embroidered in silver thread with dragons, griffins, Minotaurs and other demonic looking creatures he did not recognise. The marble pillars themselves, he now noticed, were brilliant white in colour, but naturally flecked with varying shades of red. He asked the chancellor where that particular type of marble came from.

'Hell – probably,' replied the chancellor from where he lay without opening his eyes.

Concentric steps led from the base of the pillars down to the main floor. Directly in the centre of the floor was a circular white and red flecked marble dais, maybe twenty feet in diameter, which was completely devoid of decoration save for a single red cushion in its centre. Surrounding the dais were concentric rings of wide low benches, covered in scarlet velvet. The only break in the benches was to allow a purple carpet to run from the dais under their balcony and out of sight. With the gentle light of the moon illuminating it, the whole scene had an almost dreamlike quality about it.

On the opposite side of the chamber to them, at the top of the concentric steps, was an age worn white marble slab, about seven feet by three, that had the appearance of an altar, and on which there were various large silver ornaments arranged, but he could not make out what they were. Behind the altar was a large mirror, flanked on either side by an alcove that was about nine feet high and five feet wide, topped by a graceful arch. In each was the statue of a remarkably ugly idol. One was purple skinned, the other black. Studying the nearest one, Alex could see that it had the face of a demon, with a forked tongue and large, insane-looking eyes, its open jaws lined with ferocious teeth. It had four arms, and in its taloned hands it had a sword, dagger, some sort of double-sided mace and a freshly severed human head held by the hair. Finally, under its clawed feet was sculpted the body of a prone man, arms outstretched as if pleading, his face frozen in a death agony. Alex studied the other statue, and after a few seconds realised it was identical in all respects except colour.

He turned his attention back to the mirror. It was large, maybe thirty-five feet high and fifteen feet wide, and dominated the temple. But there was something wrong with it. He varied the angle of the mirror he was holding, but no matter how he looked at it, the surface of the large mirror appeared to be jet black, as if it were made of obsidian. All around the silver frame were words inscribed in gold in a flowing script different to the harsh and angular rune-like script they had seen on the tapestry. At each corner of the frame was a huge clawed hand that appeared to act as the attachment for the mirror to the wall behind it, and between each hand, along the edges of the mirror, were seven evenly spaced stubby spikes. He was about to move on when something about the hands caught his eye. At first he thought it was just the fact that each had four taloned fingers and two opposing taloned thumbs, but then he realised it was something else. Looking at them, it seemed that the clawed hands were gently, almost imperceptibly, tightening and loosening their grip on the stone work behind them in time to the pulse of the chant. He closed his eyes, rubbed them and looked away;

he assumed he was seeing things in the cold light of the moon.

On the floor of the temple itself were a large number of the Rakshasa priesthood, maybe one hundred and fifty, their scarlet cloaks pulled snugly round them, hoods up as they sat on the concentric benches around the centre. More were coming in to join them as Alex watched.

Incense sticks burnt, supported in large sand filled vessels scattered around the room. There were also large black candles atop elegant black metal stands all around the hall, but they remained unlit. Other members of the priesthood, who he took to be novices, were dressed in simple scarlet tunics and were moving in and out of the temple with what looked like huge silver teapots. They used these to re-fill silver goblets, which stood in front of each of the chanting ones, with a steaming liquid. Occasionally a chanting priest would reach out from his cloak, down the goblet of liquid in one go, and then return to the chant. As soon as an empty goblet was spotted, it would be refilled immediately.

'You were lucky you slept,' declared Lord Charlemont after Alex had finished surveying the temple, 'this chanting has been driving me to distraction.'

'What do you think of the mirror?' Alex asked.

'Korthdan probably coiffeurs his hair in front of it every day,' was the sarcastic reply. 'Why, what about it?'

'There's something unusual about it – more than just the fact its surface is black. I can't put my finger on it.'

'Black?' exclaimed Lord Charlemont, looking puzzled. He took the mirror from Alex and peered over the balcony. 'You're right. How bizarre. It looked like a normal mirror earlier on.'

'What about those idols? Have you ever seen anything like them?'

'As a matter of fact, yes I have. They're similar to the protector demon one would find in certain Buddhist temples.'

'The Buddhists worship such idols?'

'Not exactly. The idol is usually hidden away in a side chapel, but offerings are made to it to protect the temple from *other* demons.'

Alex paused, taking this information in, and then turned to the chancellor, who was resting, eyes closed, near his feet. 'Is this where the Full Moon Feast is going to take place?'

'What?' asked the chancellor. Alex repeated the question, and he gave a deep heartfelt sigh. 'Yes,' he said, 'I am afraid it is. Please tell me when it gets near to midnight and I'll go downstairs. I witnessed one once, many years ago, and that was enough.'

'Why, what happens?' asked Lord Charlemont.

The chancellor shifted his position slightly, his manner becoming evasive. 'I don't want to tell you,' he said. 'It would bring back the memories which I'm trying to forget. I still have nightmares about it.' He then looked at them both sternly. 'I'm telling you, come downstairs with me when it starts. It is something you don't want to witness.'

'So it starts at midnight?' persisted Lord Charlemont.

'Yes,' replied the chancellor wearily. 'The chanting stops a short time before.' He closed his eyes again, laying his head back on the floor. 'And then *it* starts!'

*

More time passed, and, if anything, the chanting grew more intense and deeper, soon seeming to resonate the very walls of the temple itself. Each chant now seemed to have an almost physical force behind it, quite apart from that of the actual sound, that they all could feel each time it was expressed.

The chancellor was looking worried. 'It was not like this last time,' he said, raising his voice to be heard. 'Something different is happening tonight, I am sure of it.'

'What?' asked Lord Charlemont.

'I don't know!'

Almost simultaneously there was a palpable ripple of excitement from below and the sound of movement. Using the mirror, Alex could see that the priests' number had grown to at least two hundred. The ones on either side of the aisle were looking over their shoulders at someone making his way to the centre, their lips still moving to the chant. The figure was tall, wearing a long flowing purple cloak, but with the hood down, and was definitely male. On his head was a braided silver headband, and he had long grey hair that just passed his shoulders. Walking with a regal tread, he approached the dais. It had to be Korthdan. He walked up to the dais, stepped on to it, and then faced the direction he had come and sat down cross-legged on the cushion, wrapping his cloak round him. Alex could see that his eyes were closed, as if he was engaged in some inner concentration.

'What's happening?' asked Lord Charlemont.

'It's Korthdan – I'm sure of it,' replied Alex, handing him the mirrored device.

Lord Charlemont had a look and then passed it to the chancellor, who confirmed Alex's guess.

'He doesn't usually attend these feasts,' the chancellor said over the rising crescendo of the chant from below. 'I am going now,' he added, passing the mirror back and making as if to move.

'No,' ordered Lord Charlemont. 'He may speak. I want you here – it's all part of the deal!'

The chancellor looked at Lord Charlemont, clearly shocked at the thought of having to stay one moment longer, but then he reconsidered.

'Very well,' he said, 'but if the feast does take place, I'm leaving. Once it starts, not even Korthdan will be heard.'

'There's something happening,' announced Lord Charlemont presently as he moved the mirror round to get a view directly below the balcony. He looked intently for a few seconds, and then started back in shock. He faced Alex, a pleading look in his eyes while thrusting the mirror towards him.

'Tell me I'm wrong,' he blurted out.

At that moment the chanting stopped with an almost brutal abruptness, to be replaced by an expectant silence. Alex quickly positioned the mirror to see what was happening. Below them, walking with a slow measured pace, was a smaller figure wearing a long purple dress, decorated with obscure patterns embroidered in silver. With a start Alex realised it was Isabelle but, save for her long blonde hair, he would hardly have recognised her. She walked bolt upright, with a haughty demeanour, her head slightly tilted back as she surveyed those around her. She had large silver bangles on her wrists, with finer ones on her ankles, which glistened in the moonlight. Her long hair had been tied into two braids, with jewel encrusted clasps, and a purple silk scarf was tied loosely around her neck.

Korthdan rose as she approached, as did the rest of Rakshasa, but not one uttered a sound as she walked with bare feet over the thick purple carpet beneath her. As she reached Korthdan she looked at him briefly, then lowered her head in a gesture of respect. As he held his left hand out Isabelle took the proffered hand with her right one, and then turned to face the way she had come, their hands now formally clasped between them at her shoulder height. A dreadful realization began to fill Alex at the sight of the ancient vampire lightly clasping Isabelle's hand – but the sight of her face as she raised her head back up again shocked him to the core.

Instead of Isabelle's serene and pleasant face, he saw a harsh and pitiless visage which viewed the assembled Rakshasa calmly and coldly, lips set in a contemptuous smile below heavily lidded eyes which were now a dazzling ice blue. Still the Rakshasa made no sound, and it was impossible to know if they revered, or even feared, this lone human in their midst. The couple stood there for a while longer, then two scarlet clad priests approached, one bearing a scarlet cushion upon which lay a fine silver chain. They bowed as they reached Korthdan and Isabelle, then one stood to face the assembly and began speaking.

Lord Charlemont, over his initial shock, had moved closer to Alex so he too could view the scene below. At the priest's voice he turned his head slightly and looked questioningly at the chancellor.

'It is not the normal tongue,' the other whispered. 'I do not know what he is saying.'

Lord Charlemont shook his head in disgust and turned his attention back to the mirror that Alex held.

'Surely you know what this is?' hissed Alex, his voice shaking with anger.

Lord Charlemont stared at him uncomprehendingly for a moment, then looked back at the scene below – and realization finally dawned on him.

'My God! No – say it is not!' he exclaimed in a strangled whisper.

As one priest continued to speak, the other picked up the chain from the cushion. He then approached the couple and began gently winding the chain around their clasped hands. This done, he stood back as the other stopped speaking. Alex sensed a feeling of anticipation in the huge chamber and then Isabelle, with her free hand, began to slowly unwind the scarf from around her neck. With one last tug it was gone, and she turned slightly, tilting back her head and elongating her neck – to display two gaping punctures in her pale smooth skin, as if she had been attacked by some vicious animal.

Alex gasped in horror at what he could see, but at the sight of these hideous wounds a ripple of applause could be heard around the chamber, that quickly grew into a rapturous torrent as the previously silent Rakshasa began to cheer the couple, some of them slamming their goblets on the benches, others whooping with almost animal like cries of delight. The noise became deafening, but through it all Isabelle calmly surveyed the assembled throng with her pitiless gaze, seemingly unmoved by the outpouring of emotion around her. Alex glared at Lord Charlemont, but the other would not look at him.

At last Korthdan raised his hand and the commotion gradually died down. A priest returned to remove the chain and then Korthdan spoke some inaudible words to Isabelle. Without turning to look at him she bowed almost imperceptibly, and then released his hand and walked with a stately pace back the way she had come, and out of sight.

As she left, Lord Charlemont finally faced Alex, a haunted, devastated look in his eyes.

'What's the matter?' Alex goaded him. 'Upset for Lady Isabelle – or heartbroken over your precious treaty?'

At this, Lord Charlemont looked at him, silently mouthing the words 'The treaty', and then stared down at the floor, gasping for air, speechless for the first time since they had met.

They all sat there for a few minutes, Lord Charlemont's laboured gasps slowly returning to normal, while from below they heard the sound of goblets clinking as they knocked against the spouts of teapots, as well as a general murmur of conversation. At the sound of two claps the murmuring ceased almost instantly, replaced by another expectant silence. Shortly after that, a strong, resonant Rakshasa voice drifted up towards them.

'Korthdan,' the chancellor whispered.

Alex grabbed the mirror again and looked over. Korthdan now stood alone on the circular marble dais, giving a speech. Alex ducked back down as he realised the chancellor had started translating for Lord Charlemont.

'...Seven have just told me that the Inception was successful.' Isolated cries of joy greeted this statement, but they soon quietened down again. 'The Inception marks a new beginning for us, a new chapter in the history of the Most Holy Nation. This is a great night for us.' He paused. 'From this night forward we will begin to avenge the Day of Shame and blot it out from our memories. Almost one hundred years ago I led you here, a broken and rootless people, driven from our rightful home in fair...'

'I did not catch that,' said the chancellor.

'...and running from one land to another before the armies of the barbarians...'

'He means the armies of Man,' explained the chancellor.

'Since then we have been waiting – waiting for the stars in their courses to align favourably for us, for all the seeds we have sown since then to bear fruit, and for the world of the barbarians to turn on its axis and adjust its ways to accommodate us, while all the time planning for the future, building up our strength, our numbers and our faith in ourselves. Tonight was the night, as predicted by The Seven and our astrologer priests, for the next warrior high priest to be conceived, and the new history of the Rakshasa begins hereon from this moment. With it, in time, will come our new home – a proper homeland for us for the first time in living memory – and a security and prosperity that will last for millennia. No more will we run from the barbarians, or have to suffer their ignorance, abhorrence and gross mistreatment of our people.'

Korthdan paused as cheers burst out here and there from the gathering.

'No more will we have to hide ourselves away in fear and disguise ourselves from the vile barbarian. Henceforth, this night will be known as The Night of Glory!'

The applause gathered in strength, and then the whole assembly erupted in cheers and cries of triumph. Alex peered over the balcony again. Korthdan, his cadaverous face fixed in an expression of compassion and wisdom, had his hands held up above his head, palms outwards, and was taking the adulation from those gathered around him, slowly moving round so that all could see his face. All the priests now had their hoods down; some were weeping openly in apparent relief, while others looked up to Korthdan with undisguised love and admiration. Alex noticed that roughly half of them were female. Despite their similarity to the male priests due to their long hair, he sensed femininity in their faces, even though their fangs were now quite apparent as they smiled and cheered Korthdan. Korthdan finished his turn round the dais, and then slowly made his way off it, walking out along the aisle preceded by seven hooded priests that Alex had not noticed before. Noisy, excited conversation broke out amongst those gathered in the temple below when Korthdan had left, while on the balcony the two Englishmen were now even more despondent.

'Well,' said Lord Charlemont presently, having recovered some of his composure, 'I won't pretend I understood half of that, but it doesn't sound good. It would appear Lady Isabelle is to bear Korthdan a child – but why? Why not…' he paused, groping for a suitable word, but then gave up '…use one of their own?'

Alex shook his head. 'This whole situation is insane' was the only thing he could say. He noticed Lord Charlemont had a pencil and sheet of paper out, and was writing quickly on it. 'What are you doing?'

'I'm recording the speech,' Lord Charlemont replied without looking up. 'You never know, it might one day make sense to others.'

Alex turned to the chancellor. 'So that was it then?' he asked.

'That was what?' queried the chancellor.

'The Full Moon Feast?'

'No – in fact, I think it's just about to begin.'

CHAPTER 28

The conversation below died down, and then there was the sound of wood scraping on marble. Alex peered over with the mirror. The novices were clearing away the benches, two at a time carrying them out of the temple, while the priests stood around, yawning and stretching their arms and legs. Using long tapers, other novices were lighting the black candles, which Alex soon noticed gave off a sickly perfume. As the benches were slowly removed, Alex began to see that the floor was paved with the same white and red flecked marble as the pillars, but was decorated with inlaid black marble depicting huge profane looking symbols, arranged around the circumference of the main floor. At first he thought they were some representation of the zodiac, but then he counted and realised there were thirteen of them in total. Evenly spaced in a circle around the central dais were five pentangles which Alex at first thought were black inlaid marble, but then realised were the grates of drains, though he could not think why they would be needed in the temple.

'Look at this,' he said, passing the mirror to Lord Charlemont. 'It looks like another form of the zodiac.'

'Hmm, yes. Ancient Vedic astrology also uses thirteen signs in their zodiac,' he commented, and then returned to his scribbling.

'I'm going now,' announced the chancellor. 'And for the sake of your sanity, I would advise you to come with me!'

Lord Charlemont and Alex looked briefly at each other.

'We'll stay,' Lord Charlemont said. 'We need to know everything possible about these fiends, if we are to defeat them.'

'Very well. I will see you later.' And with that the chancellor disappeared down the stairs, taking his torch with him.

*

All the benches had now been cleared. Silence fell on the assembled priests, and Alex detected a subtle change of mood around the temple; it turned from one of relief, celebration and joy to that of excited pent-up carnal expectation. He picked up the emotion, experiencing it as if a hand were lightly gripping his stomach, his legs becoming weak and his whole body beginning to tremble slightly. Lord Charlemont was experiencing it also – his hand shook as he took the mirror from Alex. They huddled together and managed to position themselves and the mirror so that they could both see.

A number of new voices came up from below: frightened human voices. A crowd of about one hundred slaves was being herded into the temple by *kilij* wielding novices. The other Rakshasa stood back, arranged up on the steps surrounding the main floor as the slaves entered, watching them silently. The slaves undoubtedly included those that had been purchased from Mustafa, but now they were all wearing simple clean white tunics as the novices directed them on to the circular marble dais. Presently all were on it, the ones on the outer edges nervously holding on to ones further in for support. Still the Rakshasa watched silently. Then, from below the balcony came the sound of huge metal doors closing, and the mechanical sound of them being locked.

Alex's heart thumped at this sound and its implication.

The Rakshasa began to advance towards the dais. Some of the slaves on the outside, wide-eyed, cried out and tried to huddle closer together. With a shock, Alex recognised the slave girl who had temporarily escaped from the Rakshasa aboard their galley. She was at the edge of the dais closest to them and looked as if she were going to run for it again.

The Rakshasa were now at the dais. They started circling it like wolves round tethered goats, looking at those on it in intense fascination, as if they had never seen humans before.

Suddenly a female Rakshasa lunged forward with a blood-curdling cry, grasping a male slave by the neck and pulling him off the dais and on to the floor, before stooping down over him and burying her fangs in his throat. Other females leapt on his body and held him down, their mouths diving to his throat as a pool of blood quickly formed under him. Screams erupted from the dais, and then all the Rakshasa surged forward in ones and twos, pulling their victims from where they stood and out on to the marbled floor, where they were immediately slain.

Carnage was everywhere, but still Lord Charlemont and Alex could not tear their eyes away. Two of the young male slaves managed to break away from the dais, and ended up with their backs to a pillar while a group of male Rakshasa closed slowly in on them. They had picked up a metal candle stand each and were swinging them skilfully, making a good job of keeping the Rakshasa at bay until they were rushed by the Rakshasa, and overpowered.

Suddenly Alex realised he was kneeling looking at the scene of carnage – *over the edge of the balcony.* So was Lord Charlemont. There, on the floor of the balcony, was the mirror, though he could not remember them having discarded it. He quickly grasped Lord Charlemont by the arm and pulled him down. Screams and shouts of terror filled the air, echoing around the inside of the dome. They both made to move towards the spiral staircase, but the scene below had unnerved them so much that neither dared cross the threshold and descend into the darkness. Instead, they lay again on the balcony floor. Alex blocked his ears with his hands and wished he had taken the chancellor's advice, but when he closed his eyes all he could see were the terrified and pleading faces of the slaves.

*

The night wore on. The pitiful pleading, shouts and screams of terror from below had seemed to last an age before finally dying away. However, when, with shaking hands, Lord Charlemont consulted his watch, the time was barely three o'clock.

Alex sat back on the balcony, numbed at what he had seen. Lord Charlemont made as if to take the mirror from him, but then changed his mind and slumped down again. They sat there for hours, and only when the sun had actually risen above the horizon did they dare descend the spiral staircase. The chancellor was in better shape than them, having stuffed his ears with wax, and had actually managed to get some sleep, huddled by himself at the bottom of the spiral staircase. He shook his head in disgust when he saw the looks on their faces, but said nothing. The palace soon quietened down, and at around eleven o'clock they made their way to the wine cellars. From there they travelled back, without further incident, to Pyrgos with the notables on the wine cart.

CHAPTER 29

The next day Alex set off for Fira. He was dreading breaking the news about the hellish night to Helena, but he had left the chancellor in a good mood. The two young women who had been selected by the lottery the day before had made it to the watchtower, and a festival was being held in the village to celebrate their safe return.

Presently Helena arrived – in floods of tears.

'My poor sister,' she kept on repeating, shaking her head, and for a time was inconsolable, her eyes puffy with crying from the night before. At last she managed to compose herself and spoke.

'While serving food to me last night, one of Zentar's wives told me my sister had had a great *honour* bestowed on her.' She paused.

'Go on,' prompted Alex with a feeling of trepidation.

'She started talking about the Rakshasa, and how they were "a nation with no country to call their own".' Helena wiped tears from her face. 'And then she said that their priests had foretold, years ago, that an opportunity would arise whereby they could claim a whole country on this earth for their own. By some unholy means, they somehow knew about this whole trade agreement business, and that is why they kidnapped us. My sister...' She choked back more tears. 'Isabelle was to be kidnapped, and then sent on to the emir of Egypt. The Rakshasa are to ensure that the son she is to bear for him – and they are certain it will be a male – will somehow be brought up in their foul ways and will become the emir when his father passes away. In time, the Rakshasa will move to Egypt under his protection and have the mechanisms and resources of that entire country at their command.'

She lowered her voice. 'Somehow, on that night a child was conceived – but on another plane of existence – the astral plane. She said the astral child will wait there for almost a year, or rather thirteen full moons, and when the emir does actually…' she shuddered '…possess my sister, the astral child will take the place of the one conceived by him and then be born naturally.'

'This is madness!' Alex muttered.

'I know!' she retorted. 'But I can only tell you what she told me. And it somehow seems to make sense. It explains a lot of things, does it not?'

Alex made no reply, thinking through the implications of this latest piece of news.

'But what about you? Did you get into the fortress?' She grasped his hand. 'Did you see her?'

Alex hesitated.

'Well?' she persisted.

Reluctantly Alex related they had witnessed, and Helena was silent for a while afterwards.

'So… Has she has become one of them?' she finally asked.

'I don't know – but what about Zentar?' Alex demanded between gritted teeth, forcing himself to stay calm. 'Why did he not tell you all this himself?'

'He is away on some task set for him by Korthdan.'

'Taking Isabelle to the emir, perhaps?'

'What!' she exclaimed. 'I did not think of that.' She was speechless for a few moments. 'But regardless of that, I told his…*consort*' she spat the word out 'that I do not wish to see him again, unless he brings my sister back to me. I will have nothing more to do with him – I swear!'

Alex gave a silent sigh of relief. 'They may yet miss the deadline,' he said, trying to lift her spirits.

'I would like to think that were possible,' she said in a flat voice, looking away from him. 'But I fear I have lost her forever.'

*

Lord Charlemont was waiting for Alex back at the chancellor's house and was visibly shocked as Alex related the news regarding the "astral" child.

'So, what do you think?' asked Alex.

Lord Charlemont rubbed his chin, his eyes cast down. 'I have read of such a thing,' he finally admitted. 'The resultant offspring is referred to as a "moonchild" – an appropriate name in the circumstances – but usually it involves an effort to bring a physical incarnation of Satan into the world. Again, probably not too far from the truth! But even if it's true, it will be at least a dozen years before the boy can take the throne of Egypt – and a lot can happen in that time. It does, however, suggest that we were wrong all along about the Dutch involvement, and that Lady Isabelle is to be somehow brought back into the Levant Treaty process – though how Korthdan plans to do that is beyond me.'

He picked up his pipe from the table and lit it.

'In a way,' he said, looking up, 'it doesn't change a thing – we continue as planned. Now, Chancellor, we need to talk about getting me back to the mainland.'

*

It was decided that the chancellor would get Lord Charlemont into the dockyard the following day, and direct him on to a galley bound for Piraeus. Lord Charlemont's intention was that he would return a few days before a full moon with a group of his own men to prepare the way for an invasion shortly afterwards, depending on the willingness of Admiral Blake to cooperate. If Lord Charlemont had not returned by the fourth full moon, Alex was to take it that Admiral Blake would not raise an invasion force that year and make his own way back to Piraeus. By then, the stormy season of autumn would be approaching, making an invasion by sea more risky and highly unlikely.

The next day came. Lord Charlemont left at dawn with the chancellor and a few of his men. Alex stayed behind and briefly wondered if he would ever see Lord Charlemont again. He realised that, despite the other's arrogance and maddening urge to dominate all around, he had become quite attached to the man.

CHAPTER 30

Once Lord Charlemont had left, Alex resigned himself to waiting for months for any further developments. It was to his surprise, therefore, that just over two weeks later the chancellor woke him soon after dawn.

'My lookouts have seen a boat coming from the west,' he declared. 'It can only be him!'

Alex gave a shout of joy and leapt out of bed. Already, on the road outside, two of the chancellor's notables had arrived with a large cart pulled by four mules. As soon as he and the chancellor had clambered on to the back, they set off at a fast clip through the slowly waking village. Once they were clear of the village and on to the top road, Alex looked out to the west and saw a small galley sailing in on the morning breeze.

About a quarter of a mile from St Catherine's Church, they turned left off the top road down a dirt track that led directly to a copse situated at the edge of the mighty cliffs. Another eight of the chancellor's men were already waiting in the copse with half a dozen donkeys. Making their way through the trees, they came across a narrow path that dropped steeply down to their right along the side of the cliffs. It was an ancient path to the base of the cliffs that followed a natural fissure in the rocks. It led down to Port Ormos, the quay below Fira, and had been abandoned hundreds of years previously when the wider well-paved donkey track had been built. It was now forgotten to all but a few on the island, and had been overlooked by the Rakshasa.

The path widened as it descended, following the curves of the cliff. At the bottom of the track, between it and the quay, was a mass of trees, bracken and shrubbery which took them some time to hack down and pull the protesting donkeys through. Eventually they made their way on to the quayside itself. A number of what, presumably, were store rooms had been cut into the soft rock at the base of the cliff. The doors of most of them had rotted away, but two massive doors were still intact and guarded what appeared to be an entrance to a sea cave.

'What is that?' Alex asked the chancellor.

'What?' asked the chancellor, turning round. He appeared somewhat distracted. 'Oh, that. The Rakshasa built it when they first came here, but have not used it since. We think they started to build a port here, then changed their plans.'

He turned his attention back to the approaching galley, as did Alex.

As it drew nearer, Alex noticed a figure standing in a dramatic pose on the bow of the boat, one hand held over his eyes, shielding them from the sun. He smiled – it could only be Lord Charlemont.

Soon the galley came alongside the quay, and a man at each end of it threw ropes to the notables, who used them to pull the boat further in and secure it to the mooring rings.

In addition to Lord Charlemont and Fredrich, there were twelve mercenaries on board. All wore hunting jackets and weapons belts, loaded down with a wide assortment of firearms, sabres, knives and grenades.

'Chancellor!' exclaimed Lord Charlemont, stepping down from the bow and on to the deck. 'So good to see you again.'

The chancellor did not return his greeting. 'Stay where you are, Lord Charlemont,' he called out in a strong voice. 'Raise your hands above your heads,' he clearly ordered the rest.

Alex turned to him in surprise, but before he could do anything, Talus had seized him from behind and pressed a cocked pistol to his temple. The other notables had also moved fast and formed a line on either side of the chancellor, their muskets covering those on board, cocking them as they took aim.

'What in God's name is going on?' demanded Lord Charlemont.

One of the mercenaries at the stern made to go for his musket, but was spotted. A shot rang out, and the man fell back on to the deck, swearing in French and clutching his arm. The other mercenaries, who had initially tensed up at the sight of the muskets, slowly and deliberately relaxed, moving their hands up and away from their weapons.

'If anyone moves again,' ordered the chancellor, 'kill them.'

'Vot ist de problem, Lord Charlemont?' one of the mercenaries demanded without taking his eyes off those on the quayside.

A rustling caught Alex's attention; there was more movement in the undergrowth they had just hacked their way through. His blood ran cold. If the chancellor had betrayed them, they probably had only moments before a Rakshasa war party appeared – and then certain capture or death. His dream of marrying Helena and a life back in England came crashing down in a few heartbeats.

'Chancellor,' bellowed Lord Charlemont, shaking his fist, 'if this is treachery, I swear you will burn in hell for it!'

CHAPTER 31

'The pact,' ordered the chancellor, his hand outstretched.

Lord Charlemont hesitated.

'The pact,' the chancellor repeated. 'None of you sets foot on Santorini until I have seen it.'

As he spoke, out of the undergrowth appeared more of his men, leading more donkeys with large willow baskets on their backs. Alex breathed a sigh of relief.

Lord Charlemont moved slowly over to a large oilskin-covered bag on the deck. Gingerly reaching inside it, he pulled out a long oilskin-covered cardboard cylinder, and then walked back over the deck and carefully handed it to the chancellor. The chancellor moved back from the quayside and called Spyro over to him. Together they pulled the parchment out, then, kneeling down, they spread it on the quay and read through it. Alex knew that it would be written in English and Greek with all the usual insignia and seals of an official document.

Time dragged on. Lord Charlemont and his men shifted uncomfortably under the guns of the notables, beads of sweat beginning to form on their faces. Finally the two kneeling men looked at each other and nodded. The chancellor grunted in approval and stiffly got to his feet, walking back to the quayside.

'Good,' he declared. 'It is as we agreed.'

'I could have told you that!' retorted Lord Charlemont.

'You can disembark now,' the chancellor said, indicating to his men to lower their weapons.

Lord Charlemont was the first, melodramatically jumping from the deck on to the quayside and walking over to the chancellor. He cordially shook hands with him, smiling and slapping him on the back as if the recent hostilities had just been a huge prank.

'I do apologise for appearing so soon,' he guffawed to the chancellor, 'but Admiral Blake had a fleet sitting idle and is planning the attack as we speak.'

'No need to apologise,' said the chancellor impatiently. 'We will talk later. First I want to get the cargo unloaded.'

He then broke off and started to issue orders to his men.

'Alex!' Lord Charlemont exclaimed and, to Alex's surprise, came forward to shake him warmly by the hand, again with much back slapping. 'So, how's it been going in my absence?'

'Very well,' Alex replied. 'Lady Helena is still attending mass every morning at St Catherine's, and the tunnels are almost complete.'

'Good, good,' enthused Lord Charlemont. 'I have a fair bit of news from Athens, I can tell you,' he added with a conspiratorial wink.

'Any problems on the journey here?' Alex asked.

'Not really, but I can see why the Rakshasa use such trolls for oarsmen – ours were almost exhausted by the time we got through the other side of the Wall. Another five minutes and we would have lost our forward momentum and been dashed to pieces.'

'Are the oarsmen some of your men as well?' Alex queried. Glancing to the galley, he noticed that none had yet appeared on deck.

'Good God, no,' replied Lord Charlemont, laughing at the apparent naivety of the question. 'They're Russian galley slaves, man! Thirty of 'em. Came as a job lot with the ship when I bought it in Piraeus. Anyway,' he continued, placing his arm over Alex's shoulders and leading him away from the quayside as gangplanks were dropped on to it, 'we navigated around to the west of the Wall yesterday afternoon, managing the whole trip from Athens under sail – thank God! We then ploughed through it relying solely on compass bearings, managing to make the gap in the galley patrols on time. The oarsmen were getting deadly tired by then, so we decided to anchor overnight on the other side of Aspronisi, then set out at first light for here.'

'So when is the invasion to take place?' Alex asked, his excitement mounting.

'Less than two weeks from now,' Lord Charlemont replied, 'the morning after their next Full Moon Feast. But that's not the only surprise,' he warned, lowering his voice. 'I got back to Piraeus with no real problems, and I was back at the consulate barely two days after leaving the chancellor's house.'

'So what was Admiral Blake's reaction when you told him what had happened?'

Lord Charlemont gave a harsh laugh. 'He thought I was stark staring mad – until I dropped a golden egg from the hoard on to his precious table! By the time I was halfway through describing the worth of the hoard, he was already shouting out for Jenkins to come through so they could start planning the invasion. Within a couple of days he had negotiated with Admiral Yildiz to lease most of the Turkish fleet docked in Piraeus, complete with galley slaves. Most of the ships are armed with heavy guns in the bows and swivel guns along the sides, together with fifty barges. We are modifying them, of course, roofing over the oarsmen's decks to get them through the Wall of Storms. It's costing us a fortune – myself and Admiral Blake are doing the majority of the underwriting – but it will be small change once we have taken the hoard.'

'Well, what was the other surprise?'

'A *caique* turned up at Piraeus two days after me carrying Lady Isabelle herself. The fishermen claimed they'd found her wandering along the coastline in the south-west of the Morea, somehow realised she was English and brought her to the consulate. Anyway, Lady Isabelle had absolutely no memory of what had happened for the previous month, other than that there had been a large explosion on the *Fearless*.'

'Did the admiral believe you at that point, given she could not corroborate your version of events?'

Lord Charlemont sighed with impatience. 'Admiral Blake and I have known each other for years and he trusts me implicitly – but the fact that Lady Isabelle did have two fading fang marks on her throat helped validate my story. For him it was the answer to his prayers – the key to the Egyptian treaty delivered safe and sound into his hands…'

'And unsullied by the hand of corsairs,' Alex observed, shaking his head in wonder.

'Exactly. They left Piraeus shortly before I did, so by now the treaty should have been signed and sealed.' He stood back, opening out his arms. 'We did it!' he declared with a triumphal smile. He then became more serious, drawing Alex close again. 'Before I forget – remember the tapestry in the palace? Fredrich has been making some enquiries through his contacts at the Vatican. It would appear that the Holy See has had knowledge of the Rakshasa for some time now, but the Pope and his followers have seen fit to keep it to themselves. From what Fredrich was able to glean, a secret crusade took place around one hundred years ago, funded entirely by the Pope, involving members of the Spanish Inquisition, which drove the Rakshasa from a fortress in the mountains of Transylvania.'

'Maybe that's why the bishops here didn't answer the call to surrender.'

'Possibly,' Lord Charlemont conceded. 'He gleaned little else, other than the fact the crusaders initially suffered huge losses from sorcery. They managed to overcome it, and one piece of knowledge, relevant to us, has been passed down from that incident. All those who succumbed to the sorcery had fired weapons at the Rakshasa. The Rakshasa had been able to trace those who had fired the weapons by the lead shot they had handled and then attack them in their sleep on the astral plane. There is, however, a way of protecting ourselves from this: silk blocks astral emanations. Therefore, during any action against the Rakshasa we must wear silk gloves.'

'And you actually believe all that?' demanded Alex, drawing back from him.

'Yes I do – and I've brought a job lot of gloves with me,' snapped Lord Charlemont. 'All the men know the situation and why they have to wear them.' Now impatient, he looked past Alex to the ship. 'Why don't you give a hand with…'

'Wait,' interrupted Alex, grasping his arm. 'What about Helena? You have not mentioned anything about her so far.'

'Oh, do not worry on that account,' replied Lord Charlemont, brushing him off. 'The day we left Piraeus, Admiral Blake sent a signal to inform the king of what had happened. In reply, the king instructed that *both* Montagus be rescued at all costs. Which, from all our points of view, is perfect.'

'How so?'

'Think it through, man! Even though Lady Isabelle, the actual key to the treaty, has been returned, the instructions from His Majesty still give us the perfect pretext to raise an invasion force to seize the hoard. And if – God forbid – it all goes wrong and Admiral Blake is hauled before an Admiralty Board of Enquiry, he can defend himself with the direct order he received from the king himself, as long as he could prove the *primary purpose* of the expedition was to rescue Lady Helena.'

'Well, thank God for that,' exclaimed Alex as a feeling of relief swept over him.

'It couldn't have worked out better,' Lord Charlemont concluded, beaming.

*

The galley's cargo consisted of scores of small barrels of gunpowder, dozens of cases of muskets and pistols, as well as the necessary firing powder and ammunition. The cache also included half a dozen mortars with associated incendiary shells, dozens of cases of grenades and other assorted weaponry. In addition, there were several barrels of Royal Navy standard issue rations – including salted beef, Suffolk cheese and ship's biscuits – to last the whole group for several weeks.

The chancellor was not happy that they had brought such foreign food with them. 'The Rakshasa will smell you from leagues away,' he declared. 'You will stink of beef.' But there was no easy way of provisioning all the men without alerting more islanders to their presence. Eventually they agreed to eat garlic with the food, as the locals did with theirs, in order to disguise any possible smell.

Once the ordinance and provisions had been unloaded on to the quay, the crew lowered the sail of the galley, manoeuvred it to the end of the quay and began dragging a large net over it, interleaved with slender heavily-leafed foliage. When they were finished, anyone looking down from the cliffs above would just have seen an extension of the vegetation that existed between the old track and the quay, as if it had become overgrown.

The donkeys were loaded and driven up the path to the waiting cart, but it took several runs to move all the equipment up the cliffs. It was then taken to a barn about two miles east down the slope on the other side of the top road. Behind the barn a pit had already been dug, and the gunpowder cache was carefully placed in it before being covered over with manure to disguise its smell. Lord Charlemont's men took up residence in the loft of the barn, leaving two men, Oliver the skipper and the injured Frenchman, Gervais, to feed and water the galley slaves.

Lord Charlemont and Alex also moved in with the men, and they started to plan and rehearse the activities that lay before them. The chancellor then spread the word amongst the islanders that no one, on the order of the Rakshasa, was to venture north of the village of Karterados, other than to go to the church via the top road for the dawn mass.

*

One night in the barn, Alex queried Lord Charlemont on how he had assembled his men so quickly, and was told about the advertisement that had appeared in various broadsheets across Europe.

'But how did they know where to meet in Athens?'

'It's very simple, Alex,' Lord Charlemont replied in a world-weary voice. 'All of them know of one particular tavern in the capital of each major European country. To anyone else but them, the advertisement is meaningless as there is not enough information about where to meet. That way, I don't get a rag tag bunch of adventure seekers turning up and wasting my time. My men see the advert and, if they want the work, show up every night for the designated month until myself or Fredrich can get there.'

'It's a good system,' complimented Alex, 'but I do see one flaw.'

'Go on.'

'What would have happened if the taverna in Athens had been taken over by someone else who changed it to a private house, or even demolished it?'

'That's not likely to happen to that, or any of the meeting places,' retorted Lord Charlemont.

'How can you be so sure?'

'Because I own them all.'

CHAPTER 32

The next day, Alex told Helena about Lord Charlemont's arrival.

'Thank God!' she declared, a smile lighting up her face. She then caught herself. 'I never thought the day would come when I would be happy to hear of Charlemont's arrival,' she said ruefully, 'but needs must when the devil drives, I suppose.' She clasped her hands together, looking at him. 'When will it happen?'

'I don't know,' Alex lied. He had agreed with Lord Charlemont that it would be better if Helena did not know the exact day in case her manner or words accidentally gave it away – especially as he suspected Zentar was now pursuing her again, though she swore she was keeping him at bay. 'But it will be several days after the next full moon.'

'Excellent,' she said, clapping her hands. 'Now, at last I have something definite to look forward to. I presume it will happen in the church – is that right?'

'Yes. We're going to start mixing with the congregation over the next few weeks so as the Rakshasa don't get suspicious of our presence.'

'Very well. I will leave the whole matter in your hands. And now, was there any news of my sister?'

Alex brought her up to date on Isabelle's reappearance and her delivery to the emir. Though relieved to hear her sister was definitely alive, her mood darkened considerably.

'So now Isabelle has been delivered up to the emir,' she said quietly, her arms folded. 'It makes me ill to think of her, alone in that heathen's harem.'

'I agree,' Alex sympathised with her, 'but there's nothing we can do for the time being.'

She heaved a big sigh. 'You're right, I suppose,' she said, and then was quiet for a while.

'One thing I do not understand,' said Alex presently, 'is that if the Rakshasa do take over Egypt, then surely they can no longer hide away, attacking shipping to fund their kingdom – and even that hoard of gold would not last forever. At some point they will have to trade something with other nations – but as far as I can see they produce nothing of value. And what would stop other nations from attacking them, once they realised who they were?'

'Well, their priests are expert at cultivating medicinal herbs…'

'But what use would they be?' Alex exclaimed.

'Hear me out,' insisted Helena. 'Zentar told me some time ago they can cure almost any disease of man, and have created a potion that can easily prolong our lives far beyond our allotted three score years and ten. What has more value – a golden trinket or the gift of a long and perfectly healthy life? And what nation, once its rulers had tasted this "elixir of youth" and seen its effects, would attack the country that produced it and so kill the golden goose?'

They spoke of other things, but eventually the time came for them to part. As she stood to leave, she turned to him.

'There is something I would like.'

'Yes?'

'Once I'm out of the church, could I then have a pistol?'

'Why?' countered Alex, puzzled.

She became slightly evasive. 'I just want to feel,' she said, and then paused. 'I just want to feel that if it came to it…I could defend myself.'

'I don't see why not,' he replied.

The request had seemed reasonable enough at the time, but soon he was to regret agreeing to it so readily.

CHAPTER 33

At the barn, Lord Charlemont had directed the mercenaries, all ex-Swiss Guards who had been once commanded by Fredrich, to recreate the interior of the church, using bales of hay for the pews. For the Rakshasa they constructed life-size figures made up of rags, straw and broom handles, and positioned them in the appropriate places, with Helena also represented by a rag figure. Lord Charlemont took up his position three pews directly in front of her and practised turning quickly, drawing his two air guns from under his cloak and shooting her guards in the head. They had decided to use the air guns due to the risk of misfire from the flint and steel ignition of gunpowder in a pistol.

The whole sequence of events in the church would be initiated by one of the mercenaries, Henrik, who from before dawn would be keeping watch for the invasion fleet near the church. To give Admiral Blake more time to get his fleet through the Wall of Storms, they instructed Helena to request that the priest say the long form of the Latin mass each day. Following Henrik's signal – three blasts from a horn similar to that used by the Rakshasa in their hunts – those in and around the church would prepare to carry out their allotted tasks. Another man, Joachim, was stationed down by the dock, and would carry out some vital tasks there before heading back to the church.

Day after day they practised all the possible permutations of the deadly action that would follow the horn blasts, as each night the moon waxed ever larger.

*

'Fredrich, are you sure this Wolfsbane will do the job?' asked Lord Charlemont one evening, holding a bottle containing the poison up to the lantern light.

'Quite sure, my lord,' replied the other. 'It will kill any warm-blooded creature almost instantly.'

'Warm-blooded?' questioned Lord Charlemont, lowering the bottle and turning to glare at Fredrich. 'These Rakshasa are as pale as death! What if they are cold-blooded?'

'I haff no idea.'

'There's only one way to know for sure…' began Lord Charlemont.

'Don't tell me,' interrupted Alex, somewhat irritated. 'I'm to ask Helena – that fiend is bound to have held her hand at some point.'

'You read my thoughts,' concluded Lord Charlemont, with an ingratiating smile.

When Alex returned from Fira the next day, Lord Charlemont was waiting for him, distractedly tapping the palm of one hand with the tip of a crossbow bolt held in the other.

'Well?'

'Warm-blooded. Definitely.'

*

The day of the full moon finally arrived and Alex went to meet Helena in Fira. When she arrived this time, he did his best to make light-hearted conversation with her and told her he'd be back the next day. She seemed to suspect nothing.

'Oh, there's one last thing,' he said as casually as possible, just before it was time for her to leave. 'Lord Charlemont would like you to start dressing as simply as possible to aid with the rescue – no flowing dresses from now on.'

'"Lord Charlemont would like you…"' she mimicked him, and then relented and stopped. 'Oh, very well. It's not as if I have an extensive wardrobe here. I'll wear my riding dress and boots – that would be the most practical.'

'If you could do it from *tomorrow* morning…' he cajoled her.

'Yes, yes, very well. I will sort it out tonight!' she agreed, waving her hand dismissively.

They talked for a short while longer, and then it was time for her to go. He waited for a good quarter of an hour after she had gone, and then quietly made his way out of the deserted village for what he hoped would be the last time.

CHAPTER 34

The next morning Lord Charlemont, Alex and Fredrich travelled as usual by horseback to the church, which they had been attending regularly for some days. Three of Fredrich's men, armed with crossbows, were already in place, hidden around the church behind dry stone walls. Henrik and Joachim had also set off well before dawn, and they too were in position. Another two men, the Swede Axel and a Neapolitan, Filiberto, had gone and taken up positions at the copse. Alex timed his arrival for a few minutes after Lord Charlemont's, but before the Rakshasa. The other members of the team showed up in dribs and drabs, blending in silently with the waiting congregation, their cloaks drawn tightly round them. They all then waited for the Rakshasa to arrive.

There was the familiar rumble of a chariot on the paved road behind them. Alex nonchalantly turned round to catch a glimpse of Helena – and his eyes widened with shock. There, on the chariot with an uncomfortable looking Helena, was a tall purple-clad Rakshasa in the prime of youth, wearing elegant smoked glasses, his long white hair streaming back from his noble face. A murmur of surprise rippled around the crowd as they noticed the new arrival, but Alex felt uncontrollable hatred surge up within him – it could only be Zentar.

Without thinking, he began to reach for his pistol – but then felt a vice-like grip on his arm that prevented him from drawing it.

'No,' hissed Lord Charlemont. 'Calm yourself, man, or you will have us massacred!' Ignoring him, Alex tried to draw the pistol again.

'Not *yet*,' insisted Lord Charlemont. 'When the time comes, *you* take him down.'

Alex looked at him uncomprehendingly for a moment, and then realised what he was doing and released his grip on the pistol. Breathing heavily, but now containing his rage, he shrugged off the other, dropped his gaze from Zentar and blended back into the waiting congregation.

The Rakshasa checked the church as usual, and then escorted Helena and Zentar inside. As he passed, Alex noted that Zentar had two large ornate curved knives hanging from each side of his belt. As usual, Alex, Lord Charlemont and Fredrich were amongst the first few in the church. The rest of the regular congregation ignored the newcomers, probably assuming they were connected with Helena and the Rakshasa, and had strenuously avoided eye contact with them from the start.

*

Finally, everyone was in, and the priest was at the altar. Helena and Zentar were flanked on either side by their guards, and were directly behind Lord Charlemont. To Lord Charlemont's left, at the end of the pew, was Fredrich; to his right, at the other end of the pew, was Alex. Two more of Fredrich's men, Dieter and Fabian, were positioned towards the front of the church. The door was closed and the strengthening dawn lit up the stained-glass window to their right. The service commenced, its routine now so familiar to Alex that he knew it almost as well as the regular congregation. The ritual and familiarity of it – having to stand or kneel at certain points, the incantation of the prayers, the ringing of bells by the two altar boys and the sweet smell of incense – all helped calm him.

The priest was just raising the chalice to offer up the wine when, from outside, came three distinct blasts on a hunting horn. None of the team so much as flickered, but some of the locals crossed themselves in fear. The minutes dragged by. A bead of sweat formed on the end of Alex's nose that he hurriedly brushed off, not wanting his hands too far from his pistols. Finally it was time for communion. Helena, blissfully unaware of what was going to happen, stepped out first as usual and made her way up to the altar. Just before she arrived there, Lord Charlemont began to get up in a frail manner, Alex also slowly standing up as if to move into the aisle. Helena was kneeling down to receive the host when Lord Charlemont finally got to his feet, still stooped as if with a bad back. He then turned to face the window, as if waiting to file out into the aisle. Alex could see the priest stretching his hand out with the host to Helena, and then half turned towards the window himself.

Lord Charlemont then straightened to his full height and smoothly turned all the way round, while drawing his hands up and out of his cloak from waist level, an air gun in each. His cloak fell away from his arms as he levelled them and almost simultaneously shot the guards on either side of Zentar in the face. They fell heavily without a cry, one discharging his musket harmlessly into the roof as he dropped. Alex, having seen that Lord Charlemont was committed, anticipated his actions slightly, and his own shot rang out an instant later, quickly followed by three more shots from the other corners of the church. He heard Helena scream briefly from the front. For some indeterminate period of time, nothing happened; nobody else moved or reacted – and then pandemonium erupted. Men shouted, women screamed, and all scrambled to get out of the church.

Having discharged his pistol at the guard behind him, Alex saw that Zentar, having instinctively ducked down after the first shots, was now rising like a demonic jack-in-the-box, a curved knife in each hand, and leaping on to the back of the pew in front of him. Lord Charlemont had instantly holstered one air gun and was struggling to reach another pistol, but was hindered by the panicking locals.

Instead of attacking them or trying to flee, Zentar opened his mouth, clenched his fists around the hilts of his knives and thrust his head forward, emitting a blood-curdling cry that stopped all in their tracks. Lord Charlemont fell backwards, seeming to take the full brunt of the cry; Fredrich appeared stunned, while Alex fought to remain in control of himself. The cry lasted for some indeterminate time – and then Zentar leapt on top of the next pew in front of him. Like a drunkard, Alex groped madly for another pistol, thinking Zentar was going to leap on him, but to his surprise Zentar ran with the agility of a cat along the top of the pew, and then hurled himself headfirst out of the stained-glass window, arm raised in front of his face.

Everyone started to move again, the locals screaming and shouting once more. Alex shook his head to clear it and turned to the altar. Helena was still crouched down, arms raised protectively over her head. Dieter and Fabian were already on either side of her, trying to get her to stand. Alex pushed the locals back, did a large step up on to the back of the pew in front, and ran over the tops of the rest to join her. He crouched down by her, pulling one arm away from her head.

'Helena,' he said urgently, 'we must go – *now!*'

She recognised his voice and rose unsteadily to her feet, her face lightly dusted in soot from the discharge of the pistols. By now about half the congregation had got out of the church, and Alex desperately pushed those remaining out of his way as he pulled Helena behind him by the arm.

*

Outside, the team was reassembling as the frightened locals ran for their lives in all directions. Two Rakshasa lay dead near the church door, their mouths foaming and backs arched in death agonies, but there was no sign of Zentar. Henrik was there, and in the distance they could see Joachim running from the direction of the dock walls. Two of the men were trying to calm the rearing and snorting Rakshasa horses in the hope of using them to ride to the copse. Helena now regained her composure and ran with Alex away from the church door.

It took him a few moments to calm his horse, which was rearing in fright at the commotion, but a few seconds later they were on it. Looking over to where the Rakshasa had tethered their horses, he could see the other members of the team were struggling to calm the animals. They had just managed to untether one, but it went berserk, rearing up all the more and managing to knock Fabian over. It then started to trample him, deliberately aiming for his head with its powerful forelegs, the man splayed out unconscious on the grass like a rag doll.

A shot rang out and Alex's horse jumped in fright, nearly dismounting the two of them. Lord Charlemont had discharged a pistol quite close to the Rakshasa horse and it had taken fright, moving off the trampled man, but then it veered back towards one of the downed Rakshasa. It grabbed the dead warrior's tunic in its teeth and tried to drag the body away.

'Forget the horses!' Lord Charlemont ordered, shouting to be heard above the snorting and neighing of the Rakshasa steeds. 'Get Fabian on my horse, then follow on.'

Lord Charlemont mounted his horse, and the others helped him position Fabian's limp body in front of him. He glanced up and saw Alex looking at him.

'Go!' he shouted.

Alex dug his stirrups in and steered the frightened animal towards the road.

*

'We've done it!' Helena cried out, hugging him tightly as they thundered south along the top road towards the copse.

'We're not there yet,' Alex warned, shouting to make himself heard above the clatter of hooves on the cobbles. He was certain the guards back at the fortress would have heard Zentar's war cry, as well as the unfortunate shot from Lord Charlemont's pistol, and they would now be able to see the congregation scattering through their spyglasses. Still, the odds were good. He, Helena, Lord Charlemont and Fredrich would be at the copse in about a minute. The others would already be running down the paved road after them, and would cover the quarter of a mile in two to three minutes, with a head start of about the same on those coming from the fortress.

'Why didn't you tell me 'twas today?' Helena demanded, her mood suddenly changing. 'I got the shock of my life back there!'

'Couldn't be helped...' began Alex, but his attention was then caught by the watchtower high up on the mountain ahead of them. He could see flashes of light coming from it – it was the heliograph. 'Looks like they've spotted the fleet,' he observed.

'But you were expecting that, weren't...' She gave a startled squeal at the sound of a huge explosion behind them, and Alex felt the ground shake underneath the hooves of their horse.

'The dock walls,' he shouted. Over the past two weeks they had loaded a couple of tons of gunpowder into tunnels that the chancellor's men had dug for them underneath the southern wall of the dock. On hearing the blasts from the hunting horn, Joachim – a former Prussian military engineer skilled at undermining tactics – had lit five minute fuses and then run for his life back to the church. He had also set incendiary mortars up outside the wall on long fuses. Joachim had assured Alex that it would bring down one fortified tower as well as the wall on either side of it – enough of a breach to allow the invasion force to stream through.

'In my left hand jacket pocket,' Alex shouted over his shoulder, 'you'll find a pocket pistol. Take it – it's loaded.'

'Excellent!' she exclaimed, and retrieved the small weapon from him. She hugged him again, pulling herself closer into him. 'This is so exciting!' she declared, and then thrust her head forward and kissed him on the cheek. 'Our first kiss in freedom,' she laughed.

'Please,' he protested, smiling in spite of himself, 'I must concentrate.'

'Oh, you romantic, you!' she teased him.

As he glanced round at her, a movement behind caught his eye – a mounted Rakshasa female was suddenly bearing down on them at speed, raising her long barrelled musket for a shot. Alex swore under his breath – they were going at half their attacker's speed and a sitting target. There was a sudden pulling and tugging at his belt – and then a shot rang out.

'Got her!' cried Helena, and Alex glanced round again to see his smoking pistol in Helena's hand and the Rakshasa warrior crashing to the ground from her steed with an unfeminine screech. 'Longer barrel – more accurate,' she explained as she shoved it back into its holster.

'Where in God's name did she come from?' Alex shouted, spurring their horse on even more.

'She probably had just finished her watch up in the High Watchtower.'

En route they passed several of the warrior Rakshasa returning from their celebration at Ancient Thera. The first two ignored them, still intoxicated and staggering along, but the third weakly raised his fist and shook it at them as they passed.

'Hang on,' Helena shouted. 'You're passing the copse.'

'I've got to,' he replied. 'There are traps on this side of it.' He waited until they had passed the copse, and then wheeled the horse round to its southern approach. Axel and Filiberto were already stationed behind trees, each having a rack of loaded muskets within arm's reach. They turned at the couple's approach and waved them wordlessly on towards some tethered horses before resuming their positions. A part of Alex's mind noted that neither were wearing the silk gloves Lord Charlemont had brought, but he thought nothing of it at the time.

A fresh horse was waiting for Helena. She quickly mounted it, and then they set off cross-country for a small port on the east side of the island to rendezvous with a ship from the fleet. Lord Charlemont and Fredrich were to follow on, while the rest of the mercenaries would return to their ship moored in Ormos after they had dealt with the expected Rakshasa cavalry.

CHAPTER 35

Alex and Helena raced down the small drystone walled tracks, reaching the east coast about fifteen minutes later. As they rode towards the coast, Alex could see the main fleet, which was less than half a mile from the Rakshasa dock and coming in fast on the onshore wind. One galley, flying a black flag from its mast, had peeled off from the main formation and was heading to the small harbour that lay before them. Finally they reached the quay and dismounted, tethering their horses to some trees nearby. Alex then paced the quayside as they waited for Lord Charlemont to join them. The minutes dragged by, and the galley had moored up, with no sign of him or Fredrich.

Suddenly there was a sound of horses neighing in protest at being driven at a furious pace, and the two men appeared from around a bend.

Helena's euphoric mood dissipated in an instant. 'I am going on board to change,' she declared, unhitching a travel bag from her horse and walking up the gangway to the galley. 'I will not speak with that man!' she called, as the captain accompanied her below deck.

Some of the ship's crew helped take the unconscious Fabian down from Lord Charlemont's horse, and carried him onto the galley, which then cast off as soon as all had boarded.

'Alex,' exclaimed Lord Charlemont jovially, embracing him, 'we did it! Ha! Outstanding work!' He pulled away, and then spotted an officer standing nearby with a large tray containing a magnum of champagne and several flute glasses.

'Complements of Admiral Blake,' the officer declared, causing Lord Charlemont to whoop in delight.

Fredrich handed them both a glass and, for the first time since Alex had met him, gave a genuinely friendly smile. 'So, Mr Hurst,' he began, 'we haff made it after all!' He then looked past Alex. 'But no Lady Helena?' he queried.

'No,' replied Alex. 'She will probably be out later.'

'Ah well, never mind,' declared Lord Charlemont. 'Here we go!'

The cork of the magnum flew off with a loud "pop" and the men and the crew around them cheered.

'What a glorious day!' Lord Charlemont declared a few minutes later, sipping champagne with Alex up at the bow of the ship, steadying himself on a halyard as they cut through the seas ahead of them. 'By sunset we'll be on Admiral Blake's flagship, enjoying a lamb roast and a bottle of good port.' He turned to Alex. 'I tell you, this is the best caper I've been on for a long time. Good health, sir,' he said, clinking his glass against Alex's. 'And here's to a share of that hoard!'

'Good health!' responded Alex. 'Here's to a house in the country!'

'More champagne! What say you?'

Alex agreed, proffering his glass. A feeling of utter relief was beginning to sweep over him that had nothing to do with the alcohol; the further they got from the quayside, the better he felt. By his second glass of champagne, he felt totally at peace with himself and the world. Everything was perfect. They would get home with a share of the hoard, and he would marry Helena. Life was good once more, and the horror that was the Rakshasa would soon be nothing more than a memory. Lord Charlemont prattled on, telling him how they had massacred pursuing Rakshasa in the death traps set at the copse, as all the time they neared the fleet.

*

Admiral Blake's flagship, the biggest and undoubtedly the fastest galley of the fleet, was standing off about a quarter of a mile from the shore, flanked by two further galleys acting as his escort. As they got closer, they could see the sea gates to the docks had been destroyed and that the dockyard was ablaze, plumes of black smoke billowing up into the morning air from it. More galleys were positioned just off the dock walls, and were launching volley after volley of incendiary mortars into the dockyard to compound the destruction. From what they could see, only two Rakshasa galleys had made it out, and they were being blasted apart by guns fired by the British crewed galleys.

To the shore they could see that most of the barges had already been beached and had disgorged masses of marines. They had landed at the port of Kanakari, which was one of the few places where there was a gap in the small cliffs – no more than thirty feet high, but effectively impassable – that lined this part of the coast. Some marines remained back at the barges, most likely still unloading equipment from them. Most of the galleys that had towed them in stood by, one group just offshore, another group further out, protecting the rear.

'Yes!' Lord Charlemont whooped with joy, punching the air. 'It's all working out.'

He turned to Alex, punching him playfully on the shoulder.

'This will go down in history as the "Battle of Santorini",' he declared, and paused to let that sink in, taking another sip of champagne. He then held up his glass as if for another toast and looked Alex directly in the eye. '*We* will go down in history. Imagine it!'

Alex had raised his glass, but was taken aback – that was quite a thought.

After a while, Lord Charlemont calmed down as they approached the admiral's flagship and asked Alex what message the flags were currently signalling.

'I don't know,' Alex admitted.

'What?' exclaimed Lord Charlemont, rounding on him. 'You've taken part in God knows how many sea battles and you can't tell me what those flags say? That's the…'

'Every admiral uses different signals,' retorted Alex. 'Admiral Blake's will be totally different from those of the admirals I served under.'

'Ah,' remarked Lord Charlemont, taken aback by the naivety of his own question. Suddenly a look of horror crossed his face. 'My God!' he exclaimed, flinging his glass into the sea and running back towards the mast.

Something was wrong. Alex was about to follow him when suddenly the escort galley between them and the flagship, which had been slowly turning as they approached, opened up with a full barrage from its bow guns. Alex looked in horror as the cannonballs hit the water about fifteen yards short of them, rocking their galley violently. He could not understand it – why was Admiral Blake firing on them?

'Hard to starboard!' Alex shouted to the helmsman as he made to run to the mast where Lord Charlemont was standing.

The helmsman was ahead of him, and was already throwing the ship into a hard starboard turn that caught most of those on deck by surprise, causing even Alex to stagger and almost throwing him overboard. The rudder had been pushed over hard to starboard; the oarsmen on that side went into reverse while those on the port side continued forward at a furious pace to force the ship to turn completely around. The next volley landed for the most part in front of them as they tried to put clear water between themselves and the escort – though two cannonballs did strike the ship at the bow, while others screamed like banshees as they tore great holes in the sail, causing everyone on deck to duck instinctively.

Alex felt a chill run through him – he knew by heart the routine the English gun captains were working to. The first two volleys had just been ranging shots using cannonballs, but the next would find its mark with grapeshot – a deadly mixture of small iron balls and lengths of chain intended to decimate those on deck. The cannon would have already been pulled back, and the gun crews would have them reloaded, primed with grapeshot and ready to fire within two minutes of the last broadside.

'Grapeshot!' he bellowed. 'Take cover!' He raced towards the mast as the others on deck dived down companionways. Lord Charlemont, however, seemed oblivious to the danger and was intent on some task at the base of the mast.

'Get under cover, man! You'll be cut to pieces!' shouted Alex.

Lord Charlemont looked up at him as he approached, utter desperation in his eyes.

'Help me, Hurst!' he pleaded. 'For God's sake, help me!'

CHAPTER 36

As Alex approached Lord Charlemont, he could see the man was desperately trying to rig up a plain white flag to run up the mast, while a black flag lay discarded on the deck by him. Alex intuitively knew what the flag was – a signal to indicate that the galley was under their command. Without it, Admiral Blake was assuming they had been compromised by the Rakshasa and had ordered his escorts to sink them. Alex snatched the flag from Lord Charlemont, rigged it and had it run up in seconds. There was now no time to reach the cover of a companionway, so Alex hauled Lord Charlemont down behind some crates that had been left on deck, and tensed up for the expected barrage.

The seconds passed and nothing happened. After a minute or so, Alex cautiously peered over the crates and was hugely relieved to see the gun ports on the escort ship had been closed off. He sat on the deck next to Lord Charlemont, breathing heavily.

'Why in God's name didn't you tell us about that?' he demanded.

'I thought…I thought I should do it. The final act, as it were,' Lord Charlemont explained, his voice hoarse and face a picture of shock.

'It damn well nearly was the final act – of a bloody tragedy!' Alex berated him. After all their planning, he could hardly believe that Lord Charlemont had kept such a vital piece of information to himself. 'If you had been killed back there…' He realised he was still holding the sheet he had used to haul the flag up. He bunched it up and threw it violently towards Lord Charlemont. 'You bloody fool!' he shouted, getting up and turning away in disgust.

He strode away to the stern – and was surprised to see Helena had changed and was out on deck, her face pale and drawn.

'Helena – are you all right?' he asked.

'Yes, yes, fine,' she said as if distracted, and walked right past him towards the mast. He turned as she passed, puzzled as to what she was doing. Lord Charlemont was now back on his feet, walking towards her, his eyes on the deck, unaware of her presence and only looking up at the last second. He was looking shame faced, but that look disappeared to be briefly replaced by one of guilt, before an ingratiating smile formed itself on his lips. They both stopped.

'Lady Helena…' he began smoothly.

'Lord Charlemont,' she hissed.

For a moment they stared at each other. Neither moved.

'You bastard!' she shouted, her voice ringing around the ship in the silent aftermath of the broadsides. 'This is for my sister!'

With that, she raised the small pistol that Alex had given her and fired at almost point-blank range at Lord Charlemont's head.

'No!' cried Alex, and rushed towards them as Lord Charlemont collapsed lifeless to the deck.

'I'm sorry,' Helena said in a low voice, turning towards him, trying to hand the pistol to him as he pushed past her.

'You idiot!' Alex cried, and stooped down to kneel by Lord Charlemont. His face was deathly pale, one eye a bloody mess, the other rolling back in its socket, and a pool of blood forming underneath him.

CHAPTER 37

Admiral Blake personally greeted a subdued Alex as he boarded the flagship, and took Helena's frosty greeting in his stride. He was in his best uniform – an embroidered navy blue coat, with gold facings and masses of gold lace, and a gold embroidered hat. He was obviously not worried about enemy sniper fire, but his plainer working rig was draped over a nearby tailor's dummy, just in case. He looked extremely pleased with himself.

'Excellent work,' he declared, shaking Alex vigorously by the hand. 'You have earned that place on my flagship. Well done, young man! Now, where is my Lord Charlemont?'

Before Alex had a chance to answer, Lt Jenkins came over and spoke in low, urgent tones to the admiral.

'Good God!' exclaimed Admiral Blake, his face a picture of shock. He shook his head, then turned on Helena. 'Lady Helena, I order you to go below deck immediately,' he said, his voice quaking with anger. 'A cabin has been prepared – Jenkins, take her down!'

Helena looked ashamed. She briefly glanced at Alex and mouthed 'sorry', then kept her eyes downcast and followed Lt Jenkins down a companionway.

*

The leased fleet, towing a force of three and a half thousand heavily armed marines in barges behind it, had used a combination of sail and muscle to rendezvous just to the north of the Wall of Storms on the day before the full moon. As darkness had fallen, they had made their way into the Wall of Storms under muscle power, relying solely on compass readings for their course. All but two of the fleet had made it through to the other side, and the remainder were separated and scattered over quite a large area. Using copies of the maps and charts drawn by Alex, their captains had used the blue lanterns on the domes and the watchtowers to triangulate their position and then regroup as a fleet. As dawn had broken, the sun heated up the land mass of Santorini, causing an updraught that in turn created an onshore breeze, helping speed the fleet along.

'It's all gone splendidly so far,' Admiral Blake continued as Alex joined him on his observation deck, his good mood quickly restored. 'Touch wood, what?' he added, smartly tapping a handrail. 'Only the two patrol galleys managed to get out before the hellburner hit the sea gate – you should have seen the explosion that made!' He was like a schoolboy who had just let off a firework. 'Totally destroyed the gate, walls above it and to the sides, completely blocking their fleet in.'

He thrust his spyglass towards Alex. 'Here,' he said, 'have a look.'

Alex turned his attention to the scene in front of him. From where the flagship was positioned, he could see the breach in the land side of the dock wall that Joachim had made earlier in the day. Marines were already massing in front of the breach, and the crack of small arms fire could be clearly heard as they surged forward. He could see the Rakshasa had set up temporary barricades in the breach, but these would not last long once the marines had set up their field guns and begun to pound away with them. Other marines were already halfway up the long sloping hillside, making their way through the maze of drystone walls in an effort to take the top road, using mules to pull their field guns up with them.

These marines had been forced to stop now as they were coming under heavy fire from the top road, which was pining them down. One of Admiral Blake's aides was also watching the marines – he suddenly barked an order at the signaller, who immediately went to the bow and began waving two plain red flags above his head. A few minutes later a large body of several hundred Greeks appeared, armed with swords, pikestaffs and muskets, running along the top road at a furious pace, led by the chancellor and his notables on horseback. They swept along the road, surprising the dozens of Rakshasa who were defending it, then shots rang out and steel blades flashed in the morning sunlight, as the islanders engaged their hated oppressors in brutal close quarter combat.

The Rakshasa were initially overwhelmed by the ferocity of the attack, but then horns sounded from the fortress, the huge gates opened, and a horde of black-garbed Rakshasa cavalry poured out, charging down the road towards the islanders, their silver helmets glinting in the sun, kilijs held aloft. The chancellor and his notables wheeled their horses round to face the Rakshasa war party, urging their foot soldiers into a defensive formation. Pikestaffs were positioned, muskets shouldered and seconds later a volley of shots rang out. Many Rakshasa were thrown from their horses – but the main bulk of the cavalry, oblivious to the pikestaffs, tore into the massed Greeks, scattering them and throwing some into the air, such was their speed.

The flagship had fallen silent now, and all eyes were on the slaughter taking place before them. Alex felt as though an icy hand had grasped his heart as he remembered the chancellor's family and prayed the Greeks would prevail. Several more heart thudding minutes dragged by, with Rakshasa horses rearing as their riders were pulled off or shot, and Greeks falling like rag dolls as kilijs struck home. The battle continued to ebb and flow before them but it was impossible to predict the outcome, so well matched were the two sides.

'Come on chancellor!' hissed Admiral Blake through gritted teeth. 'I need that road!'

And then, almost imperceptibly, there was a sense that the Greeks were gaining the upper hand, as fewer and fewer mounted Rakshasa could be seen, though some of the dismounted ones were now fighting furiously on the ground as their riderless steeds cantered around in panic, or galloped back to the fortress. Then one mounted warrior reared his horse up – and turned to retreat back to the fortress, quickly followed by a dozen more who were now fighting for their lives as the Greeks closed around them. These remnants of the cavalry tried to regroup closer to the fortress, but even as they turned and faced, the Greeks had reformed their firing lines and sent a volley of shots that left just three warriors still mounted. The retreat turned into a rout, as the remaining riders wheeled around again and galloped furiously back the fortress, crouched low over their steeds. The last rider made it through the fortress gates, which were then hurriedly shut with an almighty boom, quickly followed by raucous cheers from those on the flagship.

'Damn fine job!' exclaimed Admiral Blake, striking the handrail with his fist. He turned to face his aides. 'Those Greeks would make the Spartans proud!'

Alex did not join in the cheering, but instead was using his spyglass to try and locate the chancellor in the mass of men now milling around the top road, cheering their hard won victory. At last he found him, dismounted and clutching his arm, but still wearing his blue cap and apparently giving orders to those around him. Relieved, he then turned his attention to the gates, thinking about how and when they were going to breach them.

'Incredible, isn't it?' observed Admiral Blake. 'These Rakshasa were so sure they were safe, they didn't even bother mounting cannon on their dock walls – or any of their walls for that matter. They've been living in the past. Well,' he declared, rubbing his hands together, 'it'll be their funeral!'

'It's Korthdan,' Alex suddenly said.

'What?' exclaimed Admiral Blake, turning to snatch the spyglass off Alex. 'Where?' he demanded.

'Up there, on the balcony of that tower to the right of the gates,' Alex replied, pointing out the direction.

With his naked eye, Alex could still just make out a blob of purple against white, high up on the side of the tower nearest to them.

'So, the General is out, surveying his troops,' commented Admiral Blake. 'And what a mess they're in. We now have the top road, and once we have taken the dockyard, they will be trapped in that elegant fortress of theirs – then we'll smoke them out!'

*

The fleet was divided into the traditional three squadrons of Red, White and Blue. Admiral Blake, as a full admiral and overall commander of the fleet, had Red Squadron at the centre of the action; a vice admiral commanded White Squadron at the vanguard, and a rear admiral commanded Blue Squadron which was standing off behind them. Each squadron was then further divided into three divisions of around seven ships each.

The day wore on, and Alex found it slightly bizarre, being safe on the flagship, watching events unfold before him. Shots would ring out; the dull thud of the field guns would carry over the water, and they could smell gunpowder and smoke as the Rakshasa ships burnt. There were the sounds of men shouting, and cries of pain as they were shot and wounded. But at the same time it all appeared to be far away, the violence being unable to actually reach out and touch him. Little did he realise he would soon be thrown back into the thick of the action.

*

Time and time again in the course of the day, the Rakshasa used their paralysing war cry, initially to great effect, but its effect was localised, and soon the marines attacking the docks appeared to become used to it and it had little further effect on them.

The day drew on, but still the Rakshasa were managing to hold out at the breach in the dock wall.

'Why they are still defending the docks is beyond me,' Admiral Blake remarked. 'The situation there is hopeless. If I were them, I'd fall back to the fortress.'

Around half past two, the signaller read out a message from Marine Colonel Walsh, who was the overall commander of the ground based part of the assault. He had set up his command post on a hillock some distance back from the wall, giving him a good view of the assault and line of sight to the admiral's flagship.

'Docks to fall within hour.'

'Excellent,' Admiral Blake exclaimed, and was about to make preparations to go onshore when the signaller informed him a second message was being sent.

'Ah-ha,' he exclaimed to his aides. 'That was the good news – this will be the bad news, I'll wager. Used that technique many times when I was a lieutenant, don't you know? Well, let's have it!'

'Large galley plus four escorts has left Port Ormos, heading south-west.'

'Where in God's name did those galleys come from?' exclaimed Admiral Blake in frustration at those around him, and then he rounded on Alex. 'You know these islands better than anyone on board. Well?'

Alex was as shocked as the admiral at this news. Desperately racking his brains, he thought back to the morning of Lord Charlemont's return. He remembered the large wooden doors guarding a sea cave – a sea cave large enough to admit a galley with oars stowed. Its doors had been firmly closed with no visible means of securing them, unless they had been barred – from the inside. He explained this to Admiral Blake.

'So, what are you saying?'

'I'm saying that there may be another way out of the dockyard,' Alex replied with reluctance. 'I think that's it. When we first arrived in the dockyard, I remember a spur that led from the dock directly into doors in the rear wall. What I thought was a boathouse could actually be the entrance to a tunnel leading to Port Ormos.'

'A tunnel running all the way under the island?' asked Admiral Blake, incredulous at the suggestion.

'It could be. A lot of Santorini is hard limestone, but also compacted ash which is quite easy to tunnel into.' Alex suddenly felt almost physically sick, all the euphoria of the early morning now just a distant memory. The dockyard had another exit and they had not spotted it – despite weeks of reconnoitring. 'They are probably using long boats to tow the galleys through the tunnel – it would not be wide enough for the galleys to engage their own oars.'

'Well,' remarked Admiral Blake with reluctance, 'that would explain why those ships have just started making an appearance – but there's one sure way to find out.' He turned to the signaller. 'Signal to Colonel Walsh: "Report activity in Port Ormos".'

'Aye, sir,' acknowledged the signaller, diving into his box of different coloured flags, but before he could send the signal another was received from Colonel Walsh.

'Lead galley has cargo.'

'Cargo?' echoed Admiral Blake, stopping dead, his face noticeably turning pale and his manner turning deadly serious. 'Request Colonel Walsh to clarify.'

A few more minutes passed before the signaller on shore replied.

'Flat object fifteen by thirty feet,' the signaller read out.

Admiral Blake said nothing for a few seconds, and then beckoned to Alex to follow him to a corner of the deck, away from his aides.

'Well, Mr Hurst, what do *you* make of this?' he asked Alex in a low voice, moving closer to him, but averting his gaze and looking out to sea.

'In what sense, sir?'

'In the sense of the *gold*, man!' roared Admiral Blake. 'The blasted gold!' His face was suddenly only inches away, contorted with fury, giving Alex a glimpse of the immense pressure he was under.

Alex did not flinch, but noted, from the corner of his eye, that some of the aides had started in surprise, intent as they were on listening in on the conversation.

'It can't be the gold, sir,' he replied, 'or, at least, not all of it.'

He paused for a moment, recalling the calculations himself and Lord Charlemont had made weeks ago.

'Go on,' ordered Admiral Blake, his usual jovial manner still absent, but calming down somewhat.

'It would take at least five and twenty of the Rakshasa galleys to transport all the gold – and even then they would only manage around two to three knots, given the weight. The figures were in the report Lord Charlemont delivered to you.'

'Ah, yes,' exclaimed Admiral Blake, heaving several huge sighs of relief. 'Remember now. Yes, of course – not enough galleys. Most of the gold *will* still be there. Good, excellent.'

He straightened up and adjusted his jacket around his shoulders before turning back to his aides as if nothing had happened, his jovial manner restored. He then leaned over the map table and studied it for a few seconds.

'So, gentlemen,' he said, turning to his aides, 'these galleys may be trying to escape, or we have to consider a possible attack on our southern flank – unlikely given they are taking the long way around the island.' He talked to them as calmly as if he were lecturing a group of cadets at the Royal Naval Academy at Portsmouth. 'In total, five galleys have broken free over the space of just under three hours. We can assume they took this long as the tunnel has apparently not been used for some time. Let us further assume they have removed all obstacles and are now emerging from the tunnel at a rate of one every half hour. Any thoughts? Suggestions?'

His aides gathered round, all eager to make their mark.

'I suggest we send Blue Squadron round the northern headland to block the tunnel entrance, sir,' said Lt Jenkins, getting in first.

'And then finish off those who have broken out at leisure,' butted in another, riding on the back of the first suggestion.

'Good. That's along the lines of what I was thinking, gentlemen, but sending all of Blue Squadron off will leave us somewhat exposed at the rear. Instead, signal the following to Blue Squadron: "One division proceed to Port Ormos. Destroy tunnel entrance. One division to cover southern flank".'

*

'Casualty report,' ordered Admiral Blake around three o'clock.

'Two hundred dead,' the message came back presently. 'Three hundred injured.'

Alex pondered the figures – the casualties were light considering the progress they had made, and once the docks fell, the battle would effectively be over – all that remained would be to dig in for a siege.

Admiral Blake now surveyed the scene in front of him at the docks. No one on the observation deck spoke as they watched the battle for the docks enter its final phase. British field guns were once more battering down the barricades, and the Rakshasa resistance appeared to be fading. Suddenly a bugle sounded and scores of marines began storming the rubble of the destroyed dock wall.

'Let us pray this is it, gentlemen,' remarked Admiral Blake, gesturing towards the heavens. 'Night will soon be upon us. Unless we have these fiends contained in their fortress by then, I fear the progress we have made thus far will be wasted.'

Onshore, more marines poured through gaps in the barricades, and soon it became obvious to those on board that the Rakshasa had been routed.

It was another quarter of an hour, however, before the understated confirmation came through from Colonel Walsh. The signal simply read: "Docks secured".

Cheers went up from all on the observation deck within earshot of the signaller, and the celebrations soon spread around the whole of the flagship and its nearby escorts. Admiral Blake's aides and junior officers surrounded him, clapping him on the back and shaking his hand as he grinned from ear to ear, his face a picture of both joy and relief.

'Damn fine job, what?' he kept saying, laughing and relishing the adulation for a good few minutes.

'Gentlemen,' he finally announced, arms raised, calming the festivities down. 'Gentlemen, prepare to go ashore. We are now in a siege scenario.'

He turned back to Alex, the warmth in his eyes now replaced with a steely gaze.

'You too, Mr Hurst. I have one more task for you to perform.'

CHAPTER 38

In less than two days a tented city had appeared around the top road, about a mile from the Rakshasa fortress. At its northern end, to one side of the road, was Admiral Blake's command tent and sleeping quarters, with other tents for his aides closely pitched around. Behind these, and spread out on the gentle slope descending from the top road, were the countless canteens, field hospitals, ammunition stores and marines' tents that made up the living and working space of an itinerant army. Alex had been assigned a tent with another lieutenant, while Helena had been given her own tent nearby, under armed guard.

Alex was outside the command tent with the chancellor, who had one arm in a sling, and other naval and marine officers, awaiting the midday briefing and wondering what his role was to be in the forthcoming siege. As he waited, he cast his eye over the tent city, all in neat rows with guy lines taut as violin strings – Admiral Blake's organisational abilities were phenomenal, and this sense of order, Alex knew, was down to his unerring eye for detail and demand for perfection from his subordinates. Alex looked back to the fortress, its walls pitted with cannon shot, smoke drifting heavenward from the blackened timbers of barricades. The invaders knew they were being observed, as occasionally there would be the glint of sunlight from a spyglass along the battlements, but otherwise the fortress was silent and malevolent, like a wounded giant biding its time to strike out again. Since the docks had fallen, there had been no attempted breakouts by the Rakshasa to disrupt the encampment, but Admiral Blake expected one at any time and had ranks of field guns and infantry positioned along the top road. The land gate to the docks was also covered by the massed heavy guns of Red Squadron, who were now anchored just offshore and ready to rain down death at a moment's notice.

A shrill whistle came from behind Alex, and he turned to see a junior aide there, waving them in.

*

'Well, gentlemen, thus far the campaign is proceeding to plan,' began Admiral Blake, beaming at the assembled officers as he paced around behind his desk, flanked by Colonel Walsh and Lt Jenkins. He looked tired, having had barely six hours sleep in the last forty-eight, but his manner was utterly determined and his mind as razor-sharp as ever. 'We estimate we have killed around three thousand of their warriors and probably wounded another thousand, which leaves around five thousand, whereas we have around three thousand marines still capable of fighting.'

He paused, and murmurs of surprise drifted around the stuffy confines of the tent, as Alex translated for the chancellor.

'Yes – we are still outnumbered, but we have them on the back foot in a siege scenario in which they cannot resupply, whereas we already have reinforcements en route from Gibraltar. However, as we all know, these fiends prefer to act by night, and so we have about a week before the moonlight will be fading to the point where they will have the upper hand should they breakout after sunset. It is *imperative*, therefore, that Merovigli falls within the next five days.'

Outright gasps of surprise met this statement.

'This can – and will – be achieved by a combination of battery and massacre,' he declared, driving his fist into the palm of his other hand. 'We will batter the walls and move up closer to them to the point where they will be forced to breakout to prevent us reaching the gates. We will then fall back and use the field guns and Brown Besses of the infantry to massacre the counterattack.' He waved away voices of protest from some of the officers. 'I know, I know – it's a crude grind, bloody and painful, but in the circumstances we have no choice in the matter. We do not have the luxury of a protracted standoff. We start today at one o'clock sharp – Lt Jenkins and Colonel Walsh will issue the necessary orders shortly.'

'Sir!' spoke up Rear Admiral Harris, the commander of Blue Squadron. 'Even with no moonlight we *could* contain them until

269

reinforcements arrive – it seems to me this strategy will be an unnecessary waste of life.'

Murmurs of agreement sprang up around the assembled officers.

'We have achieved the primary objective,' continued a captain from White Squadron, 'why the haste?'

'Good points, both of you,' commented Admiral Blake. 'But there is now a secondary objective to be achieved, which I was coming to. It has come to my attention that there is a substantial hoard of gold in a church in the bowels of that fortress,' he said. The atmosphere in the tent changed in an instant; there was no more murmuring or muttering, and all eyes were now on the admiral.

'This hoard, plundered from shipping for decades now, could pay off Great Britain's war debts, allow us to wage war on the French for a century, and give every peasant in England a herd of cows, ten acres of land and a new dwelling!'

The assembled officers were now silent at the prospect of a percentage of the hoard, the naval rules of prize distribution engraved on their minds.

'So you can see, gentlemen, if we dig in and wait for several thousand reinforcements, that increases the number of officers and ratings entitled to a share when the fortress does eventually fall.' He paused and looked around them all. 'Now, any more objections?'

Alex looked over to the White Squadron captain – his mouth was now shut as tight as a clam.

Admiral Blake then indicated to a figure who had been standing apart from the command team over in one corner of the tent. Alex recognized him as the sergeant who had challanged him at the gate, the day he had arrived in Athens.

'Following the fall of the gates, or a substantial portion of the walls, Sergeant Clark here will lead an elite platoon of marines just behind the vanguard of the attack which, at the insistence of the chancellor, will be made up of him, his notables and best fighters.'

He paused for a moment to let that information sink in. A murmur of surprise ran around the tent at this news, then several of the commanders looked to the chancellor and either touched or raised their hats in a mark of respect. The chancellor looked around the assembly and acknowledged their gestures with a curt nod.

'Following their invasion, the Rakshasa ransacked all the churches on Santorini, stealing a large number of holy Greek Orthodox relics that the islanders are desperate to retrieve before the fortress is destroyed. They are held in another part of the fortress, separate to the church. Sergeant Clark's objective will be to find and secure the church containing the hoard, otherwise I can guarantee every Jack Tar will stuff his trousers with gold plate and we will be left with a toothpick – if we are lucky!'

There was general hearty laughter at this comment, but Alex noticed Sergeant Clark remained stony-faced throughout it – the chances were he was being sent to his death in order to greatly enrich those standing before him.

'That's all very well, sir,' it was Rear Admiral Harris again, 'but how will the sergeant find the gold? I would guess the interior of that fortress has more turns than the Minotaur's labyrinth.'

'Another good point,' conceded Admiral Blake, turning to face Alex, 'which is why Lt Hurst here will be guiding him.'

CHAPTER 39

'But it's so unfair!' declared Helena later that afternoon. Alex was in her tent, as outside the air pulsated and the ground shook with the force of the field guns bombarding the fortress. 'After all you have done…'

'I know, I know,' Alex responded. 'But that is the military way: best man for the job, and all that.' He forced a smile. 'But God only knows,' he muttered, 'the last thing I expected was to have to set foot in that damn fortress again.'

'Let us pray to God that all will be well,' declared Helena, wiping tears from her eyes.

Neither spoke for a moment.

'When will you have to go in?'

'Looking at the state of the walls, I would say two days from now. The Rakshasa can only barricade them for so long.'

'And then?'

'All hell will break loose – literally. My platoon will go in just behind the chancellor's men. Behind us will be platoons of marines armed to the teeth who will kill anything they come across. They will not rest until every Rakshasa has been slaughtered.'

'Slaughtered?' exclaimed Helena.

Alex looked at her in surprise. 'Surely you do not still hold feelings for Zentar?' he demanded, jealous anger rising in his voice.

'Alex, no I do not, I swear!' she retorted. 'I told you he was using witchcraft to try and seduce me – but I never totally fell for him.'

Something then occurred to her and she was about to speak, but turned away, a look of uncertainty on her face.

'What is it?' demanded Alex.

Her shoulders slumped. 'I was not going to say…'

'Not going to say *what*?' he insisted.

'For the last couple of nights, he has come to me in my dreams…'

'Oh for God's sake!' exclaimed Alex, drawing back from her.

'I know it sounds insane, but please hear me out,' she insisted.

Alex drew nearer again, but avoided her eyes.

'In the dreams he is different than before.'

'How do you mean?' asked Alex through gritted teeth.

'Before he was…*trying* to seduce me, to persuade me to join him and the Rakshasa…'

'And now?'

'I feel he is intent on coercing me to join them in the fortress by sheer force of his will and use of the black arts. Last night, after the dream, I awoke and was standing by the entrance to the tent here – and I have never been a somnambulist. I am afraid that once I am asleep he can control me – but it is you I love, Alex, I swear!' She took his hands in hers, total conviction in her voice, but the fear of rejection in her eyes.

Alex said nothing for a few moments. Presently he calmed down and gave a heartfelt sigh. 'I believe it when you say you are mine,' he declared, taking her hands and looking wearily at her. 'But these *visitations* you speak of are just dreams – nay, nightmares! Stay strong, for soon this horror will be over – and then we can leave this cursed isle and be together.'

He stood up and was about to leave when a thought occurred to him. 'I will ask Admiral Blake to have you moved to his flagship as a precaution before the fortress falls.'

*

'Visitations? In her dreams?' exclaimed Admiral Blake, half shouting to be heard above the din of the field guns. 'Good Lord, man, it's claptrap!'

He was standing by the entrance of his command tent, sipping a brandy as he watched the bombardment of the fortress, Alex having caught him in a brief hiatus between meetings with his aides.

'Out of the question – we're here to lay a siege, not humour a hysterical female!' he continued. 'After what she did to Lord Charlemont she should be grateful to be in a tent at all – any other commander would have had her clapped in irons and thrown in the brig!' He paused, rubbed a hand over his tired eyes and sighed. 'Despite what she did, Lady Helena is under my personal protection, and I would have to answer to the king himself if anything were to befall her. No – she will remain in her tent until that fortress falls,' he declared, waving his free hand in its general direction. 'Two of my best marines are guarding her, and she is as safe there as anywhere on, or around, this island.'

*

The first day of the siege proper passed without a breakout. The guns were silenced, and Alex retired to his tent, but slept only fitfully.

'Sir, wake up!'

Alex sat bolt upright, shielding his eyes from the light of the lantern a marine was holding above him.

'What is it? Have they broken out?' he asked, instantly alert.

'No, sir. It's Lady Helena – she needs to speak to you urgently.'

'One moment,' said Alex as he pulled on his clothes, glancing outside. By the height of the moon he could tell it was around midnight, and he wondered what she could need at this hour of the night.

'Go back,' he ordered, casting around for his jacket. 'I will be with you shortly.'

'Well, she is just waiting outside, sir,' said the marine.

'What?' exclaimed Alex. 'She was not to leave the tent!'

He pushed past the man, expecting to find Helena standing there – but there was nothing except the faintest aroma of her perfume hanging in the still night air.

'She was there a moment ago…' exclaimed the marine as he emerged from Alex's tent.

'Go to her tent – see if she is there!' Alex ordered with a growing feeling of dread, and then he ran past the command tent and on to the top road, stopping to look around.

A movement caught his eye – and he gasped with shock. Helena was running barefoot along the top road to the fortress, her nightdress billowing out wraith-like behind her in the moonlight.

'Helena!' Alex called in desperation, and set off running after her.

She flitted past the night guards, startling them, but they did not move to stop her in their confusion of who she was.

'Hold your fire!' Alex shouted, desperation in his voice. 'Helena – for God's sake, stop!'

Still she ran on without a glance behind, as if she had a demon on her heels – but he started gaining on her. On one side of the road the cliffs dropped away to the darkness of the sea below; ahead the waning moon was positioned over the fortress itself, shining along the length of the road and illuminating it with a spectral light on which Helena ran, as if along a moonbeam. She cleared the front line of the field guns – but Alex now knew he had the speed to run her down before she could reach the fortress. He had passed the field guns himself, and was barely twenty yards behind her when suddenly the deep bass sound of huge horns shattered the peace of the night, and up ahead, to Alex's horror, he could see the fortress gates beginning to open.

'I still have time!' he thought, 'I can still…'

The fortress suddenly seemed to explode from within as brilliant shafts of intense blue light shot out of every opening, accompanied by a wall of sound that shook the ground as it emerged from the doors: an invisible juggernaut that thundered along the road, first knocking Helena over, and then Alex. An instant later he was caught up in a demonic cacophony of sound that overwhelmed and terrified him, rooting him to the earth. It passed as quickly as it had hit him, but left him helpless and drained of energy, sprawled on the ground.

From where he lay he could see shadows appear in front of the light emitting from the gates, and then felt abject despair as countless Rakshasa horsemen, their steeds as black as night, began to emerge from the gates in a smooth, unhurried manner, moving slickly into an arrowhead formation as they cleared the fortress.

Helena was standing ahead of him, calmly watching the squadron of Rakshasa cavalry as it bore down on her. Alex tried to cry out to warn her, but his voice died in his throat. The lead rider was now just yards from Helena and would surely run her down, but suddenly he peeled away to the right and rode past her, as did the next to her left and so on, so that they passed her and Alex on either side before reforming further down the road. The ground shook under the weight of the horses' hooves. Countless riders passed, and then seven scarlet-clad riders appeared, *kilijs* drawn and glinting in the moonlight, at the centre of whom was a purple-clad figure riding a pure white charger. With his white hair flowing behind him and red eyes flashing in the moonlight, Zentar carried with him a huge flag of the Rakshasa moon demon, billowing gently in the night air. The scarlet riders fanned out around Helena and Alex, and formed a guard around them as Zentar's horse trotted towards Helena, whose eyes never left him. He stopped by her and then addressed her in Latin.

'Are you ready, my love?' he asked, his voice measured and clear in the night air. He glanced over to where Alex lay, and then back to her. 'Are you ready to assume your destiny and become my queen?'

Alex tried to speak, but could not – and was then horrified by the imperious set of Helena's face and contemptuous curl of her lip as she briefly looked down at him before turning back to Zentar.

'Yes, I am ready, my Lord,' she replied with absolute conviction, and without a further word she gracefully swung herself up behind him.

The sound of shots, shouts and screams of terror were beginning to drift over to them from Admiral Blake's camp as Zentar's horse trotted over to Alex.

'Tonight your comrades will die in their thousands,' Zentar declared. 'But I have spared your life this night so you may know that Helena chose *me* over you. You are but an irrelevance to her, and her life is now with me and the Rakshasa.'

He turned the horse round on the road to head back to the fortress.

'Helena,' croaked Alex, barely able to speak. He looked up, and she glanced down at him again with pitiless eyes.

'Helena, I *love* you!' he managed to shout, but then Zentar spurred his horse and they set off at a canter for the fortress gates, the scarlet guard close behind. Alex collapsed, weeping, on the ground, barely able to move.

Sometime later he heard the ground shake again as the Rakshasa cavalry returned to the fortress. He staggered to his feet to get off the road, and heard a horse coming very close. He turned to face it – and was struck on the forehead with a musket butt. He crashed back down to the ground, dead to the world.

CHAPTER 40

Alex awoke shivering, just after dawn, his head pounding with pain, a metallic taste in his parched mouth and face covered in dried blood. A glance towards the fortress revealed it to be silent and apparently lifeless. In the other direction, a heavy cloud of smoke hung over the encampment, with the cries of wounded men drifting across the still morning air. As he staggered back to the camp, Alex realised something had subtlety changed in the environment, but at first he could not place it. Then the first rays of the sun struck him, and he realised with a shock that the Wall of Storms had ceased to exist and he could see the sun rising up, directly out of the sea, whereas normally it would not appear over the wall until mid-morning.

The force was in complete confusion when he arrived back, with no guard even challenging him on the way in. Feeling sick to his stomach, he saw Admiral Blake's command tent was now a smouldering ruin, as were most of the tents near it, with charred bodies lying around, frozen in their final death throes. His heart sank – surely the campaign was now finished. Who would take the place of such a man as the admiral? He suddenly felt exhausted, his belief in a rational world of cause and effect shattered, and completely wrung out of emotion. Slumping to the ground, he sat there for some time, head in his hands, and wondered if he would ever get over Helena's betrayal.

*

An hour or so later, Alex was helping with the wounded when suddenly cheers started to ring out from further down the hillside. A large group of men were making their way briskly up the lanes to the top road, and all around them survivors of the previous night's massacre were pausing in their work to run over and cheer them on. As they drew nearer, Alex could hardly believe his eyes – it was Admiral Blake, together with

Colonel Walsh, Lt Jenkins and a few of his aides, accompanied by Sgt Clark and his platoon of marines. All looked shocked to the core at the devastation around them, but were otherwise unharmed. Admiral Blake was scanning those around him, and as he drew close to Alex their eyes met.

'Hurst? Is that you? Thank God you are still alive!' he exclaimed. His eyes darted around. 'But where is Lady Helena?'

*

A few hours later, the remaining commanders assembled once more, this time in a cramped mess tent, their mood distinctly subdued. It transpired that the senior officers had decamped to the Admiral's flag-ship the previous night to carry out detailed planning for the further deployment of the fleet, and had watched horrified from the sea as the camp was overrun by the Rakshasa cavalry. The chancellor and his men had also withdrawn to Pyrgos to bury their dead from the battle for the top road, and so they too had avoided the massacre. Admiral Blake's manner was grave and completely lacking his usual jovial spirit.

'We are now down to just over one thousand fighting men,' he began. 'We cannot afford another breakout on that scale, with that...' he paused as if uncertain how to describe it '...*demonic* war cry preceding them. They could completely wipe us out in a few days before reinforcements arrive.'

The remaining officers nodded in agreement.

'They probably think they have wiped out our command layer and that we will take days to regroup and mount a response, so I intend to attack, during daylight hours, when they are least expecting it.'

'When will the attack be, sir?' asked a marine captain.

'This afternoon – at three o'clock,' replied Admiral Blake.

A shocked silence descended on those gathered.

Alex could hardly believe what he was hearing. 'But, sir,' he said, speaking up, 'Lady Helena is now in the fortress. Should we not try to negotiate with the Rakshasa to free her before the final assault?' Despite her actions of the previous night, he could not bring himself to give up on her.

'Mr Hurst,' snapped back Admiral Blake, 'from what you have told me it is quite clear she has made a choice to remain with the Rakshasa

– and therefore will have to take her chances with them.' He gave an impatient sigh and then turned to Lt Jenkins. 'Issue the order that, if captured alive, Lady Helena is not to be harmed.'

*

Barely an hour after the command meeting, marines began to haul the field guns up along the top road to get them closer to the fortress, while the chancellor and his men took up their positions. All the while they expected opposition from the Rakshasa, but none came. By three o'clock, all were in position, and the gun crews looked anxiously to their commanders, itching to fire their guns before they started taking sniper fire.

Alex, Sgt Clark and the elite marines were positioned with the Greeks just behind the guns and heard the shrill blast of Colonel Walsh's whistle – they all covered their ears at this, and an instant later the ground shook as dozens of field guns fired almost simultaneously at a weak point that had been identified in the walls.

The smoke cleared, and shouts rang out – the wall had been breached! The chancellor and his notables quickly mounted their horses, and then he turned to face his men, some looking anxious, others with their faces set in stony resolve.

'Today God has given us the chance to drive the Rakshasa from our land,' he declared, his voice strong and resolute. 'Today we will avenge our ancestors and restore our honour!'

His men cheered at this, their spirits lifted and their fighting blood raised. The next moment there was the sound of three distinct whistle blasts – the signal to attack.

At this the chancellor wheeled his horse around towards the breach, and drew his sword with his good arm. 'For God and Saint Irene!' he cried, and spurred his horse into a gallop, followed by his men shouting war cries.

Alex, Sgt Clark and his marines set off behind them, all of them expecting heavy defensive fire at any moment – but still none came. Then they were through the breach and inside the fortress walls by the stables, all of which were empty, doors open and straw strewn around on the street outside. Two of the marines were carrying a large spool of twine on a pole between them, strips of cloth crudely knotted into it every ten feet or so. They secured the free end of twine to a horse ring, and then began unspooling the twine to act as a guide to Admiral Blake. Still there was no resistance, and so Alex led the way through the maze of streets that led to the palace itself, as the chancellor and his men took off in a different direction. It was unnerving – all the streets were deserted, the doors of some houses swinging open as they passed.

'What's happened, sir?' asked Sgt Clark as they made their way to the palace gates. 'Where *are* they all?'

Alex just shook his head – he could give no reply.

The palace gates presented their first real obstacle – but they were blown down in a matter of minutes by sappers in the team who were able to fit charges directly to the hinges.

Soon they were at the ramp leading down into the wine cellars. The platoon then quickly slid down it, running through the kitchens and out into the dining room. All the tables were laid, the ghastly candelabra lit, with some of the candles just spluttering out, and plates left with remnants of food on them. Alex could even feel the heat from the embers of the two great fireplaces. It was as if the Rakshasa had had one last meal and then calmly left the dining room, without even bothering to extinguish the blue lanterns that lined all the corridors and passageways. The Hall of Trophies threw up more surprises – all the skeletons had gone, along with the oil painting that hung behind each, and the tapestries that lined the walls had been taken down.

On they went to the underground church, where Alex received another huge shock. The side door that he and Lord Charlemont had first thought was a store cupboard was now open, and the hoard of gold, instead of being seven or eight feet high, was barely up to their knees. He led the marines into the church, and for a few moments they slipped and crashed around on the uneven surface.

'It this it?' asked an incredulous Sgt Clark, holding his torch high above him, trying to see further into the gloom.

'They've taken most of it to another place in the fortress,' replied Alex, wiping sweat away from his eyes with his sleeve. 'They must have!'

He thought desperately through the possibilities. Could there be another tunnel from the fortress that linked up with the tunnel through the island? Were the Rakshasa attempting to escape en masse by sea? He stepped out of the church again and looked at the floor of the passageway. There was the odd trinket lying on the ground, jewels sparkling here and there in the darkness, with quite deep recent grooves and scrape marks on the dirt floor. It was as if the Rakshasa had scooped the treasure up in large baskets and dragged it away, the smaller items spilling out.

'They've taken it this way. Leave a dozen men to secure the church, the rest follow me!' Alex ordered, and then they set off at a run, their torches spluttering as they held them aloft, Alex's eyes glued to the ground, following the trail of gold and trinkets.

Soon they were back in the palace proper, in a large well lit passageway where the faint trail merged with a much larger one. There was now no need to scan the ground carefully; the trail of items belonged to a host of refugees that had recently passed by – plates, cutlery, clothes, ornaments and even horse droppings were strewn around. They slowed down; it was probable that such a body of Rakshasa had a rearguard to cover them, and there was no telling if that guard was in front or still bringing up the rear behind them. Rounding a corner, they found the trail stopped abruptly in front of huge bronze doors, inlaid with profane Rakshasa symbols, which were slightly ajar. The hairs on the back of his neck stood up as Alex realised where they now were.

'Wait,' ordered Alex, and he made his way to the opening in the doors. A glance though the gap confirmed what he had guessed – this was the entrance to the North Temple where the Full Moon Feast had taken place. The light in the temple was all wrong, though – it was now late afternoon and it should have been well lit with sunlight from above, but instead appeared to be illuminated by a swirling mix of all the colours of the rainbow, as if someone were wildly rotating a magic lantern within. On the circular marble dais in the centre of the temple were seven scarlet-clad figures, sitting cross-legged, chanting rhythmically. As Alex watched them, they stopped chanting, stood up and began to walk purposely over towards the large mirror directly opposite from where he stood, the surface of which was now as black as night. The ancient altar that had stood in front of the mirror on the night of the feast had been moved elsewhere, and Alex noticed that the trail of belongings they had been following was visible up the steps leading to the mirror itself – and then appeared to stop directly in front of it. Alex was flummoxed – as far as he knew, the only way in or out of the temple was via the doors he was standing outside. He turned and beckoned Sgt Clark over.

'Is the gold in there, sir?' whispered Sgt Clark, moving in close behind him.

'Can't see any – can only think they have taken it down a staircase. Prepare the men – there are seven Rakshasa within.'

Sgt Clark relayed the orders to the men, and then peered in himself.

'I can only see two!' he declared. He suddenly swore under his breath, stepped back and stared at Alex, a look of confusion on his face.

'What?' exclaimed Alex. He moved closer to the gap again – and then gasped in shock.

There, walking diagonally across the temple from the right-hand side towards the mirror, was the purple-clad figure of Zentar – closely followed by a now purple-clad Helena. With horror, Alex realised Helena had, like Isabelle, been transformed – she held her head unusually high, her eyes fixed with a steely gaze on the figure in front of her, while her countenance was hard, uncompromising and as cruel as an eagle. Her face had been powdered deathly white, her lips were vermillion and her fiery auburn hair was arranged in a large mass above her head, held in place with numerous silver grips and clasps, while her hands were adorned with silver rings, and wrists weighed down with bangles of jewel encrusted silver. Both she and Zentar had their arms outstretched, holding large silver ornaments that Alex recognised from the altar on the night of the feast, the multi-coloured light glinting off their surfaces.

There was a loud crack – and then a shot impacted the door just above Alex's head. He turned to see at least a dozen Rakshasa warriors sweep down the corridor towards them in the cold blue light, *kilijs* unsheathed.

'Get her, sir!' urged Sgt Clark. 'We'll hold them.'

Alex needed no prompting and, as the two groups began to exchange fire, was through the gap, the doors slamming behind him an instant later. The two purple-clad figures stopped dead at his appearance and turned to look at him. There was a shocked silence, giving Alex time to glance around and confirm his earlier belief that the only way out was through the door behind him – but where had the seven priests gone?

'How dare you violate this sacred place?' Zentar suddenly roared, crouching to place the ornament carefully on the floor before springing to his feet as he unsheathed his long knives and making to run at Alex.

Alex automatically raised his musket, paused for a moment to allow Zentar to close the distance between them – and then discharged it. Any other living being would have been stopped dead by the impact of the shot – but somehow Zentar seemed to anticipate its trajectory and blocked it with a sweep of his left hand knife. The blade of the knife shattered, and the impact flung the hilt out of Zentar's grip. He cried out in pain, but continued his charge. Throwing his musket to one side, Alex unsheathed his sabre, ready to meet a scything attack from Zentar. Glancing briefly behind the figure bearing down on him, Alex could see Helena was now holding the ornament at waist level, her face an expression of disgust at his very presence.

'Helena,' he shouted over to her, 'he's bewitched you!'

A flicker of doubt crossed Helena's face – and then an instant later Zentar unleashed his war cry at Alex. This time, though, Alex was prepared, steeling himself against it as Zentar fell on him, wielding his long knife with incredible force and skill, Alex only just managing to parry the blows. Alex had the slight advantage of being higher up the concentric steps of the temple; Zentar knew this and strove to outflank him and force him lower down – but Alex held his position.

'You are too late – Helena has given herself to me,' Zentar hissed through clenched teeth as both briefly drew back to reassess the other.

Latterly, a remark like that would have provoked blind rage in Alex – but he had never lost a duel in his career due to an icy calmness he could induce in himself, as well as the ability to think analytically, even while fighting for his life. Within a few further exchanges of blows, he realised Zentar had put everything into his initial assault and was already weakening, whereas Alex now began to carry out controlled set pieces that gave him time to analyse his opponent's weaknesses.

Zentar had great natural speed and strength – but he lacked the skill and discipline that could only come with continual practice and actual deadly swordplay. A few exploratory moves later, he concluded Zentar was shifting to a defensive stance, confirmed it with a feinted lunge – and then moved in for the kill, his sabre seeming to move with a life of its own as he effortlessly rained blow after blow on the retreating figure of Zentar. Then they were on the floor of the temple, and he continued to force Zentar back, past the stationary figure of Helena, until he was at the base of the steps leading up to the mirror.

Alex was suddenly aware that the intensity of the multi-coloured lights swirling around the temple was decreasing – and it appeared that Zentar had noticed it too. He skipped up a couple of steps, out of Alex's reach, and both paused momentarily, muffled shots and screams audible from outside the doors.

'Helena,' Zentar cried out, the urgency apparent in his voice, 'we must leave, now!'

Alex backed off slightly so that he could turn to look at Helena while still keeping half an eye on Zentar.

'Don't listen to him!' he implored, though he could still not for the life of him understand how Zentar could get out of the temple. 'Come with me!'

The imperial haughtiness had left her, and Helena's face was a picture of confusion; she stumbled forward a few steps until she was equidistant from both of them, and then seemingly absentmindedly dropped the large silver ornament. It crashed heavily to the marbled floor, raising a howl of anger from Zentar. Helena was looking in puzzlement at the silver rings and bangles that adorned her, then she briefly looked at Zentar before turning to Alex.

'Alex?' she exclaimed, looking at him as if seeing him properly for the first time. 'Is it you?' She looked at her hands and wrists again. 'Why am I wearing these?'

'You are my queen,' Zentar bellowed from halfway up the steps. 'Come here and take your place by my side! I command you!'

This order visibly shocked Helena and seemed to snap her back into full awareness of herself and her surroundings.

'Your *queen*?' she exclaimed, her voice initially low, but then rising with anger. 'How can you say I am your *queen* when you invaded my mind while I slept and poisoned it with your foul necromancy?' She shook her head in disbelief. 'For days now I have watched myself as if from afar, unable to control myself or direct my own actions.' She held her arms up to him. 'How can I be your queen when you crushed my will and turned me into no more than a silver-clad courtesan?' She began shaking off the silver bangles, and then brutally pulled the rings off her fingers one by one as Zentar looked on aghast. 'No, sir,' she shouted at Zentar, her voice shaking with hatred and rage, 'I am not your queen, and *never will be*. My place is not here with you and your depraved kind…' She paused, her voice choking in her throat as she turned away from him. 'My place is with Alex…'

With a cry of anguish, Zentar ran down the steps and launched himself at Helena. Alex shot over to her and barely managed to parry the knife blow while keeping himself between the inhuman attacker and Helena. He soon fought Zentar back towards the steps, and then executed a few moves to open up Zentar's chest momentarily. In the split second his chest was exposed, Alex barrelled his sabre forward – and ran Zentar full through the heart. Zentar screamed in pain, his knife bouncing off the marble floor as it fell from his hand. Alex withdrew his blade and returned to the ready position, though his foe was now surely mortally wounded. Zentar staggered back for a few steps, hands clasped to his chest, fear and shock in his eyes – and then did something that astounded Alex. He turned away, but instead of slumping to the floor as expected, he suddenly seemed to gather himself – and ran up the steps leading to the mirror. Shocked at his opponent's revitalisation, Alex then recovered and made to follow him. The mirror was set slightly back between the alcoves containing the demonic statues – so he had his quarry cornered.

Zentar stopped momentarily to face him, and then turned to Helena, his face contorted with rage.

'Treacherous harlot!' he roared.

What happened next caused Alex to doubt his sanity. Zentar ran at full pelt towards the obsidian black of the mirror's surface – and disappeared straight into it. One moment he was visible, the next the blackness of the mirror appeared to swallow him up, and he was gone, consumed by shadow. Alex had sprinted up the steps after him, and only just managed to stop himself at the threshold of the mirror, staring at it in shock. Then he carefully walked backwards down the steps to the floor and further back to the now crouched and weeping figure of Helena.

'I'm so sorry, Alex, I'm so sorry,' she wept, looking up at him in abject misery. 'He forced his will on me. I was powerless to resist. Please forgive me.'

'Where…' began Alex, still keeping an eye on the mirror, '…where in God's name did he go?'

'He just told me we were going to a place of safety,' she replied haltingly, turning away and raising a handkerchief to wipe the tears from her eyes, 'by means of their dark arts.'

'Well, come now,' he urged her, not taking his eyes off the mirror. 'We must leave.'

'Yes, yes, take me from this slaughterhouse!' she exclaimed, stifling her sobs as he pulled her to her feet and supported her shaking body back over towards the entrance.

They reached the double doors. The shooting outside had died away, and Alex now listened intently for a clue as to who, or what, was lurking beyond the threshold. Suddenly the doors began to open; Alex stepped back, pushing Helena behind him, and levelled his air pistol.

'Lt Hurst?' called Sgt Clark, stepping into the temple.

'Thank God,' exclaimed Alex, and was about to holster his pistol when Sgt Clark unexpectedly threw himself at him.

'Look out!' he shouted, as he caught Alex off balance and threw him to the floor.

There was the zip of an object tearing through the air, and an instant later Sgt Clark was lying on the floor, screaming in agony, a crossbow bolt embedded in his shoulder. Alex turned to the source of the missile – and with a shock saw the cadaverous purple-clad figure of Korthdan standing with his back to the mirror, cradling a crossbow in his hands and looking for all the world as if he had just risen from the grave. He snarled, and hatred flashed in his eyes as they bored into Alex.

'Vile *hybrida*!' he roared, the fury in his voice physically shaking them. 'Thou hast betrayed thy blood!'

Alex had no idea what that meant – but saw his chance. He shook himself, leapt to his feet and ran across the temple, levelling his pistol as he did. Korthdan saw the threat, but just contemptuously flung the crossbow to one side. The central marble dais was between Alex and Korthdan; Alex jumped up, ran over it and off the other side, and was within thirty feet of his target, but had to close the gap further still to be sure of an accurate shot. He reached the bottom of the steps, his gaze fixed on Korthdan as the gaunt figure snarled again – and then began walking backwards into the mirror. Alex was now halfway up the steps; he stopped dead, aimed at Korthdan's heart and discharged the pistol. In that instant, Korthdan's body disappeared into the blackness, the fading multi-coloured lights in the temple completely vanished, and the reflective surface of the mirror re-appeared. Alex's shot ricocheted off the surface of the mirror and into the heights of the temple, before falling harmlessly back down to the marble floor. Alex's jaw dropped; he was rooted to the spot for a moment, but then ran up the remainder of the steps as he flipped his pistol over in his hand and brought the metal butt crashing against the surface of the mirror. It bounced off, jarring his hand so much that he lost his grip on it. He stepped back from the mirror, barely able to comprehend what he had seen.

The predicament of Sgt Clark brought him back to reality – the poor man was screaming like a soul in torment. Alex retrieved his pistol and rushed back to him. Blood was issuing from everywhere – his nose and ears, and even from under his fingernails. More of his men had entered the temple, and they and Helena were now trying to pull the bolt from his shoulder. The screaming suddenly stopped as his jaws clamped together, then he shuddered once more before his body went limp, and was gently lowered to the ground by his men. Alex was stunned – due to the other's bravery he had avoided a horrific death by a hairs breath.

*

Alex took Helena by the hand and led her silently out of the Full Moon Temple, over the bodies of the Rakshasa outside it and through the maze of the fortress, pushing their way past the mass of red uniformed marines that were now sweeping through it in a frenzy of revenge, destroying everything in their path. They finally emerged from the gates of the fortress, and into the cool air of the evening outside. A large procession of mule hauled carts was already leaving the fortress, each carrying a number of strongboxes, as another empty mule train made its way in. Admiral Blake and his aides were there supervising the operation, together with a large group of marines. The admiral suddenly noticed them and looked shocked at Helena's appearance, but drew up anyway beside Alex.

'Damn fine job, Hurst!' he declared, clapping Alex on the shoulder before turning back to the mule train. 'Double it now, men! I want that church emptied by the end of this day.' And with that, he disappeared back into the noise and madness of the fortress.

Alex heard a number of horses approaching from behind, and turned to see the chancellor and his notables also emerging from the fortress. Tied to their saddles were wooden boxes, of various sizes, and some of the notables were resting larger religious statues and other objects in front of them.

The chancellor was turning to say something to one of the notables when he noticed Alex. He stopped in mid-sentence as their eyes met, a look of deep relief and happiness on his face. He trotted his horse over, reaching down to vigorously shake Alex's hand.

'Thank you Lt Hurst,' he exclaimed. 'It seems the devils have all been slaughtered or vanquished back to hell! Santorini is ours again!'

'That's…wonderful,' returned Alex, somewhat in a daze.

'It is a great day, a joyous day!' the chancellor continued. 'We will talk of all this another time, for there is much work to be done – but now we return to Pyrgos to celebrate!'

With that, he doffed his cap to Helena, then spurred his horse and quickly joined his notables and men who were heading back home along the top road.

Alex and Helena continued walking until they were well clear of the fortress, and then sat down together, exhausted, on the grassy edge of the cliffs. The sun was setting, and a golden path of warm light stretched out towards them across the shimmering surface of the sea. Neither spoke; their joy at being reunited was tempered with the knowledge that the shadow of the Rakshasa still loomed large over them.

GLOSSARY

Araba A Turkish coach, similar to a covered wagon with canvas roof.

Armenian Inhabitant of Armenia, a mainly Christian country located between Europe and Asia, occupied by the Ottomans.

Anno Hegirae The Islamic (Hijri) Calendar, with dates that fall within the Muslim Era, is usually abbreviated to AH in Western languages from the Latinised *Anno Hejirae* – "In the year of the Hijra".

Apothecary A medical practitioner.

Balkan Peninsula The peninsula bounded by the Adriatic and Ionian Seas to the west, the Aegean Sea to the east, and the Mediterranean to the south.

Broadcloth A dense woollen cloth, woven so as to have a surface of diagonal parallel ridges.

Brown Bess A standard British army musket with a 46 inch barrel.

Caique Traditional Greek fishing vessel.

Calico Coarse printed cotton fabric.

Caldera Flooded volcanic crater.

Cape of Good Hope Southern tip of Africa.

Copperplate Fine legible handwriting. The name is due to the fact that copybooks from which students learned it were printed from etched copper plates.

Constantinople Modern Istanbul.

Corsair (aka *Barbary corsairs*) Privateers licensed by the Turkish Government who operated off the north coast of Africa, known as the Barbary Coast, in the seventeenth and eighteenth centuries.

Consul-General of the Morea The most senior Levant Company consul on the Balkan Peninsula.

Dragoman An interpreter or guide.

Distemper Illness or disease.

East Indies The whole of south-east Asia, including India and the islands of Borneo, Celebes, Java, Sumatra, the islands from Bali to Timor, the Moluccas, and New Guinea.

Factory An establishment for traders conducting business in a foreign land.

Fearless, HMS A fifty gun ship, similar to HMS *Gloucester*, part of the fleet that Admiral George Anson circumnavigated the world with in 1740.

Firman Guarantee of safe passage issued by Ottoman authorities.

Franco-Ottoman alliance This was a military alliance established in 1536 between the King of France, Francis I, and Suleiman the Magnificent. It enabled the French to resist the might of the Habsburg empire. Frowned on in Christian Europe as the "sacrilegious union of the Lily and the Crescent".

Frankistan The name given to Christian Europe by the Turks, Arabs and Greeks.

Good Queen Bess Queen Elizabeth I.

Great cabin Captain Todd's quarters, at the stern of the ship, and, in HMS *Fearless* on the same level as the upper gun deck.

Haj The pilgrimage to Mecca. This is one of the Five Pillars of Faith (or duties) of Islam.

Hanger Sword that literally "hung at the side". Around 20 to 30 inches in length and slightly curved.

Haradj Capitation tax paid by non-Muslims in place of military service, as they were not allowed to bear arms.

Hellburner A ship packed with explosives and driven into the enemy.

Janissary A Turkish soldier.

Kadi Local Turkish judge.

Kasteli Fortified settlement.

Khan Inn built around a courtyard.

Kilij Turkish style sabre.

Last Dog Watch Ship's watch from 6pm to 8pm.

Levant, The The eastern part of the Mediterranean, including its islands and the countries that border it.

Magazine Area on a ship used to store gunpowder for the cannon.

Mamluk White slaves who were brought to Egypt, raised and trained as elite soldiers. They overthrew the ruling classes in the thirteenth century, but were themselves deposed by the Ottoman invasion of Egypt in the early sixteenth century.

Metope A rectangular element with carved or painted figures that alternates with triglyphs (plain rectangular stone with three vertical carved lines) in a decorative band above the columns of a Doric style building.

Morea, The Modern Peloponnese.

Mullah A Muslim man who has been educated in Islamic theology and sacred law.

Mussulman The eighteenth century term for a Muslim.

Nio The modern Cycladic island of Ios.

Papas Greek Orthodox priest.

Pasha Ottoman governor.

Porte, The (Also the **Sublime Porte**) The Sultan's court at Constantinople.

Private ship Naval ship that does not have an admiral on board.

Ragusa Modern Dubrovnik, Croatia.

Saltpetre The mineral form of potassium nitrate – used in the manufacture of gunpowder.

Salonica Modern Thessaloniki.

Sapper Military engineer.

Sherbet A liqueur made with liquorice, orange juice and water.

Shrouds Netting like rigging of a sailing vessel that gives a mast its lateral support. Used by the crew to climb up and set the sails, etc.

Spyglass Telescope.

Stone Twenty pounds weight, or approximately nine kilogrammes.

Smyrna Modern Izmir, Turkey.

Tops Platforms on a ship's masts.

Treaty of Tordesillas This 1494 Vatican sanctioned treaty divided newly discovered lands outside Europe along a meridian 1,000 miles west of the Cape Verde islands. New lands to the east (such as India, the East Indies, and later Brazil) would belong to Portugal; those to the west (the Americas and the Philippines) could be claimed by Spain.

Triangulate Determine your position by taking a compass bearing on two fixed points. The bearings form a triangle whose apex you are located at.

Turkey merchant A trader in contact with the Turks.

Twelve-pounder Ship's gun that can fire a twelve pound (approximately six kilogramme) cannonball.

Upper Gun Deck Highest of the continuous decks which run the full length of a ship without a fall or interruption.

Vaivode Local governor.

Vrykolakas Greek term for vampire.

Xebec Small three-masted vessel used in the Mediterranean by the navies of Spain and France, as well as the Barbary corsairs.

For more information about Tom O'Dornin and his work,
visit www.tomodornin.com